Nonfiction in Focus

A Comprehensive Framework for
Helping Students Become Independent
Readers and Writers of Nonfiction, K–6

Janice V. Kristo, Ph.D., and Rosemary A. Bamford, Ed.D.

Foreword by Richard T. Vacca

New York • Toronto • London • Auckland • Sydney
Mexico City • New Delhi • Hong Kong • Buenos Aires

Teaching
Resources

KH

Dedication

To the many teachers and colleagues who worked with us to envision a structure for scaffolding students' understanding of nonfiction literature. Their questions, insights, and suggestions led us to more powerful ways to support students.

Credits:

Pages 38, 39: Adapted by permission from *Investigate Nonfiction* by Donald H. Graves. Copyright ©1989 by Donald H. Graves. Published by Heinemann, a division of Reed Elsevier, Inc., Portsmouth, NH. All rights reserved.

Page 48: From *The Magic School Bus: In the Time of the Dinosaurs* by Joanna Cole, illustrated by Bruce Degen. Text copyright ©1994 by Joanna Cole. Illustrations copyright ©1994 by Bruce Degen. Reprinted by permission of Scholastic Inc.

Pages 50–52: From *All About Frogs* by Jim Arnosky. Copyright ©2002 by Jim Arnosky. Reprinted by permission of Scholastic Inc.

Page 73: Material from *The Last Safe House* by Barbara Greenwood with illustrations by Heather Collins used by permission of Kids Can Press Ltd., Toronto, Canada

Page 85: From *How Do Animals Sleep?* by Melvin Berger. Copyright ©1996 by Melvin Berger. Sundance/Newbridge Educational Publishing, LLC, a Haights Cross Communications Company.

Page 131: From *The Lewis and Clark Trail: Then and Now* by Dorothy Hinshaw Patent, illustrated by William Munoz. Text copyright ©2002 by Dorothy Henshaw Patent. Used by permission of Dutton Children's Books, a division of Penguin Young Readers Group, a member of Penguin Group (USA) Inc., 345 Hudson Street, New York, NY 10014. All rights reserved.

Page 158: From *I Am Water* by Jean Marzollo, illustrated by Judith Moffatt. Text copyright ©1996 by Jean Marzollo. Illustrations copyright ©1996 by Judith Moffatt. Reprinted by permission of Cartwheel Books, an imprint of Scholastic Inc.

Pages 161, 192: From *We Have Marched Together: The Working Children's Crusade* by Stephen Currie. Copyright ©1997 by Lerner Publications Company, a division of Lerner Publishing Group. All rights reserved. Photo acknowledgment: Corbis-Bettmann.

Page 177: From *Who Was Ben Franklin?* by Dennis Brindell Fradin, illustrated by John O'Brien. Text copyright ©2002 by Dennis Brindell Fradin. Used by permission of Grosset & Dunlap, a division of Penguin Young Readers Group, a member of Penguin Group (USA) Inc., 345 Hudson Street, New York, NY 10014. All rights reserved.

Pages 188–189: From *The Pumpkin Book* by Gail Gibbons. Copyright ©1999 by Gail Gibbons. Reprinted by permission of Holiday House, Inc.

Page 288: From *Improving Writing: Resources, Strategies, and Assessments* by Susan Davis Lenski and Jerry L. Johns. Copyright ©2000 by Kendall/Hunt Publishing Company. Used with permission.

Every effort has been made to find the authors and publishers of previously published material in this book and to obtain permission to use it.

Cover design concept by Josué Castilleja

Interior design by LDL Designs

Cover photo by James Levin

Interior photos by Michael C. York unless otherwise indicated

ISBN 0-439-36598-8

Copyright ©2004 by Janice V. Kristo and Rosemary A. Bamford

All rights reserved. Published by Scholastic Inc. Printed in the U.S.A.

5 6 7 8 9 10   23   11 10 09 08 07 06

12/21/06

Table of Contents

Part I: Nonfiction: What It Is, Why It's So Popular, and How It Fits Into a Literacy Program

Part II: Using Nonfiction Across the Comprehensive Framework

Appendices

Acknowledgments

Both of us have a long history with nonfiction. In the 1950s and 1960s, we were the only kids at school who ordered nonfiction titles from publishers' book clubs. As adults, we've held seats on the National Council of Teachers of English's Orbis Pictus Committee and worked with teachers on using nonfiction in their classrooms. We've coauthored several books on evaluating and selecting nonfiction. And our enthusiasm for and interest in the genre never waned.

Initially, our academic interest focused strictly on studying nonfiction as a genre, but we've moved on to teasing out and understanding the complexities of teaching it. Specifically, we've been exploring how to teach nonfiction in K–6 literacy programs that scaffold students' learning so that they gain a deeper understanding of how to read and write nonfiction.

This book is the product of a long but rewarding journey. We couldn't have done it without the continuous dedication, support, and flood of good ideas, questions, and nudges from a wonderful group of educators. We offer special thanks to students in our nonfiction graduate course, classroom teachers, and members of our nonfiction focus group. These educators gave over willingly their Friday evenings once a month to travel the long road to the University of Maine to talk about nonfiction. Thank you all for sharing your good thinking and wise counsel about the drafts of this book: Ellen Almquist, Heather Anzelc, Tanya Baker, Judy Bouchard, Barbara Bourgoine, Dyna Curtis, Shana Curtis, Jan Elie, Mary Evans, TammyJo Forgue, Mary Glennon, Kimberly Grant, Diane Hauser, Sharon Imbert, Berenice Knight, Valerie LaFave, Bill Meloy, Shelly Moody, Paula Moore, Eileen Nokes, Janet Nordfors, Zoanne Paradis, Raelene Parks, Sue Pidhurney, Roxanne Roberts, Kellie Tinkham, Jane Wellman-Little, Janis Poulin Whitney, Sandip Wilson, Jody Workman, and Sharon Zolper.

We want to thank Rich Vacca for his thoughtful foreword to this book and for his immense contributions to content area reading that have informed our thinking.

We are grateful for the generous support from publishers who sent us many nonfiction books to examine. We also want to thank Dottie McKenney in the Learning Materials Center at the University of Maine Library for her assistance in locating materials and Rich Pooler and Ann Sidelinker at the University of Maine Printing Service for their assistance in reproducing materials.

We also give special thanks to Mark Bamford and Roger Frey for their patience, good humor, encouragement, and strong backs. They carried many bags of nonfiction books for us, prepared meals, and had a smile for us every step of the way. We also wish to thank Ray Coutu for his extraordinary editorial skills. Ray was one of our biggest fans along the way, and we hope we've done him proud!

Foreword

By Richard T. Vacca, Professor Emeritus, Kent State University

If only my teachers had had the opportunity to read *Nonfiction in Focus*, an immensely practical and groundbreaking book, and put into practice the mother lode of ideas and strategies found in it, my life as a student would have been very different. I don't think I would have struggled as much with informational texts in or out of school. I wouldn't have developed the mistaken notion that expository or informational writing is boring. I wouldn't have been daunted by the prospect of reading about science, history, mathematics, or, as these authors put it, "the literature of fact."

Nor would I have pretended to be the reader I wasn't. Although I was an above-average student in school—and enjoyed reading fiction—I loathed reading for information. Sadly, the only models of informational texts that I was exposed to were deadly dull, five-pound textbooks. Nonfiction was a non-entity in my life as a reader in school. It wasn't until I began doctoral studies in my mid-twenties that the world of nonfiction opened up to me and I began thinking about and studying the differences between fiction and nonfiction.

In *Nonfiction in Focus*, Janice Kristo and Rosemary Bamford do much to demystify the nature of nonfiction and its indispensable role in a K–6 literacy curriculum. They show us how to help students distinguish fiction from nonfiction, how to create engaged readers of nonfiction, and how to develop strategies for reading and writing within a comprehensive framework for integrating nonfiction into a literacy curriculum. Children will learn the nuts-and-bolts of nonfiction, and how to read and write it, without having to enroll in a doctoral program as I did!

Until I began doctoral study in literacy education, I never paid much attention to the nature of text and the critical role that it plays in learning to read and reading to learn. Like so many of us, as an elementary student, I naively assumed all texts were the same—just strings of words on a printed page. And reading was just reading, regardless of whether I was reading a trade book, a poem, a biography, a newspaper article, or a comic book. Even as an English major in college, I wasn't aware of the dynamic interplay between reader and text. Nor was I aware that a text is a blueprint for constructing meaning. In other words, I didn't see the text's author as its architect, or the reader as the builder who interprets the blueprint and—in the process—constructs meaning. Little did I know that there is an underlying structure to nonfiction that is different from the text structures of fiction—structures such as problem-solution, cause-effect, sequence, and comparison-contrast— which I could use to construct meaning with the text as my blueprint. Instead, I assumed that my job as a reader was to say the words in my head and hope that something made sense in the process. I didn't approach reading as discovery (a search for meaning) and knowledge construction (using the text to build and clarify meaning). Rather, I began with the title of the text and plowed my way through the words until I was finished reading.

Not only didn't I know much about text, but I also didn't know how to read strategically. All of my reading classes revolved around Dick-and-Jane-type basal readers and workbooks which were designed for a singular purpose: to develop skills. Skills were taught mainly in isolation with little attention to the nature of the text. We read to answer questions, not to wonder, imagine, enjoy, or, for that matter, learn. I grew into a reader-of-sorts outside of school where I could read stories—for the joy and wonder of it all—without having to answer questions all the time. In junior high and high school I read mostly fiction from literature anthologies, which contained one or two obligatory nonfiction selections. I lugged around content area textbooks from class to class because it was part of the cultural expectations associated with "doing" school. Lugging around science and history textbooks, of course, is a lot different from reading them. It requires a strong back, not a strong mind.

Suffice it to say, as a student I had few school experiences with nonfiction literature as an alternative to textbooks. But that was then. With the onset of the standards-based movement in American education, learning to read the literature of fact has become an important component of the literacy curriculum. If you follow the comprehensive framework described in *Nonfiction in Focus,* you will find yourself in the position of building strong minds as well as avid readers of nonfiction. In the process, your students will discover a lot about themselves as readers. They will come to understand the differences between fiction and nonfiction texts, and what it means to engage fully in the reading process. Kudos to Janice Kristo and Rosemary Bamford for putting nonfiction into focus in ways that will make a difference in the literate lives of today's students.

Introduction

Are your students excited about reading nonfiction books? Are those books among the first your students pick up and browse? Although your students may like nonfiction, how much do they understand about how it works? Do they know about different types of nonfiction and the kinds of information to expect from each one? Do they know how to navigate complex pages that blend visual and textual information? Do they know how to use access features such as maps, time lines, glossaries, and sidebars? Are they good at generating their own informative, engaging nonfiction writing for inquiry projects or content area reports, or is their writing dull and uninspiring?

We've thought a lot about these questions, immersing ourselves in reading nonfiction, learning how it works, and appreciating it for its richness and complexity. There are plenty of professional resources on the market about teaching nonfiction and inquiry, but we think they don't go deep enough. We wanted to produce a resource that shows how to teach nonfiction not as one-shot lessons, but comprehensively in a literacy program that supports students in becoming independent readers, writers, and inquirers over time. Our notions of teaching reflect what Richard Allington (2000) writes in "The Schools We Have. The Schools We Need:" "Unfortunately, we assign children work to complete and confuse that with teaching. What all children need, and some need more of, is models, explanations, and demonstrations of how reading is accomplished. What most do not need are more assignments without strategy instruction, yet much of the work children do in school is not accompanied by any sort of instructional interaction. Rather, work is assigned and checked. Teachers talk to students when assigning, but the talk usually involves presentations of procedures, not instructional explanations of the thinking processes needed to complete the activity. Children are told to 'Read pages 12 to 15 and answer the questions at the end (or on the Ditto, in the workbook, or in a journal).'"

Many theorists and researchers informed our thinking as we wrote this book, but so did a dedicated group of Maine educators who participated in our nonfiction focus group meetings. They grappled with our tough questions and helped us wade through the complexities of teaching and learning about nonfiction. We left those meetings committed to explicitly showing students how to become effective readers and writers of nonfiction.

The major goal in our book is to show you how to do just that: model, explain, and demonstrate strategies for reading and writing nonfiction within a comprehensive literacy framework for grades K through 6. This framework includes reading aloud, shared and guided reading and writing, student-led groups, and independent reading and writing. We show you how to plan instruction for each of these components and carry out that instruction in a way that leads students toward independent learning. For example, you'll see how teaching changes from highly scaffolded, or supported, instruction in read alouds and modeled writing to less scaffolded instruction in discovery circles, where children are given the opportunity to apply strategies on their own. In other words, we explain how to teach so that students will "get it." Students will learn how to use features of nonfiction, how to distinguish types of nonfiction, and what information to expect from those various types. They'll learn ways to write nonfiction so that others will want to read it.

The book is divided into two parts. Part I lays the groundwork for why it's critical to teach students, even very young students, how to read and write nonfiction. In Chapter 1, we explore why nonfiction is so popular and how it benefits students. In Chapter 2, we explain a comprehensive framework for teaching nonfiction and the theory and research that supports it. This framework provides you with an overall way to organize instruction. It represents a complete program and gives students multiple experiences reading and writing nonfiction. In Chapter 3, we describe how to evaluate and select nonfiction. That chapter works as a mini-manual to help you learn the "anatomy" of nonfiction. In Chapter 4, we present what students need to know about reading and writing nonfiction, which will help you carry out the specific teaching approaches described in Part II.

Each chapter in Part II explains an instructional approach to reading and writing and the level of scaffolding required to carry it out. You'll find all the tips, strategies, and background information you need to get the most out of each approach. The book ends with an appendix of helpful forms and resources.

How to Use This Book

We recommend that you read the book cover to cover, because the content of each chapter builds upon what came before it. As you read, you'll gain an understanding of how scaffolded instruction works in a comprehensive framework.

When you're finished, we hope you'll understand nonfiction better, see its benefits to students, and be excited about implementing the comprehensive framework and scaffolded instruction in your classroom. We're convinced that there's no better way to lead your students to becoming effective readers and writers of nonfiction.

PART I
Nonfiction: What It Is, Why It's So Popular, and How It Fits Into a Literacy Program

Chapter 1
What's All the Fuss About Nonfiction?

"Two years ago, I was working in a second-grade classroom. One student, a boy named Jeremy, was a very unmotivated reader who was receiving special education services. Although Jeremy had shown some progress in reading, he never chose to read. I felt I needed dynamite to jumpstart him....

One day, as part of my preparation for a workshop for teachers, I brought about 75 non-fiction books to Jeremy's class. I spread them out on the floor and invited each student to choose two books that he or she would be interested in reading. Jeremy made his selections and returned to his seat. As he read through one, *Chasing Tornadoes!* (McGuffee & Burley, 2000), he repeatedly called me to his desk to point out some fact that he found absolutely amazing. When he was finished, he turned to me and announced, 'That book was so interesting. I read the whole thing, even the glossary!'"

— Betty Titcomb, veteran teacher

Nonfiction books are a powerful draw not only for at-risk readers, like those Betty teaches, but for most students, regardless of their ability or age. Teachers tell us all the time that these books make a difference in the literate lives of their students. They report that their students are excited about the books, they want to read them, and they want to talk about them. Some kids become so interested in their books that they track down additional information on the topic and enthusiastically share it with others. We've seen instances in which students, even those who are struggling, assume the role of classroom expert on their topics. Nonfiction has a way of breaking through students' indifference and inspiring them to read and write.

With that, we welcome you to *Nonfiction in Focus*. By reading it, you'll learn ways to make your teaching of nonfiction explicit and strategic and, as a result, lead your students down the road to becoming more skillful readers and writers of the genre. In this chapter, we provide the baseline information you need to teach nonfiction with confidence. We define nonfiction and describe differences between reading nonfiction and fiction. We go on to discuss why there is so much interest nowadays in nonfiction books and how these books benefit students.

What Is Nonfiction?

Nonfiction is the literature of fact—or the product of an author's inquiry, research, and writing. Its primary purposes are to provide information, explain, argue, and/or demonstrate. The form it takes—the way it's written and organized—is determined by the nature of the content, the purpose of the author, and what best facilitates understanding of the topic (Bamford & Kristo, 2000).

We find that children naturally gravitate toward nonfiction. They have a need to know, understand, and learn. It doesn't take much prodding to get children of all ages to ask questions about the world around them, and nonfiction often provides the answers. They love to pour through books with photographs of trucks, dinosaurs, pyramids, and just about anything else under the sun! Indeed, a child's interest in the world often starts with a nonfiction book. Researchers have found that even very young children can read and write nonfiction (Caswell & Duke, 1998) and that those early experiences establish a strong base for reading more sophisticated nonfiction in later grades (Newkirk, 1989; Pappas, 1991).

The terms "informational text" and "nonfiction" are often used interchangeably. Although opinions vary, we associate nonfiction with trade books—well-written, well-illustrated books on topics related to science, history, math, and the fine arts. We use the term *informational text* to cast a wider net that encompasses many kinds of expository or non-narrative writing—not only books, but brochures, articles, recipes, newspapers, and selections from Web sites.

> "The nonfiction writer must always rein in that impulse to lie, in all the subtle ways we can shade the truth into something less than—or more than—the truth. The nonfiction writer must be more truthful than we usually require of ourselves or of each other.... So when we label a piece of writing nonfiction, we are announcing our determination to rein in our impulse to lie."
>
> —Philip Gerard, from *Creative Nonfiction*, 1996

What Are the Differences Between Reading Fiction and Nonfiction?

To deepen our understanding of nonfiction, we next compare it to a mainstay in classrooms across the country—fiction. Whether we share it aloud, use it in reading lessons, or integrate it into the content areas, fiction is typically our number-one choice. Educator Vicki Benson (2002) says: "In the early grades of school, children are immersed in fiction 80 to 90 percent of the day. They read fantasy and folktales and create imaginative stories. They learn that stories have characters, a setting, and a problem that the character tries to resolve during the story."

Because of the early emphasis on fiction, students become familiar with how it sounds, how to read it, and how to write it. It stands to reason that learning how to read and write nonfiction deserves the same emphasis. This is happening to some degree; many primary teachers are weaving nonfiction into the curriculum and finding that there is much to teach students about it—how to identify its types, how to discuss the way it's written and organized, how to use access features (e.g., table of contents, index, and glossary), and how to understand visual information (e.g., diagrams, maps, and time lines). One way to do this is to teach students, in whole-class lessons, small groups, and one-on-one conferences, how reading nonfiction is different from reading fiction. Figure 1.1 lists important differences between these two activities.

To help your students understand the differences between fiction and nonfiction, pair books on the same topic and discuss them using the information in Figure 1.1 to guide you. For example, read about crocodiles in Bernard Waber's *Lyle at Christmas* (1998) and Seymour Simon's *Crocodiles & Alligators* (1999), or address the topic of frogs in Irene Livingston's *Finklehopper Frog* (2003) and Jim Arnosky's *All About Frogs* (2002). For a more sophisticated comparison, use Karen Hesse's *Out of the Dust* (1997) and Jerry Stanley's *Children of the Dust Bowl: The True Story of the School at Weedpatch Camp* (1992). Begin with simple books that are clearly defined as either fiction or nonfiction, and then move to books that blur the line. Paired books are also available commercially, such as the Magic Tree House series by Mary Pope Osborne (Random House) and Steck-Vaughn's Pair-It Books series, which are written especially for emergent readers.

Why Is There So Much Interest in Nonfiction Nowadays?

Now that we've explained how nonfiction is different from fiction, we'll discuss why it's becoming so popular. There is definitely a groundswell of interest and excitement in nonfiction for children. It is a visible genre. Books are no longer hidden on the back shelves of bookstores, but advertised extensively and placed where tiny hands can reach them. More and more nonfiction is being published as a response to diverse interests of readers. In fact, children's literature expert Susan Hepler (2003) states that "The Library of Congress (2002) reports that 'the split in our juvenile cataloging has changed from about 50–50 in the early 1990s to nearly 60 percent' in favor of nonfiction titles." What are other reasons for nonfiction's rise in popularity? We explain some here.

Figure 1.1

The Differences Between Reading Fiction and Nonfiction

When we read fiction we:

- Expect the work to be untrue. It may be classified as fantasy, a story that could never happen; contemporary realistic fiction, a story that takes place in the present but is not a "true" story; historical fiction, a story that takes place in the past and is not a "true" story.
- Expect that the work will contain the elements of story, such as plot, characters, setting, conflict, resolution, and theme.
- Rely on the first line to be the "gateway" to the text, whether it's a novel, short story, picture storybook, or play.
- Start reading at the front of the book and continue straight through to the end because it brings closure and satisfaction.
- Begin reading at the top of the page and travel to the bottom, with our eyes moving from left to right.
- Can put the book down and pick it up later at the point where we left off.
- Judge the quality of the work in terms of the quality and development of plot, theme, and characters, and the extent to which it entertains or captivates us, and holds our attention.

When we read nonfiction we:

- Expect information that is true and accurate, and depend on the writer to provide it.
- Can choose to read only part of the text. Keep in mind, though, that recent research indicates that a reader may lose meaning if he or she merely samples historical nonfiction and biography and does not read it in its entirety (Wilson, 2001). This happens because those types of books are usually written chronologically, so meaning may be lost if a reader only browses the text.
- Have the option of starting at the front of the book, the back, or somewhere in between, depending on the type of book it is, its organization, and the purpose for reading it. The first line, then, isn't always the gateway to nonfiction. For example, a reader may enter the book by starting first with the table of contents, the index, the headings, or the captioned illustrations and photos.
- May need to reread parts, so we don't necessarily need to go to the place in the book where we left off reading.
- Expect the visual elements (e.g., photographs, illustrations, diagrams, maps, graphs, time lines) to help us access information about the topic. These features can be read for meaning even when they contain few or no words.
- May be interrupted from reading the running text (the continuous writing on each page) by visual information. So we don't always start at the top and go to the bottom, nor do our eyes always go from left to right on a page.
- Read diagrams, maps, graphs, and other graphic interpretations of information from bottom to top, from right to left, or in a circular or seemingly random or zigzag way depending on the book's design and the purpose for reading.
- Compare captions to assess whether they repeat information in the text, contain new information, or describe how to process the visual elements that they support.

Educators See a Need for Including Nonfiction
In Their Classrooms

With the quantity of information available, children need to become savvy consumers of this genre—to learn what information is available to them, to ask questions and be able to locate sources for finding answers, and to be discriminating when it comes to choosing those sources. Many educators are following this lead by devoting more attention to nonfiction. It's no surprise, then, that learning about this genre is recommended and even mandated in many curriculum guides and standards documents.

The Standards Movement Is Calling Attention
To Teaching Nonfiction

Educational standards require the use of more nonfiction in reading and writing. Many district and state standards, as well as those from national organizations such as the National Council of Teachers of English and the International Reading Association (1996) place a high priority on being able to read, write, and think about informational materials. The content standards advocated by organizations such as the National Science Education Standards (National Research Council, 1996), the National Council for the Social Studies (1994), and the National Council of Teachers of Mathematics (1989) can be more easily met if students understand their way around nonfiction—how to read it, talk about it, and write it.

Publishers Are Supporting the Call for Nonfiction

Publishers are responding to the need for more high-quality nonfiction for children with an abundance of books—and seeing revenue gains. Susan Hepler (2003) says, "For years nonfiction was viewed as the fusty and lackluster cousin of fiction. Now, these books look and read better than ever with snappy graphics, clear and marvelous photographs or artwork, engaging and surprising formats, and passionate texts."

Today's nonfiction trade books are, indeed, written and illustrated in a different way than books were years ago. Researcher Richard Kerper (2003) agrees: "[Current authors and illustrators] take as much care with the illustrations, photographs, diagrams, maps, and tables as they do with the paragraphed text. Their creations speak to the reader-viewer about more than facts. They excite the senses and the imagination; they stimulate the formation of images, questions, and hypotheses. They invite a child to participate in the world of the book."

Recent nonfiction titles speak to how engaging current nonfiction is to a wide audience. Take, for example, *Audubon: Painter of Birds in the Wild Frontier* by Jennifer Armstrong (2003), *Secrets of Sound: Studying the Calls and Songs of Whales, Elephants, and Birds* by April Pulley Sayre (2002b), *Math for All Seasons* by Greg Tang (2002), *The Chimpanzees I Love: Saving Their World and Ours* by Jane Goodall (2001), *Leonardo's Horse* by Jean Fritz (2001), and *Vincent van Gogh: Portrait of an Artist* by Jan Greenberg and Sandra Jordan (2001). This is a sumptuous sampling of what publishers are offering to readers for explorations into science, social studies, famous people, mathematics, and the arts. Honors such as the Orbis Pictus Award and the Robert F. Sibert Award give trade publishers an incentive to keep the quality high.

Many publishers of curriculum materials are offering more nonfiction, too. For example, Mondo, Rigby, Pacific Learning, Shortland, Houghton Mifflin, Scholastic, and Newbridge offer multipacks and big books for guided reading and shared reading. Newbridge and Pacific Learning offer materials for guided reading and shared reading in the upper elementary grades, as well as instructional videos on using nonfiction. We'd like to see more instructional materials like these for the intermediate grades and higher, because we believe that shared reading, guided reading, and other practices typically reserved for early grades are critical in the upper grades. We'll discuss this point later in greater depth.

How Does Teaching Nonfiction Benefit Students?

Perhaps the most compelling reason for the rising tide of nonfiction is the positive impact it has on students. When you incorporate high-quality nonfiction into your program, you help students in many ways. Specifically, you:

- Meet the needs of students with a range of reading levels and interests.
- Provide examples of writing in various content areas.
- Open the door to classroom research and inquiry.
- Develop and expand vocabulary.
- Influence growth and development of primary-grade readers and writers.

In this section, we explore these benefits.

Nonfiction Meets the Needs of Students With a Range Of Reading Levels and Interests

Research (Vacca, 2002; Walpole, 1998) indicates that content area reading is difficult for many students. Textbooks, for example, may challenge even highly capable readers, because they tend to be "inconsiderate," meaning the writing is often not clear or concepts are not developed or fully explained.

As a result, students may struggle to learn from textbooks, particularly if they are the only type of text that the teacher is using. If we use science, math, and social studies textbooks exclusively, even good ones, students won't experience reading widely in content areas. They won't read other perspectives on a topic, nor will they likely read about a topic in depth. Students may not learn how to process and comprehend the discourse or vocabulary and language structures of science, mathematics, social studies, and other content areas.

Nonetheless, we expect students to be effective readers and writers of content area information. So, in addition to using the best textbooks available, it's important to choose high-quality sets of nonfiction books on topics you typically teach. A text set of well-chosen nonfiction differs in how information is presented. It will go far toward meeting a range of reading abilities and curriculum expectations and offer numerous possibilities for teaching about expository writing in the content areas. For example, you can teach how writing styles vary across types of nonfiction books or how visual information such as maps, graphs, or diagrams are used to explain concepts.

Consider this, though, before hauling loads of books to your classroom: There is more nonfiction available today than ever before. We believe that less is more. Having a lean collection of high-quality, up-to-date, accurate nonfiction books that you know well is preferable to having a library full of unfamiliar, out-of-date, or inaccurate books. In Chapter 3 we discuss how to make good selections.

Nonfiction Provides Examples of Writing In Various Content Areas

What students read influences what they write (Tierney & Shanahan, 1996). This concept is called intertextuality and is discussed in Chapter 2. When students read and write fiction predominantly, the skills and strategies that are necessary to be successful nonfiction readers and writers don't necessarily carry over. Giving students many ways to learn about and interact with nonfiction is important to help them become good readers, writers, and consumers of nonfiction. Nell Duke (2000) says, "Children must see, hear, read, and write informational texts before they have any hope of reading and writing them well."

By using well-written nonfiction books, you teach students how authors who are passionate about their topics think and write from the perspective of scientists, historians, mathematicians, or artists. You can also use them to teach how writers collect data, research a topic, and incorporate visual information. But most important, during writing instruction, you teach students how to read as a writer—to study the craft of writing nonfiction and see the many choices a nonfiction writer makes in every line of text, from selecting information to include in the text to selecting an organizational structure to selecting the lead that will open the piece (Murray, 1984). In learning to read, we are acquiring the strategies we need to make meaning of text, but in writing we are learning strategies to create meaning for others. Share a variety of nonfiction books on one topic to provide examples of how different authors think about and research a topic, as well as to show a range of writing styles, points of view, and perspectives.

Nonfiction Opens the Door to Classroom Research And Inquiry

Inquiry can take a variety of forms, from simple projects, where students collect data on their favorite kind of ice cream, to more ambitious ones, where students design and write whole books on space exploration. Regardless of their scope, inquiry investigations require a high-quality collection of nonfiction books so that students can research topics.

Certainly, students need to become savvy consumers of the array of informational sources available today, both print and nonprint sources. The Internet, for example, is an incredible source of information, but students need to learn how to use it judiciously and realize that it is not the only source for information. Some may think that technology competes with books—and could eventually bring about the printed book's demise. But educator, author, and critic Betty Carter (2000) says that there is a future for nonfiction books for children, regardless of technology. She states, "…much of what nonfiction books offer youngsters can't be replicated." We believe that the knowledge students acquire about how nonfiction books work—how they're organized, how they convey visual information, and so forth—increases their success in using other sources.

Nonfiction Develops and Expands Vocabulary

In their work on vocabulary instruction, researchers Isabel L. Beck, Margaret G. McKeown, and Linda Kucan (2002) discuss profound differences in vocabulary knowledge among students at various grade levels and with different abilities. For example, they found that first graders from high socioeconomic backgrounds have vocabularies twice the size of children from low socioeconomic backgrounds, and high-achieving third graders have vocabularies close to those of low-achieving high school seniors. The researchers believe that vocabulary isn't given the attention that it deserves in schools, and argue that "Multiple encounters over time are called for if the goal is more than a temporary surface-level understanding and if new words are to become permanently and flexibly represented in students' vocabulary repertoires."

We believe that teaching with nonfiction books in a comprehensive framework, which we describe in the next chapter, offers many opportunities to learn new content-related words, as well as strategies for figuring them out. See chapters in Part II for ideas on teaching vocabulary.

Nonfiction Influences Growth and Development of Primary-Grade Readers and Writers

One of the strongest arguments for exposing young children to informational texts is that it increases their ability to read and write it effectively in the later grades (Pappas, 1991; Sanacore, 1991). Nell Duke (2000), as well as others, states that we need to provide experiences in the early grades to help students meet the demands of informational text in the later grades. Beyond this argument, research by Linda Caswell and Duke suggests that nonfiction, rather than narrative texts, may help young children develop and grow as readers and writers. They state (1998): "...non-narrative texts provided a rich array of benefits for our students beyond simply preparing them for future encounters with these texts. Specifically, through interactions with non-narrative texts, these students became more interested, purposeful, perseverant, knowledgeable, confident, and active in their reading

IS NONFICTION ALIVE AND WELL IN YOUR CLASSROOM?

Take an inventory of your classroom environment and your instruction and see how you incorporate nonfiction.

- What do you have displayed on your classroom walls? Is it narrative? Is it nonfiction or informational text? Is it a combination of both?
- Look at your classroom library. What genres are most readily available to your students?
- Think about what you have read aloud to your students over the last month. What percentage is nonfiction?
- Think about what your students have written thus far this year. What percentage is nonfiction?
- Think about your answers. What is the status of nonfiction use in your classroom? What are your next steps?

and writing. Non-narrative texts, therefore, served as an important catalyst for their overall literacy development."

It's never too early to introduce children to nonfiction, and, indeed, we need to do this. According to Duke's (2000) research, first graders in her study were engaged only 3.6 minutes per day in written activities with informational texts, and low socioeconomic students were engaged for 1.9 minutes or less.

In later chapters, you'll see how young children respond to nonfiction enthusiastically and deeply in a variety of contexts. For example, read-aloud experiences provide the building blocks for later instruction. You'll learn how to develop children's reading and writing skills so that they eventually write their own nonfiction books, even in kindergarten. Just imagine what children would accomplish if the groundwork for learning about nonfiction were established in the primary grades and then built upon each year!

Closing Thoughts

In this chapter, we defined nonfiction and described how reading it differs from reading fiction. We also discussed why there is such an interest in nonfiction these days. We then explained the many powerful benefits of using nonfiction in the classroom.

From here, we will focus on how to become an effective teacher of nonfiction by offering specific ways to help students deal with the numerous challenges nonfiction holds for young readers and writers. In the next chapter, we describe a comprehensive framework that shows you how to scaffold instruction and move students toward independent reading and writing of nonfiction.

Chapter 2
A Comprehensive Framework For Teaching Nonfiction Reading and Writing

"Kids seem to have a hard time assimilating and understanding nonfiction....
After they have finished a report, and I ask them what it is about, many of
them say, 'Well, can I see my paper? I need to look at it to tell you.'
Or worse, 'I don't know.' We need to teach them to engage with the material
they read about—to think about it, process it, and turn it around in their
minds to see what makes sense. My kids need...processing time to make
sense of what they're reading before they start writing."

—Mary Evans, fourth-grade teacher

As we said in Chapter I, nonfiction is no longer the literary stepchild in the curriculum. Teachers across the country want to help students become good readers and writers of nonfiction. So what's the best way for them to do that? This chapter describes a comprehensive framework for weaving nonfiction into the literacy program. This framework is organized around levels of scaffolding, from heavy to light, to move students from being novice to independent readers and writers of nonfiction.

Teaching Nonfiction in a Comprehensive Literacy Program

Learning to read and write nonfiction is so important in our information age that it can't be left to chance. Teachers tell us that, in the long run, incidental or occasional teaching of it doesn't produce a high level of proficiency. We have to do much more than simply make nonfiction books available to students or teach fiction only and hope skills transfer to nonfiction.

We believe that high-quality learning is the result of high-quality teaching. High-quality teaching means helping students explore nonfiction books in deep and thorough ways. They learn how it works from the inside out—how to select books wisely, how to read and understand nonfiction in different content areas, how to use visual information, how to examine nonfiction as a tool for inquiry, and how to craft good nonfiction writing. We also must encourage students to wonder, question, and develop a deep desire to seek answers in good nonfiction books. This kind of teaching takes time because the goal is so ambitious: to transform students into independent learners. The time you invest in helping your students learn about the complexities of nonfiction will result in better reading, writing, thinking, and engagement in the inquiry process.

So how does this all happen? We believe learning happens in a literacy program that gives students many different opportunities to interact with literature. A good program should contain:

- instructional read aloud and modeled writing
- shared reading, shared writing, and interactive writing
- guided reading and guided writing
- reading and writing discovery circles
- readers' workshop and writers' workshop
- extension activities for reading and writing
- mini-lessons for reading and writing

Each of these approaches offers students different learning experiences. In each approach, the teacher's role is to "scaffold" instruction, which means that she or he adjusts instruction and expectations according to students' abilities, so that all students can learn successfully. For example, in highly scaffolded instruction (e.g., instructional read alouds and modeled writing), the teacher models, or demonstrates, strategies that are new to students. From there, the teacher moves to a more moderate level of scaffolding (e.g., guided reading and guided writing), and finally to a low level (e.g., readers' and writers' workshops) as students become more knowledgeable. (See Figure 2.1.) Educators Michael Graves and Bonnie Graves (2003), building on the work of P. David Pearson and Margaret Gallagher (1983), say that "… effective instruction often follows a progression in which teachers gradually do less of the work and students gradually do more. It is through this process of gradually assuming more responsibility for their learning that students become competent, independent learners."

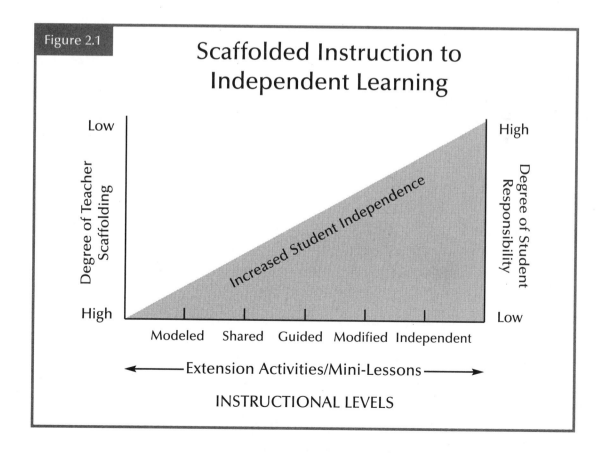

Figure 2.1

Scaffolded Instruction to Independent Learning

Here's a simple example of scaffolded instruction: If a friend who is unfamiliar with sophisticated kitchen gadgets is interested in learning how a breadmaker works, we show her by giving a demonstration. Our friend watches carefully to see how we, the more expert ones, operate the machine. That's an example of highly scaffolded instruction. Next, we might take her, step-by-step, through the procedures of working the breadmaker, repeating the demonstration, and then giving her opportunities to try each step herself. As she practices, we observe and offer assistance and feedback. Over time, our scaffolding decreases as she takes on more responsibility for learning how to work the machine on her own. Through our gradual release of responsibility, we move our friend from being a novice user of the breadmaker to becoming an independent user.

A Comprehensive Framework
Organized by Levels of Scaffolding

The same basic principles are at work as you move students from being novices to becoming independent learners. Figure 2.2 shows our framework, which clearly spells out the levels of scaffolding and roles of the teacher and student for each approach in the literacy program.

This framework is based on the notion of the gradual release of responsibility (Campione, 1981; Graves & Graves, 2003; Pearson & Gallagher, 1983), showing how the teacher's role shifts from demonstrating to leading to assisting and eventually to observing and assessing. Conversely, the student's role moves from watching to apprenticing to demonstrating and finally to doing the task independently.

Notice that each reading approach has a writing counterpart—for example, instructional read aloud has modeled writing; shared reading has interactive writing and shared writing. This is because reading and writing are strongly connected processes. Although the reading and writing approaches may be taught in tandem, they aren't always taught that way. We'll discuss this concept later in the chapter. Mini-lessons are just what the name implies: brief, teacher-directed lessons, which are taught throughout the framework as needed. Students do extension activities independently to practice what they have learned. These activities are designed for either individuals or small groups. They are used as follow-up work to instructional approaches. See Chapter 9 for a more detailed description of these.

To further clarify the framework, we define the levels of scaffolding and the approaches in the next section.

Figure 2.2

Comprehensive Framework

Level of Scaffolding	Role of Teacher and Student	Reading Instructional Approach		Writing Instructional Approach
Modeled	• Teacher demonstrates • Students watch	Instructional Read Aloud	↑	Modeled Writing
Shared	• Teacher leads • Students apprentice	Shared Reading	Mini-Lessons and Extension Activities*	Interactive Writing and Shared Writing
Guided	• Students demonstrate • Teacher assists	Guided Reading		Guided Writing
Modified	• Students work collaboratively • Teacher modifies support by observing, helping, assessing	Reading Discovery Circles		Writing Discovery Circles
	• Students work independently, with other students, and/or with the teacher • Teacher modifies support by observing, helping, assessing	Readers' Workshop		Writers' Workshop
Independent	• Students practice • Teacher observes and assesses independent practice activities	Extension Activities*	↓	Extension Activities*

* Extension activities can be used as follow-up activities with all instructional approaches, but students are working independently—either individually or in small groups. Keep in mind that extension activities should match the student's ability to practice the activities independently.

Modeled Instruction: Teacher Demonstrates and Students Watch

Modeled instruction is most appropriate for teaching something new. It can be done with large or small groups, or with individual students, at all grade levels. During modeled instruction, the teacher demonstrates the processes of reading and writing text by reading, writing, and/or thinking aloud about texts. (Think alouds are described in detail in Chapter 5.)

The teacher's primary responsibility is to demonstrate by pointing out, naming, thinking aloud, and applying the new teaching point. These are ways to help students notice important features of nonfiction and are described later in the chapter. The students listen, observing the teacher's moves and learning from the demonstration. Instructional read aloud and modeled writing are examples of modeled instruction.

Instructional Read Aloud

During instructional read alouds, the teacher reads and thinks aloud a small portion of a nonfiction book. She demonstrates how an experienced reader navigates nonfiction text. She might, for example, show how to preview a book before reading it, how to apply strategies during reading, how to understand new vocabulary, how to make sense of confusing information, how to read visual information such as time lines, and how to monitor one's own reading. Often instructional read alouds are interactive; students participate in the discussion. When reading aloud complicated nonfiction, have overhead transparencies or big book editions of the text so that students can see visual features.

Modeled Writing

Modeled writing is done in large or small groups, or with individual students, using chart paper or overhead transparencies. The teacher demonstrates how she or other authors create or revise a nonfiction text, thinking aloud as necessary to clarify her decisions and examine closely the writing of others to uncover the choices they made. Topics she might cover include what to write, how to start, what words to use, ways to revise, and how to incorporate visual features or other elements of nonfiction. As with instructional read alouds, the students' role is primarily to listen, although there may be some exchanges with the teacher.

Shared Instruction: Teacher Leads and Students Apprentice

In shared instruction, the teacher builds on what she demonstrated in modeled instruction, usually with the entire class, but sometimes with small groups or individuals. Although she decreases the level of scaffolding in shared instruction, she maintains responsibility for selecting the teaching points, leading the discussion, and directing the processing of how to read and write nonfiction. The students' role is that of apprentice, meaning they contribute to the discussion by problem solving and sharing discoveries about the text that is being read or written.

The teacher provides explicit instruction. To do this, she typically uses enlarged versions of the text, such as big books, charts, or overhead transparencies, so that everyone in the group can see what she is reading and referring to. Shared reading, interactive writing, and shared writing are examples of shared instruction.

Shared Reading

A shared reading session may consist of two stages, one being the teacher and students rereading a familiar nonfiction text and the teacher then asking questions to help students figure out how the text works by pointing out, naming, and, in the case of writing, applying different features. From there, the teacher may move on to an unfamiliar text to continue that work or introduce new concepts and strategies.

Interactive Writing and Shared Writing

Interactive writing and shared writing are activities where the teacher and students collaborate to plan, draft, and revise text. The teacher provides a high degree of scaffolding and, depending on the age and knowledge of the students, may select the topic, type of writing, and features to include. The students share responsibility for determining the final wording of the text.

Interactive writing is primarily used with kindergartners and first graders. The teacher decides on specific teaching points and students "share the pen" (McCarrier, Pinnell, & Fountas, 2000), meaning the teacher invites them to the easel to contribute letters or words. The teacher provides direct instruction as needed. For example, she might provide instruction in phonological and word analysis (hearing and recording sounds), concepts about and conventions of print, and reading to confirm what is written. Interactive writing can also be used with small groups of second graders and third graders who are struggling with writing (McCarrier, Pinnell, & Fountas).

Shared writing, unlike interactive writing, is often used in grades K through 6. Although the teacher serves as the primary scribe, students are expected to help make decisions about the piece's content. The teacher and students work together to develop and organize the ideas for the text. For example, the teacher might work with students to write a paragraph that compares and contrasts information or a typical feature of nonfiction, such as a sidebar, to include in a report. The teacher's final written product is read aloud and may be used for other mini-lessons, as well as serve as a model for students who are working on their own writing.

Guided Instruction: Students Demonstrate and Teacher Assists

Guided instruction provides opportunities for small groups of students to try out new understandings about how to read and write nonfiction. The teacher reduces scaffolding to a helping level, making students responsible for demonstrating what they know. She prompts, cues, and assists students in using and applying what they know to reading and writing text that is slightly more difficult but within the students' reach. Two examples of guided instruction are guided reading and guided writing.

Guided Reading

In guided reading, the teacher usually works with two to six students with similar needs. Each student has a copy of the same book. The teacher overviews and introduces the book and comments on the nonfiction features it contains. Students read designated sections of the book either orally or silently, depending on reading ability. When students read orally, the teacher listens to check on how they are processing the text. Following the reading, whether oral or silent, the teacher leads a discussion about the book, helping students make connections to other books or information, sort through any conflicting information, and summarize information. The teacher may ask students to continue reading portions of the book on their own or do a writing activity that's connected with the guided reading lesson.

Guided Writing

For guided writing, the teacher uses explicit instruction with either large or small groups, often after instructional read alouds, shared reading, and guided reading, or as mini-lessons in writers' workshop. There are two basic purposes for guided writing: to provide specific information about some aspect of writing expository text and to have students *try out* a particular writing strategy, skill, or technique, such as writing captions, comparisons, or bulleted lists. Students write in pairs or individually, share their writing, and receive feedback from both the teacher and peers.

Modified Instruction: Students Work on Their Own or Collaboratively, and Teacher Modifies Support as Necessary

This level of scaffolding encompasses four instructional approaches: reading and writing discovery circles and readers' and writers' workshops. Both discovery circles and workshops build on what students learn from modeled, shared, and guided instruction. In discovery circles, students read and write together in small groups. In readers' and writers' workshops, students work more independently, occasionally working in pairs or small groups, while in discovery circles they work in pairs or in small groups, but not alone. Here, students are encouraged to solve problems that come up in their reading and writing on their own and with peers, instead of relying on the teacher. However, the teacher remains available to students.

To get started, the teacher may first give a mini-lesson focusing on some aspect of reading or writing nonfiction. When the discovery circles meet, the teacher observes, listens in on groups' conversations, and sometimes participates as a temporary member of a circle if modeling is needed. During reading and writing workshops, the teacher observes, assists, and conferences with individuals or small groups as the need arises.

By closely observing students at work in discovery circles and workshops, teachers can find out what students understand about reading and writing nonfiction as they work with their peers and on their own. Taking notes is a good idea as it provides informal assessments that can help the teacher modify instruction based on what students need. From notes, the teacher can determine how much additional scaffolded instruction students need—in other words, determine the point at which to enter the comprehensive framework.

Reading Discovery Circles

In reading discovery circles, small groups of students typically meet to talk about a single nonfiction book that all members have read (although there are variations to this that are described in Chapter 8). The teacher usually selects the texts for the discovery circles, based on a content area topic or aspects of nonfiction that the class is studying. For more advanced discovery circles, these selections may be on the same topic, a variety of titles by the same author, or nonfiction written by student authors.

During reading discovery circles, groups meet to discuss what they've read and to share writing or other responses to the selections. Prior to the circle meeting, the teacher often works with students to focus the discussion. Discussion topics might include what the author wrote about, how he or she wrote it, or how he or she used visual information. Students may also talk about debatable, controversial, or inconsistent information they found.

Writing Discovery Circles

During the writing discovery circles, students collaborate on a piece of writing. Following the reading discovery circle, members draft pieces of writing that represents their collective thinking or findings. The topic emerges from the group or is assigned by the teacher. One student serves as the scribe. The group's work might include diagrams, charts, time lines, a letter to the author, or even an argument or position statement. Students can also bring individual pieces to discovery circles and share them to receive feedback from group members.

Readers' Workshop

Readers' workshop is a daily block of **time where** many literacy-related activities may take place: vocabulary work, guided reading, independent **reading of** self-selected nonfiction books, extension activities (which are described below), and so forth, but its primary focus is opportunity for independent reading. The workshop may begin with a read aloud and shared reading lesson and lead to word-level work. The teacher may follow that with independent reading and/or guided reading. Because the teacher must meet the needs of all learners, she varies her scaffolding. So, for example, some students may be involved in a guided reading lesson during this time, while others are engaged in independent extension activities.

Writers' Workshop

In writers' workshop, students write on self-selected topics associated with content areas. The block usually includes mini-lessons, small-group and individual conferences, independent writing time, and a large share session where students read their writing and receive feedback from the class. Guided writing sessions may also be included as a mini-lesson to initiate the session or time in which the teacher works with students who have similar needs.

Mini-Lessons for Reading and Writing

Mini-lessons are short, focused lessons that, like extension activities, can be carried out across the framework as needed. The teacher chooses the topic and leads the lesson, inviting students to ask questions and make observations at relevant points. Topics might include management practices, such as how to maintain reading/writing folders or complete an extension activity; how to use a particular convention, such as commas; or how to read or write a particular text feature, such as captions. Mini-lessons are often conducted at the beginning of workshops to lead students into new territories that help them grow as readers and writers. They can be done with the entire class, small groups, and even with individuals.

Scaffolding for Independent Learning: Students Practice and Teacher Observes and Assesses

Students need opportunities to practice the strategies and apply concepts they are learning during instructional read alouds, shared reading and writing, interactive writing, and guided reading and writing. Extension activities are designed to provide those opportunities. Students might practice data gathering by taking an inventory of each student's favorite color; research nonfiction books to locate information on topics that interest them or to find access features authors use as models for their own writing; or try some short exercises designed to boost their nonfiction writing skills, such as crafting captions or definitions. (See Chapter 9 for a discussion of extension activities.)

Extension activities are usually assigned immediately after guided reading or during workshops because, at that point, students have the basic background knowledge they need to carry out the activity. Extension activities can be done in centers, at desks, or even in the library.

Determining the Level of Scaffolding

A master teacher knows how much explaining, modeling, prompting, and cueing to do to ensure that students are sufficiently supported. She also sees when students are doing their problem solving without becoming frustrated. When the explanations are too detailed, students tend to forget or zone out. And conversely, when explanations aren't detailed enough, students usually wind up with way too many questions. In the first case, the teacher overestimates the student's ability to absorb lots of information; in the second, she underestimates and expects the student to figure it out on his or her own. When a teacher scaffolds effectively, she supports the student in figuring out new information without frustrating that student, thus keeping success within reach.

The comprehensive framework will help you reach that point. You may not take every student through every level for every teaching point, nor move through the framework sequentially. Because your students probably capture a range of abilities and background knowledge, you'll want to select instructional levels that best fit their needs. Determine the level by carefully assessing your students, using these questions as a guide:

- What do I want to teach about nonfiction?
- What do I want students to be able to do as readers and/or writers?
- What do students know already about nonfiction?
- Are they familiar with the topic or the content?
- What kinds of scaffolded experiences do the students need to successfully achieve independence with a new concept?

Travis Robinson, a fourth-grade teacher, puts these questions into action. A group of his students doesn't understand how to use nonfiction that includes time lines. So he plans a shared reading lesson to help the group learn how to read time lines. He makes several overhead transparencies of time lines from nonfiction books for his lesson to help the students determine how they work. He also wants students to be able to construct their own time lines, so he decides on the levels of scaffolded writing instruction that make the most sense. Since the group has never constructed a time line on its own, Travis plans a modeled writing lesson to demonstrate how he writes one. This will be followed in a later lesson by a shared writing lesson to create a time line using information from a short biography on a favorite sports figure. He may also do a guided writing lesson using another short biography, asking students to pair up to create a time line. These experiences will ensure their success at including one in their inquiry report on presidents.

Travis' decision making is strategic. It's on target, efficient, and effective. His choice of an instructional approach depends on the amount of support students need, which he determines by assessing what they know and what they need to know. See the box above for guidelines on selecting approaches based on the difficulty of the text.

The Theory Behind the Comprehensive Framework

There are two major theoretical underpinnings of the framework, which are grounded in the work of Russian psychologist Lev Vygotsky (1978): the role of assisted performance in teaching and the role of oral language in learning.

The Role of Assisted Performance in Teaching

Vygotsky's work (1978) points to the importance of interactions to promote children's thinking and problem-solving skills. With scaffolded instruction from experts (teachers, parents, and so forth), learners attempt new tasks and make cognitive progress, assuming that instruction is in the zone of proximal development (ZPD). The zone of proximal development is the area in which a child is incapable of learning a task independently, but is capable of learning it with the support of a more knowledgeable other. This reminds us of the old adage that two heads are better than one. However, in this case, one "head" is more knowledgeable and is guiding and supporting the other one, which is less informed. As the more knowledgeable one assists the learner through increasingly more difficult tasks, the learner internalizes understandings, concepts, knowledge, skills, strategies, and language (Pressley, 2002b).

This notion of assisted performance emerged from Vygotsky's observations (1978) of adults working with children to solve problems within their zone of proximal development. Adults assist performance by first observing what the child understands and then carefully teaches by adjusting the level of support needed for the child to move a step closer to carrying out the task independently, which is precisely our goal for the framework. With support, the learner can eventually perform the task without assistance, having internalized the kinds of thinking that were previously supported by an adult. Michael Pressley (2002b) emphasizes, "Without adult assistance, there are many forms of thinking that the child would not discover alone or in interaction with peers."

Our goal as teachers is to explain and model at a level that matches our students' needs. Too little modeling, too little explaining, or the inverse—too much modeling or explaining—may result in students feeling confused, overwhelmed, or just not smart enough.

The Role of Oral Language in Learning

Language is essential to learning. We use it when carrying out all higher mental functions, such as drawing conclusions, constructing meaning, and planning ahead. We use language to regulate actions and achieve goals. We use it to represent our actions, our thoughts, and the thoughts of others, as in retelling. Made up of a system of symbols (words), language helps us to communicate (talk, read, or write), record (write), and store ideas, actions, and things. Words symbolize the physical world and the abstract world of thought and ideas.

Teachers use language to assist performance. How well we use language to assist performance has a huge effect on the cognitive development of our students. In fact, in their study of exemplary fourth-grade teachers, Richard L. Allington, Peter H. Johnston, and Jeni Pollack Day (2002) report that classroom talk between teachers and students, as well as the nature of that talk, was one of the features that set those teachers apart. They report, "Classroom talk was… process oriented—what might be called strategic. Teachers encouraged students to describe *how* they accomplished things—solving a problem, selecting a topic, locating information, and so forth. 'How could we find that out?' and other such comments permeated teacher talk."

Critical Connections Between Talk and Learning

Structured time to talk is essential to thinking and writing about topics. Students need to talk about what they are learning—to you, to their classmates, and silently to themselves, in their heads. Talking, in particular, retelling, and thinking aloud helps students process unfamiliar or complex material they have read or heard; it allows them to internalize new information, vocabulary, language structures, and knowledge about how to read and write nonfiction.

Even adults use language to process information. Here's an example: During a checkup, your doctor informs you of a minor illness. When a friend asks, "How did it go?" you try to reconstruct your conversation with the doctor. You tap into early forms of oral language—simply telling what happened by retelling what the physician said. (See Figure 2.3.) You may fill in the gaps of what you don't recall or understand with knowledge you do hold. Or you may actually recall more as you retell what happened to your friend. You also might interpret the information, discuss your plan of action, or describe the procedures that the doctor suggested. You may even separate your assessment of the situation from the doctor's, making it seem less or more severe than it really is.

These oral transactions are a normal part of our daily lives and are essential to the development of problem-solving skills. They are best developed through a social process and nurtured in a context in which learners are scaffolded by greater experts, such as adults and more knowledgeable peers. Talk, then, is central to the success of the comprehensive framework. Donald Graves (1989) says: "The ability to compose a story about 'what happened' is one of the fundamental units of human thought and knowledge. Recounting in order with an interpretation of events is the underpinning of all human thought. Without it there would be no history, geology, chemistry, biology, or physics, to name but a few disciplines that rely on an orderly recounting of events."

The Underpinnings of Nonfiction Discourse

Young children have a natural enthusiasm to tell adults about events in their lives—whether it's about losing a tooth, going to the circus, or winning an award at school. These daily oral transactions build and support crucial thinking abilities—beginning early in life, as children interact with parents and caregivers, and then later as they interact with teachers. Adults help children orally construct the events of their lives by encouraging them to tell and retell. The questions, prompts, and rephrasing that adults offer help children clarify their explanations.

Here's an example. When Jan was eight years old and living near her Uncle Ben, she and her friend Gail saw an odd-looking bird near a pond where they were playing. They ran into Uncle Ben's house all excited. Both gasping for breath, they started to talk at once about the bird they had seen at the edge of the pond, describing it as "enormous with a long beak." They had never seen one like it before. They thought that it was prehistoric. They thought they had discovered something that would send the science community into a frenzy.

First, Uncle Ben asked the girls to slow down. Then he told them to catch their breath and describe everything they remembered about the bird. He had the girls show him how tall the bird stood, how big around it was, and its color. He asked again exactly where they saw it and what it was doing. He also asked the girls why they thought it was prehistoric.

Having a hint as to what kind of bird it was, but not revealing it, Uncle Ben went to the pond with the girls to have a look. The bird was still in the same spot. He knew from looking at it exactly what kind it was, but he wanted to take the girls through the process of finding out together. Out came one of Uncle Ben's many field guides. Together they scanned the different sections and, by process of elimination, came to the one on herons. They found that the "prehistoric" bird was actually a great blue heron. And, with great interest and enthusiasm, they read the information about it. Uncle Ben's questions helped to draw out more details from the girls. He prompted them to think through what they saw and to expand their responses. The girls had something exciting to relate and an adult who took the time to help them process it. Uncle Ben would've made a great teacher.

This kind of scaffolded oral interaction forms a base for effective nonfiction instruction later in school. The adult showed interest in the children's account by asking them to recount as many details as they could in order to clarify when he didn't understand, and to interpret what they were thinking ("Why do you think the bird is prehistoric?"). These important moves invite children to explore what they know and understand. They are fundamental strategies for reading and understanding material in nonfiction books and for crafting expository writing. Rich conversations need to happen at every level of the framework for all students at all ages.

Donald Graves (1989) believes there are essential oral language experiences that are linked to reading and writing nonfiction. In the left-hand column of Figure 2.3, we share these oral language experiences, and in the right-hand column, we connect them to specific examples of reading and writing nonfiction.

Figure 2.3

Oral Language Connections to Reading and Writing Nonfiction

ESSENTIAL ORAL LANGUAGE EXPERIENCES DESCRIBED BY DONALD GRAVES (1989)	CONNECTIONS TO READING AND WRITING NONFICTION
What happened. Children need to be able to give recountings of what has happened to them or of events they wish to share with others. Fundamental is the ability to recount an event in the order it happened. Most disciplines rely on orderly recountings of events.	Much of the nonfiction we read and write describes what happened or happens. Letter writing is an important first step for young expository writers. Many of the early emergent nonfiction readers are "what happened" descriptions. In nonfiction for older readers, what happened is often combined with other oral transactional forms identified by Graves.
Interpretation. Shared events need interpretation. "This is how it happened and why I think it happened that way." If others question the information, further data is needed to support conclusions.	Many of Jim Murphy's books (1995; 2000), for example, not only describe events, but also interpret the events to help readers. Reporting information is only the beginning. Helping one's audience understand and access the events requires an analytical layer of meaning.
Invention. Children (and adults) invent data to go with their accounts and interpretations. Learning to distinguish between fact and fiction for self and others is key to selecting nonfiction sources and becoming a critical consumer as well as creator of them. Further, as students engage in short-term and long-term data gathering, their appreciation for accuracy matures.	Accuracy becomes an important issue as we examine how authors of informational sources fill in missing information. Students' experiences with invention supports their learning how to read critically, to identify misinformation, to note when or how authors are identifying missing information, and to use these mentor texts for their own writing. Authors often include information on the limitations of their research. One example: Stanley and Vennema (1994), in *Cleopatra*, inform readers that all the information written on Cleopatra was done so by her enemies.

ESSENTIAL ORAL LANGUAGE EXPERIENCES DESCRIBED BY DONALD GRAVES (1989)	CONNECTIONS TO READING AND WRITING NONFICTION
Show or display. Children wish to display their skills and share the process of how they do things. Questions and requests of young children for clarification help them build schema for how they do things and eventually helps them learn how to read and write directions. Recounting a process is the foundation of observation and recording in sciences such as chemistry, physics, and biology.	How-to books, as well as books in the fields of science, use descriptions of processes and orderly descriptions of collecting information. Whether it's Jane Goodall's presentation of her work with primates (2001) or descriptions of how the water cycle works, all have their roots in this form of expression. Flow charts are often used to visually depict processes.
Planning. Children need to be able to use language to structure a future project or request, to hypothesize, or to give directions to others. Using language to affect the future is one of the most difficult composing tasks, requiring a strong sense of the planning process as well as the ability to represent the event to others, and, at the same time, to decenter and write and read the directions from another point of view.	An effective reader is able to recognize how others have planned their presentation of information. Recognition of organizational structures allows the reader to determine how to use and read an informational source. Planning one's approach to data gathering, note taking, and creation of final product all build on children's early and school experiences with planning skills. Today's nonfiction often includes information describing the author's research process.
Dual points of view. Children encounter different points of view throughout the day. They need to understand the logic behind other points of view and at the same time have their own views confirmed. Children encounter these structures and narratives that deal with other points of view in the literature that is read to them. Persuasive, argumentative, and report writing grow out of opportunities to encounter contrary points of view leading to acknowledgment of another point of view, to understand the rational facts in opposition, and to propose alternative action.	Ability to recognize limited presentations and rational facts are rooted in the ability to acknowledge other points of view. Dual points of view support searching for conflicting information as well as considering the needs of audience when presenting information. Many authors use comparison and cause/effect structures to explore dual points of view and to clarify relationships. Unfortunately, informational sources and nonfiction literature do include biased and single-perspective information.

Adapted from Graves, 1989 |

Role of Retelling in Learning How to Read and Write Nonfiction

Learning to retell is an essential underpinning of the comprehension literacy framework. When we ask students to retell after hearing or reading nonfiction text, we are asking them to specifically recall and interpret the text either orally or in writing. This ability to retell a text in a comprehensible way is at the very heart of students' learning how nonfiction works. Noted researchers Hazel Brown and Brian Cambourne (1987) connect the retelling procedure with becoming consciously aware of language and the content. Through retelling experiences, students attend to features of text that they would not typically focus on either orally or in writing. Brown and Cambourne (1987) found that by providing structured opportunities for students to engage in retelling after read alouds and shared, guided, and independent reading, students showed growth in knowledge of text forms, text conventions, the processes involved in text construction, the range and variety of text forms and conventions used in writing, control over vocabulary, reading flexibility, and confidence.

In the course of retelling a nonfiction text, either orally or in writing, students not only internalize its content, but also its conventions and features (Graves, 1989). As you and students respond to the retelling, students refine their thinking and their ability to retell. Students recognize they must retell (again, whether orally or in writing) in a way that others will understand. As you work with all the approaches in the framework, assist students in retelling. By doing so, you help them reshape the information they read and make it their own.

Advantages to Using the Comprehensive Framework

There are many good reasons for using the comprehensive framework in your classroom. Here, we point out a few beyond the ones we've already discussed.

Contains a Broad Base of Teaching Approaches

As we've discussed, the framework is made up of reading aloud, shared reading, guided reading, interactive writing, writers' workshop, and so forth. As students gain expertise about how to read and write nonfiction through these approaches, they become more independent. Gay Su Pinnell and Irene Fountas (2003) say: "No one instructional concept or approach can provide the support children need to be good comprehenders of written text. Comprehension is built through numerous and varied experiences with texts—hearing them read aloud, reading them independently, reading them with support and guidance, writing about them, and sharing the reading with others."

We heartily agree! Although Fountas and Pinnell are not strictly referring to teaching nonfiction, an instructional repertoire that allows many ways for students to interact with text is critical.

Applies to All Grade Levels

The literacy framework is designed for use in kindergarten through grade six. Although modeled, shared, and guided instruction are often used in the primary grades, when you look closely at what the teacher does in each approach to support learners, it becomes difficult to make grade- or age-level distinctions. Each approach offers students a different way to learn how to be more effective readers and writers.

As we've said before, you don't need to move through the framework sequentially, nor would it always make sense to do so. Determine what your students already know about nonfiction, what you want them to learn, how much support they will need to learn it, and then determine the best approach or approaches for them.

Provides a Common Way to Talk About Teaching Reading and Writing

No matter what grade you teach, the framework provides you and your colleagues with a common language to talk about nonfiction reading and writing instruction. This language helps you talk about curriculum both within and across grades. Students will recognize this language as they move through the grades; they won't be confused by different expecta-

PLAN OPPORTUNITIES FOR CONVERSATION

Student talk and retelling should be expected and valued throughout the framework. Here are some questions for students to get you started:
- What did you learn in hearing or reading this piece of nonfiction?
- What do you notice and discover about this nonfiction book that we are reading or hearing? Encourage students to use the vocabulary associated with aspects of nonfiction—writing style, visual information, access features. See Chapter 3 for examples.
- What questions do you have for the author?
- What connections do you make with what you already know about the content of the book?
- What connections can you make to personal experiences?
- What connections do you make with other books on the topic?
- How would you explain what you've learned to a younger audience?
- What are you learning about nonfiction as literature as you read about this topic you're investigating? For example: How did the author support readers to understand new vocabulary? How is the content organized in the book? How did the author use access features such as a table of contents? (See Chapter 3 for details.)

tions and terms for instruction at every grade level. This consistency makes transitions from grade to grade seamless and leads to greater productivity because students don't get bogged down in terminology. Teachers and students are freed from "recreating the wheel" and can devote their full attention to what needs to be learned (Pinnell & Scharer, 2003).

Helps Students Learn "Rules of Notice"

Our ability to read and write nonfiction depends upon "noticing" details within the text and visuals. As we become more informationally literate, we are able to separate important material from that which is less so, understand how to interpret information, and eventually use what we learn in our own writing. Researcher Peter Rabinowitz (1998) calls these strategies "Rules of Notice." For example, when reading nonfiction it is important to notice what type it is, its organizational structure, kinds of access features, use of words such as "may" or "perhaps," and how to interpret information in bulleted lists to fully comprehend the material.

Literacy expert Jeffrey Wilhelm (2001) suggests that we help our students develop the rules of notice best by providing instruction that progresses from highly scaffolded support to low support, as described in the comprehensive framework. You can demonstrate what expert readers and writers need to "notice" about how nonfiction works by thinking out loud during instructional read alouds and modeled writing, through discussions during shared and guided reading, and through interactive, shared, and guided writing. Here are some things to try:

- Point out and name the types of books and features, such as sidebars, captions, hedging on the author's part, or chronological structure.
- Describe the types of nonfiction and how to use their features. You might say, "I need to reread this book because...," "This book seems to be written like my journal because...," "I'm going to look at the labels in the diagram because...," or "I'll compare this section to the chart because...."
- Demonstrate how to read different types of nonfiction and interpret the features.
- Demonstrate how to write different types of nonfiction, applying various organizational structures and text features.

Promotes Active and Reflective Teaching

Sometimes we expect too much of our students too quickly. Offering a few lessons here and a few assignments there is counterproductive, as it won't produce successful students in the long run.

Rather, what makes a difference is a commitment to carefully crafted reading and writing experiences that are designed to support where students are in their learning. When teachers work within the framework, they continually monitor and reflect about how and what students are learning. Then, they decide how much assistance/support to provide in order to move students toward greater independence. This is active and reflective teaching in action—and it helps students grow, develop, and meet their potential as effective nonfiction readers and writers.

Provides a Platform for Teaching Vocabulary

Having a large vocabulary is key to being a successful reader and writer of nonfiction. However, simply asking students to define new vocabulary words in social studies and science and use them in sentences isn't an effective way to remember those words and make them their own. Instead, repeated experiences with new content area words are key to internalizing words (Beck, McKeown, & Kucan, 2002). Hearing and discussing new words during instructional read alouds, seeing and discussing them in shared reading and guided reading, and composing them in interactive/shared writing and guided writing helps students master vocabulary and use it in independent work. Activities such as these also get students interested in and excited about learning new words. So the framework is the perfect platform for developing vocabulary.

Allows You to Make Connections Between Reading, Talking, and Writing

Reading, talking, and writing work in tandem in the framework and promote "intertextuality"—how familiar texts influence what we comprehend and how we comprehend unfamiliar ones. The language and structures we use when we read, talk, and write are borrowed from or are influenced by our prior experiences with texts. Did you ever wonder why so many young children begin or end their written and oral stories this way—"Once upon a time" and "They lived happily ever after"? That's a simple example of intertextuality at work. These children have been exposed to fairytales at bedtime both from oral storytelling and from books being shared aloud. These experiences, in turn, influence the way young children write stories. No matter how old we are, the way we think, the way we read, the way we write, and how we make sense of the world are all impacted by our experiences. Think about the recreational reading that you do. Both of us have favorite authors. We've become much more aware of how much we think, write, and even use the words our very authors use in their writing—another example of intertextuality at work!

So what does this have to do with the framework? The framework supports multiple exposures to nonfiction and its features—through reading, talking, and writing. This is critical for the nonfiction writing our students produce. The more we expose students to high-quality nonfiction and encourage conversations around how it is written, the more likely students are to write their own high-quality nonfiction.

Exposing students to new information more than once helps them remember the content. For example, when we read two books about the same topic, we comprehend the second text far better than if we read unrelated texts (Crafton, 1981). The experience of reading the first text increases the comprehension of a second related text (Hayes & Tierney, 1982).

Helps Students View Inquiry as a Process

Learning how to engage in inquiry in sophisticated ways is a process that takes time. Using the comprehensive framework teaches students how to think, talk, read, and write about content in increasingly more mature and powerful ways. Even kindergartners can apply what they learn, for example, in modeled instruction to engage in small-scale inquiry projects, such as making a bar graph of favorite ice cream flavors or kinds of clocks. The inquiry process is discussed more fully in Chapter 4.

Closing Thoughts

As teacher Mary Evans said at the beginning of this chapter, "We need to teach [students] to engage with the material they read about—to think about it, process it, and turn it around in their minds to see what makes sense." We need to offer them multiple experiences reading and writing nonfiction where we actively and explicitly teach and scaffold students' learning. This will help them increase their understanding about the material they read and promote active thinking and processing.

The comprehensive framework to teach nonfiction reading and writing shows us the many possible ways there are to teach students. Each of its approaches is described in terms of the teacher's role and the students' role. Each offers students different and important literacy experiences as they move from being novice learners to independent learners.

In the next chapter, we introduce you to the anatomy of nonfiction—a guide to learning about how nonfiction works—to help you make wise selections for use in every approach of the framework.

Chapter 3
Turning a Critical Eye on Nonfiction:
Evaluating and Selecting Materials

Janet Nordfors' students are learning to become critical consumers of nonfiction as they read and discuss books together.

B arbara Bourgoine, a Title I teacher, had four second-grade reluctant readers who, like so many students, had heard and read primarily fiction in earlier grades. As a result, they were unfamiliar with the features and structures of nonfiction. They equated drawings with fiction and photographs with nonfiction. So, she conducted a shared reading lesson to help them understand the differences between fiction and nonfiction. Here is Barbara's description of that lesson:

I started by asking the four children, "Why do we have books?" The question took them by surprise. But after thinking about it, they decided that books are for learning. I then showed them an assortment of ten books with the titles masked and asked, "Can you tell me if these books are fiction or nonfiction?" The students quickly sorted the books into piles. Books with photographs went into the nonfiction pile; books with illustrations went into the fiction pile. When they were done, I picked up a book from the fiction group and revealed the title: *Dominoes Around the World* (Lankford, 1998). (See Figure 3.1.)

"What do you think now?" I inquired. "Fiction or nonfiction?"

Robin scanned the book from back to front, closed it, and confidently announced, "Nonfiction." When I asked him how he decided, he exclaimed, "Because nothing happened in the end. It's all the same!" (See Figure 3.2 for the page that prompted Robin's response.)

From there, I asked the students what they knew about the characteristics of fiction. They agreed that fiction contained characters, a setting, a problem, and a solution. I listed these elements on a comparison chart under fiction. (See Figure 3.3.)

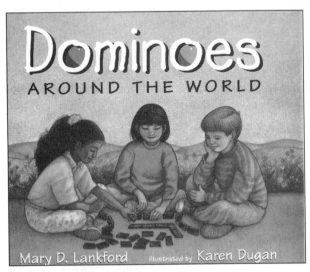

Figure 3.1: A nonfiction book from Barbara's lesson, which students initially assumed was fiction because the cover contains an illustration instead of a photograph.

Ukraine

Ukrainian Dominoes Snuggled on the edge of the Black Sea, the Ukraine is famous for its fertile farmland. Part of the former Soviet Union, the Ukraine declared independence late in 1991. Of the former republics of the Soviet Union, it is second only to Russia in population and natural resources.

Ukrainian Dominoes, or "Banging the Ivories," is often played in parks or in the courtyard of an apartment building. The game may be played on a board that leans against the wall when not being used for dominoes. Groups gather to watch, and neighbors sometimes call out the window to complain about the noise of banging tiles!

How to Play:
1. After shuffling, the two, three, or four players each draw six dominoes.
2. The player with the highest double goes first.
3. Player two must match one end of the double or draw.

4. A player must draw from the boneyard—known in the Ukraine as "going to the market"—until she can play.
5. The round is over when one player plays all her dominoes or when no one can play. Scoring is determined the usual way.

Figure 3.2: A page containing directions for playing dominoes, which made Robin realize that the book is nonfiction.

Nonfiction in Focus

We then proceeded to examine the book more closely. Robin noticed that the children were different on each page of the book, so he concluded that there were "no characters." He noticed that the setting was also different on each page, so he concluded that there were "sometimes settings." But most of all, he realized through the pictures that there was no problem or solution. We added the presence or absence of these features to our comparison chart. We then wrote the title of the book on a sticky note and put it on the nonfiction side of the chart.

As we examined the books further, we began to find ones that blurred the line: books that seemed to be both fiction

Fiction vs. Nonfiction

FICTION	NONFICTION
Characters	No characters
Setting	Sometimes a setting
Problem	No problem
Solution	No solution
Fiction (in the Library of Congress Cataloging-in-Publication Data)	Juvenile Literature (in the Library of Congress Cataloging-in-Publication Data)
Drawings	Photographs

Figure 3.3: A chart created by second graders that lists the characteristics of fiction and nonfiction.

and nonfiction. So the children applied a strategy that they learned in previous lessons: They checked for the phrase "Juvenile Literature" in the Library of Congress Cataloging-in-Publication Data on the page just after the title page (verso page). They knew that this was a good indicator that the book was nonfiction. (See Figure 3.5, page 51, for an example of a verso from a nonfiction book.) We added our findings to the chart.

The children continued to add sticky notes for each book title to the appropriate sides of the chart. Then we looked at *The Magic School Bus: In the Time of the Dinosaurs* (Cole, 1994). (See Figure 3.4.) The students all agreed it was fiction, until we looked at the handwritten reports written by the characters in the book.

"It's real," claimed Kyle.

"But it's make-believe!" exclaimed Winter. "People don't live with dinosaurs!"

Alex agreed.

"Can it be fiction and nonfiction?" Robin inquired. We discussed this possibility, and decided that the Library of Congress cataloguing wasn't always clear, that the book could be designated as nonfiction, but have some fictional qualities!

Robin placed the sticky note with "Magic School Bus" written on it on the line dividing the Fiction and Nonfiction sides of our chart. He then picked up a copy of *No, David!* (Shannon, 1998) and copied the title onto a sticky note, and placed this, too, in the middle of our chart.

When I asked him why, he told me that it was a fiction story about when the author, David Shannon, was a child. I realized the importance of reading authors' notes to students. This information empowered Robin to think about the book's factual evidence because they prompt children to think about how authors' lives influence their work. I saw this as another teaching opportunity for taking the group back to the verso page. Together we found the book was actually catalogued as fiction. I talked about how authors of fiction often use situations from their real life to write their stories, but that doesn't mean these books are nonfiction.

Figure 3.4: A page from one of Joanna Cole's books, which caused students to question whether it was fiction or nonfiction.

Barbara's students are well on their way to becoming informationally literate. They are strengthening their "ability to find and use information" (American Association of School Librarians and the Association for Educational Communications and Technology, 1998). As a result of this immersion experience, they are "noticing" (Wilhelm, 2001) the critical features of nonfiction such as types of nonfiction, titles, visual elements, organizational structure, language style, and information on the verso pages. And, even more important, they are learning how to interpret that information and make critical judgments.

Knowing how nonfiction works and selecting good examples of it will serve you well as you work within the comprehensive framework described in Chapter 2. Like Barbara, we all need to increase students' ability to "notice" the types and features of nonfiction. That starts with learning how to select and evaluate nonfiction to match our teaching purposes.

This chapter will help you become a better selector, reader, writer, and teacher of nonfiction. We provide an overview of the anatomy of a typical nonfiction book (Figure 3.5), a close examination of the various types and features of nonfiction, information on how to build text sets, and, finally, guidelines for taking stock of students' knowledge of nonfiction.

Nonfiction in Focus

Baseline Practices for Developing Informational Literacy

There are two important baseline practices to keep in mind as you select and teach nonfiction: building your own informational literacy and explicitly and continuously teaching students about nonfiction. Unless you embrace these practices, all the knowledge about nonfiction in the world won't help you.

BUILD YOUR OWN INFORMATIONAL LITERACY

To achieve informational literacy for your students, you need to achieve it yourself. We suggest immersing yourself in the genre by starting a study group that includes your librarian. Use these eight steps to guide you:

1. Read nonfiction for pleasure! Select books on topics you think your students would enjoy hearing read aloud. Think about their variety, appeal, and what attracted you to them.

2. Examine several different books on the same topic. Show the variety of approaches used by authors to convey information: organizationally, stylistically, and visually.

3. Be critical. Which books were enjoyable and easy to understand? How did nonfiction discourse change from discipline to discipline?

4. Think instructionally. How might these books meet instructional needs? Which ones would you use for read aloud, shared reading, guided reading, and mentor texts (i.e., a small set of books to use as examples of good writing)?

5. Work with your school library media specialist. Take advantage of his or her vast knowledge of nonfiction books, informational materials, and your school library collection.

6. Read widely about nonfiction. Journals such as *Language Arts, Book Links,* and *Horn Book* provide articles and reviews about nonfiction books and authors. For a list of exemplary books from the National Council of Teachers of English Orbis Pictus Award for Outstanding Nonfiction for Children, see Appendix A.

7. Create your own nonfiction book. Select a subtopic of one of your content units and design your own nonfiction book. Include in your book the features of nonfiction that you teach in reading and writing. Consider the choices you made in creating the nonfiction book and share that information with students in modeled writing lessons.

8. Immerse your students in nonfiction books and text sets. Engage them in being critical consumers of nonfiction. Which books do they like and why? Create comparison charts of their findings as you share.

EXPLICITLY AND CONTINUOUSLY TEACH STUDENTS ABOUT NONFICTION

As we examine the anatomy of nonfiction books, looking at the various types of books and their many features, think about how to help your students notice and interpret these aspects of nonfiction. Consider how knowing more about nonfiction will help your students to evaluate and select books wisely and to incorporate features of nonfiction into their writing. Keep in mind how you would scaffold instruction in an explicit and continuous fashion. This kind of instruction will take your students far.

Figure 3.5

Anatomy of a Nonfiction Book

Nonfiction books are complex—and becoming more so. They include many features that are quite different from those found in fiction. So let's take a brief tour of Jim Arnosky's (2002) *All About Frogs* to see what makes nonfiction unique and challenging to read and write.

The lily pads depicted on the endpapers introduce the concept that frogs are found in ponds or wet habitats.

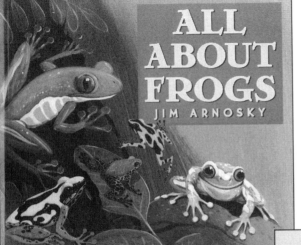

The cover and title, *All About Frogs,* suggest that this is a survey book. But since the book is only 28 pages long, it probably presents only the most important ideas about frogs. The cover displays several different frogs, alerting the reader that more than one kind of frog will be discussed.

A short note on the left-hand side of the title page informs the reader that bullfrogs depicted on some pages are shown actual size. Already, the author is providing aids to help readers notice and interpret the drawings.

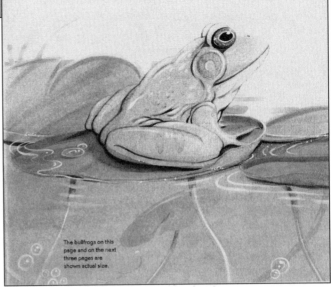

The bullfrogs on this page and on the next three pages are shown actual size.

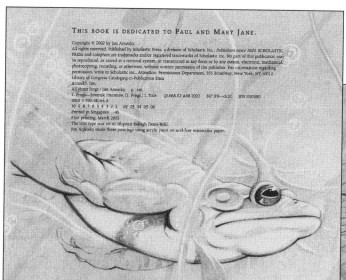

THIS BOOK IS DEDICATED TO PAUL AND MARY JANE.

Copyright © 2002 by Jim Arnosky.
All rights reserved. Published by Scholastic Press, a division of Scholastic Inc., Publishers since 1920 SCHOLASTIC
PRESS and colophon are trademarks and/or registered trademarks of Scholastic Inc. No part of this publication may
be reproduced, or stored in a retrieval system, or transmitted in any form or by any means, electronic, mechanical,
photocopying, recording, or otherwise, without written permission of the publisher. For information regarding
permission, write to Scholastic Inc. Attention: Permissions Department, 555 Broadway, New York, NY 10012.
Library of Congress Cataloging-in-Publication Data
Arnosky, Jim.
All about frogs / Jim Arnosky. — p. cm.
1. Frogs—Juvenile literature. [1. Frogs.] 1. Title.   QL668.E2 A68 2002   597.89—dc21   2001020680
ISBN 0-590-48164-9
10 9 8 7 6 5 4 3 2 1   02 03 04 05 06
Printed in Singapore   46
First printing, March 2002
The text type was set in 16-point Raleigh Demi-Bold.
Jim Arnosky made these paintings using acrylic paint on acid-free watercolor paper.

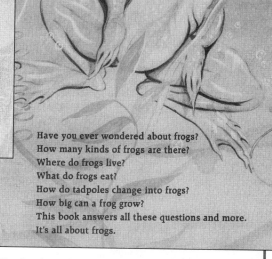

Have you ever wondered about frogs?
How many kinds of frogs are there?
Where do frogs live?
What do frogs eat?
How do tadpoles change into frogs?
How big can a frog grow?
This book answers all these questions and more.
It's all about frogs.

The verso is usually found on the back of the title page or at the end of the book. It includes the library cataloging information in the section called the Library of Congress Cataloging-in-Publication Data. This helps us to determine if the book is nonfiction in two ways: Under the first subject heading (1. Frogs) is the phrase "Juvenile Literature" rather than "Fiction." Generally, if a book is labeled Juvenile Literature, it's nonfiction. (We will discuss this point in more detail in the section on accuracy.) Also, the Library of Congress number does not begin with "PZ," which is used for fictional works.

Skipping a few pages into the book, we note that in the running text Arnosky compares frogs to toads. Nonfiction authors often compare and contrast the information to clarify concepts and head off any potential confusion.

Also note the graphics on this page—the silhouetted representations of frog shapes and jumping behaviors. In nonfiction, information is not necessarily presented in a linear fashion on the page, nor is visual information always restated in the running text. Readers' eyes need to move around the page, noting *all* information, textual and visual.

The lead on the first page begins with a series of questions. This is a technique that many nonfiction writers use to make the reader curious about the content of the book and how it's structured.

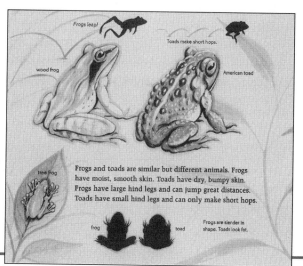

Frogs leap!

Toads make short hops.

wood frog

American toad

tree frog

Frogs and toads are similar but different animals. Frogs have moist, smooth skin. Toads have dry, bumpy skin. Frogs have large hind legs and can jump great distances. Toads have small hind legs and can only make short hops.

frog

toad

Frogs are slender in shape. Toads look fat.

continued on next page

Figure 3.5

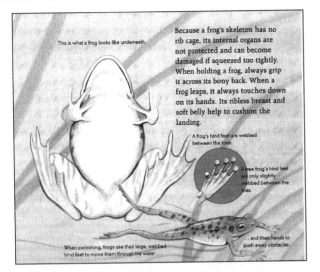

This is what a frog looks like underneath.

Because a frog's skeleton has no rib cage, its internal organs are not protected and can become damaged if squeezed too tightly. When holding a frog, always grip it across its bony back. When a frog leaps, it always touches down on its hands. Its ribless breast and soft belly help to cushion the landing.

A frog's hind feet are webbed between the toes.

A tree frog's hind feet are only slightly webbed between the toes.

When swimming, frogs use their large, webbed hind feet to move them through the water . . .

. . . and their hands to push away obstacles.

On this page, information is conveyed not only through the running text, but through labels, captions, and the circular insert that shows an enlargement of a tree frog's hind feet. To capture the meaning, the reader needs to pull together all the information consciously.

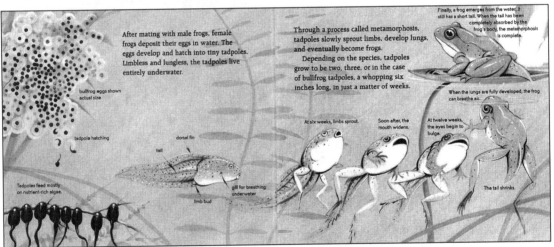

After mating with male frogs, female frogs deposit their eggs in water. The eggs develop and hatch into tiny tadpoles. Limbless and lungless, the tadpoles live entirely underwater.

bullfrog eggs shown actual size

tadpole hatching

Tadpoles feed mostly on nutrient-rich algae.

dorsal fin

tail

limb bud

gill for breathing underwater

Through a process called metamorphosis, tadpoles slowly sprout limbs, develop lungs, and eventually become frogs.

Depending on the species, tadpoles grow to be two, three, or in the case of bullfrog tadpoles, a whopping six inches long, in just a matter of weeks.

At six weeks, limbs sprout.

Soon after, the mouth widens.

At twelve weeks, the eyes begin to bulge.

Finally, a frog emerges from the water. It still has a short tail. When the tail has been completely absorbed by the frog's body, the metamorphosis is complete.

When the lungs are fully developed, the frog can breathe air.

The tail shrinks.

On this two-page spread, which appears toward the end of the book, Arnosky presents information in a linear fashion, requiring the reader to examine the visuals from left to right across the spread to understand the life cycle of the frog.

As you can see, reading *All About Frogs* requires a wide range of strategies and knowledge about how nonfiction works.

General Points to Consider When Selecting and Evaluating Nonfiction

- The nonfiction picture book format is appropriate for readers of all ages. The visual aspects of these books—illustrations, photographs, diagrams, time lines—can help *all* readers access information. The appropriate age range for nonfiction books is usually much broader than for fiction books.
- The nonfiction literature that students read serves as a model for the nonfiction they write. This, in turn, supports their ability to read increasingly more difficult nonfiction and, eventually, to apply their new understandings about nonfiction to their writing.
- Each nonfiction book that you select needs to match your instructional purposes, including the content you plan to teach. It must also fit with the instructional approach and level of scaffolded instruction you plan to employ—for example, if you're choosing a book for read aloud (high scaffolding), you could use a book that students may have difficulty reading on their own. But if you're choosing a book for extension activities (low scaffolding), you should choose books that present few challenges for students.

A Closer Examination of Types of Nonfiction and Features of Nonfiction

Now that we have presented a general overview of a nonfiction book, let's look closely at what makes nonfiction unique. There are many types of nonfiction and a wide range of features that define it, as shown in Figure 3.6. In this section, we examine each of these categories shown in the chart, using guiding questions to structure the discussion.

For a more detailed discussion of the types and features of nonfiction, we recommend our text *Checking Out Nonfiction K–8: Good Choices for Best Learning* (Bamford & Kristo, 2000). The descriptions presented in this chapter are adapted from that book.

Figure 3.6

Types of Nonfiction and Features of Nonfiction

Types of Nonfiction Books

Subgenres of nonfiction chosen by the author to meet his or her purposes for writing:

- Concept
- Photographic essay
- Identification/field guide
- Life cycle
- Biography
- Experiment, activity, craft, and how-to
- Documents, journals, diaries, and albums
- Survey
- Specialized
- Reference
- Information picture storybook/blended books

Features for Determining Accuracy

Information that indicates genre, the author's credentials, research methods used, currency of information, and expert verification of accuracy:

- Dust jacket
- Copyright date
- Author's credentials
- Illustrator/photographer's credentials
- Library of Congress Cataloging-in-Publication Data
- Acknowledgments
- Dedication
- Preface, prologue, introduction
- Use of speculative language or generalizing
- Use of fact and opinion
- Afterword, epilogue, end notes, author/illustrator notes
- Bibliography/sources, readings for further information
- Author's comparison of content to other sources (within text or materials in the appendix)

Organizational Structures

Common ways to arrange or chunk information:

- Enumerative
- Sequential
- Chronological
- Compare-contrast
- Cause-effect
- Question-answer (point-counterpoint)
- Narrative

Style of Writing

The crafting and expression of language used by the author to create an appealing and cohesive presentation:

- Clear and coherent writing
- Organization/chunked information and internal patterns of language and structure
- Language
- Figurative language/metaphors
- Vocabulary
- Voice/point of view
- Tone
- Leads
- Conclusions

Access Features

Supports that help the reader locate information:

- Title
- Table of contents
- Introduction, preface, prologue
- Headings and subheadings
- Sidebars
- Bulleted information
- Inset sections or pages
- Glossaries, pronunciation guides
- Bibliographies
- Index with no subtopics/with subtopics
- Afterword, epilogue, endnotes, author/illustrator notes
- Appendices

Visual Information

Graphics that complement and extend the running text in a variety of ways:

- Design of book/formats/layout
- Dust jackets/covers of the book
- Endpapers (sometimes called endpages)
- Labels and captions
- Illustrations/photographs/archival materials
- Diagrams: simple, scale, cross section, cutaways, flow, tree, web
- Graphs: line, bar, column, pie
- Tables (charts)
- Maps: geographical, bird's-eye view, flow
- Time lines

Guiding Questions for Evaluating and Selecting Nonfiction

Now that you are familiar with the types and features of nonfiction, here are six guiding questions related to them that will help you choose nonfiction knowledgeably and strategically. Following the discussion of each guiding question, we pose a sample of questions to actively engage you and especially your students in the process of examining nonfiction and thinking about issues around writing it. The questions for assessing the various features can be used by your students to also assess their own writing.

1. **Types of Nonfiction Books:** What is the purpose, scope, and depth of the information presented?
2. **Organizational Structures:** How does the author select and structure the information?
3. **Access Features:** How does the author help readers navigate the information?
4. **Features for Determining Accuracy:** How does the author inform readers about his or her knowledge and provide evidence of the potential accuracy of the information?
5. **Style of Writing:** How does the author's writing help the reader understand the content?
6. **Visual Information:** How does the book's appearance, inside and out, inform the reader?

The balance of this chapter is organized around these guiding questions. To give you a sense of how you might use the questions to select nonfiction books, we will apply them to a text set on insects. (See box on page 57.) We hope that our investigation helps you evaluate and select books on your own.

Guiding Question 1—Types of Nonfiction Books: What Is the Purpose, Scope, and Depth of Information Presented?

The type of book an author writes depends on his or her purpose for writing it, considering the audience and its intended use. (See Figure 3.7 for a list of types of nonfiction books.) For example, if the book is for a young audience with little knowledge of the topic, the author might create a concept book, which would contain only basic information about the topic. If the author wants to recreate an experience, such as the migration of butterflies, in a highly visual way, he might create a photographic essay. Photographic essays are written for a variety of age levels, from simple ones on the birth of a kitten to more complex ones on, for example, a family's experience at a fiesta. As you and your students explore nonfiction, check the right-hand column of Figure 3.7 to narrow down the purposes of the books you are considering.

The purpose also dictates the scope and depth of ideas. Like all authors, nonfiction authors can present topics as narrowly or widely as they wish. They must think of the topic in terms of

A Text Set on Insects

GENERAL INFORMATION

About Insects by Cathryn Sill

Bugs by Claire Llewellyn

Insects by Bettina Bird and Joan Short

Insects, Bugs, & Art Activities by Steve Parker

What's That Bug? by Nan Froman

ANTS

Ants by Paul Fleisher

Army Ant Parade by April Pulley Sayre

The Life and Times of the Ant by Charles Micucci

Looking at Ants by Dorothy Hinshaw Patent

BEES

The Life and Times of the Honeybee by Charles Micucci

BEETLES

Tooth and Claw: Animal Adventures in the Wild by Ted Lewin

BUTTERFLIES AND MOTHS

Butterflies and Moths by Elaine Pascoe

The Butterfly Alphabet Book by Brian Cassie and Jerry Pallotta

Creepy, Crawly Caterpillars by Margery Facklam

An Extraordinary Life: The Story of a Monarch Butterfly by Laurence Pringle

The Great Butterfly Hunt: The Mystery of the Migrating Monarchs by Ethan Herberman

The Life Cycle of a Butterfly by Bobbie Kalman

Magnificent Monarchs by Linda Glaser

Monarch Butterflies: Mysterious Travelers by Bianca Lavies

Where Did the Butterfly Get Its Name? Questions and Answers About Butterflies and Moths by Melvin Berger and Gilda Berger

CRICKETS AND GRASSHOPPERS

Are You a Grasshopper? by Judy Allen and Tudor Humphries

Cricketology by Michael Elsohn Ross

DRAGONFLIES

A Dragon in the Sky: The Story of a Green Darner Dragonfly by Laurence Pringle

PREHISTORIC INSECTS

Bugs Before Time: Prehistoric Insects and Their Relatives by Cathy Camper

LADYBUGS

Ladybugs: Red, Fiery, and Bright by Mia Posada

BIOGRAPHIES

Bug Watching with Charles Henry Turner by Michael Elsohn Ross

Rachel: The Story of Rachel Carson by Amy Ehrlich

REFERENCE BOOKS

Beginner's Guide to Butterflies by Donald Stokes and Lillian Stokes

The Kingfisher A–Z Encyclopedia by Ben Hoare (Ed.)

National Audubon Society First Field Guide to Insects by Christina Wilsdon

Scholastic Encyclopedia of Women in the United States by Sheila Keenan

SCIENTISTS IN THE FIELD

Backyard Detective: Critters Up Close by Nic Bishop

The Bug Scientists by Donna M. Jackson

Hidden Worlds: Looking Through a Scientist's Microscope by Stephen Kramer

Types of Nonfiction Books

Figure 3.7

Types of Nonfiction Books	Purpose
Concept Books	Describes the basic characteristics of a set, class, or abstract idea (e.g., shoes, dogs, seasons, freedom). Example: *About Insects* by Cathryn Sill (2000)
Photographic Essays	Confirms and authenticates with photographs taken during the gathering of information of a particular event or personal experience. Example: *Monarch Butterflies: Mysterious Travelers* by Bianca Lavies (1992)
Identification/Handbooks	Identifies the specifics of a class (e.g., trees) and characteristics of specific members of the class (e.g., maple or oak). Example: *National Audubon Society First Field Guide to Insects* by Christina Wilsdon (1998)
Life Cycle Books	Describes the series or stages both in form and function that an organism passes through from egg to maturation—its life history (e.g., frogs, butterflies, or a log). Example: *An Extraordinary Life: The Story of a Monarch Butterfly* by Laurence Pringle (1997)
Biography	Documents part of or the entire life of an individual. Example: *Bug Watching with Charles Henry Turner* by Michael Elsohn Ross (1997)
Experiment/Activity/How-to Books	Describes the sequence or stages of conducting an experiment or activity. Example: *Cricketology* by Michael Elsohn Ross (1996)
Survey Books	Provides an overview and specific information about a topic, but not necessarily all the information (e.g., an "all-about book" about bats, hurricanes, the brain, cowboys, etc.). Example: *Insects* by Bettina Bird and Joan Short (1997)

Types of Nonfiction Books	Purpose
Document/Journal/Diary/ Album Books	Includes original documents, interviews, or first-person accounts providing a personalized perspective. Example: *Tooth and Claw: Animal Adventures in the Wild* by Ted Lewin (2003)
Specialized Books	Offers specific and limited information on a narrow topic for which there are few sources (e.g., Chicago Fire, volcanic island of Surtsey, Robert Louis Stevenson's train trip across America). Example: *Hidden Worlds: Looking Through a Scientist's Microscope* by Stephen Kramer (2001)
Reference Books	Provides useful facts and information in abbreviated and easily accessible form and format (e.g., dictionaries, almanacs, atlases, encyclopedias). Example: *The Kingfisher A–Z Encyclopedia* edited by Ben Hoare (2002)
Informational Picture Storybooks	Carries the qualities of fiction due to narrative writing style and possibly invented characters. General and specific information are provided on a topic (e.g., a walk at the beach with Grandma, who identifies and describes various sea animals found along the shore). Example: *Magnificent Monarchs* by Linda Glaser (2000)

scope (how broadly to cover the topic) and depth (what level of detail to include)—and, from there, select the most sensible type of nonfiction to convey their ideas. We like to think about scope and depth using a triangle, with its top representing the scope of the topic and its length representing the depth of the topic. Figure 3.8 shows how the triangle changes shape to represent the scope and depth of the books.

Depending on the intended audience and use of the book, the size of the lines of the triangle increase or decrease. If the book is for young readers, the lines will probably be very short, with limited scope and depth. But if the book is for older, more knowledgeable readers, the scope or depth increases.

Figure 3.8

Scope and Depth of Books in
The Text Set on Insects

▽ *About Insects* by Cathryn Sill. Limited scope, with single-line statements for each general characteristic about insects with few details.

▽ *A Dragon in the Sky: The Story of a Green Darner Dragonfly* by Laurence Pringle. Narrow scope limited to one insect with extensive details about the insect.

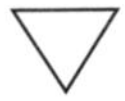

▽ *Bizarre Bugs* by Doug Wechsler. Medium scope, covering several bizarre bugs with some details for each one.

▽ *What's That Bug?* by Nan Froman. Broad scope, with some historical information about categorizing insects and some detailed information on each order of insect.

Why Is It Important to Teach Types of Nonfiction Books?

It's important to select types of books that best match our teaching purposes. For example, if we wanted simple definitions for an introduction lesson on insects, a dictionary would suffice, such as *Scholastic Children's Dictionary* (2002). To help students broaden their understanding of the general characteristics of insects, a concept book such as *Bugs! Bugs! Bugs!* (Dussling, 1998) or an encyclopedia entry from *The Kingfisher A–Z Encyclopedia* (Hoare, 2002) would most likely give the information we needed.

If the purpose is to give students a resource that explains a variety of insects for brief reports they're writing, we'd select a book that is more detailed than a dictionary or concept book, such as Llewellyn's *Bugs* (1998). If we want students to identify specific insects they find in the woods on a field trip, a field guide such as the *National Audubon Society First Field Guide to Insects* (Wilsdon, 1998) is ideal.

However, if a student were engaged in a more in-depth inquiry about the various orders of insects, a survey book—or "all-about" book, as it's often called—such as *Insects* (Bird & Short, 1997) would be more useful than a field guide. Many of the books in your school library's non-

Create Text Sets

Developing text sets on single topics to support the comprehensive framework is important. To ensure a diverse, well-rounded set, it's important to select books that represent a variety of perspectives on the topic. Also, choose books that capture many writing styles to give students a range of options to apply in their own writing. Finally, select a variety of types of books to familiarize students with the many subgenres of nonfiction that are available to them. You may not be able to include every type of book, but that's all right. The majority, most likely, will be survey books or "all-about" books, which are the most common nonfiction book for children (Bamford & Kristo, 2000).

Once you've narrowed down your selections, ask yourself these questions before you use the books for teaching:

- How well does the entire text set cover the scope and depth of the topic?
- Will this set provide introductory information for my least knowledgeable students and advanced information for those who know more?
- Does the set include a variety of nonfiction types, organizational structures, styles of writing, access features, and visual information to expand students' experiences?
- Does the set offer a variety of books that can be used instructionally across the scaffolded literacy framework (e.g., read alouds, shared reading, guided reading, discovery circles, mentor books for writing, and independent research)?

Also, examine the text set with your students. Ask them whether the books contain the content they need. Together, create comparison charts to identify the features and content of each book. Encourage students to examine books critically to determine the difficulty level of each book. Which ones present information that is understandable? Once you have taken students through this immersion process a few times, their "noticing" of features improves, as does their ability to appraise the quality and usefulness of the books.

fiction section are probably survey books. Survey books vary in their depth of coverage, from introductory to advanced, depending upon the intended audience. They can provide specific information, such as *A Dragon in the Sky: The Story of a Green Darner Dragonfly* (Pringle, 2001), or more general information, such as *Bugs Before Time: Prehistoric Insects and Their Relatives* (Camper, 1999). Survey books may be very broad or very specific, which makes them excellent resources for inquiry studies.

As you and your students notice types of nonfiction, and their scope and depth of information, you'll find that your selections will better match your purposes and meet your needs. You'll also find that students are more apt to return to these books as mentor texts for writing. (More on mentor texts later in the chapter.)

Questions to Assess Types of Nonfiction Books

Encourage your students to ask themselves the following questions as they select nonfiction books that meet their needs:

- What kind of information am I seeking?
- Does this book contain the scope and depth of information I need on the topic?

To find the right books for a writing task, have students ask themselves the following questions:

- What kind of information do I need to answer my inquiry (i.e., introductory information on a topic [concept book], information on a topic and subtopic [general survey book], or information to identify specific kinds of things, such as rocks [field guide])?
- Based on the information I have found, which type of book should I write?

Guiding Question 2—Organizational Structures: How Does the Author Select and Structure the Information?

The nature of the information often determines the organizational structure the author uses. (See Figure 3.9 for a list of organizational structures.) For example, if the information is made up of a main topic with several subtopics—say, ants and their characteristics—then an enumerative organization might work well. But if the information is made up primarily of similarities and differences between two main topics, for example moths and butterflies, the author may choose a compare-and-contrast organization. If the information provides the steps on how something works, then a sequential organization may be the ideal choice. The organizational structure provides the skeleton on which the information is built.

Authors also embed structures within other structures to support the readers' exploration and understanding of the information (Bamford & Kristo, 2000). For example, in the survey book *Insects,* Bird and Short (1997) use an enumerative structure to frame the book, but also include structures such as comparing and contrasting of specific insects, sequencing to explain the life cycle of insects, and cause and effect to describe their eating habits. The insect field guide is structured alphabetically. However, its introductory section is structured enumeratively, with the main topic (i.e., insects) and subtopics (i.e., their characteristics).

Figure 3.9

Organizational Structures

Organizational Structures	How Information Is Organized
Enumerative	Introduces general information usually followed by a discussion of the subtopics. Typically a survey book. Example: *Ants* by Paul Fleisher (2002)
Sequential	Presents information in step-by-step order, alphabetical order, or numerical order. Examples include ABC books, counting books, how-to books, books on experiments, cookbooks. Visuals may include diagrams. Example: *Insects, Bugs, & Art Activities* by Steve Parker (2002)
Chronological	Explores information over time of occurrence. Chronological organization is used in life cycle books, biographies, diaries, a history of events or a topic that unfolds over time. Often the overall framework for the book is chronological, but other organizational structures are used internally. Visuals may include time lines. Example: *Rachel: The Story of Rachel Carson* by Amy Ehrlich (2003)
Compare-Contrast	Compares and contrasts information, characteristics, or qualities of the topic. Less often used as a framing structure and more often as an embedded internal structure. Example: *Butterflies and Moths* by Elaine Pascoe (1997)
Cause-Effect	Explores a causal relationship between the cause and its effect or a problem and its solution. Similar to compare and contrast, cause-and-effect organizational structure is often an embedded internal structure. Example: *Looking at Ants* by Dorothy Hinshaw Patent (1989)
Question-Answer (Point-Counterpoint)	Organizes information by presenting a question and then answering it. Some nonfiction series use this

continued on next page

Organizational Structures	How Information Is Organized
	organizational structure throughout. Example: *Where Did the Butterfly Get Its Name? Questions and Answers About Butterflies and Moths* by Melvin Berger and Gilda Berger (2002)
Narrative	Presents information using the narrative structure of beginning, middle, and end in picture storybook nonfiction or blended book. More recent nonfiction is written by or in the voice of the researcher using narrative organization. Used as an introduction or lead to set stage for the information. Example: *Magnificent Monarchs* by Linda Glaser (2000)

Why Is It Important to Teach Organizational Structures?

Knowing about organizational structures is important both as a reader and a writer. When students recognize the structure, it aids in processing and recalling information, building schema or background knowledge about the topic, and even taking notes. For example, if you're reading information that describes a process sequentially, such as building a birdhouse or the international space station, you need to process the information in steps—first, second, third, and so on. However, if you are reading a compare-contrast about domestic turkeys and wild turkeys, you will process the information in terms of how the birds are alike and how they are different. You may even create a comparison chart or Venn diagram to show the information visually.

By paying attention to the author's overall and embedded structures, readers can better employ comprehension strategies, such as making connections, questioning, inferring, determining importance of information, and synthesizing (Harvey, 1998). Use some of your favorite nonfiction books to examine organizational structures and to serve as mentor texts for your students' writing.

Questions to Assess Organizational Structures

Encourage students to assess books for scope and depth, using the questions on page 62. Then have them ask questions such as these to determine organization:

- How do I think the information is organized? How is the information chunked?
- Am I finding other structures embedded in the text?

Nonfiction in Focus

- How do the table of contents and headings help to inform my decisions?

The following questions will help your students organize their own writing:

- What kind of information have I collected on my topic?
- How might I chunk or divide up the information?
- What kind of organization would help my readers?
- Are there other structures I might employ to further clarify information for my readers?

Guiding Question 3—Access Features: How Does the Author Help Readers Navigate the Information?

Locating information is usually the key objective of the nonfiction reader. (See Figure 3.10 for a list of access features.) Using access features such as titles, tables of contents, and indexes helps the reader navigate through the book by identifying the specific location of information. Introductions, prefaces, prologues, afterwords, epilogues, endnotes, and author/illustrator notes speak directly to the reader about the topic, issues surrounding the topics, future considerations, or sources used in collecting the information. Sidebars, inset pages, bibliographies, glossaries, pronunciation guides, and appendices provide extra pertinent information. When a nonfiction book lacks these features, our search for information is often impeded. Access features make a book reader-friendly.

Why Is It Important to Teach Access Features?

Increasingly, access features are being included in nonfiction books even for young readers. Knowing how to use them saves time and frustration. By skimming and scanning the book before reading, students can quickly determine what access features are available to support their reading. Access features also support the reader's use of comprehension strategies. By using the title, for example, students can make predictions about the content, scope, and depth of coverage, and whether the book matches their needs. Important strategies like this can be taught through instructional read alouds and shared reading, as well as in follow-up extension activities.

The table of contents, headings, subheadings, and index inform readers about the contents of a book and often serve as key guideposts to locate specific material. The level of detail these features contain, however, differs from book to book. For example, the table of contents in *Looking at Insects* (Glover, 1998) is simple, with each body part listed as a separate heading. However, the table of contents in *Butterflies and Moths* (Pascoe, 1997) has both headings and subheadings, thus providing more information to the reader about the contents of the book. You may be able to

Figure 3.10

Access Features

Access Features	How Features Provide Access to Information
Title	The name of the book. Identifies the topic and may provide clues to type of book or organizational structure. Example: *The Life and Times of the Ant* by Charles Micucci (2003)
Table of contents	An ordered list of the names of the sections and/or chapters of the book with page numbers. Example: *The Life Cycle of a Butterfly* by Bobbie Kalman (2002)
Introduction, preface, prologue	An overview of the topic, possibly describing research methodology, sources, and significant issues or limitations of the content. Example: *Insects* by Bettina Bird and Joan Short (1997)
Headings and subheadings	Bolded subtitles describing either by word, phrase, or question the content of individual sections of the book. Example: *Hidden Worlds: Looking Through a Scientist's Microscope* by Stephen Kramer (2001)
Sidebars	Boxed information set off next to the margin in listed format or running text that may summarize information by listing key points or provide supplemental information. Sidebar information is usually related directly or tangentially to the rest of the page. A useful feature for information that is difficult to include elsewhere. Example: *What's That Bug?* by Nan Froman (2001)
Bulleted information	Listing of terms or information preceded by a bullet (•) that makes information easier to scan. Example: *Bugs Before Time: Prehistoric Insects and Their Relatives* by Cathy Camper (1999)

Access Features	How Features Provide Access to Information
Inset sections or pages	Usually larger than a sidebar with more extensive information that would interrupt the flow of ideas if included in the running text but adds new perspectives or dimensions; often printed on colored pages to alert readers to the new information. Example: *Ants* by Paul Fleisher (2002)
Glossaries/pronunciation guides	A list of definitions and pronunciation of new terms usually found in the end materials, but occasionally following the title page or on individual pages. In shorter books, a glossary is sometimes combined with the index. Example: *Bugs* by Claire Llewellyn (1998)
Bibliographies/sources for further reading	List of recommended sources for information on the topic (e.g., books, web sites, organizations, museums at the end of the book). Example: *The Bug Scientists* by Donna M. Jackson (2002)
Index with no subtopics/with subtopics	An alphabetical list of the key topics discussed in the book with pages where information can be located at the end of the book. Subtopics may be listed vertically under the main heading or in running text style that is more difficult to read. Example: *Insects* by Bettina Bird and Joan Short (1997)
Afterword, epilogue, endnotes, author/illustrator notes	Notes at the end of the book from author and/or illustrator providing additional information or explanations about the topic, research findings, and decisions made regarding inclusion of information. Example: *Rachel: The Story of Rachel Carson* by Amy Ehrlich (2003)
Appendices	Variety of materials at the end of the book may be included (e.g., experiments, summary page of information, recipes, time lines, environmental appeals). Example: *Ladybugs: Red, Fiery, and Bright* by Mia Posada (2002)

locate where specific information is from the table of contents, or you may have to refer to the index at the back of the book. A successful reader has learned how to make these decisions.

Because introductions, sidebars, inset pages, and appendices provide valuable information but are often skipped over by readers, it is important to teach students how to access information from them and to use them in their writing. Closer examination of these features in instructional read alouds, shared reading, and guided reading will help students see their value. Your instruction will help students become more strategic in deciding when to use these features and to what extent.

Finally, by encouraging students to skim books for glossaries and bibliographies, you support their growth as readers by exposing them to valuable features for building vocabulary and finding other sources related to the topic under investigation.

Questions to Assess Access Features

Encourage students to ask questions like these as they browse books to learn what access features are available:

- Are the main access features included, such as a table of contents and index?
- If not, does the author provide an introduction or headings to support locating information?
- Does the author help clarify my understanding by discussing issues or special considerations about the topic in introductory materials, such as the prologue, preface, or foreword? Or is this information in the end materials—author/illustrator notes or epilogue?
- What other features does the author use to provide additional information? Are there sidebars, bulleted sections, inset pages that enrich the running text, and other appendices such as sources to support further research on the topic?
- How does the author help me deal with new vocabulary? Is a glossary/pronunciation key provided?

When writing, students can adapt these questions to determine how they can support their readers as well as ask themselves these additional questions:

- Have I included access features such as a table of contents or index to help my reader locate where the information is in my report?
- Have I included headings and subheadings to chunk my information?

Guiding Question 4—Features for Determining Accuracy: How Does the Author Inform Readers About His or Her Knowledge and Provide Evidence of the Potential Accuracy of the Information?

Assessing the accuracy of a nonfiction book is often difficult, especially when you are unfamiliar with a topic. The features described next will help you to potentially assess accuracy. (See Figure 3.11 for a list of features for determining accuracy.)

The verso page (i.e., the page usually following the title page) often includes features for assessing the accuracy, such as the acknowledgments, dedication, copyright date, and the Library of Congress Cataloging-in-Publication Data (LC). First check the LC subject heading to see if the book is identified as "Juvenile Literature" or "Fiction." "Juvenile Literature" is often a good indication the book is nonfiction. Acknowledgments and dedications can provide clues about the quality of an author's and illustrator's research or whether experts reviewed the manuscript. The copyright date helps determine if the information about the topic is current. This is especially important if that information changes frequently, such as recent findings about dinosaurs, capabilities of computers, and how the brain functions.

Other features such as the dust jacket, preface, prologue, introduction, afterword, epilogue, endnotes, author/illustrator notes, and bibliography help to determine the quality of the author's and illustrator's credentials. From these features, you can also learn how information was gathered, what decisions were made regarding information that was included or omitted, and what experts the author consulted.

It's important to read the running text closely, too, because even when a nonfiction book is current and reviewed by experts, it doesn't guarantee that there isn't erroneous information. Also, comparing information from the book to your own knowledge and other sources may uncover possible inaccuracies. However, when the text doesn't match what the reader believes is correct, problems can arise. Researcher Donna Alvermann and her colleagues (1985) found that readers are more apt to hold to their own strong beliefs and assume the text is wrong. To help students become critical readers, it is crucial to show them how to resolve conflicting information by checking other resources, rather than discounting it.

Paying particular attention to the author's use of language, generalizations, and distinctions between fact and opinion may alert students to possible bias or attempts to manipulate the reader's emotions. Being a critical consumer of nonfiction requires exercising high standards and expectations of authors. We want to be sure that the author knows the topic well and is able to help us understand complex information.

Figure 3.11

Features for Determining Accuracy

Features for Determining Accuracy	How Features Support Information About Potential Accuracy
Dust jacket	The paper cover that wraps around the book. The front includes a cover with title and illustration and an inside flap with summary of content. The back inside flap includes information about the author and illustrator and research conducted on the topic. The back cover may include reviews of the book, information on other books if in a series, and/or visuals related to the book. Example: *A Dragon in the Sky: The Story of a Green Darner Dragonfly* by Laurence Pringle (2001)
Copyright date	Date when book was published, indicating potential currency of information. Example: *Army Ant Parade* by April Pulley Sayre (2002a)
About the author	Credentials of the individual who wrote the book. Is this their field and how did they obtain their information? Example: *The Butterfly Alphabet Book* by Brian Cassie and Jerry Pallotta (1995)
About the illustrator/ photographer	Credentials of the individual who photographed or did the illustrations. Is this their field and how did they obtain or create the visuals? Example: *Backyard Detective: Critters Up Close* by Nic Bishop (2002)
Library of Congress Cataloging-in-Publication Data	The cataloging description that includes a summary and subject headings that also indicate genre. If the content is nonfiction, the term "Juvenile Literature" is used, and the LC number begins with letters other than PZ. Example: *Creepy, Crawly Caterpillars* by Margery Facklam (1996)

Features for Determining Accuracy	How Features Support Information About Potential Accuracy
Acknowledgments	Individuals or institutions that provided information or reviewed the book for accuracy. Example: *Tooth and Claw: Animal Adventures in the Wild* by Ted Lewin (2003)
Dedication	A statement of affection and/or recognition of contributions to the researching of the information. Example: *Rachel: The Story of Rachel Carson* by Amy Ehrlich (2003)
Preface, prologue, introduction	A section that may provide an overview of the research involved in acquiring the information. Example: *Insects* by Bettina Bird and Joan Short (1997)
Use of speculative language or generalizing	Explanations within the text where author uses words such as *may* and *believed* to alert readers to what is known/unknown. Example: *Bugs Before Time* by Cathy Camper (1999)
Use of fact and opinion	Clear distinctions made by author of what is known versus an opinion of the author or other individuals. Example: *The Bug Scientists* by Donna M. Jackson (2002)
Afterword, epilogue, endnotes, author/illustrator notes	Explanations by author about the thoroughness of the research and how missing or contradictory information was addressed. Example: *The Life and Times of the Honeybee* by Charles Micucci (1995)
Bibliography, sources, readings for further information	Bibliographic information that may indicate the extensiveness of the research and other materials. Example: *A Dragon in the Sky: The Story of a Green Darner Dragonfly* by Laurence Pringle (2001)
Author's comparison of content to other sources	Author may compare sources in the front matter, running text, or end materials. Readers also may need to compare the nonfiction book to other sources to determine accuracy. Example: *Bugs Before Time* by Cathy Camper (1999)

Why Is It Important to Teach About Accuracy?

We usually read nonfiction to learn about a topic, which means, most likely, we are not experts on that topic. This makes assessing books for accuracy very difficult—especially for students, who have even less knowledge about most topics than we do as adults. But once we open the door to helping students compare information to other sources and warn them that they can't assume all nonfiction is accurate, even kindergartners rise to the challenge. Teaching students to have high expectations for accuracy and a hearty dose of skepticism leads to critical reading behaviors of the nonfiction they read and write.

Teaching students to use copyright dates to determine accuracy can be tricky. For example, students might reject the book *The Life and Times of the Honeybee* (Micucci, 1995) because they thought the copyright date was old. This might be problematic for third or fourth graders because a book written about the time they were born might seem out of date. We need to help them modify their notion of copyright dates to evaluate what information might go out of date rapidly. Make a list of topics and their potential for being out of date to provide a perspective on how to judge the currency of the information in a book by more than its copyright date.

Questions to Assess Features for Determining Accuracy

The following questions help readers determine the probable accuracy of nonfiction books:
- What information do I have about the author's background and knowledge about the topic?
- How does the author provide evidence of using experts for collecting the information or reviewing the final manuscript?
- What language does the author use to signal the differences between fact, opinion, and changes in what we know about a topic?

Students can ask similar questions to assess their informational writing:
- How have I informed the reader about the sources I used to find information?
- Has an outside expert reviewed what I have written to check it for accuracy, and have I acknowledged my expert(s)?
- Have I distinguished between fact and my opinion or what may be believed about a topic?
- Have I informed my reader of problems experienced in gathering the information, such as incomplete sources or contradictory findings?

For some books, disagreement on whether they are fact or fiction will prevail. Periodically, a book classified as "Juvenile Literature" is, in our opinion, "Fiction," and another classified as

Look for Clues on the Verso Page

To help students become adept at identifying genres, examine a set of multi-genre books together. Have students scan each book first, specify the genre, and then check the Library of Congress Cataloging-in-Publication Data on the verso page. If the verso page says "Juvenile Literature," chances are the book is nonfiction. And, of course, if it says "Fiction," the book is just that. Be sure to caution students that sometimes "blended books" (those that include fictional and nonfictional information) are identified as both "Juvenile Literature" and "Fiction." *The Last Safe House: A Story of the Underground Railroad* by Barbara Greenwood (1998) is an example of a blended book, as indicated on the verso page. Also, in the acknowledgments, the author informs the reader that she created a fictional family for the book. (See Figure 3.12.)

"Fiction" we'd label "Nonfiction." Nothing is fail-safe. Conversely, some books may be a blending of both fiction and nonfiction, but the cataloging information may not indicate this. However, we are finding that, increasingly, blended books are being listed as both "Juvenile Literature" and "Fiction."

For my children: Edward, Martha, Adrienne and Michael — great readers all.
BG

For my favorite designer, Blair.
HC

Canadian Cataloguing in Publication Data

Greenwood, Barbara, 1940-
The Last Safe House : a story of the underground railroad

Includes index.
ISBN 1-55074-507-7 (bound)   ISBN 1-55074-509-3 (pbk.)

1. Underground railroad — Juvenile literature. 2. Fugitive slaves — United States — Juvenile literature. 3. Fugitive slaves — Canada — Juvenile literature. 4. Underground railroad — Juvenile fiction. 5. Fugitive slaves — United States — Juvenile fiction. 6. Fugitive slaves — Canada — Juvenile fiction. I. Collins, Heather. II. Title.

E450.G73 1998   j973.7'115   C98-930345-4

Text copyright ©1998 by Barbara Greenwood
Illustrations copyright © 1998 by Heather Collins

All rights reserved. No part of this publication may be reproduced, stored in a retrieval system or transmitted, in any form or by any means, without the prior written permission of Kids Can Press Ltd. or, in case of photocopying or other reprographic copying, a license from CANCOPY (Canadian Copyright Licensing Agency), 6 Adelaide Street East, Suite 900, Toronto, ON, M5C 1H6.

Neither the Publisher nor the Author shall be liable for any damage which may be caused or sustained as a result of conducting any of the activities in this book without specifically following instructions, conducting the activities without proper supervision, or ignoring the cautions contained in the book.

We acknowledge the support of the Canada Council for the Arts and the Ontario Arts Council for our publishing program.

Published in Canada by   Published in the U.S. by
Kids Can Press Ltd.   Kids Can Press Ltd.
29 Birch Avenue   85 River Rock Drive, Suite 202
Toronto, ON M4V 1E2   Buffalo, NY 14207

Edited by Valerie Wyatt
Designed by Blair Kerrigan/Glyphics
Music (pages 92-93) arranged by Matt Dewar

Printed and bound in Canada by Kromar Printing
CM 98 0 9 8 7 6 5 4 3 2 1
PA CM 98 0 9 8 7 6 5 4 3 2 1

Acknowledgments

This is a story of a family in St. Catharines, Canada West, in 1856, whose lives are changed when they are asked to help Eliza Jackson, a black girl escaping from slavery. Although the families are fictional, the background is fact, based on information from many reliable sources.

I am indebted to Daniel G. Hill's authoritative history of the life of escaped slaves in Canada, *The Freedom Seekers: Blacks in Early Canada* (The Book Society of Canada/Stoddart, 1981), and to a number of museums that house artifacts and collections pertaining to black history. The North American Black Historical Museum and Cultural Centre in Amherstburg, Ontario was particularly useful. These, along with many other sources, helped me understand the realities of the Canadian portion of the Underground Railroad. Along with various social histories of the time, they also helped me envision Johanna's initial reaction to the arrival of Eliza Jackson and her subsequent growth in understanding.

In creating the background for my fictional Jackson family, I drew on many first-person accounts of escapes. Particularly useful was Benjamin Drew's *The Narratives of Fugitive Slaves in Canada*, published in 1856. William Still also recorded the stories of escaped slaves who passed through his safe house in Philadelphia. Many of these appear in Charles L. Blockson's *The Underground Railroad* (Prentice-Hall, 1987). Blockson's *The Hippocrene Guide to the Underground Railroad* (Hippocrene, 1994) provided detailed information on various escape routes.

A book of this nature needs a talented illustrator dedicated to historical accuracy. Many thanks to Heather Collins, not only for her painstaking attention to detail but also for the warmth and energy her art projects. And more thanks than I can express to two people who gave me constant encouragement and support through all the vicissitudes of such a large project: my husband and tireless researcher, Robert E. Greenwood, and my editor, Valerie Wyatt, who combines great creativity and sensitivity with her impressive editing skills.

Figure 3.12: The verso page from *The Last Safe House*, which clearly indicates that it is a blended book.

Guiding Question 5—Style of Writing:
How Does the Author's Writing Help the Reader Understand the Content?

Children's literature expert Amy McClure (2003) defines style as "the author's ability to creatively combine words, form, and content with a creative vision that guides these elements." An author's style is the result of how he or she combines organization, language, voice, and tone with a passion for the topic to create a piece of writing that not only informs the reader, but touches him or her on an emotional level. (See Figure 3.13 for a list of writing style features.)

Nonfiction's purpose is to impart new, often complex information, so the author must write with clarity and coherence to inform the reader. To be clear, the writing needs to be well organized, logically developed, and use understandable language accompanied by examples that ground the reader. When the writing is coherent, the reader experiences "ahas!," not "huhs?" The author alerts readers to the organization of the information, explains that information clearly, and helps them understand the connections between details. Authors such as Sandra Markle, Laurence Pringle, Joanna Cole, and Jim Murphy are especially skilled at creating clear, coherent nonfiction.

Just as in fiction, many nonfiction authors have a distinctive voice and a point of view. For example, when you read Laurence Pringle's *A Dragon in the Sky: The Story of a Green Darner Dragonfly* (2001), a rich, highly descriptive narrative with informative sidebars told from the conversational third-person point of view, it propels you into the world of this dragonfly. In contrast, the text and drawings of *The Life and Times of the Ant* (Micucci, 2003) offer the reader a humorous presentation with information divided into small chunks.

Good language choices are critical in nonfiction. Because the author is describing information, he or she needs to be precise, but wants the writing to be enticing, too, filled with vivid imagery, meaningful metaphors, and a rhythm that captures the reader's attention. Vocabulary selection is particularly important when explaining complex concepts. Although the inclusion of the glossary is helpful, more important to understanding and retention is how well the author presents and describes new terms in the running text.

Beginning and endings frame a nonfiction book. The lead draws the reader in and initiates the unfolding of the information. Leads in nonfiction are often very similar to those in fiction. What is different is that the information is accurate and begins to frame the scope and depth of the discussion, as well as the overall tone of the text. The ending of a nonfiction book is equally important because often it summarizes key points, raises new issues, or speaks directly to readers about their own connections to the topic (e.g., pollution and its impact on insects). It's important

Figure 3.13

Style of Writing

Style of Writing: Elements	How the Elements Help Readers Understand the Content
Clear and coherent writing	The primary goal of the author is to write clearly and coherently by developing a logically organized text written in understandable language. It explains and informs the reader about the topic by providing chunked information, explanations, and pertinent examples using strong figurative language and metaphors. Clarity and coherence is enhanced by meaningful generalizations and supportive details, with important information appropriately emphasized. Example: *The Bug Scientists* by Donna M. Jackson (2002)
Organization/chunked information/internal patterns of language or structure	Dividing or bringing together information into manageable chapters, sections, and subsections to build schema for the reader. May include embedded cause-and-effect and compare-and-contrast structure to support explanations. Example: *Cricketology* by Michael Elsohn Ross (1996)
Language	The rhythm and flow of the language is determined by the choice of words, phrases, verbs, descriptive language, and length of sentences working together to create memorable text and content. Even the choice of words for chapter headings will capture the reader's attention. Example: *Army Ant Parade* by April Pulley Sayre (2002a)
Library of Congress Cataloging-in-Publication Data	The cataloging description includes a summary and subject headings that indicate genre. If the content is nonfiction, the term "Juvenile Literature" is used, and the LC number begins with letters other than PZ. Example: *Creepy, Crawly Caterpillars* by Margery Facklam (1996)
Figurative language/metaphors	Analogies that relate new information to readers' prior

continued on next page

Style of Writing: Elements	How the Elements Help Readers Understand the Content
	knowledge enhance comprehension. Example: *Magnificent Monarchs* by Linda Glaser (2000)
Vocabulary/definitions within text	New terms, content, and explanations are potentially difficult to understand. The careful selection of terms and how authors choose to embed definitions within the text or on the page supports comprehension. Continuous use of new vocabulary is critical to recalling these terms. Example: *Insects* by Bettina Bird and Joan Short (1997)
Voice and point of view	The emotional involvement of the author is evident, as is a sense of the person behind the facts. Point of view here means both author's perspective and possible bias, and a literary point of view in that the author may write in the first person, second person, or third person. Example: *Are You a Grasshopper?* by Judy Allen and Tudor Humphries (2002)
Tone	The way the author talks to the reader, i.e., conversational, humorous, neutral, or partisan. On occasion, less appropriate tones that are condescending, patronizing, didactic, or authoritative may be used, but they are not appealing to readers. Analyzing tone may uncover evidence of bias and attempts to manipulate readers' emotions. Example: *Backyard Detective: Critters Up Close* by Nic Bishop (2002)
Leads	Leads include a question, a description, a problem, an idea, a provocative statement, or a personal narrative. Successful leads draw in readers and alert them to the parameters of the topic. Example: *Bugs* by Claire Llewellyn (1998)
Endings	Endings include summaries of key points, new directions to consider, invitations to become actively involved in the topic, and questions to think about. Example: *A Dragon in the Sky: The Story of a Green Darner Dragonfly* by Laurence Pringle (2001)

for authors to know their topic, but it's equally important for them to be able to craft their writing, because it's the quality of the writing that keeps us reading!

Why Is It Important to Teach Style of Writing?

What makes nonfiction interesting and understandable is the author's style of writing, the weaving together of words, sentences, and paragraphs into what Professor William Strong calls "the voice of the text, echoing in our ear, that pulls us along" (2001). The author's style helps readers visualize, make connections, question, draw inferences, separate the important information from the supporting details, synthesize information, and so forth. So when we teach students to attend to the style of writing, we not only help them note how an author helps readers navigate the information strategically, but we also show them how to process that information. In addition, we are making explicit the variety of stylistic choices they have available to them as writers.

Stylistic features should be taught through every approach of the comprehensive framework. As you examine your text set in preparation for teaching, think about how the same or similar information is presented in several books. Is the style of some books less appealing than others? Do some have language that is captivating? Style is an elusive but critical feature because, after all, it can determine whether you stop reading or keep going. Finally, helping students attend to an author's style is important to their own writing. Authors can become mentors to your students.

Questions to Assess Style of Writing

The following questions can help your students critically examine style in nonfiction books and in their own writing:

- As you started to read did you want to continue reading? Did the lead capture your interest?
- How did the book sound when you read it aloud? Did the language flow naturally? Did the word choice and sentence variety help to clarify the information?
- Was the writing clear and understandable? Were you able to understand the information?
- How did the author use descriptions, explanations, and metaphors to interpret and clarify the information?
- Was the tone of the author appropriate to the topic and inviting to you as a reader?
- How did the conclusion or closing chapter support your overall understanding of the topic? Did it cause you to think about the topic in a new way?

Guiding Question 6—Visual Information: How Does the Book's Appearance, Inside and Out, Inform the Reader?

Today's nonfiction is very visual. We no longer rely solely on text to explain because the visuals typically allow readers to see what is being described. In high-quality books, they help to illuminate the topic and clarify the information. And like a well-written picture storybook, the text and visuals support one another. Even pages that may appear chaotic initially, filled with many kinds of text and graphics, are often carefully designed so readers can navigate them with ease. No matter what kind of visual, its presence on the page should make sense and be integrated with the content of that page. (See Figure 3.14 for a list of types of visual information.)

The dust jacket or cover begins our journey into the book by identifying the topic and its scope and depth through words and images. Endpapers may provide further information or just complement the color theme of the cover. The size, shape, format, and layout of pages need to be visually appealing, but also work to inform readers.

The placement of labels and captions for illustrations is crucial to supporting the reader. Can you tell what label or caption goes with what illustration? When you read a few of the captions in a typical nonfiction book, and then the running text, you'll notice that often the caption expands upon ideas in the text and the illustrations. In cases where a flow chart depicts a process such as how milk gets from the cow to the kitchen table, the running text and/or captions may describe the diagram.

New technology has led the way to magnificent-looking books. The full-color photographs by Dennis Kunkel in *Hidden Worlds: Looking Through a Scientist's Microscope* (Kramer, 2001) capture remarkable images of minute microscopic life and objects. Bob Marstall's botanical paintings of the green darner dragonflies in *A Dragon in the Sky: The Story of a Green Darner Dragonfly* (Pringle, 2001) are as visually captivating as Kunkel's photographs. Diagrams such as cutaways and cross sections take the reader inside an insect in *The Life and Times of the Ant* (Micucci, 2003) and *Insects* (Bird & Short, 1997).

Graphs and time lines present detailed information and complex concepts in a visually appealing, accessible way. For excellent examples of graphs and time lines, we recommend Ann Whitehead Nagda and Cindy Bickel's *Tiger Math: Learning to Graph From a Baby Tiger* (2000) and *Chimp Math: Learning About Time From a Baby Chimpanzee* (2002). These books trace the development of each animal, using a variety of graphs and time lines to clarify information.

Maps are becoming more common in nonfiction books. They come in many forms and, like diagrams, should connect clearly to the running text and be easy to read. A word of caution, though: Maps become obsolete quickly, so be sure to check them for accuracy before using them to teach.

Figure 3.14

Visual Information

Types of Visual Information	How Types of Visual Information Inform the Reader
Design of book, formats, and layout	Overall appearance of the book sets the tone and presentation of the information, including the dust jacket, book shape, page layout, typography, paper quality, ink, color, and other physical aspects of the book. Example: *A Dragon in the Sky: The Story of a Green Darner Dragonfly* by Laurence Pringle (2001)
Dust jackets and cover	Dust jacket and cover with title visually present information on the topic and may suggest degree of coverage while creating visual appeal. Example: *Where Did the Butterfly Get Its Name? Questions and Answers About Butterflies and Moths* by Melvin Berger and Gilda Berger (2002)
Endpapers (sometimes called endpages)	Sturdy sheets of paper that hold the interior of the book to the front and back covers and continue the theme of the dust jacket and cover or may contain important illustrative and photographic information, such as archival photos, maps, or time lines. Example: *Hidden Worlds: Looking Through a Scientist's Microscope* by Stephen Kramer (2001)
Label and captions	Single words, phrases, or short paragraphs labeling the parts of an illustration or describing the illustration. Description may duplicate or extend running text. Example: *The Life Cycle of a Butterfly* by Bobbie Kalman (2002)
Illustrations, photographs, and archival materials	Drawings, paintings, photographs, and reproductions of archival materials such as photographs, maps, postcards, posters, and historical documents that explain and expand upon the running text. Example: *Scholastic Encyclopedia of Women in the United States* by Sheila Keenan (2002)

continued on next page

Types of Visual Information	How Types of Visual Information Inform the Reader
Diagrams: simple, scale, cross section, cutaways, flow, close-ups, tree, and webs	Scale diagrams depict size relationships; cross sections show the internal parts of an object; cutaways show both internal and external parts; flow charts show sequence of processes or cycles; and close-ups magnify a part of an object. Tree diagrams and webs show how information is organized. Tree diagrams show hierarchical relationships vertically and webs link the main idea to subtopics. Example: *The Bug Scientists* by Donna M. Jackson (2002)
Graphs: line, bar, column, and pie	Line graphs show changes in size, value, or patterns of the same subject over time, such as temperature. The bar graph compares information across the page and the column graph compares the units vertically. The pie graph divides a circle to represent the information proportionately. Example: *The Great Butterfly Hunt* by Ethan Herberman (1990)
Tables (charts)	Tables are graphic presentations of information usually made up of columns and rows. Headings describe the subject matter, such as birds and their favorite food. Example: *Insects* by Bettina Bird and Joan Short (1997)
Maps: geographical, range, bird's-eye view, and flow maps	Maps provide a visual presentation of spatial relationships. They are usually geographical, but also may be architectural (room layouts, for example). Bird's-eye view shows varied perspectives, such as looking down at a site, at an angle, or from the side. Flow maps show changes and processes, such as weather patterns. Example: *Beginner's Guide to Butterflies* by Donald Stokes and Lillian Stokes (2001)
Time lines	Time lines present major events in someone's life or a historical event chronologically. They may be presented in diagram format, charts, or as a graph. Example: *Bugs Before Time* by Cathy Camper (1999)

Why Is It Important to Teach Visual Features?

The old saying that pictures are worth a thousand words may be true—and learning how to read and create them requires explicit instruction. We need to help students look critically at the visual presentation of information from cover to cover. We should not assume that students have the strategies for reading and creating visual information. Figuring out the sequence in which to read visual information needs to be taught. Learning how to connect visual information with the rest of the text is crucial to making sense of how the information on a page fits together. Because information is complex and can be represented visually in a variety of ways, learning how to read and create diagrams, tables, graphs, time lines, maps, and other graphic elements is crucial.

Create a Set of Mentor Texts to Support Students

Now that you have examined the many types and features of nonfiction books, it is a good time to create a mentor text set (Anderson, 2000). A mentor text set is a small, very select set of books to use with your students as models of well-written, well-designed texts—in this case, nonfiction. Although not as advantageous as having a living, breathing expert at each student's side, these books make good coaching tools to support your students' reading and writing. Your collection should include books from several subject areas—especially science and social studies.

We encourage you to refer to your mentor texts repeatedly in immersion lessons, mini-lessons, and conferences with students to provide specific examples of how authors handle a particular type of nonfiction or feature of nonfiction. It's a good idea to introduce some of these books early in the year during immersion lessons, using instructional read alouds and shared reading, focusing on the features that you want students to gain control over. Also, include them in extension activities and encourage students to study them on their own when attempting a particular feature, type of book, or language style in their own writing. Your constant reference to these books will be contagious. You'll find students taking their cue from favorite authors in no time.

Questions to Assess Visual Features

Here are questions about visual features that students can ask themselves when considering nonfiction books and examining their own writing:

- Is the function of the visuals clear in describing or explaining the information? Do the visuals help readers understand the content?
- Are the visuals appropriately placed in the book to connect directly with the text?
- Are the visuals clear and easy to read?
- Where appropriate, are keys provided to explain how to read the visuals?
- Is there sufficient information in the running text to understand the visuals and, conversely, are there sufficient visuals to understand the text?

Next, we present ways to immerse students at the beginning of the school year to jump-start their learning about nonfiction as well as to assess their knowledge of it and its features.

Jump-Starting Your Study of Nonfiction Through Immersion

Familiarizing your students with nonfiction books and how they work is key to successful reading, writing, and inquiry. To do this, plan genre immersion experiences early in the year (Parkes, 2000). Since conventions of nonfiction depart considerably from conventions of fiction, immerse students in nonfiction by reading it aloud, examining and talking about nonfiction features, and encouraging lots of browsing—these are all practical first steps.

Immersion experiences provide intense exposure to nonfiction features with less attention given to the content. Plan these experiences by combining brief instructional read alouds with shared and guided reading and writing with lots of problem-solving opportunities. Taking a close look at nonfiction raises the critical level of "noticing" (pointing out a feature, naming it, and telling how it's used) and helps define the qualities of good nonfiction.

Students who haven't had much experience with nonfiction, particularly older ones, will benefit from immersion practices at the beginning of the school year, before starting inquiry instruction. Immersing students in a lot of nonfiction to examine features is invaluable for taking inventory of what your students know about nonfiction. (See Appendix C, Student Assessment Checklist: Types and Features of Nonfiction.)

The teachers we know approach immersion experiences in three ways:

- Use a few nonfiction books to examine a variety of features.
- Use many nonfiction books to examine a variety of features.
- Use many nonfiction books to compare a single feature.

Use a Few Nonfiction Books to Examine a Variety of Features

The goal of this kind of immersion experience is to acquaint students in a short time with a basic knowledge of nonfiction features and vocabulary, setting the stage for more in-depth discussions in later lessons. Choose one or two well-written nonfiction books on a similar topic that will appeal to your students' interests, and over several days read them aloud together. By reading aloud you'll be able to acquaint students with the content as well as the books' features. We recommend reading aloud a few pages a day, unless the books are short. Combine instructional read alouds, think alouds, and shared reading to model good reading strategies and to draw out what students notice about nonfiction. We find that within a short time students are making a lot of discoveries about nonfiction and sharing those with one another.

We suggest selecting books that have many features of nonfiction, such as a table of contents, captioned illustrations, headings, diagrams, glossaries, definitions within text, an index, and a good, clear writing style. Some of our favorite books for this immersion experience are:

- *Beavers* by Helen H. Moore
- *Giant Pandas* by Gail Gibbons
- *Hurricanes: Earth's Mightiest Storms* by Patricia Lauber
- *It's Disgusting—and We Ate It! True Food Facts From Around the World—and Throughout History!* by James Solheim
- *Meet the Octopus* by Sylvia M. James
- *Safari Beneath the Sea: The Wonder World of the North Pacific Coast* by Diane Swanson
- *The Life and Times of the Ant* by Charles Micucci
- *The Life Cycle of a Lion* by Bobbie Kalman and Amanda Bishop

Second-Grade Comparison Chart

Multigrade primary teacher Sue Pidhurney plans an in-depth examination of three short books on bears with her top reading group of second graders. She selects books with a variety of visual features that her students will compare and contrast and then apply to their own writing. Over a three-day period, they examined: *Growl!: A Book About Bears* (Berger, 1998), *The Big Bears* (Berger, 1996a), and *How Do Animals Sleep?* (Berger, 1996b). On the first two days they focus on *Growl!: A Book About Bears* (Berger, 1998) and *The Big Bears* (Berger, 1996a).

Sue uses a combination of browsing, mini-lessons, guided reading groups, and interactive writing—each about 30 minutes long. In these lessons, she wants students to:

- Make connections between the nonfiction features in these books to other books they have read or heard read aloud.
- Identify and name the features.
- Describe how the features help readers.
- Talk about the characteristics of high-quality features.
- Compare and contrast the content of the books and their features.
- Make reading/writing connections.

Each day as they examine a new book, they use interactive writing to record on a chart the nonfiction features they notice, as seen in Figure 3.15.

On the third day, Sue introduces the last book, *How Do Animals Sleep?* (Berger, 1996b), in a guided reading group so that students can compare it to the other two bear books. She first asks that they examine the book for its access features. Students note on the feature chart that this book includes similar access features found in the others, such as an index, table of contents, photos, and captions.

For Amy this is an "aha!" moment when she realizes books can have some of the same features. Since this book describes the sleeping habits of several animals, Sue asks, "Do you see any other features that help you find out more about bears?" She particular-

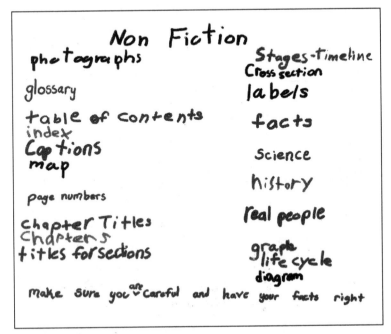

Figure 3.15: The chart that Sue's students created during interactive writing, showing the nonfiction features they identified in a selection of books on bears.

Nonfiction in Focus

ly wants them to notice the bolded words and the corresponding definitions in the caption. Here is a sample of the discussion:

SANA: Can I read page 5 where they show the bears? [Reads the text.] (See Figure 3.16.)

SUE: What do you notice about that paragraph that she just read? Is there something different than what you've seen in the other books?

AMY: *Hibernate* is in bold letters.

SUE: Yes, *hibernate* is in bold letters. Why do you think it is? Is there anything in the book that tells what *hibernate* means? Is there a glossary?

AMY: No, there is no glossary.

SUE: But look on the page where *hibernate* is. Is there something on this page that tells us what *hibernate* means?

REGAN: Next to the photos, there's a caption that tells about hibernation.

SUE: That's right. Some of the captions

Most American black bears and grizzly bears **hibernate** in sheltered areas, or dens, from 4 to 8 months out of the year, depending on how long the winter is. When not hibernating, these bears are mostly active at night and early in the morning. They spend the rest of the time resting or sleeping.

During hibernation, the bear's body temperature drops and its breathing slows down. But during warm days the bear may interrupt its sleep by taking short trips outside of the den.

The American black bear lives mostly in forested areas. Sometimes it sleeps in trees, at other times it sleeps on the ground.

Grizzlies live in forests and along coastlines. These two grizzlies in Alaska are sleeping—one on a rock in the water, ready to catch a salmon when it wakes up; the other one sprawled out in the snow on its back.

Figure 3.16: A page showing how one author uses photo captions to define boldfaced terms within the running text. Sue helps her students read for this information.

in this book explain what the bolded words mean. Are there any other sections in this book on bears?

ZEEK: The next page is about bears.

SUE: Zeek, how did you find that information?

ZEEK: I just turned the page.

SUE: So the table of contents didn't help you then?

ZEEK: No, I would have to go through the whole book to find that information or use the index.

SUE: Zeek made a good point when he said that we would need to go through the whole book. It's important when we take our first careful look at a book to see what access features are included to help us read it.

Figure 3.17

Comparison Chart of Features in the Bear Books

Books	Table of Contents	Page Numbers	Pics & Captions	Photos	Drawings	Maps	Diagrams	Glossary/ Bold Words	Index
Growl!	No	No	No	X	No	No	No	No	No
The Big Bears	X	X	No	X	No	No	No	No	X
How Do Animals Sleep?	X	X	X	X	No	No	No	No	X

Sue and her students compare the other books to *How Do Animals Sleep?* and complete a comparison chart of the three books. (See Figure 3.17.)

As the conversation continues, the students note that *Growl!* didn't have page numbers, an index, or a table of contents to help them, even though the information was useful. Sue asks, "When you write nonfiction, what do you want to include in your work that will help readers?"

REGAN: A glossary for bold print words.

AMY: An index with page numbers. You can't use the table of contents or index if you don't number the pages.

ZEEK: Pictures with captions.

REGAN: Photos and drawings.

SANA: Table of contents.

SUE: How about a map? [Heads nod yes.] The next time you work on writing your inquiries, think about the nonfiction access features you know, why they are helpful, and ones you want to include for your readers.

Sue ends the guided reading by having them reread the list of features they explored. These books included other features, such as bulleted lists and photo credits, but were not included in this lesson.

Use Many Nonfiction Books to Examine a Variety of Features

Another immersion experience used by teachers in grades 3 to 6 involves engaging the students in a more advanced genre study, usually extending from one to three weeks. Rather than limiting the in-depth examination to one or two nonfiction books, these teachers use a selection of different types that include a variety of features and topics.

Share what nonfiction features you notice in several of your favorite books that are large enough for the whole group to see. You can also prepare overheads or use a big book edition. Take lots of time to point out, identify, and talk about the purpose of the features and whether they're effectively crafted to support a reader's understanding of the text, as well as which books seem easier to read and why. Use the guiding questions in this chapter as you share sample passages of text, captions, front matter, and end materials. These will help you organize what you want to share about the books.

Then give small groups or individuals a selection of books to browse, starting with the cover. Key to this type of immersion experience is having a variety of nonfiction books. While some may be less well crafted than others, they serve as good contrasts to the excellent examples. This guided browsing focuses on pointing out, identifying, and discussing features and is an important time for students to share and talk about what they find with one another. Have them list their findings on a large comparison chart and/or include them in their own nonfiction feature dictionaries.

Dictionary of Nonfiction Features

Second-grade teacher TammyJo Forgue, third-grade teacher Shelly Moody, and fourth-grade teacher Janet Nordfors all have success with students creating their own nonfiction feature dictionaries. Each teacher has a special name for these dictionaries and different ways she leads students into the process of creating them. The dictionaries are similar, though, in that they include definitions and examples of the features.

Although Shelly's and Janet's students are older, their goals are similar to TammyJo's and Sue's because their students also need to develop baseline understandings about nonfiction. Each teacher also wants her students to learn how to look more critically at nonfiction books, develop a common vocabulary for discussing the features, be able to describe the purpose of them from a reader's perspective, and eventually include them in their writing.

Alphabet Book of Nonfiction Features

TammyJo Forgue created a big book called the *ABC Book of Nonfiction Features* as a model for her students. (See Figure 3.18.) For examples of nonfiction features, TammyJo used a combination of photocopies of specific nonfiction features from books they knew and her own photographs and drawings. Her book serves as a model for her students as they create their own feature books. TammyJo's ABC book is a popular resource for students as they conduct inquiry projects and incorporate the features into their own writing.

Text Feature Searches

Shelly Moody created a Nonfiction Feature Search sheet for her students to check off nonfiction features they find during a book browse. (See next page.) This activity helps her students become aware of the variety of features and is Shelly's first step in having them create their own nonfiction feature glossaries.

Before Shelly introduces the Nonfiction Feature Search sheet using *Whales* by Deborah Hodge (1997), she makes sure that each student has a different nonfiction book that includes lots of features and a copy of the search sheet. As they exam-

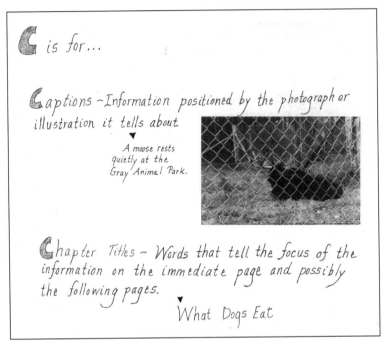

Figure 3.18: A page from TammyJo's big book on nonfiction features, which provides multiple definitions per page as well as examples and illustrations.

ine *Whales* together, she points out and explains each feature. After each explanation, students do a feature search of their book. If they find the feature, they check it off on the Nonfiction Feature Search sheet.

Then Shelly plans an extension activity designed for students to work in partners with a small collection of selected books. The students do this search with the goal of identifying the book they think is the best in terms of features.

When Shelly's students become proficient at identifying and naming features, she helps them design their own nonfiction feature glossaries using a three-ring notebook. Shelly uses shared writing to develop a definition for each feature. Students then create their own example of each feature as they design their glossary. As they learn about new features of nonfiction, they add additional pages. Students consult their feature glossaries throughout the year for models to use in their own writing.

Shelly reported that when her students began their inquiry projects, she observed them first browsing books and checking copyright dates and access features. She learned that they were doing this because they wanted to determine how helpful the books would be for their projects.

Nonfiction Feature Search

TITLES					
Endpages					
Title Page					
Verso Page					
Dedication					
Copyright Date					
Table of Contents					
Headings					
Bold Print					
Glossary					
Index					
Introduction					
Author Notes					
About the Author					
Appendices					
Sidebars					
Inset (text box)					
Bullets					
Captions					
Photographs					
Labels					
Diagrams					
Maps					
Question Format					
Bibliography					

Guides to Nonfiction Books

Fourth-grade teacher Janet Nordfors also supports her students in creating their own spiral-bound Guide to Nonfiction Books. She begins by working with her students to survey lots of nonfiction books and makes individual class charts on types of nonfiction, access features, visuals, and organizational structures. Through shared reading lessons using a common magazine, such as *Time for Kids,* she helps them refine what they notice. Students create their own guides to nonfiction books, with each page labeled with the name of the feature, a definition, and a student-created example. Figure 3.19 shows Elisabeth's definition page for diagrams. Figure 3.20 shows an example of the diagrams she included in her inquiry book, *Rainbows of the Sea.*

Use Many Nonfiction Books to Compare a Single Feature

The investigation of one feature across many books heightens students' awareness of the variations they'll find in their reading and could include in their own writing. We offer two examples of immersion in a single feature at second grade and fifth grade.

Nonfiction Book Introductions

Janis Poulin Whitney, a second-grade teacher, and Sandip Wilson, a Title I director, worked with second graders during the spring in a six-week nonfiction genre unit. They examined a

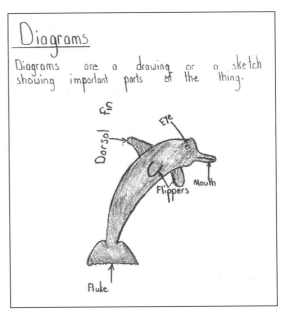

Figures 3.19 (above) and 3.20 (below): Diagrams that a student, Elisabeth, created for her Guide to Nonfiction Books, and her inquiry book, entitled *Rainbows of the Sea.*

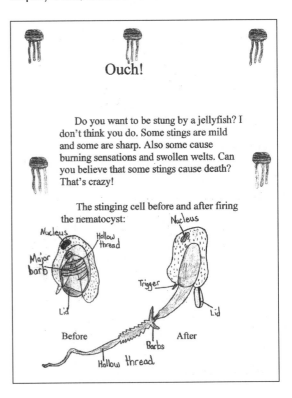

single nonfiction feature at a time across a collection of nonfiction books and topics. During the fall and winter, the students had a solid range of nonfiction experiences through instructional read alouds and shared and guided reading dealing with a myriad of topics, including the rain forest, plants, and animals. Janis wanted the students to begin the process of comparing how features are presented in different books.

To expose students to a more in-depth study of individual features, once a week, Janis and Sandip use an immersion experience in the nonfiction genre unit. Following their discussion and comparison of lots of books, the students complete a page in what they call their Pamphlet on Nonfiction Features by adding a definition and an example provided by Janis.

Janis begins by introducing the feature and the working definition of the feature written on the easel. "An introduction tells you what the book is going to be about. This book has the heading 'Introduction.' Listen to the words in it." She shares aloud a sample selection from a big book, *Animal Shelters* (Bolton & Cullen, 1987). Students sit on the floor in pairs, each with books to explore for introductions.

AJ: Is this heading like an introduction? It tells about what the book is going to be about.

ABBY AND KAYLA: This book doesn't have a heading, but it sounds like an introduction. In our book each thing in the introduction has its own section.

JANIS: Abby and Kayla have an introduction that is different from other books. Mine says "Introduction." Does yours?

ABBY: Ours says "World of Insects."

JANIS: Did it give you general information?

ABBY: Yes.

JANIS: Josh and Nick also have a different kind of introduction.

JOSH: Wow, this guy talks about himself. This introduction tells you more than what the book is about. It is about the author. He loves dinosaurs. [*Feathered Dinosaurs* (Sloan, 2000)]

SANDIP: Where did you get the information about the author in the text?

NICK: What does text mean?

[Sandip comments that the conversation provides a chance to fill in areas of their knowledge that are germane to the study. Vocabulary is critical and what might appear as simple words, such as *text*, also become topics of inquiry.]

JANIS: We found out that sometimes there is a heading but it doesn't say introduction, and sometimes there is no heading but the information in that first section tells about the book.

Cutaways and Cross-Section Diagrams

When Sandip joins the class a few weeks later, the students are on the floor and at tables with their features pamphlet, their Nonfiction Books Checklist (see next page), and books spread around them. They are perusing books to look for cutaways and cross-section diagrams. For example, AJ found a cross section of land in a book about Earth and compared that to an illustration of an underground nest in an ant book. These students use what they identify successfully in one book to verify what they discover in another. They continue adding entries to their pamphlets and include a list of books that used the feature.

Janis' students eagerly search nonfiction books, which increases their awareness of the variety of nonfiction features and how those features are used for different topics.

photo: Sandip Lee Ann Wilson

Identifying features was the task for these second graders, but as time went on, Janis and Sandip reported that they moved well beyond pointing out and naming features to becoming more interested in actually reading the books and looking more deeply into how the features help readers.

Fifth-Grade Comparison Chart

By fifth grade, the students Sandip Wilson works with already have a basic knowledge of the terms for nonfiction features and some of their characteristics. Sandip wants to heighten their critical examination of features and to begin making judgments about the quality of the nonfiction. Her immersion experience with fifth graders is similar to Janis' work, but students examine the feature in three books at a time. Sandip uses a collection of books from the Orbis Pictus list. (See Appendix A.) As they examine the feature, Sandip asks them to open all three books so they can see the feature across three texts. Spreading the books out so they can look back and forth easily is new to them, but it is an efficient strategy for comparing features. The students discuss how the features differ from book to book, the kind of information provided, and which book is easier to read. Over several days, they examine a variety of features and create a comparison chart to record their findings. For example, one kind of table of contents contains descriptive information and another uses subtopics. (See Figure 3.21.)

Nonfiction in Focus

Nonfiction Books Checklist

Look through the book and check the conventions that you find.

List the page or pages where you found these conventions.

Book title: _____

_____ Captions _____

_____ Close-ups _____

_____ Comparisons _____

_____ Cross Sections _____

_____ Cutaways _____

_____ Glossary _____

_____ Headings _____

_____ Index _____

_____ Introduction _____

_____ Labels _____

_____ Maps _____

_____ Photographs _____

_____ Table of Contents _____

_____ Types of Print _____

Samples of Text Set Comparison Charts

Author	Title	Table of Contents	Introduction	Author Notes	Index	Glossary	Afterword/ Epilogue	References

Author	Title	Table of Contents	Author Notes	Inserted Boxes	Captions	Graphs	Labeled Diagrams	References	Copyright Date

Why Immersion Experiences Are Important

Whichever approach you use to immerse your students in nonfiction, you'll no doubt be surprised by how much information and vocabulary they've internalized about how nonfiction texts work. Combining instructional read alouds, shared reading, and interactive/shared writing to examine nonfiction serves to jumpstart learning by preparing students to be more observant and critical about how nonfiction is written. This work also gets them ready to participate in shared and guided reading and writing lessons.

Closing Thoughts

Developing students' informational literacy should be a primary goal for all of us. To do that, we need to ensure that students read high-quality nonfiction literature and have ample opportunities to examine it, read it, and write it. Nonfiction that is engaging, organized well, accurate, and has useful access features and clear visuals enhances a reader's understanding of content. Immersion experiences are good beginnings toward helping students learn how nonfiction works and the features authors use to support readers. Planning rich immersion opportunities helps build and develop our students' informational literacy.

Now that we've explored nonfiction in depth, let's consider what our students need to know to be able to read and write it well. In Chapter 4 we discuss this topic and offer insights into planning curriculum.

Chapter 4
What Students Need to Know About Reading and Writing Nonfiction as Tools for Inquiry

"One day I heard a chair slam to the floor as Chad jumped out of his seat. 'Mrs. Moody, I found it! I found it! You can hear a lion roar from five miles away!' he shouted. When Chad found that answer to one of his key questions about lions, he had accomplished so much. He had been absolutely adamant about finding out how far a lion's roar reaches. His persistence finally paid off when he located the answer in *The Dominie World of Animals: Lions* [Meadows & Vial, 2000] after days of patiently searching through book after book.

"That is what learning how to read and write nonfiction is all about—
learning how to be an inquirer, taking delight in finding out—in knowing
how to answer the questions that fill my students' minds every day. They
learn how to use nonfiction books and the features in them to answer their
questions. This process allows them to become experts and authors as they
share their passion and excitement about learning with others."

—Shelly Moody, third-grade teacher

Shelly's goals for her students—to be excited about learning, inquisitive, and able to use nonfiction to read and write about their interests—are goals we share. We want students of all ages to be eager to learn, to inquire, and to become independent readers and writers of nonfiction. This chapter first describes inquiry as a way of thinking and the importance of fostering this state of mind beginning in the primary grades. Next, we look at how focused, purposeful teaching will help you reach these goals. We describe what students need to know about how nonfiction works and how to be inquirers. Lastly, we discuss the strategies that effective readers and writers use and how these strategies apply to reading and writing nonfiction for inquiry. There is a lot to consider in helping students become engaged learners. So look closely at what we offer, and use the material to inform your own nonfiction curriculum.

Classroom Inquiry: A State of Mind

What if Abraham Lincoln had not become President? Do butterflies grow bigger once they hatch from the chrysalis? How are sneakers made? Inquiry is a state of mind—a way of thinking. It is natural to wonder and learn about our world, from infancy to old age. We engage in inquiry whenever we seek information—whether we're checking the temperature, looking for a way to make ice cream, figuring out how to get rid of a wart, learning how to swim faster, or finding out how gravity works.

Classrooms are a natural place for all kinds of inquiry to bloom and flourish. It can take many forms—from simple surveys of the kinds of shoes classmates wear to favorite movies to keeping a daily record of the length of the day to long-term inquiry projects. As teachers, our job is to help students learn how to use reading and writing strategies to successfully carry out their inquiry work. Whether the inquiry project is a long-term one or very brief, it's important to give students opportunities to engage in a variety of data-gathering strategies, including talking with experts, collaborating with peers, reading nonfiction materials, viewing videotapes and DVDs, contacting agencies and organizations that do work related to their topics, or doing Internet searches.

Data can be recorded and shared in a variety of ways. For example, if students are interviewing an expert, use shared writing so that you serve as scribe, recording responses on a chart. Reporting information doesn't need to be limited to just crafting running text. Steve Moline (1996) reminds us that nonfiction writing includes visuals because these often communicate information more clearly and succinctly than running text does. It's important that students learn how to craft both kinds of text.

Teach students how to read and write nonfiction and carry out inquiry projects through approaches in the comprehensive framework. The inquiry process includes four components—new content to learn, reading and processing nonfiction resources, inquiry strategies for gathering information, and creating and writing nonfiction products. These are shown in Figure 4.1.

There are many instructional paths to doing classroom inquiry. No matter the route, most likely each of the components in Figure 4.1 figures into the process. Consider what your students need to learn and incorporate that instruction into the framework. For example, an instructional read aloud is a good approach to use to introduce new content and to talk about how the author conducted research. Incorporate a think aloud on how to read a particular nonfiction feature. During modeled writing, you may show another way to share information and how to write it.

In Figure 4.2 we offer ways to think through the instructional issues for each inquiry component. Use these questions to help you plan what to teach about conducting inquiry, what nonfiction selections to use, and the level of scaffolding needed by your students.

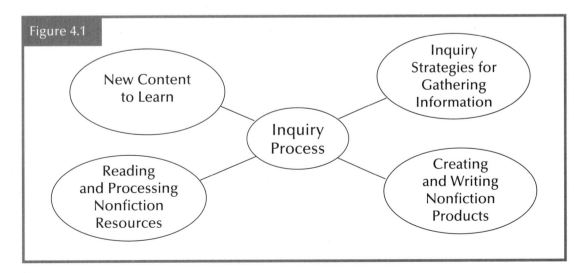

Figure 4.1

New Content to Learn

Inquiry Strategies for Gathering Information

Inquiry Process

Reading and Processing Nonfiction Resources

Creating and Writing Nonfiction Products

Figure 4.2

Inquiry Process:
Definitions and Planning Questions

Inquiry Process	Questions to Consider for Planning
New Content to Learn. The purpose for engaging in inquiry is to acquire new information and add to or reevaluate prior knowledge.	• What are the major goals and objectives? What state and local standards and expectations will be met by teaching the content? • Which nonfiction will best present the information?
Inquiry Strategies for Gathering Information: The process of inquiry may include tasks such as how to select and refine the topic, how to gather information on the topic, and how to keep records on what we find.	• What strategies do the students already know? • What are the new strategies that will be learned in each content unit? • What new strategies do we want them to learn about gathering data? • What nonfiction books and materials provide models for how we research topics?
Reading and Processing Nonfiction Resources: To determine the appropriateness of the information, we need to read and process it by comprehending the text, visuals, and support features, and learn how to use the Internet and gather and process information from experts.	• What content area reading strategies do students already have under control? • What new reading strategies can be taught using the nonfiction selections? • What nonfiction can build general content understandings about the topic through instructional read alouds and shared reading? • What nonfiction can be used in shared and guided reading to expand the ability to read text or comprehend nonfiction features? • Which books can be used for independent work? • Which books will serve as mentor texts showing or explaining ways individuals gather data and their methods for reporting out information to readers?

Inquiry Process	Questions to Consider for Planning
Creating and Writing Nonfiction Products: To create and write new products for others, such as a nonfiction book, report, documentary, experiment, persuasive essay, magazine article, speech, or artistic presentation, we need to address organizing information, writing the text, designing or finding appropriate visuals, organizing the layout, and acquiring experience in using and creating new technologies, such as PowerPoint®, videos, and Web pages.	• What products can the students currently create with assistance? • What products can the students currently create independently? • What new outcomes and products do we want students to learn how to create, such as field notes, catalog description, a children's nonfiction book, a written observation, a report of an experiment, a diagram, a model, a photographic essay, a newspaper feature story, a report of an interview, or a handbook? • What special features of these new products need to be taught?

The Role of Focused, Purposeful Teaching

In Chapter 2, we described how a comprehensive framework for teaching nonfiction supports students as they grow in their understandings about the complexities of the genre. We consider the components of the framework to be what Michael Pressley (2002b) calls "happy environments," where children learn to do difficult things well because they are actively engaged. Pressley suggests that when teachers plan instruction that progresses from high levels of scaffolding to low, there are fewer disciplinary problems because supported and engaged learning promotes harmonious classroom relationships.

Teacher Cathy Tower (2000) believes deeply in creating those environments. She says, "Before students can begin doing research and inquiry on their own, they need to experience nonfiction reading and writing and learn to generate questions and find resources." We want students to read, write, and talk about nonfiction texts as the tools for inquiry and to build understandings about content. We need to help students fill their "nonfiction toolboxes" with strategies for reading and writing it. Teaching that is focused and purposeful is an effective way to do that. Focused and purposeful teaching means you identify key aspects or features of nonfiction that you believe are important for your students to learn. You want students at any age, then, to be able to do these things—point out that aspect or feature, name it, describe how to use it, read and understand it, and use it in writing.

We know that nonfiction is a complex genre—there's a lot to learn about it. But consider this: Your students won't learn everything about nonfiction in one year. We advocate designing a curriculum by zeroing in on exactly what you need to teach. If you try to cover too much, that's exactly what you've done—covered it, but not taught it. Being focused and purposeful means that you are both specific and explicit about your instruction. You won't try to cover so much information that students are confused over what they're supposed to learn. Consider with your colleagues how instruction about reading, writing, and inquiry is distributed over the K–6 curriculum so that students grow and develop in their understandings over the grades. See Appendix D, Checklist for Designing a K–6 Curriculum Based on Types and Features of Nonfiction.

Specifically, focused, purposeful teaching means that you identify what strategies you want students to learn for reading and writing nonfiction, and then you scaffold instruction to help students meet those goals. You give clear explanations for what you want students to do and learn.

DON'T LOSE SIGHT OF THE CONTENT

As your students read, write, and talk about nonfiction across the comprehensive framework, they will typically deal with two content areas—science and social studies. At times it might be easy to lose sight of the content in the midst of teaching students how to read and write nonfiction. But keep in mind that learning content is key. So, while teaching, always bring students back around to it. For example, if you're talking about how an author uses a bulleted list, ask students how that list contributes to their understanding of the content. Or, if you're showing students an excellent diagram, talk about how it helps them understand the content better.

You demonstrate new skills and strategies to add to their nonfiction toolboxes. You design opportunities for practice, and assist when needed. This way of thinking recognizes the instrumental role and responsibility we have for insuring that our students learn. We introduce novice learners to skills and strategies in reading and writing nonfiction and continue our work with them until they are able to use what they learn independently. To do this, we use the scaffolded instructional approaches that we introduced in chapter 2 and describe in chapters 5 to 9. Next, we examine typical goals for studying nonfiction to give you a sense of what you might teach.

Goals for Studying Nonfiction in the Literacy Program

In this section, we present major goals for studying nonfiction, which we organize into four categories:

- Learning how nonfiction works.

- Learning to craft nonfiction writing.
- Learning to read nonfiction texts.
- Learning to inquire.

These goals are not age or grade specific, nor are they listed in any particular order. The goals you select depend on what your students already know about nonfiction from prior experiences and what they need to know. No doubt you'll come up with additional goals, or you may modify what we offer based on the needs of your students, your curriculum, or district and state standards.

To design instruction around goals, we suggest "backwards planning" (Wiggins & McTighe, 1998). When you plan backwards, you first create a short list of the goals you want to address. Then, take a look at the Student Assessment Checklist: Types and Features of Nonfiction in Appendix C for specific features or aspects to teach to help you reach your goal. The checklist lists the features of nonfiction with the levels of "noticing" so you can determine not only what features your students know, but also the level at which they understand and apply them. From there, teach students using the approaches within the comprehensive framework.

We hope these goals are helpful for organizing your instruction. At the end of each set of goals, we have included a teaching or assessment idea that targets a goal in each set.

Learning How Nonfiction Works

These goals focus on two important concepts—being able to differentiate between fiction and nonfiction and distinguishing characteristics that define text as nonfiction.

You might teach students to:

- Distinguish nonfiction writing from fiction and be aware that the primary purpose of nonfiction is to provide information, to explain, to argue, or to demonstrate, and is a product of an author's inquiry, research, and writing.
- Size up a book to know whether it will be useful; use access features to locate information. (See Figure 4.3.)
- Appreciate that there are various types of nonfiction, differing in organizational structure, scope, depth, and presentation of content.
- Recognize typical organizational structures of nonfiction (e.g., survey, sequential, chronological, compare and contrast, cause and effect); recognize that structures can be embedded within structures, depending on the content, purpose of the author, and intended audience.
- Examine and learn from visual information such as diagrams, maps, and graphs.

Figure 4.3

Assessing Access Features of a Nonfiction Book

The teacher and students can use this chart to assess the usefulness of access features in a nonfiction book.

Access Features	✓ If Used	How It Is Used
Title		
Table of contents		
Introduction, preface, prologue		
Headings and subheadings		
Sidebars		
Bulleted information		
Inset sections or pages		
Glossaries, pronunciation guides		
Bibliographies		
Index with no subtopics/with subtopics		
Afterword, epilogue, endnotes, author and illustrator notes		
Appendices		

- Determine that the information is accurate and know ways to assess an author's efforts to ensure this (e.g., checking acknowledgments, sources cited, the foreword or introduction, author's notes, bibliography).
- Determine the relationship between special features, such as diagrams, captions, labels, and the running text (i.e., whether the information in those features repeats what's in the running text, extends it, or is completely different from it).

Learning to Craft Nonfiction Writing

We not only want students to read nonfiction well, but to write it well. Here are some goals to consider that will put students on the road to crafting high-quality nonfiction.

You might teach students to:

- Understand that nonfiction writing is different from one discipline to another (i.e., that writing in science is different from writing in social studies).
- Select and narrow topics.
- Use the organizational features (e.g., organizational structures, headings) that are appropriate to the content and purpose of the book.
- Vary their style of writing to match their purpose.
- Use words and organizational structures or visuals in their writing that signal readers to the type of nonfiction they are writing.
- Use signal words and phrases that help to support readers' comprehension of organizational structure (e.g., compare and contrast, cause and effect). (See Figure 4.4.)
- Select and create visuals such as illustrations, captions, diagrams, and charts that support and expand the running text.
- Process and coordinate writing the running text with including visual features (e.g., photographs, diagrams, flow charts).
- Include features that support understanding of specialized language or terminology (e.g., definitions included within running text, boxes, glossaries) in their writing.
- Use access features that support and extend understanding of the content (e.g., table of contents, introduction, index, sidebars).

Figure 4.4

Teach Signal Words and Phrases

When teaching within the comprehensive framework, point out and discuss signal words and phrases and what they mean in the text. Encourage students to include those words and phrases in their own writing. For example, signal words that indicate cause and effect (Lenski & Johns, 2000) are:

- *as a result*
- *because*
- *consequently*
- *eventually*
- *due to*
- *for that reason*
- *if*
- *leads to*
- *so*
- *then*
- *when*

For a complete list of words and phrases that signal information, see Appendix G.

Learning to Read Nonfiction Texts

Effective readers of nonfiction pay attention to an array of things related to how nonfiction works, such as how the writing is organized, how new vocabulary is defined, and how visual information supports their reading. Good nonfiction readers also build a repertoire of strategies to use before, during, and after reading.

You might teach students to:

- Develop their ear for how nonfiction text sounds to appreciate an author's style and build awareness of fluency.
- Apply comprehension strategies before, during, and after reading nonfiction: making predictions and connections, questioning, visualizing, inferring, determining importance, analyzing, synthesizing, and summarizing what they read. (See pages 107–110 for more on reading strategies.) (See Figure 4.5.)
- Use a repertoire of strategies to match purposes for reading (e.g., using keywords in table of contents or index to find specific pages, browsing to get an overall sense of content or organizational structures).
- Coordinate the running text with visual features (e.g., photographs, diagrams, flow charts).
- Be aware of methods authors use to support understanding of specialized language or terminology (e.g., definitions included within running text, boxes, glossaries).
- Understand that certain features of text alert us to the type of literature we are reading (e.g., organizational structures, access features, illustrative materials).
- Recognize and understand that access features support and extend understanding of the content (e.g., table of contents, introduction, headings, index, sidebars).

Learning to Inquire

To engage successfully in inquiry, students need to have some knowledge about the topic under investigation, understand the inquiry methods being used, be skilled in using and gathering information from nonfiction books and other sources, and be skilled in presenting that information to others. Helping students to become independent inquirers is our ultimate goal because it requires them to use all their knowledge to learn more about their world and share it with others.

You might teach students to:

- Develop a spirit of inquiry by asking questions as a way to learn from nonfiction books,

Figure 4.5

Teach Reading Strategies Across the Framework

Tracking students' use of reading strategies across the comprehensive framework is important to success. This chart lists a sample of reading strategies that will assist in ensuring that you're covering all strategies, in each approach of the framework. Charts such as these can be used to track books used, dates of lessons, evaluative comments regarding students' progress, and notes about the lesson.

Reading Strategies	Comprehensive Framework Approaches					
	Instructional Read Aloud	Shared Reading	Guided Reading	Discovery Circles	Readers'/Writers' Workshops	Extension Activities
Making Predictions						
Making Connections						
Questioning (Monitoring & Correcting)						
Visualizing						
Inferring						
Determining Importance						
Analyzing						
Synthesizing						
Summarizing						

from conversations with others, and from sharing writing with others.

- Select and narrow a topic for inquiry.
- Activate and use all that they know about both the content and reading and writing nonfiction to answer their inquiry questions.
- Read nonfiction to study both the content and the craft of writing (reading like a writer), and write their own non-fiction with their audience in mind (writing for the reader).
- Select the most appropriate research methods for conducting their inquiry (e.g., reading, interviewing, experimenting). (See Figure 4.6.)
- Select the most appropriate nonfiction for their inquiries.
- Develop strategies for synthesizing information from several sources and methods for interpreting and clarifying what is known about a topic.
- Feel comfortable about their topic—know about it from the "inside out"—be able to talk about it with ease with others and then be able to write about it.
- Access what they know about good nonfiction and apply their understandings to the nonfiction they write.

Figure 4.6

Interview an Expert: A Checklist of Things to Do

Gathering information from an expert involves a variety of strategies. If you're planning classroom interviews, use this checklist to make sure you cover all the bases—or give it to your students to make sure they cover theirs.

1. Contact expert to schedule an appointment for the interview.
2. Develop questions to ask the expert.
3. Send questions to the expert before the interview.
4. Prepare for interview by reviewing current notes on the topic and your questions.
5. Keep track of what expert says by:
   a. taking notes during the interview
   b. audiotaping the interview
   c. videotaping the interview
6. Review interview notes.
7. Summarize the notes from the interview.
8. Select quotes to be incorporated into the final report.
9. Write final report. Send a copy of the report to the expert to ensure you haven't misquoted him or her.

Strategies for Reading and Writing Nonfiction

Setting goals is extremely important. But the truth of the matter is, we'll reach none of them unless we teach students strategies for comprehending and writing nonfiction. So in this section, we describe strategies for reading nonfiction effectively, followed by strategies for writing nonfiction. In Part II, we provide plenty of ideas for teaching these strategies.

Strategies for Reading Nonfiction Effectively

Understanding how nonfiction works is important, but we also want students to become thoughtful, independent, engaged readers who understand deeply what they read. We do this through strategy instruction. Our advice is grounded in the work of Pearson, Roehler, Dole, and Duffy (1992), who state, "We really do expect *all* readers of *all* ages to engage in all of these strategies at some level of sophistication. We really are arguing that there are no first-grade skills, third-grade skills, sixth-grade skills, and so on." Our work is also informed by educators such as Irene C. Fountas and Gay Su Pinnell (2001), Stephanie Harvey and Anne Goudvis (2000), and Ellin Oliver Keene and Susan Zimmermann (1997). These are key strategies that research demonstrates expert readers use to build comprehension. Readers apply them to all kinds of texts, at different points in the reading process—before, during, and after. Thoughtful and active readers need to:

- Use existing knowledge to make sense of texts—making connection to self or other texts, or the world.
- Monitor their comprehension throughout the reading process (i.e., knowing when they're not understanding).
- Determine what's important in texts.
- Ask questions.
- Draw inferences during and after reading.
- Synthesize information when they read.
- Make predictions.
- Visualize or make mental images while reading.
- Analyze and critique what they read.
- Summarize.

Now let's examine how effective readers apply these strategies to nonfiction texts (Bamford & Kristo, 2003; Bamford & Kristo, 2000; Duke & Pearson, 2002; Keene & Zimmermann, 1997;

Paris, Wasik, & Turner, 1996; Pressley, 2002a; Pressley, 2002b). Notice how the general strategies listed above are infused throughout the more specific ones listed below.

Before reading a nonfiction book, good readers:

- Determine their purposes and goals to guide their selection of nonfiction books.
- Select sources by title, abstract, or catalog description; analyze cover illustration to determine if the book will meet their purposes.
- Preview by:
  — Checking key words in table of contents and/or index.
  — Examining headings, subheadings, and visuals.
  — Activating prior knowledge to access the potentially new information.
  — Assessing the scope and depth of the content.
  — Noting organizational structures (e.g., cause-effect, compare-contrast) and access features (e.g., table of contents, glossary, index).
  — Noting where important or desired information is located and what parts to read in detail versus those to skim or ignore.
  — Making connections to other books, to themselves, and to the world.

During the reading of a nonfiction book, good readers:

- May read only a section of the book, skim sections from front to back, view visuals only, or skip irrelevant information depending upon what was read during the selection process.
- Reread important information or content that is difficult to understand.
- Reflect on ideas by underlining, highlighting, and writing notes in the margins; adding stick-on notes; or creating graphic organizers to assist with synthesizing, integrating, or summarizing information (e.g., comparison chart on different kinds of whales).
- Use knowledge of organizational structures and how nonfiction books work to make predictions about content.
- Carefully read topic sentences, topic paragraphs, summary sections in paragraph form, bulleted/numbered lists, and sidebars.
- Notice words or phrases that signal explanation or definition, persuasive writing, compare and contrast, and perspective/biases or author interpretations of the content. (See Appendix G, Words That Signal Information.)
- Alter predictions or assumptions of the content based on reading.
- Reevaluate or reaffirm prior knowledge based on reading.

- Visualize or make images in the mind while reading text.
- Compare information from one source to other sources, such as other nonfiction books, documentaries, web pages, or interviews with experts.
- Attend to new or contradictory information, possibly stopping to directly compare with other sources.
- Continue to make connections to self, text, and the world.
- Use prior knowledge, making conscious and unconscious inferences about the content (e.g., comparing and contrasting an event in history that repeats itself, looking for causes and effects, determining why an author emphasizes a point or hedges, recognizing turning points in events and consequences).
- Analyze visual features and their captions in relationship to the running text to determine similarities in information, differences in information, and text explanations of visuals such as diagrams and flow charts.
- Analyze the text for main ideas.
- Question what they read by querying the author directly or indirectly.
- Work backward and forward to construct a main idea because the author's organization was confusing or the information was initially read too quickly.
- Modify or shift reading rate, attention to details, and decisions to reread depending on whether the content is challenging, difficult to understand, or confusing.
- Draw conclusions about the ideas based on author's reputation, copyright date, experts noted who reviewed the information, resources or primary sources identified by the author, perceptions of the author's purpose(s) for writing, tone of the writing, author interpretations of the information, and author's choice of examples.
- Decide on the quality of the information and whether the presentation of the topic is interesting, the visuals clarify or add to the information, the arguments or interpretations of the author are credible, the organization assists the reader in understanding the topic, and the style of writing is appealing.
- Monitor their own comprehension, keeping in mind their reading goals, which lead to decisions about whether to continue to read or move on to another book.

After reading a nonfiction book, good readers:
- May reread select pieces to clarify or confirm information.
- Summarize by retelling verbally, in writing, or visually.
- Determine accuracy and credibility of the content compared to other sources. Decide if fur-

ther information is needed because all questions were not answered or new questions arose as a result of the reading.

- Consider how to use the information depending upon the original purpose for reading it (e.g., share with peer group, use it to write a section of a report, create a comparison chart).
- Critique what is read to see if the book presents information consistent with what is known about the topic.

Strategies for Writing Nonfiction Effectively

Like reading, writing needs to take place in an environment where students are actively engaged and instruction progresses from high teacher support to low. This environment should be a community of readers and writers, where students interact and support one another's learning. Students should have easy access to a collection of high-quality nonfiction books and opportunities to hear and discuss nonfiction during instructional read aloud, shared reading, guided reading, and other components of the framework, so that they are continually exposed to good models of nonfiction. In writers' workshop mini-lessons, students need opportunities to critically examine individual features of nonfiction and to consider how the author made choices in creating that feature. Students need to see their teacher demonstrate writing, thinking aloud about the choices she is making as she composes. They need time to discuss how to write nonfiction—challenges they encounter and strategies they use. Students also need plenty of opportunities to write nonfiction as a group, in interactive writing, shared writing, and guided writing; to practice writing short pieces such as captions, diagrams, bulleted lists, comparing and contrasting; and, finally, to engage in inquiry to write short and longer pieces collaboratively or individually.

FROM THEORY TO PRACTICE: AN EXAMPLE OF STRATEGY USE IN ACTION

The strategies described in this chapter offer you a multitude of ways to help students become strong, skilled readers of nonfiction. But where do you even begin applying them in the classroom? Let's look at what fifth-grade teacher Frank Dragone did with one of his students, Lee, who is exploring questions about outer space. In Figure 4.7, we show how Lee uses some of the strategies she is learning before, during, and after reading *Space Station Science: Life in Free Fall* (Dyson, 1999). The left side of the chart lists the reading strategy, and the right side explains how Lee applied it and what Frank did to help her.

Figure 4.7

What a Good Reader Does to Understand Nonfiction

Strategies to Comprehend Nonfiction	How One Fifth Grader Applies Strategies and What Her Teacher Does to Help
	BEFORE READING
Good readers size up a book before they start reading. They look at such things as how the book is organized and the structure of the text.	Nonfiction readers determine the type of nonfiction book they're about to read, its organization, and access features or where to find information. Lee knows from how her teacher described types of nonfiction books that *Space Station Science* (Dyson, 1999) is an "all-about" book or survey book. She also knows this from the information on the book jacket, the listing of topics in the table of contents, and browsing through the book. Lee also knows that a survey book is usually organized by subtopics, so she may not need or want to read the entire book. She may decide to read specific chapters in order to find the information that she needs. (Information on how to determine the type and organization of a nonfiction book is found in Chapter 3.)
Good readers preview the book by checking for key words in the table of contents and/or index to locate information.	Lee has questions about her topic on living in space, so these will guide her as she reads. She wants to know how living in space affects the body. Using the table of contents she finds an entire section on her question. She also checks the index using the key words and phrases *living in space, body,* and *health* and finds nothing. Frank intervenes and together they scan the index: Under the subheading *astronaut,* they find *"health of"* with several pages listed. Lee decides she will need to read section 3 and section 5. Frank decides to use this index for a shared reading lesson because of its organization.

continued on next page

Strategies to Comprehend Nonfiction	How One Fifth Grader Applies Strategies and What Her Teacher Does to Help
	DURING READING
• Good readers make predictions as they read. • Readers who are active question the author as they read. • They continually monitor what they read by making decisions about what parts to skim and scan and what sections to examine carefully.	Lee's inquiry questions are important because she uses them to make predictions to guide her reading, which triggers a new ripple of questions. These are "I wonder" questions and "what if" questions (Zarnowski, 2003). The more she reads, the more her reading inspires her to think about *What would happen if?* This new round of questions leads to more predictions about what answers she'll find next, and then another round of questions. She skims and scans to find information she is looking for based on her questions.
Good readers literally talk to themselves. This internal speech is a dialogue the reader experiences as a way to question, modify, and formulate new understandings, as well as to confirm or make changes about prior knowledge.	Lee's teacher has taught her to think aloud, so as she reads some material and skims other parts, it will look like she is having a conversation with herself. The think alouds help to scaffold her knowledge about the topic. (More on think alouds in Chapter 5.) Lee was fascinated with the question in *Space Station Science* that asked, "If people stayed in space, would they end up as blobs?" In this book the author said that astronauts really have to do a lot of exercise and other things to keep healthy. This made her wonder about how being in space affects animals that are on board. She wonders if astronauts have ever taken a dog or their favorite pet when they travel in space.
	AFTER READING
Effective nonfiction readers reflect on what they've read and make a plan for what to do next.	Lee decides to write a bulleted list of notes to share in her reading discovery circle. She also plans to see if *Space Station Science* has information about animals that have traveled in space. Her alternate plan is to look at additional sources if this book doesn't contain answers to her questions.

In the next section, we share what effective writers do before, during, and after they write. These writing strategies emerge from four sources: educators who have written extensively on student inquiry, the research process, and the expository writing process; our work with K–12 teachers who create their own nonfiction books to serve as mentor texts for their students; our interviews with authors of nonfiction trade books; and our own work with nonfiction literature (Atwell, 1998; Bamford & Kristo, 2000; Bamford & Kristo, 2003; Graves, 1994; Harvey, 1998; Harvey & Goudvis, 2000; Hoyt, 2002; Maxwell, 1996; Moline, 1996; Murray, 1984; Piazza, 2003; Portalupi & Fletcher, 2001; Short, Harste, & Burke, 1996). Now, let's briefly examine a sample of the before-, during-, and after-writing strategies effective nonfiction writers use.

Before writing nonfiction, good writers:

- Select their topic and create webs, KWL charts, and other graphic organizers to determine scope and depth of information.
- Select research methods appropriate to the discipline, such as reading nonfiction books, interviewing an expert, going on-site to collect data (for example, learning how the post office operates), and using sources such as the Internet.
- Process and coordinate information sources and select material from them for future use.
- Use newly gathered information to reconsider the scope and depth of their final piece.
- Review gathered information to select the type of nonfiction and organizational structure that best fit their purpose for their audience.
- Regularly share orally what they are learning about their topic in order to think more deeply and internalize their information, discover what they know and don't know about the topic, and pinpoint conflicting information.
- Use graphic organizers to create a plan for the piece.
- Refer to text sets on the topic and mentor texts to get ideas for presenting the information.

During the writing of nonfiction, good writers:

- Select and chunk information to fit the organizational structure they've chosen (e.g., if describing a process such as making maple sugar, then it will be important to chunk the information sequentially).
- Do not rely on notes too heavily. This will preserve their voice and perspective on the topic. In draft stage, they can check the piece against notes for accuracy.
- Select information to be displayed visually and create or select visuals (e.g., illustrations, photos, diagrams, maps, tables) that expand the running text and support readers' comprehension.

- Select extra but important information to include in sidebars, inset pages, or author notes.
- Select strategies for including new terminology and consistently use the strategies in writing the piece (e.g., define the term in running text, boldface terms, include definitions in a glossary).
- Include access features to support readers, such as headings, subheadings, captions, labels, table of contents, and index.
- Begin with a strong lead that engages readers and establishes scope and depth of the text.
- Support generalizations with details and explanations.
- Distinguish clearly between fact and opinion.
- Identify where information is contradictory.
- Use metaphor and descriptions effectively to connect with readers' prior knowledge, such as describing an elephant as being as large as a school bus.
- Reread to assess for clarity and consistency of style.
- Include a conclusion that summarizes the main idea and provides points for further thought.
- Add appropriate materials at the back of the piece, such as epilogue, author/illustrator notes, glossary, bibliography, or sources for further reading.
- Include information about the author and the research done to create the text.
- Select an appropriate format for the informational piece and layout for individual pages.

After writing nonfiction, good writers:
- Request that a teacher, parent, or more knowledgeable peer edit their piece.
- Ask an expert to review the piece for accuracy.
- Share their piece so others can learn about their topic and share the decision they made as a writer of nonfiction.

QUESTIONS FOR CONNECTING AND IMPROVING NONFICTION READING AND WRITING

As we discussed in Chapter 2, reading and writing are inextricably linked, but also different. In reading we are gathering information from the text, where as in writing we are creating meaning by constructing text. Many of the questions good readers ask themselves are very similar to the questions good writers ask. See Figure 4.8 for a comparison of some of those questions and note the extent to which they overlap. Then share them with your class, as you work within the comprehensive framework. Chances are, your students will be empowered to know that similar questions can improve their reading and writing.

Figure 4.8

Questions for Helping Readers and Writers Make Decisions About Nonfiction

Questions Good Readers Ask Themselves	Questions Good Writers Ask Themselves
What is the topic of the text I am reading?	What topic am I going to write about?
What kind of information is provided on this topic?	What kind of information do I want to share with my readers?
What is the author's purpose in writing this book?	How do I want my readers to use my information?
How is the information organized?	How will I organize my information to make it more accessible to the reader?
How does the author tell me how the research was conducted to ensure accuracy?	How will I inform my readers about how I did my research?
What do I already know about the topic? What do I know about how this author presents information?	How can I draw on readers' prior knowledge to help them understand my message?
How does the author lead off the information? Does the lead tell me anything about the type of book this is, the author's writing style, or the author's perspective on the topic?	How will I begin my informational piece? What style of writing would be appropriate for the type of book I am writing? What would best convey my perspective on this topic?
What kind of visual information does the author use to clarify and explain the information in the text? Does the visual information make sense and what do I need to do to comprehend it?	How will I extend and support my text so readers can "see" the information? What visuals will best explain the information?
How can I find specific information using key words in the table of contents and index?	What access features should I include to assist the reader in locating specific information on my topic? How is my information chunked? Would a table of contents or index be helpful or do I need both?

Taking Stock of Your Students' Knowledge of Nonfiction

Good instruction is based on assessing students' knowledge about the types and features of nonfiction. So track evidence of what your students can do independently and with your assistance. A student who is mastering this body of knowledge can:

- Point out and name the various types of nonfiction and their features.
- Explain the purposes of the various types of nonfiction and their features.

Figure 4.9

Sample Checklist

This checklist represents what a second grader knew about visual information at the beginning of the year.

Visual Information	Point It Out	Name It	Describe How to Use It	Practice in Reading	Practice in Writing
Design of book/ formats/layout	✓	✓			
Dust jackets/covers	✓	✓	✓		
Endpapers	✓	✓	✓	✓	
Labels and captions	✓	✓	✓	✓ simple ones	
Illustrations/photos/ graphs/archival materials	✓	✓	✓	✓ illus. & photos	✓ illus. & photos
Diagrams: simple, scale, cross section, cutaways, flow, tree, web	✓	✓	✓	✓ simple diagrams	✓ simple diagrams
Graphs: line, bar, column, pie	✓	✓			
Tables (charts)	✓	✓	✓	✓ simple chart	
Maps: geographical, bird's-eye view, flow	✓	✓	✓	✓ simple map	✓ simple one
Time lines	✓	✓	✓		

- Read different types of nonfiction, using features to locate and explore information.
- Write different types of nonfiction and demonstrate their expertise in interpreting information for readers.

See Appendix C for a record-keeping chart that will help you assess your students on all these fronts. Figure 4.9 shows an excerpt from a filled-in chart.

Closing Thoughts

In this chapter, we showed you that the nonfiction toolbox is, indeed, full of strategies to teach students about reading and writing nonfiction. There's no doubt about it—there's a lot to learn, and there's a lot to teach. Now the good news: Your students won't and shouldn't learn everything they need to know about nonfiction in a month or even a year.

Meet with your colleagues to design a nonfiction curriculum. Focus your teaching on what your students understand at this point about nonfiction and where you want to take them. Keep in mind the strong bond between reading and writing—how the two processes influence and impact one another. Doing this will jump-start your thinking for what's ahead in Part II—Using Nonfiction Across the Comprehensive Framework, which explores each approach of the framework in detail. It will give you a base for making decisions about what and how to teach—and plenty of ideas for getting started.

Chapter 5
Instructional Read Alouds and Modeled Writing:
Demonstrating Strategies for Students

"I love listening to you read, especially those weather books. Like the
time you read that book about hurricanes and the author kept saying
stuff that really made me feel like something was going to happen.
The author kept saying over and over again that in 1938 no one knew
about this hurricane. I couldn't believe that. I mean it was so weird
because now we know when we're going to have bad weather.
I was really at the edge of my seat waiting for it to happen!"
—Tiffany, fifth-grade student, speaking to her teacher

Tiffany is referring to the book *Hurricanes: Earth's Mightiest Storms* (Lauber, 1996). In a section of the book, author Patricia Lauber writes in the style of a newspaper reporter, repeating the line "No one knew..." to create rhythm and build tension and a sense of drama. This technique grabs the audience's attention when the book is read aloud. It also provides a good example of fluent reading. Tiffany's teacher, Judy Bouchard, frequently reads aloud books like this to share what good science writing sounds like. As she reads, she thinks aloud, too, so that students become aware of her questions and comments about stylistic choices.

Another reason Judy selected *Hurricanes* was because it is an excellent example of how an author writes about science in an exciting, unexpected way. She wants her students to hear how Lauber uses words to pull readers along and to try that in their own writing. Before she asks them to do that, though, Judy does a modeled writing lesson to show her students when, how, and where to use the techniques that Lauber uses. She also plans several more instructional read alouds to help students notice techniques other science writers use to make their content interesting and exciting to read.

Here are Judy's overall goals for her instructional read alouds and modeled writing lessons. She wants students to:

- Develop an ear for what good nonfiction sounds like.
- Become aware of ways authors craft their writing to make it appealing to readers.
- Make their writing interesting by using techniques they have learned through instructional read alouds and modeled writing.

In this chapter we:

- Define modeled instruction and its subcategories, instructional read alouds, and modeled writing, and show where they fit on the scaffolded literacy framework.

Nonfiction in Focus

- Identify the benefits of using modeled instruction.
- Describe think alouds as a key component to modeled instruction.
- Define instructional read alouds and discuss the role of think alouds as a key component.
- Offer lesson ideas and tips for reading aloud nonfiction.
- Define modeled writing and discuss the role of think alouds as a key component.
- Offer lesson ideas and tips for modeled writing of nonfiction.

What Is Modeled Instruction? Teacher Demonstrates/ Students Watch

Modeled instruction is when the teacher demonstrates something new or unfamiliar about nonfiction, as students watch and learn. It is usually done with large or small groups at all grade levels, but sometimes with individual students.

Depending on the purpose of the modeled instruction, teachers may invite students to participate. See the shaded area in Figure 5.1 for where modeled instruction falls on the comprehensive framework. Note that two approaches we recommend for modeled instruction are instructional read aloud and modeled writing, which we cover in depth in the next section.

Modeled Instruction: Quick Points

- **Purpose:** To introduce a new or unfamiliar aspect about reading or writing nonfiction through models of nonfiction and teacher think alouds. When we think aloud, we model how a more experienced person reads and writes nonfiction.
- **Kinds of Modeled Instruction:** Instructional read alouds and modeled writing
- **Scaffolding Level:** Highest
- **Teacher Role/Student Role:** Teacher demonstrates/students watch. Teacher primarily demonstrates, models, and explains using examples, while students listen and learn, although teachers may invite student interaction depending upon the purpose.
- **Instructional Context:** Typically done with the whole class or a small group, with students of all ages and grades.
- **Types of Materials Typically Used:** Nonfiction books, magazine articles, and nonfiction writing by the teacher and students.
- **Next Steps:** Modeled instruction can be followed up by another instructional read aloud or another modeled writing lesson, a shared or guided writing lesson, or independent extension activities.

Figure 5.1

Comprehensive Framework

Level of Scaffolding	Role of Teacher and Student	Reading Instructional Approach		Writing Instructional Approach
Modeled	• Teacher demonstrates • Students watch	Instructional Read Aloud		Modeled Writing
Shared	• Teacher leads • Students apprentice	Shared Reading		Interactive Writing and Shared Writing
Guided	• Students demonstrate • Teacher assists	Guided Reading	Mini-Lessons and Extension Activities*	Guided Writing
Modified	• Students work collaboratively • Teacher modifies support by observing, helping, assessing	Reading Discovery Circles		Writing Discovery Circles
	• Students work independently, with other students, and/or with the teacher • Teacher modifies support by observing, helping, assessing	Readers' Workshop		Writers' Workshop
Independent	• Students practice • Teacher observes and assesses independent practice activities	Extension Activities*		Extension Activities*

* Extension activities can be used as follow-up activities with all instructional approaches, but students are working independently—either individually or in small groups. Keep in mind that extension activities should match the student's ability to practice the activities independently.

Think Alouds: A Key Component of Modeled Instruction

Think alouds give students opportunities to learn firsthand what we do as we read and write nonfiction. This is important because reading and writing are invisible and complex processes. Students can't see how we comprehend text, apply strategies, and make decisions as more expert readers and writers (Roehler & Duffy, 1984; Wilhelm, 2001). According to Jeffrey Wilhelm (2001), author of *Improving Comprehension With Think-Aloud Strategies*: "A think-aloud of reading is creating a record, either through writing or talking aloud, of the strategic decision-making and interpretive processes of going through a text, reporting everything the reader is aware of noticing, doing, seeing, feeling, asking, and understanding as she reads. A think-aloud involves talking about the reading strategies you are using and the content of the piece you are reading."

While reading aloud, we can share images and patterns we see, questions and confusions we have, and connections and choices we make as readers. While modeling writing, we can think aloud how we plan, narrow a topic, change our minds, revise, confront problems, consider options, make decisions, and use the features of nonfiction so our piece is clear and well organized. We also use think alouds to examine nonfiction writing of others and consider how that writing was composed. Although think alouds are important for all students in grades K to 6, they are especially important for intermediate and middle-school students who did not have the advantage of reading and writing nonfiction in the primary grades (Ehlinger & Pritchard, 1994). Think alouds help readers and writers:

- Size up a nonfiction book to determine whether it meets their purpose for the reading. For example, the teacher could ask in the think aloud, "Will this book answer my questions

The Benefits of Modeled Instruction

- Engages all students in reading and writing because the teacher is doing the primary work.
- Enables the teacher to model, through think alouds and other techniques, how to read and write nonfiction so that students can hear and see strategies in action.

- Makes learning manageable for students because lessons are brief and focused.
- Prepares students for more implicit and explicit instruction because students have been introduced to strategies and features of nonfiction.

about the topic I'm writing about or want to learn more about?"

- Activate background knowledge, enabling them to make connections to the content of their reading and writing.

- Locate and examine the access features the author uses, such as the table of contents and index, to support their understandings and to consider using them in their own writing.

- Understand new vocabulary to boost their understanding of the content and give them words to use in their own writing.

- Examine the visual information (e.g., photos and captions, diagrams, graphs, cross sections, flow charts) to learn when authors use it, for what purpose, and how it contributes to understanding the topic.

- Consider the style of writing for words and phrases that signal literary devices (such as metaphors), bias or perspective, hedging or hypothesizing, or facts versus opinions.

- Determine how the writing sounds when it's read aloud. Is it clear, interesting, and understandable?

- Build upon literal understanding of the text to infer what the author doesn't state.

- Recognize similarities or differences in information among books on the same topic.

- Be strategic readers by knowing what to do before, doing, and after they read.

- Visualize what the author is saying and make predictions based on what they see.

- Summarize and synthesize information, recognize the difference between these two processes, and see reasons to use these strategies.

- Determine what to do if the text becomes confusing or too difficult: reread sections, abandon the text, or read only sections or captions.

> ## USE THINK ALOUDS ACROSS THE COMPREHENSIVE FRAMEWORK
>
> Think alouds needn't only be used during modeled instruction. Use them in any component of the comprehensive framework—shared and guided reading lessons, shared and guided writing, discovery circles—when you want students to understand how a more proficient reader and writer makes decisions and solves problems.

Instructional Read Aloud

An effective way to learn something new is to have someone more experienced show you how to do it. That's the principle behind instructional read alouds. The more experienced person—the teacher—demonstrates something new about nonfiction, such as comprehension strategies to use before, during, or after reading a nonfiction book, ways to figure out new vocabulary, what to do when you encounter conflicting information, and how to understand visual information. The teacher usually accomplishes this by thinking aloud—or sharing his or her thoughts about the text out loud, while reading the text aloud to the group.

When you plan an instructional read aloud, choose a nonfiction book that does a good job illustrating the point you want to make. This is important for teaching visual information such as photos and captions, time lines, maps, and diagrams. Create an overhead transparency of the page or pages with the visual information you want students to see as you read aloud. This is critical if you're reading aloud to a large group so that everyone can easily see the material. We discuss this further in the section on lesson ideas later in the chapter. The enlarged pages can also be used for a shared reading, which we cover in Chapter 6.

How to Incorporate Think Alouds Into Instructional Read Alouds

To help you get started with instructional read alouds, we provide explanations and examples of how Mary Evans, a fourth-grade teacher, plans and conducts a think aloud using *Growing Up Wild: Penguins,* a picture book by Sandra Markle (2002), as part of her unit on Antarctica. These suggestions are based on the work of Jeffrey Wilhelm (2001). (See Figure 5.2.)

Mary is working on helping her students recognize ways authors support readers in understanding new vocabulary. In *Growing Up Wild: Penguins,* new vocabulary is italicized and defined in a glossary at the end, making the book perfect for the lesson. Mary plans to focus on these text features in her think aloud. She also wants students to see that they can use them in their own nonfiction writing.

Because it's important for Mary's students to see certain pages clearly during the instructional read aloud, she gathers them on the floor close to her. Mary will hold up *Growing Up Wild: Penguins* for all to see as she reads, but she'll put the book down when she's ready to think aloud. This reinforces that her think aloud is not part of the text but rather a sharing of her thoughts as she reads.

Figure 5.2

An Instructional Read Aloud With Think Aloud

Procedures for Doing Read Alouds	Example from Mary Evans' Fourth-Grade Classroom
1. Decide on your purpose. Your read aloud should focus on an aspect or feature about nonfiction that you want to introduce or review. Have a focus even though the text you choose might be appropriate for many purposes. Trying to do too much during a think aloud usually confuses students; they most likely won't remember what is important.	Mary's focus is on helping her students determine how authors support a reader's understanding of new vocabulary.
2. Carefully choose a high-quality book, based on what you want to teach about nonfiction. Picture books work well, even for older students. If you choose longer books, select excerpts. Remember this is a short lesson, not an extended read aloud as you might plan for another purpose.	Mary chose *Growing Up Wild: Penguins* by Sandra Markle (2002), a picture book describing the life cycle of Adelie penguins. This lavish book is perfect for her unit on Antarctica. The way the author identifies new words by italicizing them and defining them in a glossary at the end of the book gives her students a new strategy for working with words. Mary may decide to read aloud the entire book later so that students learn about the complete life cycle of these penguins. But for the purpose of the think aloud, she'll only read sections that present new vocabulary.
3. Prepare by carefully examining the book and what it has to offer, keeping your purpose foremost in mind.	Mary plans to read the first couple of pages of this book, using sticky notes to mark the passages with italicized words. She also places

Procedures for Doing Read Alouds	Example from Mary Evans' Classroom
Select brief portions to share aloud. Place sticky notes at points where you want to stop to think aloud and jot down notes of what you plan to say. Practice with the book so that you're comfortable doing the think aloud and you're clear about what you want to say and what reading or writing strategies you want to model.	a sticky note in the glossary and jots down what she plans to say to the class.
4. Gather students together and tell them the reasons for doing the think aloud and to listen to the strategies you use, and why and when you use them.	**MARY:** Let's look at the chart we are creating of ways that authors help readers understand new words. **ERIN:** So far, we found that the author might give us a definition right next to the word in the same sentence. Or the author might explain the word if we keep on reading. We also said that some authors have mini-glossaries on pages in the book or at the back of the book. **MARY:** Okay, good. Those are some examples. Today we'll add another one to our list. I have a book by Sandra Markle on penguins. [Holds up the book and shows students the cover.] There's a map at the beginning of the book of Antarctica where Adelie penguins live. [Holds up the book so everyone can see the page.] I'm going to do a think aloud right at the beginning of the book because I want you to listen carefully to what I say and what I do when I see a word that the author has italicized. [As Mary holds up the book and points to an italicized word, Joseph reminds everyone about how you can italicize words on the computer.] *continued on next page*

continued on next page

Procedures for Doing Read Alouds	Example from Mary Evans' Classroom
	MARY: That's right; as writers we can italicize words so that readers notice them. Some times we find words that are highlighted or bolded. Listen carefully to learn what I think about as I come to italicized words.
5. Read the text aloud and do the think aloud. Wilhelm (2001) suggests "[using] verbs like *I wonder, I think, I predict, I bet, I'm confused* to spotlight the kinds of mental moves you are making. Use phrases like *I'm going to reread, I'll have to read further,* or *I don't know* to both highlight reading strategies and show kids that as an expert reader stitches together an understanding of a new text, it's okay that he has some loose threads—it's okay that he doesn't know, that he is going to have to read on to find out. That's what predictions are—best guesses that we suspend in our heads, that the text will either prove we're on target or in need of correction."	Text excerpt that Mary reads: "Adelie penguins live in one of the coldest places on Earth, Antarctica. They spend most of the year in the Antarctic seas living on the *pack ice*, resting on floating ice rafts and diving under the ice to catch food." MARY: The phrase *pack ice* is italicized, and I wonder why. I know that authors make words look special or have them stand out to readers for good reasons. I think I'm going to read further. I bet these words will be defined. [Continues reading.] TEXT EXCERPT: "Then in September and October, they head for the coast of Antarctica. That's springtime in the southern hemisphere, and thousands of Adelie penguins gather in *colonies* to mate and raise their young at places like Cape Royds and Cape Bird on Ross Island." MARY: *Colonies* is another word that is italicized. Let me see. I'll reread the sentence and see if the word *colonies* is defined. [Rereads the last sentence.] No, it isn't. Does anyone know where I should look? JESS: How about seeing if there's something at the beginning of the book like on the verso page? Maybe the author said why the

Nonfiction in Focus

Procedures for Doing Read Alouds	Example from Mary Evans' Classroom
	words are italicized. MARY: Bravo, Jess. Let's take a look. Where should I look? [Jess notes that the verso is at the beginning of the book, but all Mary finds is a title page, and the page before it lists the author's other books. She notes that there is no table of contents in the book.] MARY: Let's look at the end of the book. Remember that some books have a verso page at the end. [Finds the verso page and reads an author's note aloud to the students.] But this tells us about different kinds of penguins, not about the italicized print. I think I'll go back one page to see what I can find. Okay, wow! There's a glossary, pronunciation key, and index all on one page. There's even a note that says, "Glossary words are italicized the first time they appear in the text." I know as a reader that when words are in special print or highlighted, it probably means that the author is going to define them, and those definitions will most likely be in a glossary at the end of the book. [Reads the definitions for *pack ice* and *colonies*.]
6. Debrief about the think aloud. Discuss the focus of the think aloud and how it can be applied to reading and/or writing.	MARY: What did you notice I did when I came to an italicized word? RON: You kept thinking that there had to be a reason why the author did that. You just didn't let it go. You kept thinking that it was in that special print for a good reason.

continued on next page

Procedures for Doing Read Alouds	Example from Mary Evans' Classroom
	MARY: Good. I persevered, didn't I? I know that authors give us signals sometimes that they're doing something special for readers, so I needed to pay attention. DALE: She made us look in another spot in the book. MARY: Right! So what should we remember about this to put on our list about how authors help us understand new words? MARCOS: Some authors use italics to tell us to look in the glossary to define new words.
7. **Plan your next teaching steps based on your students' needs and your teaching goals.** How will students use the strategy in their own reading? Are some students ready to apply it in their own writing? Or will you need to do some modeled writing? Will you plan additional think alouds?	Mary wants to make certain that all her students understand how the author supports a reader's understanding of new vocabulary, so she next plans a shared reading lesson. (See Chapter 6 for more on shared reading.)

A Middle-School Example of an Instructional Read Aloud That Includes a Think Aloud

Eileen Nokes, a middle-school teacher, regularly incorporates think alouds into her instructional read alouds of nonfiction to help students understand content and features. For the read aloud described here, she chose *The Lewis and Clark Trail: Then and Now* by Dorothy Hinshaw Patent with photographs by William Muñoz (2002). She feels that it is a good choice because students are studying the Lewis and Clark expedition in history, and reading it will extend their knowledge. It contains photographs with examples of complex captions (see Figure 5.3), which Eileen knows her students have trouble reading. As Will said, "It's just extra stuff, and if we were really supposed to read it, why didn't the author put it in with everything else?" Jessie added, "Sometimes captions are just too long and look too hard to read. They look like something grownups would read. I don't think they're for kids, anyways."

Eileen's goal for this is to help students appreciate that captions are supposed to be read. Some captions hold surprises because the information they include is not always part of the running text, so that readers who skip them could miss important facts.

This caption is packed with information for her to incorporate in a think aloud—what a word such as *foreground* means, how the caption enhances and extends information in the photograph, or how information in the caption compares to information in the running text. She has lots of options and needs to decide on what her focus will be.

The following is a brief excerpt from her instructional read aloud—the point where she stops reading, sets the book down, and begins her think aloud about the caption.

EILEEN: My prediction was right. I thought that the caption was going to say something about the equipment and supplies Lewis and Clark took on the expedition. That makes sense

EQUIPMENT AND SUPPLIES

"30 Sheep skins taken off the Animal as perfectly whole as possible, without being split on the belly as usual and dressed only with lime to free them from the wool; or otherwise about the same quantity of Oil Cloth bags well painted." —From Lewis's list of equipment and supplies

One of Lewis's biggest headaches was deciding what items it was necessary to bring along. There would be no supply stations along the way, so the men of the expedition had to depend on what they already had, on what they hunted and gathered, and on what they traded for with the Indians.

Altogether, the expedition carried twelve tons of equipment and supplies. The list of items Lewis purchased ranged from ink and pencils to axes and fishhooks. Many of the things he needed are very different from what we use today. Instead of matches, he had to buy "30 steels for striking or making fire." Insect repellent was unknown, and since mosquitoes thrived along the Missouri River, mosquito netting was vitally important.

There were no man-made fabrics; everything was made from natural fibers such as cotton, wool, and linen. That meant cloth items could easily rot during the trip, and the clothing Lewis purchased was bit by bit replaced by Indian-style leather clothing. There was no such thing as plastic back then, so Lewis bought oilskin bags and metal boxes to carry the precious journals and scientific instruments. He purchased 8 x 10-foot sheets of oiled linen, which served multiple purposes. They were used as tents, sails, and covers to protect goods from rain. He needed to make sure he brought along enough wool blankets, since there were no sleeping bags.

Food was a special challenge. No one knew how long the expedition would take or how much food could be obtained by hunting and gathering. Since there was no refrigeration in those days, only food that stayed unspoiled at air temperature was brought along.

Each man in the Corps of Discovery had his own gear. Some of these copies of the items they had, such as the metal plate, are easy to identify. The square wooden plate was also used for food, which was put into the big depression, while salt went into the small one. Such plates are the origin of the phrase *three square meals a day*. On the right is old-fashioned shaving gear. In the foreground are materials needed to start a fire—a flint, striking steel, and fine fibers, called tow, that burn when a spark hits them, starting the fire.

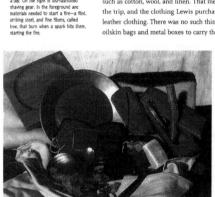

Figure 5.3: The page from *The Lewis and Clark Trail: Then and Now* by Dorothy Hinshaw Patant that Eileen used to think aloud about photographs and captions.

because that's what this page is all about, but I notice that there's extra information in the caption that's not on the page. I'm going to read the caption again. Does anyone know why?

MIKE: Because there's so many words in that caption? How can you remember everything? I thought captions were supposed to be short.

EILEEN: Well, not always. Sometimes I learn even more about the topic from reading a caption because it's a way for the author to elaborate or give additional information. I'm going to show you an overhead transparency of the page, so that you can see all the details as I read. Pay close attention to what I say and do during the next think aloud. [Opens the book again and, as she continues reading where she left off, uses the overhead transparency to point to the objects in the photograph.]

EILEEN: "In the foreground are materials needed to start a fire—a flint, striking steel, and fine fibers...." Mmmm...I'm thinking about what that word *foreground* means. I'm going to infer that it means *in front of* or *in the center* because I already pointed to everything else as I read. The things in the front are the only ones left. I'll need to look that word up later in the dictionary to make sure I'm right.

But what are "flint" and "striking steel"? Those are mentioned on the page, too. But I'm not sure what they are, so it's hard to find them in the photograph. I'm confused because the author didn't describe those things anywhere on the page. I'll have to read ahead to see if the author gives more information about this. If she doesn't, I need to figure out where to find that information. Maybe there is a glossary. What do you think I should try next?

REBEKKA: There's tons of stuff that you read in that caption that's not on the page you read. I think that you should read some more.

MIKE: I guess you have to read the whole shootin' match—the whole page and the caption. I think the really cool stuff you read is in the caption. I'm going to ask my dad about the striking steel. I wonder what else Lewis and Clark had with them.

Eileen believes she is making some progress helping her students become aware of information that captions can contain. What will she do next? Her immediate plans include following up with students on the definition of *foreground* and phrases that signal direction or location in captions, such as *upper right* and *lower left*. She also wants to be sure everyone is clear about the objects in the photograph and where to look for more information on them.

> ### HAVE STUDENTS DO THEIR OWN THINK ALOUDS
>
> Teaching students to think aloud as they read is an effective way to support their own learning about nonfiction. When we do this, we help them to internalize the language they need to be successful readers and writers. Once students master think alouds for texts that are easy for them to read and write, they can use the strategy to guide them as they take on more sophisticated texts.

How Reading Nonfiction Aloud Helps Students

Children's literature expert Sylvia Vardell (2003) says, "There are many works of nonfiction which are so well written and so beautifully designed that they come alive through the read-aloud experience." Reading nonfiction books aloud is appropriate for every grade level and for all students in every content area—science, social studies, math, and fine arts. It helps them hear how high-quality expository writing sounds.

Depending upon your purpose, nonfiction can be read aloud to open a unit, introduce new understandings about content, help students become aware of a new strategy about reading and writing nonfiction, or simply expose them to the joys of well-written nonfiction.

In the next section, we explore the benefits of reading nonfiction aloud more closely.

Students Develop an Ear for How Good Nonfiction Sounds

Good nonfiction isn't dull. Like high-quality fiction, it has style, clarity, and flow that will seduce even resistant listeners. Students need to hear what good nonfiction sounds like to appreciate its cadence and rhythm. By offering a variety of nonfiction books with strong and appealing texts and visual information, students will see all the ways writers think about their topics and craft their writing. In her book *Listen to This: Developing an Ear for Expository* (1997), Marcia S. Freeman says: "You can help your students become better expository writers by regularly reading well-written, lively and amusing, people-centered expository literature to them. Children's listening vocabulary is larger then their reading vocabulary. They can understand material read to them that is well beyond their own reading ability. Take advantage of this."

Students Become Immersed in High-Quality Nonfiction

Immersing students in nonfiction is an essential way to help them discover and learn about nonfiction books. You can do that in a variety of ways, including reading aloud excerpts. Organize a display of high-quality nonfiction books that embody a variety of topics, authors, types, and kinds of visual information. Invite students to browse the display and then read aloud excerpts from books that interest them most. Make careful and thoughtful choices about what books to read aloud and what features to discuss. Have these books readily available so your students can explore them on their own, after the read aloud.

Immersion experiences can also focus on how to choose books to match purposes for reading. Effective readers are aware of their purposes when they select a book; they don't blindly choose a book from a shelf. They know how to size it up to see if it has potential to provide the information they seek. So in the read aloud, model different purposes for selecting nonfiction books—to get information on a topic of interest, to read more by a favorite author, to find reliable sources for a research project, and so forth. Talk about how to read the front and back covers and flap copy for information, use the table of contents and index to locate information, and browse the book to see how well it matches the purpose for selecting it. See Chapter 3 for examples of immersion experiences.

Students Learn About Visual Information

Read aloud is the perfect context to teach students about visual information, such as maps, photographs and captions, diagrams, sidebars, and time lines. But because of the book's size and the students' distance from you, it's not always easy for everyone to see visual information. Don't let this stop you. If a visual is important enough for you to share during a read aloud, then it's worth taking time to create an overhead transparency of the page so that everyone can see it. This read aloud can easily become a shared reading lesson in which you and your students read and process the text together.

Students See How Writing Differs Across Disciplines

Help students appreciate history, famous people, science, fine arts, and mathematical concepts from nonfiction writers who "do their homework" and are well versed in their topics. Each discipline has its own specialized vocabulary, visuals, writing style, and organization. Read aloud texts from a variety of disciplines, and compare their similarities and differences. Create a cross-discipline text set of books on one topic, such as space exploration or the Lewis and Clark expedition, to help students build understandings about that topic and see how authors from various fields write about their respective content areas.

Students Generate Common Understandings About Content

Reading aloud nonfiction books is a great way to spark interest in a unit and tap prior knowledge about a topic. It also creates a common knowledge base about the content. This is important because not all students come to a unit with the same experience. Some may already know a lot about the topic; others may know little. When you read aloud high-quality nonfiction, it levels the playing field to some extent. It gives all students the baseline information they need to continue learning. From there, students can examine, challenge, and re-examine information on their own or in other learning contexts.

Many teachers begin instructional read alouds by creating KWL charts with their students, where they chart what they know about a topic and what they want to know before the read aloud, and what they learn about the topic after it. In addition to building common understandings among students, weaving KWL into your instructional read aloud can also enhance question-asking abilities because it encourages students to think deeply about what they know about a topic.

Students Learn Strategies for Comprehending Nonfiction

Instructional read alouds are an excellent time to introduce students to comprehension strategies such as inferring, predicting, and making connections. (See Chapter 4 for a list of strategies that good readers use before, during, and after they read.)

Here's how early literacy expert Ellen Almquist introduces the strategy of making predictions and determining the organizational structure of a book to second graders. Using the book *Century Farm: One Hundred Years on a Family Farm* by Cris Peterson (1999), Ellen encourages the children to look carefully at the title and dust jacket. She tells them, "Usually there is so much to look at before you even open a book, that if you look really carefully, you'll know a lot before you even begin reading!"

Ellen wants students to learn to take their time—to learn to look carefully at a title and a dust jacket to see what they say about the book's content. Indeed, by closely examining the dust jacket, students get clues to what the book contains and what the title means. In this case, Ellen discovers that the word *century* is not familiar to some of her students. However, once they start talking about the photographs on the dust jacket—a small colored one of a modern farm surrounded by black-and-white ones of older farms—they begin to make predictions about what the word *century* means and what information about farms the book might contain. Later, Ellen takes students on an informational tour of the book to help them understand its unique organization: The author compares and contrasts what it is like to live and work on the farm now versus a century ago by showing photographs of old and new farms on facing pages. Ellen talks about how knowing the way an author organizes his or her writing helps us make predictions when we read. Ellen provides this solid introduction to the book to launch her read aloud. Instructional read alouds are perfect for introducing students to the strategies required for reading.

Tips on Reading Nonfiction Aloud

- Let your purpose for the read aloud guide your choice of book and how much of the book you read aloud.
- Test out books by reading aloud sections to yourself before reading them to students. This will help you discover whether the book is a good choice. Sylvia Vardell (2003) recommends, "…if the language captures you or the information (and perhaps the illustrations) 'grab' you, then it might be a candidate for reading aloud."
- Don't necessarily read from cover to cover. When we read aloud fiction, we usually always read it from start to finish. It's not the same with nonfiction. Some nonfiction books are just right for browsing or reading single chapters aloud. For example, you might want to browse a concept book, look at the table of contents in a survey book, or sample entries from trivia books or almanacs of facts (Vardell, 2003).
- Sandip Wilson's (2001) groundbreaking research points out how important it is to read most historical nonfiction and biography from start to finish, so that readers keep track of events and don't lose the flow of ideas.
- For more help in planning instructional read alouds and selecting nonfiction for them, see *Making Facts Come Alive: Choosing & Using Nonfiction Literature K–8* by Bamford and Kristo (2003). Read Sylvia Vardell's chapter "Using Read Aloud to Explore the Layers of Nonfiction," the chapters specifically about choosing and using nonfiction, the interviews with nonfiction authors, and the annotated bibliography of Orbis Pictus award-winning nonfiction for lots of possibilities for read alouds, text sets, and mentor texts.

Modeled Writing

In this section, we describe another form of modeled instruction: modeled writing. First we define it. From there, we offer general points on using it and more specific guidelines for weaving think alouds into modeled writing lessons. Finally, we provide a classroom example of modeled writing in action.

The purpose of modeled writing is to demonstrate to the whole class or small groups what we do as writers, such as selecting a topic, collecting information, sorting through information to determine what to include, getting started, crafting the piece, choosing just-right words, incorporating visuals, using appropriate conventions, and almost any other topic you can think of. As with the instructional read aloud, modeled writing lessons are teacher-centered: The teacher shares examples of the features and demonstrates using think alouds as students watch and occasionally interact.

The teacher may begin a series of lessons on a feature by sharing examples of that feature from high-quality nonfiction of her own or a student's. Using examples, she identifies the characteristics of the feature and helps students examine how the feature is constructed. As the series of lessons progresses, she crafts text in front of the students, using think alouds to expose and explain her decision-making and using chart paper or overhead transparencies. (See examples below.) Modeled writing lessons are focused and short (about 5 to 15 minutes), usually occur at the beginning of writers' workshop, and are often called mini-lessons. Teachers can also use modeled instruction to demonstrate routines and procedures for participating in writers' workshop, but we will only address learning to write nonfiction. In this section, we focus on how to conduct these two types of mini-lessons used for modeling nonfiction craft lessons:

- Demonstrating how to craft nonfiction using read alouds to identify characteristics of a feature.
- Demonstrating how to craft nonfiction using writing by the teacher or student.

Demonstrating How to Craft Nonfiction Using Read Alouds to Identify Characteristics of a Feature

Read alouds are also used within the modeled writing lesson to share multiple examples of a specific technique authors use. Here the teacher points out, names, and describes the nonfiction technique the authors used to construct the feature, with an eye toward helping students apply that technique in their own writing. These read alouds help students make discoveries about how specific nonfiction features are written and set the stage for the teacher or a student to compose in front of the students who are writing.

Take Shelly Moody, third-grade teacher. She wanted

SHELLY MOODY'S STEPS TO CARRYING OUT A READ ALOUD FOR WRITING A NONFICTION FEATURE

1. Determine the purpose for the instructional read aloud, focusing on a feature you plan to demonstrate in a follow-up modeled writing lesson.
2. Select high-quality nonfiction texts that demonstrate the target feature well.
3. Identify the portion of the text to read aloud.
4. Gather students and explain what they need to listen for.
5. Carry out the read aloud, making your thoughts about the target feature visible by thinking aloud.
6. Debrief with students about the texts that were read aloud.
7. Decide on next teaching steps, based on how the students respond.

her students to try different kinds of leads in their writing. Her seven planning steps are in the box on page 137.

Shelly used two examples. She shared *All About Sharks* by Jim Arnosky (2003), which begins, "Have you ever wondered about sharks? How big do they grow? How sharp are their teeth? What do they eat? Why do they attack people? This book answers all of these questions and more. It's all about sharks!" She also shared Seymour Simon's *Animals Nobody Loves* (2001), which begins "Did you know that one blow of a grizzly bear can crush the skull of an elk?" Here is Shelly's think aloud about these leads: "Arnosky and Simon begin their books by asking me questions. Arnosky's questions sound almost like a table of contents. As I read this, I am curious to learn more about sharks. Simon's question contains surprising information and really gets me thinking about how strong a grizzly must be. These kinds of leads make me curious about the information that will follow." Shelly encouraged the students to look for other examples of nonfiction books that use question leads.

Shelly continued the focus on question leads for several days, thus increasing the intensity and duration of experience with them. (See box Nonfiction Books With Leads That Spark Wonder). Specifically, she:

- Examined more examples of leads with her students and talked about why it is important to have well-crafted leads and how these capture a reader's attention. They decided that leads that ask questions or stimulate the imagination increase the reader's interest and, therefore, would be the first ones they would work with.
- Modeled how to write a question lead by composing one for her classroom book *Sloths: The Slowest Mammals on Earth*. As she wrote, she thought aloud her decisions.
- Encouraged students to look for other examples and to try the leads in their own writing.
- Used as a good example her student Kelsey's lead in her nonfiction book, *The Fantastic Red Fox*: "Zzzz! Zzzz! Did you know that red foxes sleep with their tails over their nose? There are a lot of

NONFICTION BOOKS WITH LEADS THAT SPARK WONDER

All About Sharks by Jim Arnosky

A Drop of Water by Walter Wick

Are You a Snail? by Judy Allen and Tudor Humphries

Drip! Drop!: How Water Gets to Your Tap by Barbara Seuling

Ice Age Mammoth: Will This Ancient Giant Come Back to Life? by Barbara Hehner

It's Disgusting—and We Ate It! True Food Facts From Around the World—and Throughout History! by James Solheim

Safari Beneath the Sea: The Wonder World of the North Pacific Coast by Diane Swanson

Sea Soup: Phytoplankton by Mary M. Cerullo

Figure 5.4

Types of Leads

Question	Legend related to the topic
Exclamation (Zzzz! Psst! Splash!)	Opinion of the topic or myths
Describe the setting	Cool facts
Quotation	Vivid verbs and great description
Part of a story related to the topic (Peter Rabbit)	Tongue twisters (alliteration)
Action	What makes the topic famous
Sounds	Humor
Comparison (to animal relatives)	Present a problem
Drama, exciting situation	

interesting facts about their tails, like their tails help them balance. Also their tails help them hunt. Isn't that cool?" Shelly wanted to discuss further the decision-making process when creating question leads. This interesting lead really grabbed the attention of her classmates and the students were eager to talk about why it was effective. Shelly asked several questions such as "What do you notice about this lead?" and "What information do we learn in this lead?" Because Kelsey had added sounds to her lead, Shelly asked Kelsey how she came to write that kind of lead. "Did an author use that kind of lead in one of the nonfiction books used for the report?" "Did someone else in class try it?"

• Explored other types of leads in subsequent lessons. Shelly and her students created a reference chart and gave each lead a name that was meaningful to them. (See Figure 5.4.)

Demonstrating How to Craft Nonfiction Using Writing By the Teacher or Student

Using high-quality nonfiction as Shelly did is a good first step toward helping students become aware of what it takes to write good nonfiction. A smart second step is showing students how to do it. During modeled writing, we demonstrate how writers use specific techniques of nonfiction writing. (See the end of the chapter for topics you might cover.) You may plan your lessons as a series on one feature with each one expanding to the next. Then, design a chart with students listing what they learned from these lessons to use as a resource for writing, as Shelly did with leads.

The teacher's role varies depending upon the purpose of the modeled writing lesson. For example, the teacher could tell how she created headings or a table of contents ("First I do this, then I do this," and so forth.) Or she could present a set of guidelines, such as how to do a bibliography or photo credits. Or she could compose text in front of students, thinking aloud and inviting student input.

Many teachers we know create their own nonfiction reports working right along with their students as they create theirs. As the teacher develops the report, she uses it as a model to discuss how to solve various crafting problems. The teacher often does most of the talking, explaining how she makes decisions about writing.

Think alouds during modeled writing are invaluable because they make what goes on in the mind of the writer explicit to students—issues related to planning, such as webbing and brainstorming, making word choices, using visuals, and so forth.

The product you create in modeled writing lessons can be used in other lessons. For example, you can revise the piece by adding a metaphor to clarify a concept, embedding a definition within a sentence, using more detail to describe an event, identifying other kinds of visuals to explain the information, or deciding on an entirely different format for the information. These lessons build awareness of new aspects of writing nonfiction and can be followed by explicit lessons in shared writing and guided writing, as well as in independent extension activities to practice new skills.

A Third-Grade Example of a Modeled Writing Lesson That Includes a Think Aloud

Jody Workman's third graders had experience writing brief reports. However their leads were uninteresting. They didn't draw the reader into the text. So, like her teaching partner, Shelly Moody, she decided to do something about it. To build awareness of different kinds of leads, Jody read aloud several nonfiction books. From there, she conducted a modeled writing lesson, showing students how to write a lead using a question. Figure 5.5 shows the script from that lesson, based on a report she had started on toucans.

> ### SIX STEPS TO PLANNING AND CARRYING OUT A MODELED WRITING LESSON
>
> The procedures for modeled writing are similar to the ones for instructional read alouds.
>
> 1. Determine the purpose for the modeled writing lesson.
> 2. Decide what to write based on your purpose.
> 3. Gather students around you and explain what you will show them in the lesson.
> 4. Compose the piece, thinking aloud as you go.
> 5. Debrief with students about the piece and your process.
> 6. Decide on next steps based on how students respond.

Figure 5.5

A Modeled Writing Lesson With Think Aloud

Procedures	Jody's Think Alouds and Comments	What Jody Wrote
1. Determine and share the purpose for the modeled writing lesson. Composing text and sharing think alouds at the same time takes planning. Decide beforehand what you plan to write and how you will explain your decision-making. Begin with brief introductory comments, connecting the lesson to the needs you've identified in students' writing.	I noticed in the reports you wrote on planets, you had a hard time coming up with leads that really grabbed the reader. Over the last couple of days I've read the leads of several nonfiction books that use questions or ask us to imagine something. We liked the examples I shared, so I'm going to show you how to write a lead like that.	
2. Explain what you are going to show students. Remind them of the work you've been doing as a class and introduce what your goal is for this lesson. This is especially important if this lesson is part of a series on one feature.	As you know, I wrote my report on toucans, but I felt that my lead was flat and not very engaging. Today, I want to show you a strategy I am using to revise the lead. Remember when we talked about authors who use a big question for their leads and have unusual or surprising information, we wanted to continue reading the books? There are a couple of ways to decide what questions to use to draw in readers. I want to show you one way that uses the information you found out and wrote about for your topic.	Jody's original lead: "The colorful, beautiful toucan can be found flying through the rainforests of South America and from Southern Mexico to Northern Columbia."

continued on next page

Procedures	Jody's Think Alouds and Comments	What Jody Wrote
	I'm going to do a think aloud as I develop the lead that includes a question. After I finish sharing, we can debrief about using this approach.	
3. As you compose, think aloud about the decisions you are making. This portion of the lesson needs to be clear, focused, and brief; only engage students periodically. To reinforce the concept that writers experiment with writing until they find the text they like, work through a couple of attempts as you create the piece in front of students. Read aloud what you wrote to be sure students know what you are writing and to reinforce the concept that writers reread as they write.	The information I used to start my report was important, but it just doesn't grab my interest. Does it grab yours? Instead, I want to begin with something that is unusual about toucans like the authors did in the books I read aloud to you. 　So, last night I reread my whole report to find unusual information about my topic. I put a tiny checkmark next to information that might surprise the reader. I also looked at what I had written about the most. What I noticed was that on several pages I described the toucan's bill. I ended up putting checkmarks on page 5, where I wrote about the color of the toucan's beak. [Shows overhead transparency of the page.] 　I checked the second and third paragraphs on page 6 where I wrote about the beak being large and hollow and that it was so big it made the toucan look like it could fall over. I also put a check on page 9 about how he uses the beak to reach for food. 　As I thought about my lead, I decided that I should try to build it around that beak and how it makes him look like he will fall over. Some of the authors we read began with sounds like "Zzzzz!" Others used "Did you ever wonder?" and some	**1st attempt:** Did you ever wonder how big a toucan's beak is? **2nd attempt:** Did you ever wonder how the toucan can stand up? **3rd attempt:** Did you ever wonder how the toucan can stand up with that big bill? **4th attempt:** Did you ever wonder how the toucan can stand up with that big bill? The toucan's bill is hollow. **5th attempt:** Did you ever wonder how the toucan can stand up with that big bill? The toucan's bill is very light because it is hollow.

Procedures	Jody's Think Alouds and Comments	What Jody Wrote
	began with a "what" question. I really like "Did you ever wonder?" So I'm going to start with that and write "Did you ever wonder how big a toucan's beak is?" [Reads aloud what she wrote on her first attempt.] That isn't quite it yet. I want to include some information in the question so the reader can visualize this bird with a really big beak and that it almost looks like it will tip over, like I wrote on page 6. I don't want to use the words *tip over* again, but I could use the words *stand up*. What if I write "Did you ever wonder how the toucan can stand up?" [Reads aloud her second attempt to the group.] I like that better, but I really don't have the idea of the bill being the problem. What if I added "with that big bill?" That seems to include more unusual information that may catch a reader's attention. [Revises the lead.]	**6th attempt:** Did you ever wonder how the toucan can stand up with that big bill? The toucan's bill is very light because it is hollow. Even though it can be as long as the toucan's body, he can still sit and fly."
	My third attempt is "Did you ever wonder how the toucan can stand up with that big bill?" I really like my question, but most of the authors we read seemed to add more than just the question in their leads. I think I need to add more, so it explains what I mean. On page 6, I talked about the bill being hollow and about the toucan's flying ability. This would be a good place to add some additional information to capture the interest of the reader. I'm going to add this to the end of the sentence: "The toucan's bill is hollow." [Reads	

continued on next page

Procedures	Jody's Think Alouds and Comments	What Jody Wrote
	her addition.] As I read this I see a problem. The reader knows it's hollow, but they don't know that it is very light because it's hollow. I am going to change that sentence to read "The toucan's bill is very light because it is hollow." [Reads the revision.] I think I need to add one more idea about it being able to still sit and fly even though its nose is so long. I think I'll write the last sentence: "Even though it can be as long as the toucan's body, he can still sit and fly." [Reads her sixth attempt.] What do you think? Would you want to learn more about the toucan? (The students like the final piece.)	
4. Debrief with students. Read your new lead and the text that immediately follows it to see if it makes sense. You may want to return to the piece the next day to see how it sounds and if you still like it. Encourage students to try revising leads in pieces they've written.	Let's briefly review what I did to get ideas for my question. First, I reread my piece to find interesting or unusual information about my topic. Then, I put a little checkmark next to those places. Next, I also read to see what I was emphasizing most in the piece. I found that I had described the toucan's beak and that the size of it was very large. I also thought about other techniques we've seen our mentor authors use to start their pieces and picked one to try. Tomorrow, I may add one more paragraph to my report. I want to tell readers what information they can find in my report. [The next day, Jody adds a second paragraph, with her students' input. She	**Final addition to the lead:** There are many interesting and fun facts to learn about the toucan. Let's read on…

Procedures	Jody's Think Alouds and Comments	What Jody Wrote
	reminds them how to use ellipses, which they have seen in books they have read. She ends her lesson encouraging students to try the strategy to revise their leads.]	
5. Decide on your next teaching steps. Depending on your assessment, you can do either a shared writing lesson or a guided writing lesson in which students create question leads for their reports, while you coach and support them.	Some of the more advanced students got the idea right away and used my modeled writing to help them create their own leads. We examined additional leads in shared reading and constructed one together during shared writing. I followed this by doing guided writing lessons where we reviewed the strategy, and the students worked in pairs on one of their reports, trying out different leads. These lessons over the year led to others on how to write the leads we identified during instructional read alouds.	

Sample Lessons for Modeled Writing

We offer a list below of sample ideas for modeled writing lessons. These ideas are not grade specific and could also be used for shared writing, interactive writing, and guided writing. The determining factors are the needs of your students and the degree of scaffolded instruction they require.

- Selecting or narrowing a topic.
- Taking notes while reading about a topic, for example, choosing key words and phrases.
- Determining the best order for information.
- Chunking information and selecting organizational structures, based on the scope and depth of the topic. See Chapter 3 for types of organizational structures.
- Developing an active voice in writing.
- Crafting leads, such as use of questions, exaggeration, stating the author's position, and so forth. See Marcia Freeman's *Listen to This: Developing an Ear for Expository* (1997, Maupin House) for ideas on teaching leads, ranging from simple sentences to full paragraphs, to grades K–6.

- Creating sidebars that summarize information or supplement the running text.
- Presenting information in bullets.
- Writing various kinds of captions for visuals, such as simple one-line descriptions or more sophisticated captions that compare and contrast information, show cause and effect, or describe a process.
- Selecting a consistent style for headings and subheadings, such as single word, questions, or phrases.
- Using metaphors, similes, and other literary devices.
- Using or defining terminology related to a topic.
- Designing various types of diagrams and other visuals. Refer to Arnosky's drawing and sketching books published by Lothrop, Lee, and Shepard, and to *Field Trips: Bug Hunting, Animal Tracking, Bird Watching, and Shore Walking with Jim Arnosky* (2002), which shows how to create detailed field notes and drawings. Also see Steve Moline's *I See What You Mean* (1995) and his resource series, Dominie Information Toolkit: Using Non-Fiction Genres and Visual Texts (2002).
- Writing an acknowledgment of or dedication to experts or agencies that assisted in completing the research.

Closing Thoughts

The primary goal of modeled instruction is to introduce and build awareness about nonfiction types and features. Two examples of modeled instruction, instructional read alouds and modeled writing, are practiced frequently, and their success is based largely on effective use of think alouds. Think alouds are an excellent way for teachers of all grade levels to demonstrate for students what strategies they use to read and write nonfiction.

In Chapter 6, we present the next level of the comprehensive framework: shared instruction. At this level, the teacher and students work together to read and write nonfiction.

Chapter 6
Shared Reading, Interactive Writing, and Shared Writing:
Apprenticing Students

"I am amazed at the vocabulary and understandings about nonfiction
the students acquire through shared reading and writing lessons.
My students know many nonfiction conventions, [and] how to use
them.... Most of all, when they leave my class, they know how to
craft exciting nonfiction. Their nonfiction is full of voice and
their style shines through."
—Janet Nordfors, fourth-grade teacher

What Janet has learned is that if we want students to read and write nonfiction, we need to show them how. We can start with instructional read alouds and modeled writing, as described in Chapter 5, where the teacher assumes primary responsibility for the instruction. From there, we move into the apprenticeship level—or shared instruction. This chapter shows you how. We:

- Define shared instruction and discuss its benefits.
- Explore two forms of shared instruction in depth, shared reading and interactive/shared writing.
- Offer sample lessons of shared instruction at the end of the chapter.

Shared Instruction: Quick Points

- **Purpose:** To teach how to read and write nonfiction texts systematically and explicitly by leading students in using effective skills, strategies, and behaviors, and by problem-solving together.
- **Kinds of Shared Instruction:** Shared reading, interactive writing, and shared writing.
- **Scaffolding Level:** High
- **Teacher Role/Student Role:** Teacher leads/students apprentice. Discussion occurs before, during, and after the reading and writing with a high degree of interaction. Opinions, ideas, and interpretations are shared and exchanged.
- **Instructional Context:** Typically done with the whole class or in a small group, with students of all ages and grades. Lessons vary from 10 to 30 minutes daily depending on the content of the lesson and the teacher's goals for the lesson.
- **Types of Materials Typically Used:** Informational texts such as nonfiction trade books, commercial instructional materials, magazine selections, newspaper selections—in big book format or on overheads so all students can read the text together. For writing, teacher and students work together on sentence strips, chart paper, or blank overheads.
- **Next Steps:** All materials read or created are available for students to reread independently and to use for further work in extension activities. These materials may be added to or used as models for student writing or reread in subsequent shared reading lessons. Teaching points can be followed up with additional shared and guided reading lessons, shared and guided writing lessons, or independent extension activities.

What Is Shared Instruction?
Teacher Leads/Students Apprentice

Shared instruction is the "workhorse" of your literacy program. It leads students naturally from the highly scaffolded instructional read aloud to the more independent guided reading, and from highly scaffolded modeled writing to the more independent guided writing.

There are two primary kinds of shared instruction: shared reading and interactive/shared writing. In shared reading, students examine a piece of writing to figure out, with the teacher's guidance, how it works. In writing, whether interactive (students share the pen with the teacher) or shared (the teacher is the scribe), the teacher leads students in composing a text by asking questions, summarizing, and helping them reread what has been written.

While shared instruction is usually conducted with the entire class, the teacher may work with small groups or individuals to build on what was demonstrated in modeled instruction. Although the level of scaffolding is lower in shared instruction, the teacher is still responsible for selecting what will be taught and does most of the teaching. The teacher leads the discussion and directs the processing of how to read nonfiction or compose it. The students apprentice, meaning they contribute to the discussion or the creation of text by problem solving along with the teacher, asking questions, contributing ideas, and sharing discoveries. In other words, the teacher uses a combination of implicit and explicit instruction to teach specific strategies and to unpack the features of nonfiction, with the goal of students applying what they learn to their own reading and writing. In both versions the teacher uses enlarged versions of the text. See the box at right for definitions of implicit and explicit instruction. See the shaded area in Figure 6.1 for where

IMPLICIT AND EXPLICIT INSTRUCTION DEFINED

Implicit instruction is open-ended. During shared instruction, you might encourage students by saying:

- What do you think this book is about?
- What did you notice that you never noticed before?
- Your description tells me that you've been watching carefully.
- You seem to be noticing something new on this page. Would you like to share it?

Explicit instruction is usually used to clarify, expand, or teach a concept, strategy, or skill by:

- Directing students' attention to specific features of nonfiction: "Let's look at this table of contents. Do you notice that there are main headings and subheadings? Why do you think the author did that?"
- Processing information: "How did you know that? Have you seen it before?"
- Giving specific directions on how to do something, such as writing captions or comparing information.

shared instruction falls on the comprehensive framework. The approaches we recommend for shared instruction are covered in depth in the next section.

<table>
<tr><td colspan="5">

Figure 6.1

Comprehensive Framework
</td></tr>
<tr>
<th>Level of Scaffolding</th>
<th>Role of Teacher and Student</th>
<th>Reading Instructional Approach</th>
<th rowspan="6">Mini-Lessons and Extension Activities*</th>
<th>Writing Instructional Approach</th>
</tr>
<tr>
<td>Modeled</td>
<td>• Teacher demonstrates
• Students watch</td>
<td>Instructional Read Aloud</td>
<td>Modeled Writing</td>
</tr>
<tr>
<td>Shared</td>
<td>• Teacher leads
• Students apprentice</td>
<td>Shared Reading</td>
<td>Interactive Writing and Shared Writing</td>
</tr>
<tr>
<td>Guided</td>
<td>• Students demonstrate
• Teacher assists</td>
<td>Guided Reading</td>
<td>Guided Writing</td>
</tr>
<tr>
<td>Modified</td>
<td>• Students work collaboratively
• Teacher modifies support by observing, helping, assessing</td>
<td>Reading Discovery Circles</td>
<td>Writing Discovery Circles</td>
</tr>
<tr>
<td></td>
<td>• Students work independently, with other students, and/or with the teacher
• Teacher modifies support by observing, helping, assessing</td>
<td>Readers' Workshop</td>
<td>Writers' Workshop</td>
</tr>
<tr>
<td>Independent</td>
<td>• Students practice
• Teacher observes and assesses independent practice activities</td>
<td>Extension Activities*</td>
<td>Extension Activities*</td>
</tr>
</table>

* Extension activities can be used as follow-up activities with all instructional approaches, but students are working independently—either individually or in small groups. Keep in mind that extension activities should match the student's ability to practice the activities independently.

The Benefits of Shared Instruction

We all face classrooms filled with students who come from different cultural backgrounds, speak different languages, and have different instructional needs. Noted researcher Don Holdaway (1979) developed shared instruction to address these differences. Both the teacher and students benefit from shared instruction.

Teachers can:

- Demonstrate and problem-solve with student about how nonfiction works.
- Gain insights into students' thinking about content and how nonfiction text works, and detect and clarify any misconceptions.
- Demonstrate how to set purposes for reading and writing.
- Modify teaching as necessary, from implicit open-ended remarks or questions such as "What do you notice?" or "What should we write about?" to more direct and explicit statements such as "Let's look at the index. How do we use it to find information on our topic?" or "How many labels do we need to add to this diagram for it to make sense?"
- Introduce, reinforce, and prompt students through think alouds or questions.
- Provide the understandings students need to move successfully into extension activities and guided reading and writing.

Students can:

- Activate prior knowledge, connecting new understandings to personal experiences, other texts, and other lessons.
- Acquire new strategies for reading and writing. As students analyze text and compose it themselves with the teacher, they build schema and language for the content and features of nonfiction.
- Work in a safe environment where the teacher and peers support their participation. Even students who are unable to read and write the text independently gain entry as they share their knowledge with all members of the class.
- Simultaneously see and hear the text as they read aloud. This is particularly important for students who are learning to speak, read, and write English.
- Participate in repeated experiences over several days with mentor texts, thereby learning how information is conveyed in a specific book, in a specific content area, or by an author or illustrator, and to use these texts to inform their own writing.
- Socially construct learning with ample opportunities for lots of talk about the text's content and how to read or write the text. These rich conversations allow students to "try on" the technical language of the specific content and the writing style of the author.
- Experience a sense of accomplishment at having figured out how to read a text or create new text, which motivates them to attempt strategies on their own.

Shared Reading

Instructional read alouds build an awareness of specific features and content of nonfiction and strategies for comprehending it. But we cannot stop there and assume students are prepared to apply the knowledge they gain from read alouds in guided reading, discovery circles, or in situations where they're working independently. Because those features, content, and strategies are unfamiliar, students need supported opportunities to apply knowledge and practice new strategies before trying them on their own. In other words, they need shared reading.

Shared reading is defined as a collaborative learning activity, during which, in the early grades, the teacher and a large group of children sitting closely together read and reread in unison carefully selected enlarged texts (Holdaway, 1979; Parkes, 2000). This enjoyable extended experience allows the primary teacher to introduce students to a variety of authors, illustrators, and ways these books are crafted. The goal is not only to teach students how to read, but to encourage them to want to read. Fiction has traditionally been the genre of choice. Teachers use it to focus on alphabetic principles, concepts about print, phonics, written language conventions, and perhaps a few basic reading strategies, using enlarged text (i.e., big books or overhead transparencies) or multiple copies of the same book for more fluent readers.

However, shared reading is about much more than reading aloud together and working with conventions of print. It's about systematically and explicitly teaching students how to read, by modeling effective reading behaviors, strategies, and skills, and engaging the students in using them. And it should not be restricted to primary classrooms. Largely because of the work of Brenda Parkes (2000) and Stanley L. Swartz, Rebecca E. Shook, and Adria F.

IMPORTANT CONSIDERATIONS FOR SHARED READING

- Decide the overall *purpose* for the shared reading session, such as teaching new vocabulary, a new feature of nonfiction, new content, or a different perspective on content.
- Limit instruction to a few well-chosen teaching points. These can be planned, as well as those that come up during problem solving.
- Pace the lesson to avoid overwhelming students with too much new information.
- Make sure all students are participating to some degree, and the lesson is not being dominated by only a few.
- Directly connect the discussion of nonfiction features to the content, and encourage students to articulate what they are learning. Students should not only be able to identify features of nonfiction books, but use those features to understand the content better.

Klein (2002), we believe shared reading should happen in grades K–6. This powerful approach of the comprehensive framework can help all readers, from the most emergent to the most fluent.

Shared reading provides an opportunity for all readers to work with an expert—the teacher—who shows how to read increasingly more challenging texts by focusing directly on particular types of nonfiction or its features, or on strategies for reading nonfiction. (See Chapter 3 for a list of nonfiction types and features on and Chapter 4 for a list of reading strategies.) It is the implicit and explicit teaching that we employ to help students use their problem-solving skills, background knowledge, and comprehension strategies to analyze successfully the running text, illustrative materials, and access features.

Selecting Materials for Shared Reading Lessons

Big books, overheads of published materials or student writing, and multiple copies of magazine articles are all excellent choices for shared reading. Be sure they:

- Can be read aloud in ten minutes or less to allow time for discussion.
- Provide a clear example of the strategy or feature being taught and offer challenges for problem solving, whether it's to teach concepts about print, comprehension strategies, new vocabulary, or some other aspect of reading.
- Provide the right level of information, given what your students already know about the topic. Too much information can overwhelm students, and too little can bore them. This is especially critical for emergent and early readers, who are acquiring control over the basic process of reading. Is the information at the introductory or advanced level? Even if it is advanced, it still may be worth using if the book's introduction helps readers build a base of knowledge.
- Are about two levels lower than most students' independent reading level for fiction to compensate for difficulty of content and nonfiction features.
- Have high appeal and connect to your curriculum somehow. Topics might include the water cycle, the "Big Dig" in Boston, dinosaurs, or nutrition.

Types of Informational Materials for Shared Reading

Traditionally, teachers use big books, stories, songs, poems, and student-created materials for shared reading. They can also select from a growing body of high-quality nonfiction literature and other informational materials. Consider:

- Nonfiction books. (See Appendices A and B for Orbis Pictus award books and sources that review nonfiction and present other awards for nonfiction.)

- Teacher-created and student-created expository materials, such as group books, one-page reports, lists, directions, recipes, time lines, charts, sidebars, and summaries of information.
- Periodicals for students, such as *National Geographic for Kids, Weekly Reader, Time for Kids, Scholastic News,* and *Ranger Rick.* (See Appendix F, Children's Magazines Featuring Nonfiction.)
- Information sources such as newspapers, Web pages, game rules, catalogs, announcements, advertisements, and weather forecasts.
- Primary sources, such as famous documents, maps, and archival materials.
- Commercially produced big books, charts, and accompanying little books.

Conducting a Shared Reading Lesson: General Procedures

Here are the general procedures for conducting a shared reading lesson. Following these procedures, we present two lessons in action, one with primary readers and one with intermediate readers.

Do You Have a Sufficient Supply of Nonfiction Big Books?

Check out your classroom library, school library, and book room for big books. You may be surprised by what you find.

- Do you have a substantial core collection of nonfiction big books in your room to use for shared reading lessons?
- If so, are they engaging and do they cover the topics you teach?
- Are they written at different levels so that there is appropriate material for all students? Can some of the books be used as mentor texts?
- If the big books have accompanying little books, do you keep those accompanying books in students' browsing boxes?

Before Shared Reading

1. Select teaching point(s) for the lesson based on a needs assessment of your students. For example, your students are working on the strategy of predicting to assess scope and depth of coverage of a topic from the title. You want them to determine from the title what a book is about and what it might include.
2. Select appropriate nonfiction books that will help you meet your teaching points—an old favorite and a new one. Consider four basic aspects of nonfiction: meaning, structure, vocabulary, and visual information. If the book is not available in big book form, make overhead transparencies of target pages.

3. Organize the room so students can come together on a rug or chairs. Be sure all students can easily see the text.

4. Identify and gather additional materials as needed: easel, pointer, highlighter tape, Wikki Stix®, or word windows to draw attention to specific aspects of text, and overhead transparency markers.

During Shared Reading

Reread an Old Favorite

1. As a group, reread a familiar text for enjoyment, emphasizing fluency and expression. The purpose is to get ready to review the content, a reading strategy, or a feature.

2. Depending upon the ages and levels of your students, reread the familiar text several times to increase fluency, continue building students' confidence and skills, and set the stage for the new reading. With students in grades 3 to 6, base the number of repeated readings on students' prior level of success and fluency. However, additional rereading may be valuable if your class membership includes students for whom English is a second language.

3. Discuss the text's content and features, focusing on new discoveries and elaborating on points you covered in earlier readings.

Read a New Text

1. Introduce the new text by browsing through it with the students. Encourage participation by directing students' attention to specific features and asking implicit questions such as "What do you notice about the cover?" "What do you notice about how the author starts the book?" "As you look at this page, what do you think you should read first?" "This visual is unusual. What are you thinking about it?" and "There are many new words in this book. What do you notice the author does to help you understand them?"

2. Read aloud the text, encouraging students to join in.

3. Shared reading involves discussion before, during, and after the reading. It allows for a high degree of interaction where opinions, ideas, and interpretations are shared and exchanged. Encourage students to continue noticing and naming features and applying reading strategies to unlock meaning.

4. Engage students in an explicit lesson on the teaching points that you chose before the lesson, showing them through modeling, thinking aloud, and explaining how to process the text for meaning.

5. Provide an opportunity for the group to practice new strategies and review old ones using another page from the text.

Following Shared Reading

1. Make all shared reading texts available for students to reread independently and to use as mentor texts for their writing.

2. Assign students extension activities that require them to practice new strategies using other pieces of nonfiction.

3. Create additional shared reading lessons on the same text or a new text to deepen understandings of content, strategies, and features—especially those that are giving students difficulty. Nonfiction features vary in difficulty. For example, students may know how to process a simple table of contents. However, there are more complex ones that are divided into sections with subheadings or use poetic language that require additional support.

4. Continue the discussion of content, strategies, and/or features that you taught as you moved into guided reading and guided writing.

5. Refer back to shared reading texts as you explore other texts in whole-class, small-group, and one-on-one work, to help students make connections and apply what you've taught.

Primary-Grade Example of a Shared Reading Lesson

Raelene Parks and her kindergarten and first-grade students are studying the physical characteristics of water as part of a unit on the water cycle and weather. Prior to conducting the shared reading lesson that we are about to describe, Raelene read aloud several books on water and its many forms to build her students' background knowledge and vocabulary, including Barbara Seuling's *Drip! Drop!: How Water Gets to Your Tap* (2000), *Water: The Elements* by Ken Robbins (1994), and *Snowflake Bentley* by Jacqueline Briggs Martin (1998).

Before Shared Reading

Based on her assessment of students' needs, there were several teaching points Raelene selected for this shared reading. We will focus only on the following: predicting what will come next by drawing upon prior knowledge

> ### BUILD MOMENTUM THROUGH THE COMPREHENSIVE FRAMEWORK
>
> When you use the comprehensive framework, students make spectacular progress in reading and writing nonfiction. What you do today are the building blocks for what you teach later in the day or tomorrow. As we move into the framework, you'll notice we describe more about what happens before and after the lessons because we want to show you how the lessons connect and build on one another.

and other experiences with books, noticing how nonfiction authors use a variety of illustrations, including cartoons and photographs, and recognizing that sometimes authors write about inanimate objects as if they were human. Raelene chose these teaching points because her students needed more practice drawing on prior knowledge. They still associated nonfiction with photographs and fiction with illustrations, and they had not dealt with anthropomorphic language in nonfiction books. She wants to help them attend more to the content rather than just illustrations to determine genre. Normally, she conducts these lessons over a three-day period.

Raelene selected two big books: *Many Kinds of Weather,* written by her first-grade class (see Figure 6.2), for the "rereading of a favorite book" component of shared reading, and *I Am Water* (Marzollo, 1996) as the new text. *I Am Water* uses cartoonlike drawings for illustration and has the water referring to itself as "I." (See Figures 6.3 and 6.4.) She organizes the room so students can gather easily on the rug and see the texts, which sit on a chart stand. She has also gathered materials she thinks she might need, such as a pointer, highlighter tape, Wikki Stix®, word windows to draw attention to specific aspects of text, and sticky notes to cover words.

During Shared Reading

At the beginning of the shared reading lesson, Raelene informs the students that they are going to reread their own big book, *Many Kinds of Weather.* The students are very excited. They completed the book in interactive writing only a few days earlier. The text contains one sentence per page and reads:

> *We love sunny days.*
> *This is a cloudy day.*
> *Do you love rainy days?*
> *Snow is falling.*
> *Look at the wind blow.*

Figure 6.2: Cover for *Many Kinds of Weather,* a big book written by first graders.

Raelene begins the reading and the students quickly join in. To provide practice with fluency, they repeat the reading with one student using a pointer to highlight each word. After rereading, Raelene asks them to identify all the kinds of weather and writes them on the white board. The students decide they would like to include some additional pages to this book later.

When Raelene asks the students whether their book is fiction or nonfiction, they decide it is nonfiction because all the information in it is true. She asks, "What kinds of water did we write about in *Many Kinds of Weather*?" The students call out "rain" and "snow." Building toward the new reading, she elicits background knowledge about water and asks, "Where could we see water?" and "What can you do with water?" The students' answers include "puddles," "ice cubes," "snow," "for swimming," and "having a bath."

Raelene introduces the new book, *I Am Water*. She and the students read the title together, and then she asks them to predict "Is this book fiction or nonfiction and why?" Students had different opinions.

by Jean Marzollo
Illustrated by Judith Moffatt

SCHOLASTIC

I am ice for cooling.

Figures 6.3 and 6.4: The cover (above) and a page spread (left) from *I Am Water* by Jean Marzollo, a big book Raelene uses for shared reading.

HAIDEN: It is fiction—there aren't photographs on the cover.

SABRINA: But *Drip! Drop!* has cartoons and it was nonfiction.

KATIE: Doesn't it have to have photographs to be real?

MITCHELL: It's teaching us about water, so isn't it nonfiction?

GREGORY: But water can't talk!

[Several children suggest it could be both fiction and nonfiction.]

RAELENE: [Decides to emphasize genre distinctions during this shared reading, since there is still
confusion.] Let's read on and we will talk more about whether it's fiction or nonfiction when
we are done.

Raelene reported: "The students finally decided *I Am Water* was nonfiction because the illustrations contained things that could happen and the book was teaching about water. However, the
anthropomorphic language—'I am…' 'Watch me. I am water. I am home for the fish' and 'I am
ice for cooling'—resulted in thoughtful problem solving, as students wondered who 'I' was. Can
water talk? Can it tell us all the things it does? As we read on, we identified more information
about water: Water is rain, people drink water, and we go sledding on snow. The students decided
to revise their assumptions about nonfiction: It can be illustrated with cartoons, drawings, or photographs, and sometimes things talk about themselves as if they were human."

Following Shared Reading

As an extension activity during guided reading, Raelene offers groups a small collection of fiction
and nonfiction books at their independent reading levels. She asks students to examine the books
together and place a pink sticky note on the ones that are fiction and a yellow sticky note on the
ones that are nonfiction.

Sixth-Grade Example of a Shared Reading Lesson

Literacy specialist Tanya Baker and a group of sixth graders are doing an inquiry project on child
labor, past and present. One of her objectives for the unit is to help students notice language that signals the presence of the author's opinion and to infer what it means. More specifically, she wants to
raise their awareness of how historians take opportunities to insert their interpretations and perspective in their writing, often through use of hedging language. (See box on page 161 and Appendix G,
Words That Signal Information.) She hopes that as her students notice these language cues and examine their meaning, they will increase their ability to interpret nonfiction texts critically and also consider how the author's choice of words impacts their reaction to the information.

A Text Set on Child Labor

In preparation for her inquiry project on child labor, past and present, Tanya gathered this text set of books that vary in scope, depth, and reading difficulty. She uses books from the set across the comprehensive framework.

Cheap Raw Materials by Milton Meltzer

Coal Country by Susan Campbell Bartoletti

Good Girl Work: Factories, Sweatshops, and How Women Changed Their Role in the American Workforce by Catherine Gourley

Iqbal Masih and the Crusaders Against Child Slavery by Susan Kuklin

Kids at Work: Lewis Hine and the Crusade Against Child Labor by Russell Freedman

Kids on Strike! by Susan Campbell Bartoletti

Listen to Us: The World's Working Children by Jane Springer

Mother Jones: One Woman's Fight for Labor by Betsy Harvey Kraft

No Time for School, No Time for Play: The Story of Child Labor in America by Rhoda Cahn and William Cahn

Stolen Dreams: Portraits of Working Children by David L. Parker with Lee Engfer and Robert Conrow

We Have Marched Together: The Working Children's Crusade by Stephen Currie

We Need to Go to School: Voices of the Rugmark Children by Tanya Roberts-Davis

Working Children (Picture the American Past) by Carol Saller

Before Shared Reading

To build background knowledge about child labor, Tanya reads aloud Carol Saller's *Working Children (Picture the American Past)* (1998) and shares the photographs in Russell Freedman's *Kids at Work: Lewis Hine and the Crusade Against Child Labor* (1994). The candid photos and description of the working conditions surprise her students. They ask, "Is everything in these books real?" They have many questions, so to answer them, she initiates another instructional read aloud, using Stephen Currie's *We Have Marched Together: The Working Children's Crusade* (1997). For the passage headed "The Most Heart-Rending Spectacle," she thinks aloud: "What does the author mean when he says, 'We don't know how these children reacted to Mother Jones.' What if the author doesn't know all the answers? I think he is trying to tell us this by using this hedging language. I think he is cuing us that he couldn't find all the answers to his questions."

After reading several chapters, Tanya selects additional passages from the book to use in a series of shared reading lessons. She enlarges them and puts them on overhead transparencies. She wants to

Nonfiction in Focus

work further with the students to point out and discuss why Currie uses the hedging language and how to interpret it.

During Shared Reading

Tanya introduces the shared reading session by telling students that she will be reading selected passages from Currie's book to look at the language he uses to discuss the children's march. "I want you to pay attention to where Currie uses hedging language and how you are figuring out what he is saying." Even though these are older students, their experiences with reading historical nonfiction and reading between the lines are limited. Plus, the class includes some struggling readers. Therefore, Tanya reads aloud a passage and asks them to join in. (See Figure 6.5.) She wants to be sure they all hear the language and know what events Currie is describing.

TANYA: What do you think this passage is about?

KIRSTEN: I think he is describing the kids—like who marched in the crusade.

THE ARMY'S YOUNGEST MARCHERS

We don't know much about the children who joined this crusade. So far as we know, none kept journals, and none wrote their experiences down as part of their memoirs years afterwards. They were displayed to crowds frequently during the march, but they never gave speeches themselves. Nor did they do much talking to newspaper reporters. As a result, the names of most of the children are now lost.

We don't even know how many of the marchers were boys and how many were girls. Newspaper accounts differed widely. According to some reporters, girls made up about half of the marchers who left Philadelphia. Other reporters, however, insisted that every single child on the trip was a boy. Several witnesses said that the girls all returned to Kensington by the end of the second day. As the trip continued, some local newspapers mentioned girls as part of the army. Others didn't. After the march, even Mother Jones gave conflicting reports. We may never know the answer.

Figure 6.5: Tanya reads this passage from Stephen Currie's *We Have Marched Together: The Working Children's Crusade.*

EXAMPLES OF "HEDGING" LANGUAGE

When authors don't have all the information or are providing an interpretation for readers, they "hedge" points by using some of the following words and phrases:

Almost

Appears

Depending on our viewpoints...

From the evidence, it seems to me that...

May

Might

Generally

Historians are not certain

Historians estimate...

Occasionally

No historian has been able to...

Not sure

Perhaps

Possibly

Probably

We don't know for sure

We just don't know

The events will always be unclear

SAM: Yeah, but it sounds like to me he doesn't really know much about them.

TANYA: What makes you think that?

SAM: Well, he starts out by saying "We don't know much about the children," and then uses the words "so far as we know." I think he is telling us there isn't much information out there.

TANYA: How do we know this?

JARED: He says there are no journals, no memoirs, and they never gave any speeches so nothing got written down.

BONITA: But he does say "so far as we know." I think that means we could still discover something one of them wrote. We just haven't yet. We only know this much right now.

TANYA: Let's look at that sentence that Bonita is referring to. Who is *we*? What do you notice about the use of that word in this passage?

JAMAL: It's used a lot—he starts both paragraphs with it and even the last sentence, "We may never know." But there is only one author. I think he is saying that lots of people believe these things—that he did lots of research and other people found what he found—that we don't know much about these kids.

TANYA: You are all doing some good thinking here. Let's see if we can take it a step further. If I come in and say, "I don't know much about these children," as opposed to "We don't know much about these children," how would you interpret those statements?

KIRSTEN: I think "we" would be taken more seriously. I mean, it's like if lots of people believe something or say it's true, we believe it more than when one person says it. So does that mean when a person uses "we," we don't question them as much?

TANYA: Something to think about, isn't it? I think as we dig into more of these selections, we want to really think about how the presence of the author's perspective, what he thinks and believes, and how the language could be used to manipulate a reader's response.

Following Shared Reading

In preparation for guided reading and discovery circles, Tanya plans to continue shared reading lessons on this book to address other understandings about nonfiction features, including a further focus on language, use of quotes, archival photographs and documents, and inset pages.

Interactive Writing and Shared Writing

Shared reading helps students understand how nonfiction works. It also provides important background in preparing your students to write nonfiction. At the same time, the writing helps to inform the reading. The purpose of interactive writing and shared writing is to engage students in writing with you in order to practice and refine their own writing, decision making, and problem-solving skills. You are also continuing to teach them to read like a writer as they study their writing and the writing of others to uncover the many choices they have in composing text.

In modeled writing, you assume all responsibility for the writing. You create the text yourself as the student observes. In interactive writing and shared writing, you maintain the role of expert and provide a high degree of scaffolding. However, instead of writing *for* the students, you write *with* them. You collaborate on the piece.

Depending on your students' age and knowledge base, you may select the topic, the type of writing, and the focus of the piece. You will carefully guide their decision making about the text. With younger students, you will also focus on all aspects of forming the text, including how to hold the pen; concepts and conventions of print, such as how to form letters; how to space; how to sound out words; and how to move in the right direction. Teacher and student think alouds, as described in Chapter 5, will help students understand how to process their ideas for their topic and address the challenge of putting words on paper.

There's virtually no limit to what you might write: a response to a read aloud, a list of supplies, a recipe, a daily record of a science experiment or science observations, a description of an event or object. What is important about choosing a topic is connecting to students' common experiences and your content areas while at the same time building on the other approaches in your comprehensive framework, such as shared or guided reading lessons or modeled writing. That way, you kill two birds with one stone. You not only teach students about writing, but about important content as well.

Interactive Writing and Shared Writing: What's the Difference?

What distinguishes interactive from shared writing is who is holding the pen. In shared writing, you do. You serve as scribe for the students, while asking them questions, summarizing their ideas, and prompting them occasionally to make decisions on concepts about print and spelling, with their primary energy devoted to the piece's content. We try to get students' thinking down quickly so they don't lose track of their ideas and can maintain a greater focus on language, organizational structures, features, and style of writing. The shared writing pieces generally wind up longer than a few sentences.

In interactive writing, you and the students write the piece jointly. The students not only share responsibility for determining what will be written, they also scribe. They participate in the process of getting the text on paper as well as assist in crafting the message. In the process, you provide explicit instruction on the concepts and conventions of print, and continually help them read and confirm what the group has written. You select who does the writing based on your students' capabilities. Often we select students to write because we know they will learn something

Shared Writing in Upper Grades:
Why Stop a Good Thing?

Shared writing generally gets left behind when students move beyond second grade. This is unfortunate because, although they may have acquired control over concepts and basic conventions of print, they still have much to learn about more complex language structures and issues of craft. However, too often we skip the group processing that occurs in shared and guided writing and depend solely on mini-lessons and writers' workshop in the intermediate grades. Students need instruction at all levels of scaffolding, regardless of grade. You can demonstrate, guide, and help students work through the decisions about how to write a piece. Together you think through all the choices a writer has and the reasons for making final choices. Shared writing is the perfect context for teaching those skills.

The pieces you create in modeled writing, interactive writing, and shared writing can be displayed in the room as both informational pieces and models for writing. If you teach upper elementary or middle school, we urge you to incorporate shared writing into your literacy program.

new with our support and that of their peers. "The goal is to support them in using what they know to get to what they do not know," say literacy experts Andrea McCarrier, Gay Su Pinnell, and Irene Fountas (2000). But even in interactive writing, you still decide when to share the pen with students. For example, if they know the word to be written, then you may want to write it yourself to save time, so more energy can be devoted to the new understandings and applications.

Both shared and interactive writing are essential parts of an effective literacy program. Students not only learn to write better, but read better as they work hard to generate text and continually reread to keep track of where they are or to improve upon it. Reading and writing connections are greatly enhanced when you use interactive and shared writing, which not only lead to independence in writing, but independence in reading as well.

Conducting Interactive Writing and Shared Writing Lessons: General Procedures

Here are the general procedures for conducting interactive writing and shared writing lessons. Following these procedures, we present two lessons in action—an interactive writing lesson with kindergartners and a shared writing lesson with third graders.

Before Interactive Writing and Shared Writing

1. Select the teaching points for the lesson. Be sure to have general goals, such as helping students get their ideas down on paper through discussion, negotiating decisions with their peers, using conventions of print and language accurately, and producing text that makes sense, as well as more specific goals related to writing nonfiction. (See Chapter 4.)

2. Select nonfiction materials and/or a classroom activity to stimulate discussion and build knowledge about the content you will address. The writing may follow a read aloud, classroom activity, field trip, observation of an ongoing science experiment, or continue work on a longer piece of an inquiry project.

3. Identify and gather additional instructional materials needed:
   - Pointer, highlighter tape, correction tape, Wikki Stix®, and word windows to draw attention to specific aspects of text.
   - Markers or overhead transparency markers.
   - Magna Doodle® or magnetic letters and board to show how to write words.
   - White board or chalkboard, chart paper, or overhead transparencies.

4. Bring students together to write. We prefer to bring even older students to a central area away from their desks so their full attention is devoted to the group writing.

During Interactive Writing and Shared Writing

1. Engage students in a discussion about their common experience, such as a read aloud or field trip and/or your purpose for teaching the lesson. Help them select their topic.

2. Help students agree on the exact wording by ensuring all ideas are heard and considered. For example, if your teaching point is to show students how to create a labeled diagram of an animal or object, you may have to add a caption as well, if students present a good argument for doing so.

3. For younger children, repeat the text several times, enunciating and even counting the words to help them retain the message. For more knowledgeable students who may be working on a longer piece, shift your emphasis from word level to sentence and paragraph level. Periodically reread the text with students and help them summarize what have they written thus far. Focus on the purpose of the piece, audience needs, and how ideas fit together.

4. In interactive writing, the focus is usually at the word level—helping students to apply strategies for getting words on paper using analogies and words from the word wall. In shared writing, the focus is primarily on content and crafting, and is composed more rapidly. During shared reading, you may select a few conventions and word work activities for explicit instruction.

Following Interactive Writing and Shared Writing

1. As a group, enthusiastically reread the completed text. As you read, model fluency and expression. Also review the content and teaching points.

2. Encourage students to identify other writings in the room or in books that connect with the lesson's point. As a group, decide what needs to be done next with the piece, such as whether to add to it or where to display it, and assign extension activities.

3. Use the piece for additional lessons to teach new concepts or reteach concepts that are still giving students difficulty. Urge students to apply what they learn in their own writing. Continue the discussion of the strategies and features in guided reading and writing lessons.

4. Make interactive and shared writing texts available for students to reread independently and to use as mentor texts for their writing.

Kindergarten Example of an Interactive Writing Lesson

Sharon Imbert's work with her rural kindergartners is an excellent example of how using the framework results in more student gains than we might expect. Sharon used interactive writing with her class on crafting a book on bears. This lesson did not occur out of the blue. Sharon worked hard on nonfiction during the school year, using other parts of the framework to build momentum for interactive writing.

Several of her students did not believe they had personal stories to write and were reluctant to participate in writers' workshop. Their out-of-school experiences consisted mostly of watching television, playing in the backyard, playing computer games, or just hanging around the house. But through her work with nonfiction books within the framework, Sharon provided her students with information that, as she put it, "gave them a chance and desire to write." Her boys especially became vested in literacy.

During the fall, mostly through instructional read alouds, Sharon exposed her students regularly to nonfiction, helping them to notice and name the features, as well as figure out "what it all meant."

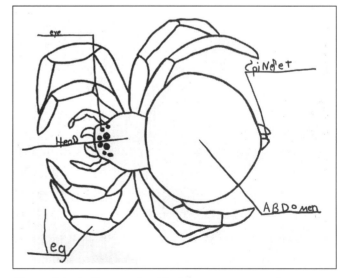

Figure 6.6: A diagram that kindergartners created during interactive writing.

One of the early topics was on insects and spiders. She also invited them to craft their own non-fiction by conducting interactive writing lessons regularly. Early pieces of interactive writing consisted of single sentences, a couple pages of connected texts, or diagrams of insects and spiders. (See Figure 6.6.) In these lessons, she concentrated mostly on the concepts and conventions of print. That said, the discussions about the content and the features students noticed in the books were rich.

Before Interactive Writing

In February, Sharon began a unit on bears. She introduced the unit by reading aloud a few concept and survey books about bears. (See box below entitled A Text Set on Bears.) From there, she read aloud sections of books on specific kinds of bears. This enabled her to "front-load," or build background knowledge about the information before trying to draw on it for interactive writing. It also helped activate prior knowledge, built a common knowledge and language about bears for all students, and certainly raised lots of questions to pursue.

Sharon has several teaching points for interactive writing. She wants students to create a longer piece of writing—specifically, a book about bears that is organized and sounds like the books that Sharon has been reading to them. Her second objective is to include some of the features they learned about in the fall, such as a cover, table of contents, dedication, index, photo credits, "about the author" section, and back cover reviews. Following the read alouds, the students decide they will write about four of their favorite bears: polar bears, brown bears, panda bears, and sun bears, and include a few facts about each one.

A Text Set on Bears

Bears by Rebecca Stefoff

The Big Bears by Melvin Berger

Black Bear: North America's Bear by Stephen R. Swinburne

Do Bears Sleep All Winter? Questions and Answers About Bears by Melvin Berger

Giant Pandas by Gail Gibbons

Giant Pandas by Lynn M. Stone

The Grizzly Bear Family Book by Michio Hoshino

Growing Up Wild: Bears by Sandra Markle

Growl!: A Book About Bears by Melvin Berger

How Do Animals Sleep? by Melvin Berger

Ice Age Cave Bear: The Giant Beast That Terrified Ancient Humans by Barbara Hehner

Pandas by Jinny Johnson

Polar Bear Cubs by Downs Matthews

Polar Bears by Gail Gibbons

During Interactive Writing

Writing the book takes several days and includes additional read alouds and modeled writing. For each interactive writing lesson, Sharon assigns every student a special role, such as spacer, punctuation wizard, editor, and meaning maker. The students are responsible for checking the writing according to their role. This increases students' involvement and focuses their attention on specific nonfiction features as well as the content. For example, the meaning makers had to check for whether the sentence made sense and was accurate, which required lots of rereading by them. When they question information, Sharon asks, "How do we check? Where do we need to go?" The meaning makers quickly return to the bear books text set. She encourages them to skim and scan to find where the answer might be. When they're confident they've found it, Sharon reads the passage for them.

Now let's take a look at the text of *Bear Facts,* the book these kindergartners wrote in interactive writing lessons, and examine the process they went through to craft each page.

Bear Facts	Looking Closely at What Students Do
Bear Facts by Mrs. Imbert's Class [cover] (See Figure 6.7.)	Because they were writing about a variety of bears, the students knew that their title had to be broad.
Photograph of a bear [frontispiece, the photograph at the beginning of a book usually opposite the title page]	A photograph was chosen for the frontispiece because the students were dissatisfied with their drawings. Sharon helped them select appropriate photographs from other sources. She assigned a page from *Bear Facts* to each child. She then gave students a sticky note with their page number on it. Each child placed the sticky note on a photograph in another book that went with their text and then Sharon photocopied it for the page.
Bear Facts by Mrs. Imbert's Class [title page]	From read alouds, the students knew that the title page repeats the information from the cover.
We dedicate this book to our families and our friend Mrs. Withee. [dedication]	As they were completing the book, the students deliberated over the dedication because they realized it was important. Mrs. Withee was another teacher working in the class.

Bear Facts	Looking Closely at What Students Do
	Initially, the students organized the table of contents similar to one in the text set. But as they organized and reorganized their chapters, they discovered that they had to change the table of contents.
Page 1: Photograph of polar bear on left page and chapter title "Polar Bears" on right with page number 1 at the bottom right page.	The layout was organized as two-page spreads with a photograph on the left-hand page and text on the right. Only right-hand pages were numbered.
Page 2: They stay in their den for 60 days with their babies.	The students originally wrote "30 days," but the meaning makers had a hunch that the information was incorrect. They reviewed the nonfiction book and found it was 60 days and corrected the text.
Page 3: They can swim for 50 miles without a rest!	The photograph selected shows a bear swimming in the water. The students used an exclamation mark because this was an unusual fact.
Page 4: Photograph of a brown bear on the left page and chapter titles on right page that reads "Brown Bears."	One student noticed that other books had what he called chapter titles. Sharon had not taught that feature, so she seized the opportunity to do so, and the students decided to include them in the book.
Page 5: Some brown bears eat a lot of fish. Page 6: Some brown bears eat nuts, ground squirrels, and insects. (See Figure 6.7.)	Originally the students wrote: "All brown bears eat..." The meaning makers questioned whether this was true since they had read that brown bears eat other things, too. After deliberating about the accuracy, they decided to change *all* on pages 5 and 6 to *some*. Note also the language structure of writing nouns in a series.
Page 7: If they get scared, they might attack people.	At the beginning of the unit, the students insisted bears ate people. However, after reading several

continued on next page

Bear Facts	Looking Closely at What Students Do
	books, they learned that bears only harm people if they're frightened. So they thought it was important to include this information [Note the cause-and-effect statement is prefaced by the signal word *if*.]
Page 10: Hunters try to kill panda bears for their fur.	The students read several books that stated that polar bears were endangered species because hunters killed them for their fur. They felt this fact needed to be included in the book.
Page 11: Baby panda bears' cries sound like human babies' cries.	The students were fascinated that baby panda bear cries are similar to human babies' cries, and so it was no wonder they used this analogy in their book.
Page 13: Some sun bears have yellow bibs on their chest.	One student suggested describing the chest of the sun bear as a yellow bib because it reminded her of the bibs her baby brother wore.
Page 14: The sun bear is bowlegged and he has an extremely long tongue.	The words *bowlegged* and *extremely* are examples of intertextuality in action, because they came directly from one of the read alouds.
Page 16: Index Brown Bears pp. 4–7 Panda Bears pp. 8–11 Polar Bears pp. 1–3 Sun Bears pp. 12–15	Students already knew that a table of contents made looking up information easier. So Sharon introduced how an index works and how it helps the reader find information because it lists important topics in alphabetical order.
Photo Credits: (Sample of Photo Credits) *Amazing Bears* by Theresa Greenaway, Dave King (1992), pp. 13a, 14a, 15a, 16a *Bears* by Barrows (1995), p. 6a *Bears* by Helen Gilks, Andrew Bale (1993) front cover, pp. 1a, 2a, 3a, 12a	Sharon thought it was important for students to know how to credit the photo sources. So she showed them how to do a photo credit list by modeling this portion of the writing. [Information is presented as it was originally in the book.]

Bear Facts	Looking Closely at What Students Do
About the Authors: The students in my kindergarten class listened to many nonfiction books and chose the facts that they found most interesting. They were thrilled with how their book came out, and look forward to writing another. They think it might be a dinosaur book. Whatever topic they end up choosing I know it will be good! Mrs. Imbert Dexter Primary School	When the class was almost finished with the inquiry and book, Sharon decided to do the About the Authors page herself because she felt that the students weren't ready to talk about themselves in third person.
Back Cover: Listen to what readers are saying about *Bear Facts*… I learned so much about bears. —Mrs. Withee, Dexter Primary School The pictures are absolutely wonderful. —The Dexter Primary School News The most informative nonfiction book ever written by a kindergarten class. —Baby Bear	The idea of including endorsements came from a graduate course Sharon was taking from Rosemary Bamford. Mrs. Withee wrote the first endorsement and Sharon made up the rest. For books that her students are writing these days, Sharon includes a blank readers' comment page and encourages family members to jot down a quick comment after they read the book with their child. Each day the book comes back, the comments are shared with the class.

Following Interactive Writing

When the text was complete, the students illustrated the book and placed it in the literature center where they can return to it again and again. Extension activities included examining other bear and animal books. Since these students are emergent readers, they read lower-level books and browse and study the illustrations in higher-level books. For other extension activities, children used sticky notes to label nonfiction features they could identify in other books. They also wrote captions and titles for books in which Sharon had masked or covered the information. Some of

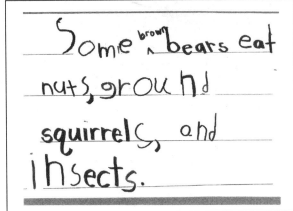

Figure 6.7: Cover and sample page from the book that kindergartners created during interactive writing.

the more advanced students ventured into creating their own short nonfiction pieces.

Sharon emphasized to us that *Bear Facts*, which was generated largely in interactive writing lessons, was the culmination of thoughtful teaching over many months. "My students were engaged throughout the process. I couldn't begin to plan for their insightful responses. Because much of the processing occurred out loud, my students knew that it was safe to voice their thoughts, opinions, and questions." Carefully orchestrated shared and modeled learning experiences like this, even for our youngest readers and writers, can have amazing results!

Third-Grade Example of a Shared Writing Lesson

Shelly Moody's third graders were in the process of writing nonfiction books on animals and were ready to add headings to the sections of their text. They consulted Seymour Simon's books for their research, but found them hard to use because many of them lack headings, chapters, a table of contents, or an index. They recognized that Simon's books lacked access features, in other words. Shelly used this as an opportunity for them to examine one of Simon's books in shared reading, analyze the content, and together in shared writing create headings for some of the sections.

Before Shared Writing

In preparation for the lesson, Shelly selected *Muscles: Our Muscular System* (Simon, 1998), a book from a previous unit, and prepared overheads of the first four two-page spreads. She also collected some of her students' favorite books to review the different styles used for headings. In previous shared reading lessons, they had examined headings from a reader's perspective. She wanted them now to look at them from a writer's perspective.

During Shared Writing

Shelly began by handing out a couple of the books to pairs of students and asking them to look again at the headings. "Many of you are ready to put headings in your animal books. Today I want to do a shared writing with you, but first let's look again at a variety of our favorite books. What do you notice about the headings? Do you see any patterns? What might we call them?" As students talked together and then responded, Shelly listed their ideas on the board with an example from the text.

- Questions: *What is a mummy?* or *What is a life cycle?*
- Word or words that describe the topic: *Habitat* or *Hot Spots* or *Smoke Jumpers*
- Words that tell what part of the book it is: *Introduction* or *Recommended Further Reading*
- Directions to the reader: *Be a Hotel Detective* or *Follow That Question*
- Quote: *"Look at me!"* or *"I will be heard"*

From there, Shelly showed the first two-page spread from the Seymour Simon book on the overhead and had the class read it aloud. She then encouraged the students to think about the page's main ideas. The first page was easy because it was very general. Since it was about muscles in general, there was a quick consensus to use "Introduction" as a heading.

For the second two-page spread, which was about how the muscles move different parts of the body, the students considered four possibilities: "Contracting Muscles," "How Muscles Work," "Muscles and Tendons," and "How Muscles Move Your Body." They rejected "Contracting Muscles" and "Muscles and Tendons" because they were too narrow. They decided "How Muscles Work" was too broad. They selected for this heading "How Muscles Move Your Body," since it captured Simon's main idea much better than the other three.

Following Shared Writing

Shelly collected a variety of other books without headings and applied sticky notes to pages where students might add them. She chose books that were less complex than Seymour Simon's books, but still had information that was well organized and chunked. This extension activity was carried out in the writing center. She also planned a modeled writing lesson on creating headings for her animal book, *Sloths: The Slowest Mammals on Earth*.

Closing Thoughts

Shared instruction affords students the opportunity to participate in reading and writing at an apprentice level. Every student, regardless of ability, can see and hear the text being read, and can share in the problem solving and decision making. Through your comments, observations, prompts, think alouds, and explicit instruction during shared reading, you can support your students' ability to read the text successfully. Every student can feel successful as a writer, too, because the same kind of support is available to them in interactive writing and shared writing. All ideas and suggestions for composing the text are valued. As you identify areas of difficulty, you can provide the explicit instruction necessary to ensure that students increase their mastery over whatever task you're asking of them.

As students' knowledge of nonfiction features, content, comprehension strategies, and composing strategies grows, identify books and writing tasks that will give them an opportunity to practice what they're learning under your guidance. Guided instruction is discussed in Chapter 7.

IDEAS FOR SHARED READING AND SHARED WRITING LESSONS

- How to identify nonfiction text by its features (e.g., organizational features, access features, and visual features).
- How expository is different from fiction (e.g., the purpose of the author is to inform, not to entertain).
- How the reader's purpose determines how a nonfiction text will be read (e.g., using key words, going to the index to select the page where specific information is and then only reading those pages).
- How organizational features and access features help readers (e.g., indexes, table of contents pages, glossaries, and headings).
- How specialized language and language structures are used to convey information.
- How information in captions and labels works with running text to convey information.

Chapter 7
Guided Reading and
Guided Writing:
Supporting and Assisting Students

During guided reading, students demonstrate new understandings of how to read nonfiction as they learn about new information.

Tim, a fifth-grade teacher, is using biographies in his four guided reading groups. Two of the groups are reading sophisticated picture book biographies by Diane Stanley, and the two other groups are reading longer chapter book biographies, one by James Cross Giblin and the other by Russell Freedman.

Before Tim started using these biographies in guided reading, he immersed his students in the genre through instructional read alouds, during which he modeled what to look for in high-quality biographies. Tim thought aloud about how biographies are organized and showed his students different types. Next, he did shared reading lessons, examining writing styles, access features, and visual information typically found in biographies—time lines, archival photographs, and primary source material such as actual diary and journal entries.

Tim is currently working with a guided reading group, using *Who Was Ben Franklin?* by Dennis Brindell Fradin (2002). Because the students in this group already read a picture book biography of Ben Franklin, Tim feels they are ready for this short chapter book. He selected *Who Was Ben Franklin?* because it offers new challenges. It will give the students experience reading a longer biography containing a variety of visual information, such as labeled illustrations and more sophisticated time lines.

At the start of the guided reading lesson, Tim builds awareness of this biography's features by asking the students to size up the book—browse through it and talk about what they notice. By doing this, Tim gets a good sense of what nonfiction features they identify right from the start.

TIM: Okay, you noticed that this is a chapter book biography. It has a table of contents. That's good. We'll come back to that in just a moment. What else did you notice?

CHAD: It's long. It's maybe the longest book I've ever read. It has 105 pages.

TIM: Right, the other kind of biography you read was a picture book biography. Everybody, take a look at the table of contents and scan the titles of chapters. How does this help you read the book?

JOSHUA: Well, it sort of organizes us because the title of one of the first chapters is "Young Ben" and the last chapter is called "A Rising Sun."

TIM: Excellent. Let's scan that last chapter and read the first sentence of that chapter silently.

[Everyone in the group reads the sentence silently, and then Tim asks:] Ann, what does it say?

ANN: "Ben returned home a hero."

TIM: When do you think that happened to Franklin? When was he made a hero?

ANN: Maybe when he was older. So maybe the last chapter is about what he did when he was old, and the first one tells about him when he was a kid.

TIM: Excellent prediction, Ann. What does that tell us about this table of contents?

JOSHUA: That it gives Ben Franklin's life in order.

TIM: Right. You'll often find a table of contents for a biography when it has chapters, and sometimes the chapter titles are written so you have a sense of that person's life from beginning to end. Remember what word we used to describe how biographies are organized?

CHAD: Chronologically?

TIM: Indeed! Good work, Chad. We have to pay attention to all the things a nonfiction author does. We're sort of like reading detectives when we read nonfiction. Now, what did you notice at the end of the book?

CHAD: The two last pages are time lines: one of Ben's life and the other is a time line of the world. What does that mean?

TIM: Let's look at those pages carefully. What do you notice?

JOSHUA: The dates aren't the same but almost. Like it says that in 1706 Ben is born. On the other time line it says what was happening in 1707 someplace else in the world.

TIM: That's good. How does having two time lines at the end of the book help us as readers?

ROBYN: Because then maybe we can see how two things were going on at the same time—things in Ben's life and other stuff in the world?

TIM: Yes, very good! Remember how we talked about time lines and how they help us keep track of events? Time lines can help us organize information as readers because they summarize key events—in this case it's events in Ben's life compared to events that were happening around the world at the same time. As you read this book, see if you refer to the time lines. We'll come back to them later. As you browsed through the book, did you find anything interesting or different about some of the pages?

JACKIE: I like how there are little pictures on most

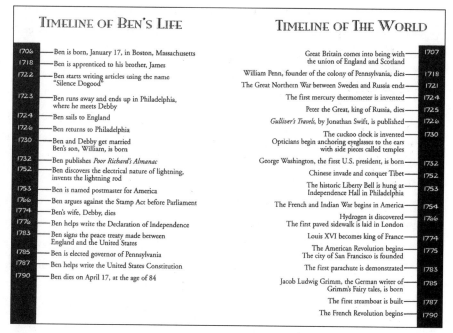

Figure 7.1: Time line from *Who Was Ben Franklin?* by Dennis Brindell Fradin, which Tim uses for guided reading.

of the pages. That's different for a chapter book, right?

TIM: Ann, what do you think?

ANN: There are pictures and some of them are kind of funny. There's also a diagram on page 4. That's kind of weird because this isn't a science book, and then there's a whole page that has mostly a picture on it and only a little writing.

TIM: This biography has a variety of visual information, even different kinds of diagrams. You're going to see a diagram on page 4 and one on page 8 when you read today. Notice what you do as a reader when you come to these pages. Think about two questions: Do these diagrams remind you of anything that you've read before about Ben Franklin? How do the diagrams help you understand the text on the page? I'm curious to know your responses to both of these questions. I've written them on chart paper to help you remember them as you read.

Tim's introduction shows how he challenges his students and, at the same time, supports them before they start reading this book. He doesn't rush students into the book; instead he prepares them. He wants them to apply two effective reading behaviors—activating prior knowledge about content and understanding diagrams—which will be part of the follow-up discussion after students finish reading.

After the introduction, Tim asks the students to start reading the book silently. While they read, Tim checks in to see how everyone is doing. From there, he asks each student to read a short segment aloud to him. This tells Tim how each student is processing the text and where he can assist and support that student's efforts.

Tim believes that all his students, even the most gifted ones, benefit from guided instruction. He says, "Guided instruction is a great way for me to see what my students know as they are actually in the process of reading or writing. I'm an eyewitness to their learning as it's happening. It's really exciting because it helps me see what I've done well in my teaching and where I need to go next."

We agree that the power of guided instruction, which includes guided reading and guided writing, offers tremendous teaching and learning opportunities. In this chapter we:

- Provide an overview of guided instruction and its subcategories, guided reading and guided writing, and show where they fit on the scaffolded literacy framework.
- Identify the benefits of using guided instruction.
- Define guided reading and describe how to plan lessons.
- Define guided writing and describe how to plan lessons.
- Offer ideas for guided reading and guided writing lessons.

Guided Instruction: Quick Points

- **Purpose:** To give students an opportunity to demonstrate what they know as readers and writers, providing support as needed, and to teach new skills and strategies that are within their grasp.
- **Kinds of Guided Instruction:** Guided reading and guided writing
- **Scaffolding Level:** Moderate
- **Student Role/Teacher Role:** Students demonstrate/teacher assists. Teacher introduces the lesson, asks questions, and explains; students demonstrate what they can do as readers and writers.
- **Instructional Context:** Typically done in small groups organized according to needs, with students of all ages and grades. Writing may occur with the entire class.
- **Types of Materials Typically Used:** Nonfiction books, informational materials such as magazine selections, and nonfiction writing done by the teacher and students.
- **Next Steps:** Guided instruction may lead to independent work or back to modeled or shared instruction, depending on need.

What Is Guided Instruction?
Students Demonstrate/Teacher Assists

In guided instruction, you might say that students go public with what they know about nonfiction. The teacher prompts, encourages, and guides students to use what they already know about reading and writing nonfiction. She also "nudges" learning forward by teaching students something new—something they may not have tried before, but is within reach. In other words, she decreases the level of scaffolding. Figure 7.2 shows where guided instruction falls on the comprehensive framework.

The high level of scaffolding in modeled instruction and shared instruction prepares students to take the "driver's seat" in guided instruction and demonstrate what they know. It's seductive to think that once we've carried out modeled and shared instruction, our major teaching responsibilities are done. We can sit back and enjoy the fruits of our labor! But we shouldn't; too often direct and explicit teaching stops too soon. Students are hurried through a massive amount of new learning and then expected to make sense of it all independently, which results in frustration, failure, and an "I don't know" or "I can't do" attitude. Students of all ages need a continuous stream of sup-

Figure 7.2

Comprehensive Framework

Level of Scaffolding	Role of Teacher and Student	Reading Instructional Approach		Writing Instructional Approach
Modeled	• Teacher demonstrates • Students watch	Instructional Read Aloud		Modeled Writing
Shared	• Teacher leads • Students apprentice	Shared Reading		Interactive Writing and Shared Writing
Guided	• Students demonstrate • Teacher assists	Guided Reading		Guided Writing
Modified	• Students work collaboratively • Teacher modifies support by observing, helping, assessing	Reading Discovery Circles	Mini-Lessons and Extension Activities*	Writing Discovery Circles
	• Students work independently, with other students, and/or with the teacher • Teacher modifies support by observing, helping, assessing	Readers' Workshop		Writers' Workshop
Independent	• Students practice • Teacher observes and assesses independent practice activities	Extension Activities*		Extension Activities*

* Extension activities can be used as follow-up activities with all instructional approaches, but students are working independently—either individually or in small groups. Keep in mind that extension activities should match the student's ability to practice the activities independently.

port and assistance. That is exactly what guided instruction provides—a context for students to use new skills and strategies and to try new challenges with the support and assistance of the teacher.

Consider this analogy: If you've been through driver's training, you remember that the more experienced driver was seated next to you, offering guidance. You demonstrated your level of understanding about driving from the minute you put the key into the ignition. If you had a good driving instructor, he or she came to your assistance when you needed it, reinforced what you were doing correctly, and complimented you when you figured out how to do something. From there, he or she determined what to teach you next.

In guided instruction, like driving instruction, the teacher's presence is critical to introduce the lesson, to provide an overview of the nonfiction piece, to listen to students, to observe students, and to recognize and compliment, prompt, and assist with difficulties. Ideally, what the teacher learns from these interactions informs his or her next teaching steps.

Guided instruction falls into two main categories: guided reading and guided writing. In guided reading, students with similar needs and abilities meet with the teacher with his or her own copy of a nonfiction text that the teacher chooses beforehand. The teacher introduces the text. From there, students read the text aloud or silently, depending on their abilities and the text's demands. The teacher listens and monitors progress as students read. Following the reading, the teacher debriefs with students and assigns further reading or extension activities.

Guided writing often occurs after instructional read alouds, shared reading, or guided reading, or as mini-lessons. During writers' workshop some of the mini-lessons may be guided writing instruction. The purpose is now to give students, without as much assistance from the teacher, the opportunity to try out a particular writing strategy, skill, technique, or feature.

Prompting as an Effective Tool for Guiding Students

As you observe students during guided instruction, you might ask yourself, "What strategies do students try when they're stuck?" "What strategies do students know, but aren't applying when they're stuck?" or "How do they problem-solve when they read and write?" Your responses should inform you of your next step, and that step might be a prompt to help students use what they know so that they can move along. Stanley L. Swartz and his coauthors (2003) say, "A prompt is a question or suggestion from the teacher that focuses the students' attention on a way to solve confusions they are having as they read. A prompt is like a nudge in the right direction." For example, the text should have enough supports that build on what students already know, so that with teacher prompting, a student facing a challenge in the text can say,

"Hey, I know how to figure that out!" Supports might be in the way the author defines new terms, the use of a pronunciation key, the use of subheadings that clearly lead from one main idea to another, or captions that match what is discussed in the running text.

As with guided reading, guided writing lessons build on what students know and can already do, but take them a step forward by presenting some challenges based on that. Here is an example of prompting in action: Jennifer, a fourth grader, is working on a piece of writing about the rain forest and is having a hard time deciding on the best way to define new terms for her readers. So, in a guided writing lesson, Jennifer's teacher, Mary Evans, prompts her to look at the class-made chart that contains all the ways nonfiction authors define new words, such as in the text, in a caption, or in the glossary. Mary assists Jennifer in selecting a strategy, reviews how it works by looking at mentor texts, and encourages her to give it a try. Mary returns later in the session to give Jennifer feedback on her attempt. As a next teaching step, Mary plans a mini-lesson using all the charts the class has produced to help students with their writing.

Be careful about overusing prompts. In guided instruction, give students a good chance to figure things out on their own without coming to their aid too quickly. Only use prompts when you think students aren't tapping into what they know to move forward. The ultimate goal is for students to become independent learners. The prompt that you give today should contribute to a student's learning tomorrow, so that the next time he or she faces that reading or writing challenge (Swartz et al., 2003), he or she can overcome it independently.

PROMPTS TO USE DURING GUIDED INSTRUCTION

Prompts should support what students know and help them problem-solve. Here are some examples:

- Think about that again. What makes sense here?
- What do you need to do to find out what that means?
- Could you make a diagram to explain what you want readers to know?
- Where do you think you start reading on that page? Why?
- That's a word that signals the reader about what to do next. What do you need to do?
- What do authors do to signal that they are unsure? Do you need to do that in your writing?
- What can you do to explain how to do that in your writing? Would a list work? What else?
- What does the caption tell you? How does it help you understand what is in the text?
- What does the author say in the introduction? Does that change your mind?
- Listen to that. Does it sound right to you? Try that again.
- Does knowing what the book is about help you with that word?

The Benefits of Guided Instruction

Teachers can:

- Group students according to needs and change the groupings based on how students are progressing.
- Present new challenges about reading and writing nonfiction that build off the knowledge students have acquired in modeled instruction and shared instruction. Provide scaffolding that propels students forward and prepares them for new learning. Guided instruction puts success within reach because of the teacher's coaching and assistance.
- Use it for all students. Guided instruction is appropriate for all grade levels and ages. It's also effective with special education students and English language learners.

Students can:

- Demonstrate what they know about nonfiction and how well they use problem-solving skills when they meet challenges as they read and write it.
- Demonstrate what they know about reading and writing nonfiction in a safe environment, where the teacher is right there for them, offering coaching and assistance.
- Feel successful because the teacher doesn't allow them to fail. Guided instruction ensures that students are successful at reading and writing nonfiction.

Guided Reading

Stanley L. Swartz and his coauthors (2003) say, "Guided oral reading is one of the most powerful teaching methods available. Good readers and struggling readers alike can be supported during a guided reading lesson. Teacher support can be adjusted to meet the specific needs of individual students."

In guided reading, the teacher meets with a small group of up to six students with similar needs, usually at a table or seating area where students face the teacher. This arrangement is important so that the teacher can easily observe and offer assistance as needed. The groups are flexible and change based on students' evolving needs.

Before the lesson, the teacher carefully chooses a nonfiction text based on its difficulty level and its topic. Students should be able to handle the text with some assistance and be somewhat familiar with its content. At the start of the lesson, the teacher introduces the text and then has students read orally, silently, or both depending on the purpose of the lesson, the challenges involved, and the reading skills of the students. Throughout the lesson, the teacher makes careful observations to see how students approach and think through the text. They coach and assist by prompting students as they come up against challenges.

Following the lesson, the teacher leads a discussion about the content of the book and reading-related topics, such as identifying additional questions, making connections, sorting through conflicting information, making comparisons, and summarizing information. Students may continue reading portions of the book on their own or work on a related writing activity or extension activity.

Planning and Carrying Out Guided Reading Lessons

In this section, we show you how to plan and carry out guided reading lessons, using examples from second-grade and sixth-grade classrooms. Specifically, we discuss how to:

- Prepare for the lesson.
- Introduce the text.
- Guide students as they read.
- Follow up.
- Keep records.
- Plan extension activities.

Each of these steps is described below and may occur over several days, depending on the needs of the students and the length and complexity of the text.

Before Guided Reading

Preparing for the lesson

Select small groups of students, typically from two to six, who are similar in terms of:

- What they know about nonfiction and how familiar they are with the content of the text that you're considering.
- What they need to know next about nonfiction. Choose a strategy or concept that challenges the students, but that they can overcome with your support and assistance.
- Reading level. Choose a text that is within the reach of readers yet provides some challenges.

With these considerations in mind, select an appropriate text for the group, making sure that each member has a copy.

During Guided Reading

Introducing the text

Your introduction should engage students, make them want to read, and get them ready to read. Introduce the text by:

- Tapping prior knowledge about the topic by including hands-on experiences, such as feeling a starfish before reading about ocean animals, or using visuals to increase your students' understandings and awareness of the content.

- Asking students to browse through text. Encourage talk about what they notice, as Tim did in the introduction at the start of this chapter. Ask: "What do you notice as you look through this book?" "What clues tell you that the selection is nonfiction?" "How is this book different from other books you've read or we've read together?" "How is it the same?" and "What do you already know about this topic?" This reminds students of what they already know about nonfiction and the topic and prepares them for new challenges they'll meet as they read.

- Discussing specific aspects of nonfiction, such as visual features (photos, captions, diagrams, and so forth), access features (such as sidebars, glossary, and index), how the text and graphics are organized, and where to start reading on the page.

- Inviting students to make predictions about what they will learn about the topic or asking them to read it for a specific purpose.

Guiding students as they read

Next, have students read the text. If you're working with young children, have them read aloud quietly at their own rate. Listen to each child, assisting when he or she struggles and complimenting when he or she is successful. This is an opportunity to do a running record. If you're working with older students, you may have them read the text silently, but occasionally ask them to read a passage aloud to get an impression of how they are processing the text.

Following up

Once the reading is complete, invite the group to discuss the content, features, and strategies that students used. What was easy for students? What was challenging? And how did you work together to figure it out?

Following Guided Reading

Keeping records

Record keeping is a must in guided reading. If possible, take running records or observational notes during the lesson. But if you find that to be too cumbersome, take them immediately after the lesson on sticky notes or some sort of record-keeping form, while ideas are still fresh in your mind. You might write about how students responded to the selection, what difficulties they encountered, how they problem-solved their way through the text, and what progress individual students made. These notes are invaluable because they tell you what students can do on their own, what they can't do at all, and what they can do with some assistance. Thus, they are crucial in guiding decisions about the skills and strategies students need, the configuration of future groups, and what to cover in the next guided reading lesson or whether you should return to a modeled or shared reading.

Planning extension activities

Extensions may be planned that involve writing or an activity related to the text that students can do as a group, with partners, or independently, such as using a graphic organizer for note taking. The book or material used for the guided reading lesson can be read again alone or with a partner and placed in an accessible location, such as a book bin or display shelf.

Second-Grade Example of a Guided Reading Lesson
Before Guided Reading

Shana Curtis and four of her students are reading *The Pumpkin Book* by Gail Gibbons (1999) for their guided reading lesson. She chose this book because the class is doing an author study of Gail Gibbons. It is also October—time to go to local farms to pick out pumpkins and get ready for Halloween. Shana chose *The Pumpkin Book* because of its supportive sequential organization, strong links between text and illustrations, the use of signal words that cue time (such as *once, after, until, eventually,* and *when*), and the abundance of familiar high-frequency words, making it the perfect choice for her group.

In this lesson Shana plans to discuss the variety of pumpkins, how pumpkins are grown and used for food, and the use of an appendix for adding interesting additional information. The challenges Shana anticipates for these children include understanding Gibbons' use of cause-and-effect explanations, the metric system to describe the size of certain objects, cross-section diagrams, captions, and terminology such as *tendrils, stems, stamen, pollen, male flower, female flower, nectar, pollination,* and *stigmas.*

During Guided Reading

Introducing the text

Shana starts the lesson by reminding the students of their author study of Gail Gibbons. "This week, we're studying Gail Gibbons and reading some of her works in our guided reading group. What have you noticed about her style?" The students tell Shana that Gibbons writes about how things grow (referring to her books on plants, berries, and trees), how to do things (referring to *The Bicycle Book* [1995]), and how to make things (referring to *How a House Is Built* [1995]).

When Shana asks what kind of books she writes, the students say, "They're nonfiction." In response to that, Shana shares a quote by Gibbons: "I like to come away from a book with the feeling I've learned something. That's why I write nonfiction." She asks the students to listen one more time to the quote and they briefly discuss what they have learned from reading her books.

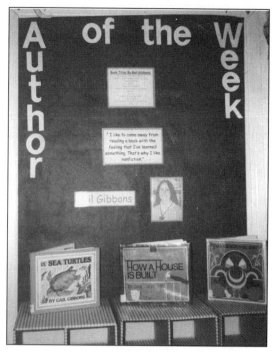

An "author of the week" display featuring the works of Gail Gibbons.

With that connection to Gail Gibbons' books, Shana introduces *The Pumpkin Book*. The students almost immediately begin talking about where they go for their pumpkins and how their

A Text Set of Books by Gail Gibbons

Apples	*Knights in Shining Armor*
The Berry Book	*The Milk Makers*
The Bicycle Book	*My Soccer Book*
Exploring the Deep, Dark Sea	*The Pumpkin Book*
From Seed to Plant	*Soaring with the Wind: The Bald Eagle*
The Honey Makers	*Spiders*
How a House Is Built	*Tell Me, Tree: About Trees for Kids*

families carve them. They read the title and predict what they might find in this book. Shana quickly notes some of their ideas. As the students peruse the book, Shana encourages them to make further connections to the other Gibbons books on plants, such as ones on preparing the soil, planting the seeds, or watering and tending the garden. She also asks them questions to familiarize them with the content. Here is a sampling of those questions.

Pages 1–2: In writing, we have been talking about the importance of leads and ways to introduce your topic. Before we look at the first two pages, what information do you expect to find in Gibbons' introduction? Now skim these first two pages. Did she include information that you expected?

Pages 3–4: On these two pages, Gibbons describes pumpkin patches. Based on what you see in the illustrations, what are the differences between the ways the farmer and the children prepare their patches? Skim the text. Do you notice any special language that describes their methods?

Page 5: Look at the diagram of a pumpkin seed. [See Figure 7.3.] What do you notice? What are the parts of the seed? Skim the text and find information about the size of the seed and the size of the pumpkin. Gibbons is telling us about the cause and the effect. As you read today, see if you find other places where she helps us see the cause and effect.

Page 6: Skim the page and see if you can find what words are used to describe the different ways pumpkins are planted.

Page 7: What do you notice about this illustration? Can anyone remember what we call this kind of diagram? [In Figure 7.4, a cross section shows the side of the pumpkin hill so the germinating seed is visible.] Why has Gibbons illustrated it this way? Can anyone remember the term Gibbons used to describe this stage of a plant's life? As they go on examining the book, Shana continues to draw their attention to the pages and the dia-

Figure 7.3: A page from *The Pumpkin Book* by Gail Gibbons showing the diagram of a pumpkin seed.

Nonfiction in Focus

grams that depict the growth of the plant, the parts of the plant, and the role of insects in pollination. She continues to encourage them to look for the language of cause and effect.

End materials: The students know that Gibbons includes interesting information at the end of her books. Shana suggests they save those pages until the next day and compare this book with several other books by Gibbons.

Guiding students as they read

"Now I want you to go back to the title page and quietly read this book to yourself. I am going to listen to each of you read. As you read, see what you can learn new about the way pumpkins grow."

A pumpkin seed won't sprout until the dirt is warm and water has soaked the seed to soften its coat. Once the seed coat breaks open, a root begins to grow down into the soil. It takes in water and minerals from the soil for food.

Figure 7.4: A page from *The Pumpkin Book* by Gail Gibbons showing a cross section of a pumpkin hill.

Shana asks individuals to read aloud for a few moments to monitor their strategies for dealing with new words and comprehending information in illustrations. See a sample of Shana's anecdotal notes on page 190.

Following up

When all students have finished the book, Shana asks, "Let's look back on your predictions. Did this book tell us how to grow pumpkins?"

After the discussion of predictions, Shana asks, "What did you learn?" They discuss all the different kinds of pumpkins that Gibbons describes, making connections to ones they have seen at the state agricultural fairs.

Next, Shana focuses on the many pages of labeled illustrations that depict how the pumpkin grows. Together she and the students review the parts of the growing plant (e.g., vine leaves, stems, tendrils, flower and its parts, stamen, pollen, male flower, female flower, and nectar) and how plants are pollinated.

Shana then asks them to reread select pages that contain the cause-and-effect statements and together they discuss what each of them means. For example, the students learn that a pumpkin seed won't sprout until the dirt is warm and water has soaked the seed's shell. Shana helps them connect the cause of warmth and water to the effect of the seed finally growing.

As follow-up, Shana does word work on *huge* and *hug,* and *circular.* These words were selected because the students had difficulty with them. During that lesson, she and the students also identify signal words Gibbons uses to alert readers that time is passing, such as *first, after, until,* and *eventually.* They add them to a class chart of signal words.

Following Guided Reading

Keeping records

Shana's anecdotal records indicate:

- Barbara had trouble with *slice,* but was guided to use context and beginning letters to figure out the word.
- Of all the words, *eventually* and *circular* were the most difficult. Need to come back to discuss.
- Lance read each page with ease.
- Josef was unsure of the phrase *seed coat* but when I pointed out the diagram, he read it with more understanding.
- Need to remind them of how to tell the difference between *huge* and *hug.*
- Students need to work more on cause and effect. During discussion, I'll go back to those pages to tease out the relationships.

Planning extension activities

Working in pairs, the students reread *The Pumpkin Book* to each other and created a flow chart illustrating the steps involved in growing pumpkins. Since they have done similar charts in shared and guided writing sessions, they are comfortable with this activity. The students also made a book in the shape of a pumpkin that contains facts that they learned from *The Pumpkin Book.* (See Figure 7.5 for an example.)

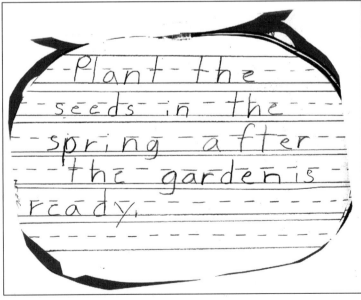

Figure 7.5: A page from the students' book on pumpkins.

Sixth-Grade Example of a Guided Reading Lesson

Before Guided Reading

As we discussed in Chapter 6, Tanya Baker is conducting an inquiry project with sixth graders on child labor, past and present. While reading aloud a piece of historical nonfiction related to the project, Tanya was intrigued when students questioned whether the read aloud contained accurate information. She designed the instructional read alouds and shared reading to help students distinguish between factual information and speculative information in historical nonfiction. She wanted students to see how authors cue readers when they don't have all the facts. (See Chapter 6 for an example of Tanya's lesson.)

Tanya's purposes for this guided reading lesson are for students to read a piece that includes speculative language on their own, and to discuss why a historian uses speculative language, what it means, and how she or he feels about it. She works with six students, using a chapter entitled "Across the Hudson River" from *We Have Marched Together: The Working Children's Crusade* by Stephen Currie (1997).

During Guided Reading

Introducing the text

Tanya begins the lesson by saying, "As we've read *We Have Marched Together* [Currie, 1997], we've talked a lot about how kids around your age and much younger were put to work in factories and mines in the early 1900s. We even looked at other books and discussed how that same thing is happening today in some parts of the world. We've also talked about how the information we're reading about is so new to us, that we're not quite sure how true it is. Could these horrible things have really happened to children as young as yourselves?

"We've learned that we need to read carefully because authors often give readers signals that indicate when they're unsure of what they're writing—that maybe they can't find all the facts. We've also learned that sometimes authors insert their own opinions. As you read, watch for the words the author uses to signal or cue readers that he is unsure of what actually happened or is sharing his perspective. Let's think about what this tells us about the importance of accuracy in nonfiction."

Tanya distributes the books to the students. She prompts them to summarize what has happened thus far. They say that Mother Jones, a crusader for workers' rights, was organizing a huge parade in New York City that included many children. They also recall that Mother Jones is trying to march the children to President Roosevelt's summer estate in Oyster Bay just outside Manhattan, and that when they stopped reading, the children were on the New Jersey side of the Hudson River. Together, they examine a map of southern New York and northern New Jersey.

Low answered, "No, Mother, he was not." Realizing he was beaten, Low called Ebstein and urged him to change his policy. The army got permission to march—and meet—that night and the next.

The children arrived in New York City shortly after Mother Jones's meeting with Low. They came in by ferryboat across the Hudson River, and they must have marveled at the sights. From the boat, the children would have had quite a view of the wide river, the Statue of Liberty, and the skyline of Manhattan, home even then of some of the tallest buildings in the world. Philadelphia was a big city in its own right. Still, to the mill children, the crowds and excitement of New York City must have seemed like a different world. No doubt they were also relieved to have finally reached their main destination.

CHILDREN IN IRON CAGES

The parades were well attended. Both were also peaceful, although Major Ebstein called out police reserves from 11 different stations around the city just to make sure. As usual, the band led the way. The remaining children carried signs. Many local working children followed along. According to one newspaper, "The noise they made was equal to the combined efforts of a whole regular regiment."

During both parades and meetings, the marchers held out an American flag to be filled with donations. According to a Philadelphia reporter who was on the scene the first day, "Coins poured into the flag until at last it resembled a huge bag of money." Mother Jones displayed 12-year-old Eddie Dunphy, one of the marching mill children, and then spoke briefly. Asked what she thought about visiting President Roosevelt, she replied: "I think he will see us. Why shouldn't he? We are law-abiding American citizens."

The highlight of the children's stay in New York came a few days after the meetings. Frank Bostock, the owner of a carnival, had invited the army to come visit his "wild animal show" at Coney Island. Many of the marchers had never been to a zoo before, let alone a carnival. The crusaders spent two nights at the carnival as Bostock's guests. A few of the

children even told a reporter "they would be willing never to go back to the mills if they could only live with the show."

The carnival was more than just fun, however. Bostock had arranged for Mother Jones to speak there. She was a popular attraction, and the building where she gave her speech was filled well before the starting time. The stage was covered with empty animal cages left over from the last show, and Mother Jones decided not to let them go to waste. Before she began her speech, Jones put some of the young marchers inside the cages—and locked the doors. To the startled crowd, the message must have been clear. Just as the animals were prisoners of the carnival, so too were the children prisoners of the factories in which they labored.

A wealthier visitor to Coney Island poses with a member of the wild animal show.

Figure 7.6: Excerpt from a chapter in Stephen Currie's *We Have Marched Together: The Working Children's Crusade,* which Tanya uses for guided reading.

Tanya then asks students to survey the chapter they will read for the lesson "Across the Hudson River," paying particular attention to its photographs and subsection entitled "Children in Iron Cages." (See Figure 7.6.) When they're finished surveying the chapter, she has them partner up for a "think-pair-share." They make predictions about the text, share them with their partner, and then with the whole group. When one student speculates that the subtitle might be a metaphor for the lives of all these children, Tanya is impressed.

The students notice the quote that opens the chapter, and Tanya encourages them to think about what it means and why Currie might have selected it. They notice the photograph of the New York City skyline and the map of New York City. They also notice a photo of a child from a wealthy family pictured with an elephant. She asks, "What does that photograph have to do with the march and why is it in a section called 'Children in Iron Cages'?" She asks them to flip through the book and look at the other photographs, which depict mill children in contrast to this wealthy child. "What's the point here?" she asks. One student finds the heading "We Want Time to Play" and remarks, "Mill children didn't have time for fun things." Tanya prompts further, "So why do you think the author has this photo on this page? As you read, think about that." Tanya is helping the students to synthesize all the information, including the visuals, rather than just solely focusing on the speculative words.

Guiding students as they read

Tanya asks students to begin their silent reading, keeping in mind their predictions about the subtitle. She also asks them to look for language the author uses when he is speculating, or hedging, about the facts. She asks them to think about how the author's words make them feel. As students read, Tanya moves around the table and checks in with each of them. She asks if they are having any problems. She also asks each student to read several sentences aloud to get a sense of how they are doing. See a sample of Tanya's anecdotal notes under "Keeping records" below.

Following up

Tanya invites students to reflect back on their predictions about the subtitle. Next, she asks them about the language the author used to signal that he was unsure about what really happened. Students discussed how the author used the words and phrases "they must have marveled at the sights," "children would have had," "New York City must have seemed like," "According to all accounts," "no doubt," "very likely," "probably," and "apparently." They discuss why authors who write nonfiction—both historical nonfiction and science nonfiction—use speculative language like that. She talks about how responsible authors research their topics extensively. If they are unable to find evidence for how people thought or what they actually said or did, then they don't make it up. If they did, it would be fiction. Authors use speculative language to show that their research isn't conclusive.

Following Guided Reading

Keeping records

Tanya's anecdotal record-keeping form indicates:

- Denise and Janet stumbled over direct quotes from historical documents. I think the syntax isn't something they're used to. I need to discuss this with the class—that people in the past didn't speak as we do today. Students seem to get caught up in the formality of how people spoke in the past, which makes fluency difficult for them.
- Everyone in this guided reading group pointed out and identified the examples of speculative language correctly. They also understood why authors needed to use this convention. I need to see how they carry this over to other readings and in their own writing.

- Everyone talked about how Mother Jones put the children in cages and how that might have felt to the children.
- Need to teach the concept of irony in nonfiction more, because most students struggled to understand the juxtaposition of the photographs of the wealthy child and the mill children.

Planning extension activities

For the extension activity, Tanya asks partners from the group to skim and scan another book from the text set on child labor and record at least five examples of speculative language. Depending on the skill level of the students, this activity could also have been done in a shared reading and writing activity or in a discovery circle on another day.

Tanya asks the students to compare and contrast how different authors writing about the same topic cue or signal readers. She also asks them to look at what information is included or excluded about the children's march in each book. The students compare *Kids on Strike!* by Susan Campbell Bartoletti (1999) (pages 108–129), *Mother Jones: One Woman's Fight for Labor* by Betsy Harvey Kraft (1995) (pages 53–61), and *We Have Marched Together* (Currie, 1997) (pages 49–75). From there, they create a comparison chart of cue words and facts presented in each book.

Selecting Nonfiction Materials for Guided Reading

It's important to choose nonfiction wisely for each guided reading group. The selection should be "just right," meaning that reading is neither too easy nor too difficult for the students. It should be within the reach of readers, yet at the same time present some challenges "to stretch the students a little" (Learning Media, 1997).

In this section, we identify important points and questions to consider in making nonfiction selections for guided reading. After that, we discuss book leveling as it pertains to using nonfiction for guided reading.

It's important to select nonfiction that addresses content that is familiar to your students, whether through experiences inside or outside the classroom. For example, you may find a book that contains visual features you want to teach, but the topic is totally unfamiliar to students. Reconsider that book because it puts an extra burden on them. You're asking them to read and understand material, without having the appropriate background.

It's also important, as we said before, to select nonfiction material that your students can read, but that also has challenges for them to tackle with your support. This might not always mean an entire high-quality book. Excerpts or even individual pages may be a better choice. They might give

What Do the Other Students Do While You Work With Guided Reading Groups?

In modeled or shared instruction, more often than not, the entire class participates. That's not the case for guided instruction, though, which is normally done in small groups. So how do you keep the rest of the class engaged?

One solution is to plan extension activities for the rest of the students. Extension activities are important adjuncts to guided reading and writing. Students work on specific reading and writing tasks that build on what they know, as well as new strategies learned through guided instruction. (See Chapter 9 for ideas.) Activities need to be carefully designed to give students the opportunity to practice independently what they've been taught, without your assistance. You need to prepare students to work on these activities. Design mini-lessons to teach students the routines and procedures for doing extension activities. The bottom line is that students need to know exactly what to do, so you can concentrate on working with guided reading groups without interruption.

you the opportunity to focus in on visual or textual features and observe more precisely what strategies your students use to deal with these features. You might consider other nonfiction resources as well, such as articles from children's magazines and newspapers that may contain the features you want to address in the lesson. Articles are usually brief, and you can get multiple copies easily.

In general, as you make selections, keep in mind the challenges the text presents in terms of vocabulary, page layout and format, font size and spacing, writing style and language structure, visual information, access features, and accessing meaning. What can your students handle? What may be too difficult? What may be too easy? Here are questions to keep in mind to help you make good decisions:

- What can your students handle? What do they know about nonfiction and what do they need to learn?
- Is the text reader-friendly? Specifically, does it contain diagrams, graphs, and other visual features that are easy to follow? Is the running text easy to follow? Are the pages uncluttered and well designed? Are new terms clearly defined?
- What new challenges does the text contain? Can your students handle them with your assistance or are they too difficult at this point?

How Aspects of Nonfiction Figure Into Stages of Reading Development

A lot has been written about the characteristics of readers as they progress from emergent to fluent, and the importance of matching them with appropriately leveled books for instruction (Fountas & Pinnell, 2001). According to Stanley L. Swartz et al. (2003), the instructional reading level is "where the student is able to read with 90 to 95 percent word-identification accuracy and 75 percent comprehension." Taking running records can help to establish reading level (Clay, 1985). Also see the record of oral reading and observation guide described by Swartz et al. in *Guided Reading & Literacy Centers* (2003).

How difficult a book is depends on a number of things, such as vocabulary, text length and structure, sentence complexity, content, and language features (Fountas & Pinnell, 2001). It isn't within the scope of this chapter to offer a comprehensive description of book leveling. However, we offer a brief guide to stages of reading development in Figure 7.7 (adapted from Fountas & Pinnell, 1996, 1999, 2001; Moore, 2003), with the approximate grade levels indicated and nonfiction features that students may be ready to handle at each of these levels. We hope this guide helps you determine if the books you're considering are right for your students.

When you select texts for guided reading, take into consideration the needs of your students, the content of your curriculum, the challenges of the text, and the purpose of the lesson. When you do that, guided reading experiences are more fruitful. Educator Anthony Fredericks (2001) echoes this sentiment. He says guided reading "is an opportunity for students to create a positive relationship

---

Figure 7.7

Stages of Reading Development, Typical Reading Behaviors, and Nonfiction Materials to Consider

EMERGENT READERS

Approximate grades: kindergarten to early first

Typical behaviors: Students are just learning how print works on a page and that there is a direct match between speech and the words on the page (i.e., a one-to-one match). They know some letter-sound relationships, can identify some letters, use clues from pictures to understand new vocabulary, and know that print is read from left to right and from top to bottom.

Nonfiction materials to consider: Use highly predictable, simple, and repetitive text with one or two lines of print. The font size should be large and spacing between words ample. Concept books may be appropriate, with simple language structures and patterns for those having difficulty with directionality or making speech-to-print connections. The books should have a predictable page layout, clear and uncluttered visual matter that is highly supportive of the text and clearly separated from it, and few to no access features to distract the reader.

EARLY READERS

Approximate grade: first

Typical behaviors: Students know many sound-symbol relationships and most high-frequency words; make use of information from pictures to help understand new vocabulary; use meaning, syntax, and graphophonemic relationships to figure out unknown words; can determine the difference between fiction and nonfiction; can figure out new vocabulary words based on how they are used in the sentence; begin to understand basic content vocabulary if concepts are discussed before reading; have a basic understanding of how visual information works on a page and its relationship to print; and begin to read familiar books fluently with juncture, pitch, and stress.

Nonfiction materials to consider: Use texts with high-frequency words, straightforward language structures, visual information with clues to aid understanding, clear and uncluttered visual matter that supports the running text, consistent page layout and format, simple captions for illustrations and photographs, and common access features such as table of contents, glossary, and index.

TRANSITIONAL READERS

Approximate grades: second and third

Typical behaviors: Students use more word-solving skills; know more words at sight; use pictures to enhance understanding of text rather than relying on them for understanding; read well silently and are developing oral reading fluency; have a repertoire of strategies for dealing with specialized vocabulary; can deal with more complex and sophisticated language structures, such as compound sentences; can begin dealing with varied page layout and format where lines of print may go across two pages or where there is a variety of formats; are learning how to examine print and visuals; and understand that visuals support the text but don't carry all the meaning.

Nonfiction materials to consider: Use simple chapter books and sophisticated informational picture books containing integrated text and visuals, such as labeled diagrams and captioned photographs.

continued on next page

SELF-EXTENDING READERS

Approximate grades: third and fourth

Typical behaviors: Students use more sophisticated word analysis strategies for understanding words, sentences, and longer text; can engage in silent reading and fluent, well-paced oral reading; bring background knowledge to reading and see the importance of it; have a repertoire of strategies for dealing with specialized vocabulary; understand how visual information works in nonfiction; and can vary silent reading speed as necessary for comprehension.

Nonfiction materials to consider: Use more sophisticated chapter books and informational picture books.

ADVANCED READERS

Approximate grades: fourth to sixth

Typical behaviors: Students view reading as a way to understand and learn about the world; use sophisticated comprehension strategies going beyond the text to make connections; apply advanced word analysis strategies, such as using base words and affixes; hold a sophisticated set of strategies for understanding new and specialized vocabulary; and know how to determine when fictional material is inserted into nonfiction material.

Nonfiction materials to consider: Use a variety of complicated yet well-written and well-designed nonfiction texts of all types.

Adapted from Fountas & Pinnell, 1996, 1999, 2001; Moore, 2003

with text by combining *what they know* with *what they can know*." And although doing it well takes time and effort, don't let this deter you, because guided reading is so important for all learners.

Guided Writing

The main purpose of guided writing is to provide an opportunity for students to briefly *try out* or do a quick write of a new feature of writing nonfiction with support from the teacher. As in guided reading, the teacher's role is to coach, assist, and prompt students to problem-solve as they write, as a whole class, in small flexible groups, or individually. In other words, the teacher's role is to scaffold instruction moderately by supporting students as they write.

Since guided writing is often a brief attempt to write a nonfiction feature, we recommend limiting the students' writing time to three to eight minutes. Educator Carl Anderson (2000) describes guided writing as "have-a-go," an opportunity for students to try out a strategy or technique. As Anderson says, it "helps them remember what we've taught when they're ready to use it later that day, or several days later" in their own writing. He promotes the use of this kind of writing because it may be the nudge students need to incorporate new nonfiction features in their writing.

Guided writing lessons often emerge from work done in instructional read alouds, shared writing, shared reading, guided reading, or as mini-lessons in writers' workshop. From that work, the teacher notes that students are now ready to write more independently and plans guided writing lessons accordingly. For example, she might note that students are ready to write a comparison and plans a guided writing lesson to address the issue.

During guided writing, students may practice a writing task that was originally done as shared writing. Students may go back to the nonfiction they read in shared or guided reading to now examine an aspect of it through the eyes of a writer—to figure out how an author crafts a particular nonfiction feature. For example, they might look at how an author uses bullets or sidebars or labels for a diagram, or how she or he writes a comparison to describe or explain. Depending on the assistance students need, the teacher might first identify the feature, find it in the text, and then discuss how and when to use it, and what distinguishes this feature. For example, headings are often questions or phrases that summarize the content that follows. Then, the teacher guides students as they try using the feature in their own writing.

Students might also return to pieces they started earlier to try out strategies that they learned in mini-lessons in writers' workshop. For example, they might add a caption or try revising their lead. As with guided reading, it's important to choose activities for guided writing that offer challenges but are within the abilities of the writers.

Planning and Carrying Out Guided Writing Lessons

In this section, we show you how to plan and carry out guided writing lessons, using an example from a fourth-grade classroom. Specifically, we discuss how to:

- Prepare for the lesson
- Guide students as they write
- Follow up and keep records

Points to Consider for Guided Writing

In modeled writing and shared writing, we show students how to write nonfiction. In guided writing, we give them a chance to demonstrate what they've learned, bringing them one step closer to independence. As you plan guided writing lessons, there are several considerations to keep in mind:

1. Select the focus based not only on what your curriculum guidelines demand, but also on the types of nonfiction and its features that students are attempting in their writing or that will somehow enhance their writing. Students are more apt to incorporate what you teach them into their independent writing if they see value in it. For example, if the guided writing lesson focuses on how to sequence information using flow charts, knowing how to do that may not make sense if students are writing about the eating habits of a giraffe. However, a flow chart might make sense if the students are writing about the postal system and the steps involved in the delivery of a letter.

2. Focus on one strategy or feature at a time, as students may get overwhelmed. For example, suppose in shared reading you're looking at how some authors incorporate definitions for new terms within the text. In guided writing, use a passage where the author hasn't included a definition within the text, and have students experiment with adding one.

3. Choose prompts that connect to writing strategies, techniques, or nonfiction features students have learned or are learning at other points in the framework (for example, something from a mini-lesson, an instructional read aloud, shared or guided reading, or shared writing).

4. Whenever possible, build guided writing lessons around what students are learning in shared reading and guided reading. This gives students the opportunity to read and discuss together how authors choose and use nonfiction features and to apply what they learn about authors' techniques and decision-making processes to their own writing. It's intertextuality in action.

Preparing for the lesson

- Choose the students. The group, large or small, should contain students with similar needs.
- Select a focus based on topics you're covering in shared reading, shared writing, or guided reading, and on an assessment of student needs from their writing in social studies and science.
- Gather reading materials used in instructional read alouds, mini-lessons, shared reading

and writing, and/or guided reading and writing to serve as models to illustrate a technique or concept.

- Select examples of writing by you or students for use as models as well. As in shared reading, enlarge the text (using chart paper, big books, or an overhead transparency) so all students can easily see it.

Guiding students as they write

- Introduce the lesson by identifying its focus.
- Create a text in front of students, thinking aloud as you go. Or read aloud an example and invite students to discuss it. Identify the feature, why it's used in writing nonfiction, and how to apply it.
- Ask the students to "have-a-go" at creating a piece on their own. This can be a quick write of an original piece or a revision of an existing piece from their writing folder. Depending on the task, their level of understanding, and their age, students can work in small groups, pairs, or individually.
- Ask students to share their work with the group or the entire class.
- Provide feedback by prompting. Encourage students to talk about the challenges they faced, the decisions they had to make, what worked well, and how they might revise their pieces to improve the information's clarity.
- End the lesson by encouraging students to apply what they've learned in their own writing. Review the feature that helps communicate information in the best way, what kind of information to use, and strategies for creating the feature. For example, a sidebar usually contains additional, but interesting, information.
- If this lesson is conducted during writers' workshop, ask students to indicate if they plan to try the strategy in their writing that day. Remind them to be selective about the features of nonfiction they use.

Following up

- If students attempt to apply the strategy or concept in writers' workshop, be sure to check in with them to see how it's going.
- Collect the pieces to review for the next steps. If the students are maintaining a folder on writing lessons or a notebook on nonfiction features, they can put the quick-write example in the notebook as a resource for future writing.

Following Guided Writing

Keeping records

As with guided reading, record keeping is a must. If possible, take observational notes during the lesson. But if you find that to be too cumbersome, take them immediately after the lesson on sticky notes or some sort of record-keeping form. You might write about how students responded to the task, what difficulties they encountered, how they problem-solved their way through the writing, and what progress individual students made. These notes are invaluable because they tell you what students can do on their own, what they can't do at all, and what they can do with some assistance. Thus, they are crucial in guiding decisions about the skills and strategies students need, the configuration of future groups, and what to cover in the next guided writing lesson or return to in modeled or shared writing.

Fourth-Grade Example of a Guided Writing Lesson

Bulleted lists are an efficient way to present information because they are easy to read, address main points, and/or summarize important facts. In nonfiction books, bulleted information is often set apart from the running text and contain at least two items and usually no more than eight. Language consistency within the list—words, phrases, or sentences—should be constructed in a parallel manner. Typically, a heading or stem begins the list, and each item begins with the same part of speech (e.g., verb, noun, or gerund) to finish the stem.

Bulleted lists are appealing to young writers because they are brief, interesting, and enhance the overall look of their pieces. They are useful as sidebars, inset pages, and end material. However, creating these lists does call for thoughtful decision making about when and how to use them.

Janet Nordfors, a fourth-grade teacher, used a series of lessons on reading and writing bulleted information with her students. Through instructional read aloud, shared reading, and guided reading, she shows them a variety of ways to create bulleted lists by looking at published examples. (See box on page 204 for books with good bulleted lists.) She also uses her own writing as a model. In shared writing, she and her students create simple lists. In fact, her class has created a chart of rules for using

Bulleted Lists

- Use bullets only when the order isn't important.
- Use simple round bullets.
- Use between 2 to 8 bullets.
- Don't mix phrases and complete sentences.
- If the list begins with an introductory phrase (i.e., a stem), finish the phrase using the same part of speech.

Figure 7.8: A chart of rules for using bulleted lists, created by fourth graders.

bulleted lists based on previous lessons. (See Figure 7.8.) Following an instructional read aloud of John Crossingham's *Lacrosse in Action* (2003), students review the chart. Janet puts pages 14 and 15 on the overhead. (See Figure 7.9.) She asks students to do a quick write of bullets for the information on those pages. She is pleased with their success and encourages them to consider using bulleted lists in their informational writing.

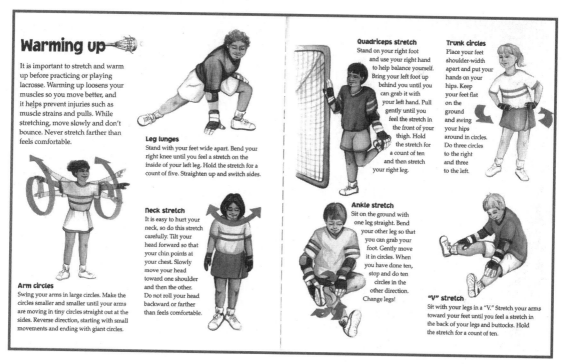

Warming up

It is important to stretch and warm up before practicing or playing lacrosse. Warming up loosens your muscles so you move better, and it helps prevent injuries such as muscle strains and pulls. While stretching, move slowly and don't bounce. Never stretch farther than feels comfortable.

Leg lunges
Stand with your feet wide apart. Bend your right knee until you feel a stretch on the inside of your left leg. Hold the stretch for a count of five. Straighten up and switch sides.

Neck stretch
It is easy to hurt your neck, so do this stretch carefully. Tilt your head forward so that your chin points at your chest. Slowly move your head toward one shoulder and then the other. Do not roll your head backward or farther than feels comfortable.

Arm circles
Swing your arms in large circles. Make the circles smaller and smaller until your arms are moving in tiny circles straight out at the sides. Reverse direction, starting with small movements and ending with giant circles.

Quadriceps stretch
Stand on your right foot and use your right hand to help balance yourself. Bring your left foot up behind you until you can grab it with your left hand. Pull gently until you feel the stretch in the front of your thigh. Hold the stretch for a count of ten and then stretch your right leg.

Trunk circles
Place your feet shoulder-width apart and put your hands on your hips. Keep your feet flat on the ground and swing your hips around in circles. Do three circles to the right and three to the left.

Ankle stretch
Sit on the ground with one leg straight. Bend your other leg so that you can grab your foot. Gently move it in circles. When you have done ten, stop and do ten circles in the other direction. Change legs!

"V" stretch
Sit with your legs in a "V." Stretch your arms toward your feet until you feel a stretch in the back of your legs and buttocks. Hold the stretch for a count of ten.

Figure 7.9: A double-page spread from John Crossingham's *Lacrosse in Action*.

Each pair of students crafts a title and a bulleted list of the exercises, using phrases. This is an easy task for these writers because they do not have to maintain consistency with a stem or begin each phrase with a verb. It also is a fairly close match to language in the text.

She then reviews rules for using a stem and asks them to "have-a-go" on finishing the stem "A lacrosse player needs to learn…." Students work

Essentials to Playing Lacrosse

A lacrosse player needs to learn:
• Warming-up exercises
• Cradling the ball in the pocket
• Catching the ball
• Passing the ball
• Chasing the ball
• Face-offs and draws

Figure 7.10: An example of a bulleted list created by fourth graders.

A Text Set of Books With Bulleted Information

Achoo! The Most Interesting Book You'll Ever Read About Germs by Trudee Romanek

Aliens From Earth: When Animals and Plants Invade Other Ecosystems by Mary Batten

The Amazing International Space Station by the editors of YES Mag

Baby Lion by Aubrey Lang

The Environment: Saving the Planet by Rosie Harlow and Sally Morgan

Eat Your Words: A Fascinating Look at the

Language of Food by Charlotte Foltz Jones

How to Babysit an Orangutan by Tara Darling and Kathy Darling

Ms. Frizzle's Adventures: Medieval Castle by Joanna Cole

Lacrosse in Action by John Crossingham

Rolypolyology by Michael Elsohn Ross

Safari Beneath the Sea: The Wonder World of the North Pacific Coast by Diane Swanson

in triads and create their bulleted list. (See Figure 7.10 for an example from one triad.) This lesson required retelling and also working to find a consistent structure for the bullets. As groups work, Janet circulates among them, providing support and assistance as needed. When they are done, they compare what they had included about lacrosse and how they had varied the sentence structures to maintain consistency in each list.

Closing Thoughts

Even the most capable students are challenged by certain texts. Consider the difficulties students have when we ask them to step out of their comfort zone to try something new or different in reading or writing. Think about how as adults we find certain reading and writing tasks challenging. Guided instruction provides that moderate level of support all learners need in a comprehensive literacy program.

Chapter 8
Reading and Writing Discovery Circles:
Observing, Helping, and Assessing Students

Students in Janet Nordfors' class support their ideas by pointing out specific evidence and features during discovery circle discussions.

Judy Bouchard's fifth graders are studying immigration and diversity in a unit called Faces of America. As part of the unit, Judy plans discovery circles—small groups in which students read, write, and talk about a variety of nonfiction books on a similar topic. Discovery circles are different from traditional literature circles, because they focus only on using nonfiction. Students typically work together with or without the teacher to critically examine content area information in science and social studies.

To prepare students for their discussion on immigration in their discovery circles, Judy shared historical nonfiction in instructional read alouds, shared reading, and guided reading to engage them in conversations about the choices people make as they go from an old life to a new life. Because she is using historical nonfiction, she believes it is important that students understand that people make choices in their lives and those decisions impact their future and maybe history as well.

One discovery circle is reading Carol Bierman's *Journey to Ellis Island: How My Father Came to America* (1998), the story of the difficult journey of 11-year-old Yehuda, his mother, and his sister Esther, who immigrated from Russia in 1922. In the process of escaping from the Germans, his sister Mindl is killed and his father never returns from war. Throughout their reading, the students are struck by the many directions in which life for Yehuda's family could have gone. Judy wants them to consider these changes in direction as "turning points" and to speculate on the "what ifs?" of this family's history. This is an effective way for students to consider the long-term effects of choices that people make (Zarnowski, 2003). Judy believes learning to recognize and discuss turning points encourages rich analytical and critical thinking about the events in history.

So in preparation for their discovery circle discussion, each student identifies and writes a brief piece about a turning point from the book. Here is an excerpt from their discussion. Note how Saladin begins with an important observation about the organization of the book.

SALADIN: The book starts with his family getting on the boat to come to America, but then in chapter two it goes back to before, when they were in Russia.

TAMARA: I liked that because you find out how Yehuda injured his arm, and even though this is a biography, there is suspense. In the first chapter you don't know if the purser is going to let them on the boat because Yehuda's arm is in the sling. It isn't until the third chapter that you find out what happens. I thought this was the first turning point.

CLARIS: Right. It's the first turning point in the book, but not in their lives. Look at all that happened to them in Russia.

TAMARA: Yeah, that's true. There were lots of times they could have died like Mindl. I think the first turning point was when Yehuda's father came back from America and he was ordered to join the Russian army.

VLADISLAV: Yeah, if he hadn't come back to Russia, he might not have died and he would have gone back to America with them to see Abe.

DONNA: When Mindl got shot and her mother took her to find a doctor, I thought for sure that Yehuda and his little sister would never find her. The decision to go look for her seemed dangerous. [Others in the group nod in agreement.]

CLARIS: I was really surprised that the Mayor sends them to look for their mother. There were so many things that could have happened then, like getting lost—

TAMARA: Or when they crossed the river, they could have fallen in and drowned.

SALADIN: Yeah! And even after they found her, trying to find their way around battles, there were lots of times they could have all died or been taken prisoners.

CLARIS: What if the doctor had cut off Yehuda's arm? They probably never would have let him in.

DONNA: I think the two biggest turning points were getting the purser to let them on the boat at the beginning, and when the doctors were trying to decide whether to let Yehuda stay in America.

VLADISLAV: When Momma wouldn't let him throw the ball, what if no one had understood Yiddish?

CLARIS: Right! Or, what if she never explained why? They might have thought she wouldn't let him throw the ball because his arm was bad.

Following the discussion, the discovery circle prepares a chart of the turning points they identified and a list of what could have happened instead. The chart is used as part of the discussion on immigra-

TURNING POINTS (What important decision changed Yehuda's and his family's life?)	WHAT IF? (What if a different decision had been made?)
Yehuda's mother would not let the Russian doctor cut off the arm and insisted he only fix the finger.	The doctor convinces Momma that he must remove the arm to save Yehuda's life. Because he is not healthy, the purser refuses to let them aboard.
The purser allows Yehuda's family on the boat even though he knows they may not be allowed to enter America.	The purser refuses to allow the family to board the ship and they can't travel to America. They decide to stay in Holland, where Momma gets a job managing a tulip company and eventually can arrange for them to leave for America.
The doctors question whether Yehuda is well enough. They ask him to run around Ellis Island twice and to throw a ball.	The doctors do not give Yehuda a chance to prove that he is strong and the family decides to return to Holland.

tion and the kinds of choices people made and the implications of deciding to immigrate to America.

Students wondered how the experiences of Yehuda's family compared to those of other immigrants. In the next discovery circle, Judy recommended that the group examine the information in the archival photographs and captions from *Journey to Ellis Island* to see if they could find that out.

Judy knows the challenges her students face talking about a nonfiction selection and how it is a different experience from when they discuss fiction. As your instruction moves through the framework, your students develop skills and strategies for working with nonfiction that can be put to use in discovery circles. Your instructional support adjusts or is modified according to the needs of your students. In this chapter we:

- Define modified instruction and its approaches, reading and writing discovery circles, and where they fit on the comprehensive framework.
- Identify the benefits of using modified instruction.
- Explain how to plan, implement, and assess discovery circles.
- Describe strategies to teach students to use in discovery circles to strengthen their reading and writing of nonfiction.

A Text Set on Immigration and Diversity

Coming to America: The Story of Immigration by Betsy Maestro

Ellis Island: Doorway to Freedom by Steven Kroll

I Am an American by Charles R. Smith Jr.

I Was Dreaming to Come to America: Memories From the Ellis Island Oral History Project selected and illustrated by Veronica Lawlor

…If Your Name Was Changed at Ellis Island by Ellen Levine

Journey to Ellis Island: How My Father Came to America by Carol Bierman

97 Orchard Street, New York: Stories of Immigrant Life by Linda Granfield

Remix: Conversations With Immigrant Teenagers by Marina Budhos

What Are You? Voices of Mixed-Race Young People by Pearl Fuyo Gaskins

Modified Instruction in Discovery Circles: Quick Points

- **Purpose:** To allow students to work in small collaborative groups to read, talk, and write about content and nonfiction features.
- **Kinds of Modified Instruction:** Reading and writing discovery circles
- **Scaffolding Level:** Low
- **Student Role/Teacher Role:** Students work collaboratively/teacher modifies support by observing, helping, and assessing. Discussion occurs before, during, and after circle meetings. There is much exchange of opinions, ideas, and interpretations.
- **Instructional Context:** Typically done in small groups, but occasionally in pairs. With young students, the teacher may read aloud and follow with discovery circle discussions and brief writing activities. Discovery circles can meet several times a week from 10 to 30 minutes, depending on the purpose, age of students, length of the reading and writing tasks, and content.
- **Types of Materials Typically Used:** Multiple copies of informational texts—such as books, instructional materials, and magazines—often connected with a unit of study.
- **Next Steps:** Students can reread reading and writing materials for discovery circles independently, use them for further work with extension activities, or share them with the class as part of an ongoing unit of study.

What Is Modified Instruction in Discovery Circles? Students Work Collaboratively/Teacher Modifies Support

Once you've steeped students in a healthy amount of modeled, shared, and guided instruction, they'll probably be ready to work more independently and collaboratively to read and write nonfiction. When you modify instruction, you shift more of the responsibility for scaffolding from yourself to your students. The extent to which you modify depends on the needs of students and the focus of instruction. For example, initially you might provide a high level of support by explicitly teaching students how to work together in discovery circles. As students meet in their circles, you adjust, or modify, support according to needs. You might serve as an active member of a circle or as an outside observer. Decision making about factors such as book selection and focus of the discussion and writing is carried out by you or by you and the students. Figure 8.1 shows

Figure 8.1

Comprehensive Framework

Level of Scaffolding	Role of Teacher and Student	Reading Instructional Approach	Mini-Lessons and Extension Activities*	Writing Instructional Approach
Modeled	• Teacher demonstrates • Students watch	Instructional Read Aloud		Modeled Writing
Shared	• Teacher leads • Students apprentice	Shared Reading		Interactive Writing and Shared Writing
Guided	• Students demonstrate • Teacher assists	Guided Reading		Guided Writing
Modified	• Students work collaboratively • Teacher modifies support by observing, helping, assessing	Reading Discovery Circles		Writing Discovery Circles
	• Students work independently, with other students, and/or with the teacher • Teacher modifies support by observing, helping, assessing	Readers' Workshop		Writers' Workshop
Independent	• Students practice • Teacher observes and assesses independent practice activities	Extension Activities*		Extension Activities*

* Extension activities can be used as follow-up activities with all instructional approaches, but students are working independently—either individually or in small groups. Keep in mind that extension activities should match the student's ability to practice the activities independently.

The Benefits of Discovery Circles

In discovery circles, students draw from all they know about reading and writing nonfiction. Discovery circles:

- Provide a forum for learning how to agree and disagree with one another respectfully, as students may present different perspectives on a single text.
- Provide a social setting for students to enjoy nonfiction.
- Provide an opportunity for students to try out what they know and work collaboratively to solve problems as they read and write nonfiction.
- Encourage risk taking and, as a result, build confidence as students try out new writing techniques in a supportive, collaborative situation.
- Offer students the chance to assess how they work collaboratively.
- Encourage interaction among students who otherwise might not work together.
- Enable teachers to observe and informally assess how students are reading, talking, and writing.

where modified instruction and discovery circles fall on the comprehensive framework.

Discovery circles are small, peer-led groups in which students share, talk, write, and learn from one another. They are also a good venue for students to share oral progress of reports or drafts of individual research. Although reading discovery circles and writing discovery circles are presented separately on the comprehensive framework, most teachers combine reading and writing in discovery circles. Teachers modify their instructional support based on what students need. For example, the teacher may work with students to help them develop effective ways to discuss content and learn more about nonfiction features. Students learn how to talk about debatable or controversial issues or inconsistent information found in their reading.

During the discussion, students talk about a nonfiction text that they've all read. They share their thoughts about content and how it is presented. They may also share written responses to the reading.

Following the discussion, students write a response. They can work on their own, perhaps journaling about what they learned about the topic, or they can work collaboratively, with one group member serving as scribe. Often teachers encourage students to include nonfiction features such as bulleted lists, time lines, diagrams, and charts as a way to apply what they've learned about in their reading.

Teachers using peer-led groups to discuss fiction may find that discovery circles are a good complement. These groups go by a variety of names, such as literature circles (Daniels, 2002; Day, Spiegel, McLellan, & Brown, 2002), literature conversations (Cole, 2003), student-led discussion groups (Robb, 2000), or book clubs (Raphael, Pardo, & Highfield, 2002).

Discovery Circles:
What Theory and Research Say

Discovery circles are grounded in important theories of literacy related to the advantages of social interaction in learning how to read and write (Almasi & Gambrell, 1994; Mazzoni & Gambrell, 1996; Raphael & Goatley, 1997; Short & Pierce, 1990). The collaboration that occurs during discovery circles prepares students to work together in life, to process information, and to make decisions and share them in writing. Students learn to ask and answer "thin" questions, such as "Who is…?," "What is…?," and "Where is…?," and "thick" questions, such as "What might…?," "How could…?," and "What if…?"—the more typical questions that we face in daily life to solve problems (Cole, 2003).

Janice F. Almasi and Linda B. Gambrell's research (1994) indicates that students are more likely to help one another clarify confusions when the discussion is student-led. When students discuss what they read, they refine ideas, argue and debate, clarify misunderstandings, reconsider opinions, learn new words, and build new understandings about content. All those things happen as a result of talk and lively and stimulating exchanges—it's what is at the heart of the social nature of learning.

Susan Anders Mazzoni and Linda B. Gambrell (1996) suggest that "In order for children to become active, independent readers and thinkers, they need to recognize and resolve their own discrepancies with text. One way to encourage this process is to provide children with opportunities to participate in peer discussions." They further observe: "Opportunities to discuss informational texts within a social context are one way that children can begin to develop higher order language expression and knowledge of content material." Planning and implementing circles requires some different considerations, so read on!

Planning and Carrying Out Discovery Circles

In this section we discuss points to consider as you plan discovery circles: organizing circles, understanding the students' role and the teacher's role, determining what students know, making nonfiction selections and sharing what they can learn next, and teaching strategies for active and engaged discussions.

Organizing Discovery Circles

We suggest having two to six students in each discovery circle, but this will vary according to your purpose. For example, if students are meeting to discuss a book, then usually four to six is a good number. However, if they are new to discovery circles or they're meeting to discuss inquiry projects or to share written reports, then pairs might be a better choice. Plan the composition of each circle so that students who will benefit from working with one another are grouped together. Circles may be configured so that students of mixed abilities work with one another, or they can be more homogeneously grouped.

If you group students heterogeneously, several in the group may read aloud sections during discovery circle time so that all hear the content, and then talk and write about it together. Or students may read on their own or as partners and convene in their circles for their conversation and writing.

Young children may first listen to the teacher read aloud the nonfiction selection and then talk and write in small discovery circles. As you can tell, there are many possibilities for ways to assemble circles and how they function.

> ### ORGANIZE DISCOVERY CIRCLES TO MEET SPECIFIC PURPOSES
>
> Some purposes for discovery circles include:
> - Reading and discussing a single nonfiction selection or multiple selections and then sharing findings, which is usually called *jigsaw groups* (Aronson & Patnoe, 1997; Daniels, 2002), as described on pages 232–233.
> - Reading and discussing texts related to inquiry topics.
> - Sharing oral and written progress reports of individual inquiry projects.
> - Debating issues raised in instructional read alouds, shared reading, guided reading, or independent reading.

Understanding the Students' Role and the Teacher's Role

Students play a major role in discovery circles. As we've already mentioned, typically they come to the circle prepared to share their thoughts about what they have read, heard, or written. Writing often follows the discussion, too, which can be done alone, in pairs, or in collaboration with others.

Usually, students lead the discussion. However, the teacher may actively participate in a discussion, as needs arise. For example, you may show how to keep a conversation focused or how to extend a response to a question if you observe students struggling in those areas. Be cautious, though, about dominating discussions. Assist when needed, then leave the group to see if students can do whatever you modeled on their own.

The teacher may play a less direct role by sitting by the side of a circle to listen and observe, but not intervene. Or she may "float" to observe and listen to several circles in action. If she wants to assess how a group is conversing, she may stand or sit nearby. If she wants to assess generally how the groups are doing, she may move from group to group. If it looks like the teacher's assistance would move the group along, she might participate for a short time. When observing and listening, teachers can use this as a data-gathering opportunity to record brief notes about what students are doing successfully or not doing so well. For example, the teacher may observe how quickly one group convened and began talking, and how another one did not. Examples of questions teachers can use for record keeping while discovery circles are in action are discussed in the section "Assessing What Happens in Discovery Circles" (see page 234). A student can also be assigned as a data collector or roaming observer (Cole, 2003), recording positive notes about how circles are working. The teacher can design a mini-lesson about how to do this.

The teacher may also designate the amount of reading or negotiate that decision with students. She may assign specific strategies for the group to try and offer students ways to structure and organize their talk. We describe ways to help students organize and enrich their discussions in the section "Teaching Strategies for Active and Engaged Circle Discussions," which begins on page 219.

Determining What Students Know

When discovery circles work well, it's probably because of previous good teaching. Good teaching, after all, yields excellent dividends, including independent learning, which is an essential ingredient for discovery circles. Consider the instructional route that will get your students there. Tally up all the experiences they've had with nonfiction. Think about the instructional approaches you've used to help students gain experience, confidence, and success reading, writing, and talking about nonfiction. Have you given them multiple opportunities to hear nonfiction read aloud? Have you demonstrated how to comprehend and write nonfiction? Have you given students opportunities to problem-solve their way through reading and writing nonfiction through shared and guided instruction? Experiences like this help students work successfully in discovery circles.

Our colleague Jane Wellman-Little is a fabulous thinker. She views what students talk and write about in discovery circles as rich ground for determining what students know about nonfiction and what still needs to be taught. So, typically, she remains in close proximity to students when they meet in discovery circles to observe how they work together and to hear how they talk about nonfiction. Or she has students share with the class how they talked as well as wrote about nonfiction. Here are the kinds of things Jane looks for. Seeing evidence of them, or lack of evidence, helps her to determine what to teach next in modeled, shared, and guided instruction:

- Substantiating statements about content or features of nonfiction and finding evidence in the text.
- Making judgments about the author's points and going back to the text for evidence.
- Specifying whether statements are facts or opinions.
- Understanding the signals authors use when they hedge or speculate about what they write.
- Checking the credentials of authors.
- Being able to retell what is read as a way to interpret facts.
- Using the organizational structure to use appropriate strategies to read the text.
- Understanding how to question the author.
- Being able to read and understand a variety of visual information in text, such as captions, diagrams, and flow charts.
- Understanding that visual information shouldn't be skipped but read and processed.
- Being able to make inferences verbally and in writing.
- Being able to synthesize and summarize information verbally and in writing.

Students should also understand the social skills of talking with one another about nonfiction—specifically, how to take turns, how to listen, how to agree and disagree, and how to be cooperative. How does scaffolded instruction help them acquire these skills? For example, in instructional read alouds, students get a taste of interactive discussions by talking about texts with the teacher. In shared instruction, they are apprenticed in taking turns, listening to and building on ideas, and problem solving together. In guided instruction, they read on their own, share their thoughts with the group, and work together to write text. By using the literacy framework over time, teachers prepare students for the independent and collaborative work necessary for

SOCIAL SKILLS FOR WORKING EFFECTIVELY IN DISCOVERY CIRCLES

- Being respectful of everyone's point of view.
- Avoiding digressions and learning ways to refocus the discussion when they occur.
- Being flexible enough to try different ways of talking or writing about nonfiction within the group.
- Building on a group member's comments to carry on a discussion.
- Giving wait time to one another.
- Getting a discussion started.
- Being mindful of hearing from each member of the group.

success in discovery circles.

As you determine gaps in students' abilities, you may need to plan mini-lessons that focus on a topic, such as how to take turns and avoid interrupting the speaker. From there, you may ask a small group of students to model the skill for the rest of the class. A list of social skills appears in the box on page 215.

Making Nonfiction Selections for Discovery Circles

Making wise text selections is key because the selections need to target the content being studied and the nonfiction features need to be ones the students understand or can process in collaboration with their peers. In this section, we address three questions that teachers frequently ask us: What criteria should be used for selecting nonfiction? Should students select nonfiction for circles? Is it wise to mix nonfiction and fiction in circles?

What Criteria Should Be Used for Selecting Nonfiction?

Figure 8.2 offers a sample of nonfiction titles that will engage and stimulate discussion. When making selections, think about the demands placed on your students in terms of content and complexity of writing, vocabulary, concepts, and text features. Are you choosing materials your students will be able to read and understand on their own? Is the style and organization of the writing accessible to them? Do students know how to read and use access features? Are you making choices that expand on what students already know about content? Do they know enough about the topic to read, write, and talk about the text with understanding? Remember, in discovery circles, students no longer have you guiding them through the selection. You may think a book is perfect for a discovery circle, but upon a more thorough inspection, you may discover that it makes a better read aloud at the start of a new unit, a good text for shared reading lessons, or a source for research.

Use sources such as the Orbis Pictus list (Bamford & Kristo, 2003), *Adventuring With Books: A Booklist for Pre-K–Grade 6* (McClure & Kristo, 2002), and the criteria in Chapter 3 to find high-quality nonfiction. Our best advice is to read lots of nonfiction and choose books that fit into your curriculum, that your students can read with ease, that have nonfiction features your students already know, and that will ignite a desire for discussion. And, as a rule of thumb, always familiarize yourself with the books you ask students to read for discovery circles, even those that are recommended, to determine whether they are right for your students and for your purposes.

Figure 8.2

A Sample of Good Nonfiction Choices for Discovery Circles

Books that pull students in because of the spectacular nature of the event or circumstance they address:

Aunt Clara Brown: Official Pioneer by Linda Lowery

Blizzard! by Jim Murphy

Trial by Ice: A Photobiography of Sir Ernest Shackleton by K. M. Kostyal

Books that contain whimsical illustrations and a witty writing style but don't sacrifice accuracy:

Hairdo! What We Do and Did to Our Hair by Ruth Freeman Swain

How to Talk to Your Cat by Jean Craighead George

What You Never Knew About Fingers, Forks, & Chopsticks by Patricia Lauber

Books that build an argument or contain a position about an issue or event:

Hurry Freedom: African Americans in Gold Rush California by Jerry Stanley

If a Bus Could Talk: The Story of Rosa Parks by Faith Ringgold

Kids on Strike! by Susan Campbell Bartoletti

Nest of Dinosaurs: The Story of Oviraptor by Mark A. Norell and Lowell Dingus

The Great Fire by Jim Murphy

We Rode the Orphan Trains by Andrea Warren

You Forgot Your Skirt, Amelia Bloomer! A Very Improper Story by Shana Corey

Books that contain information that may be controversial to some readers:

One More Elephant: The Fight to Save Wildlife in Uganda by Richard Sobol

The Chimpanzees I Love: Saving Their World and Ours by Jane Goodall

Books that don't have all the answers and speculate about evidence:

Dinosaurs to Dodos: An Encyclopedia of Extinct Animals by Don Lessem

Hatshepsut: His Majesty, Herself by Catherine Andronik

Books that tell a good story, as well as provide facts:

At Her Majesty's Request: An African Princess in Victorian England by Walter Dean Myers

Shipwrecked! The True Adventures of a Japanese Boy by Rhoda Blumberg

Tough Beginnings: How Baby Animals Survive by Marilyn Singer

Vincent van Gogh: Portrait of an Artist by Jan Greenberg and Sandra Jordan

Books that help students appreciate differences among people:

Cuban Kids by George Ancona

One Belfast Boy by Patricia McMahon

Should Students Select Nonfiction for Circles?

Because of all the factors to consider when making book selections, we don't advise letting students make those selections completely on their own. Books need to be matched as closely as possible to students' reading level and interest. They can't be too difficult or too easy. They must help you meet your teaching purpose and the content. They must enable students to tap into everything they know about reading and writing nonfiction, as well as the content. They need to complement skills and strategies students already know and enable them to apply new ones. In a nutshell, there's a lot at stake—so you, as the teacher, need to take the lead in choosing books. We feel that giving students control over book selection is best for independent reading.

However, like other kinds of peer-led book groups, you can offer choices by narrowing down the number of titles and asking students to vote for the one they want to read for the circle discussion.

Is It Wise to Mix Nonfiction and Fiction in Circles?

Some historical fiction is written so well that students are convinced that it actually happened. We even hear our college students say that it's such a good story, it must be true. Here's a case in point. Karen Hesse's Newbery-award-winning book, *Out of the Dust* (1997), a narrative written in free verse, tells the story of a young girl's life during the Great Depression in the Dust Bowl of Oklahoma. Some students have not heard of the Dust Bowl, but Hesse's writing is so beautiful and convincing that students believe the story really happened. But here's the clincher: It's a story that could have happened, but Hesse made it up. She did extensive research about the time period— good writers need to do that. From her research, she wrote a superb story. Is it informative? Can we still learn about the time period? Absolutely, but students need to know that it's fiction and, therefore, read it with a discerning eye and not accept all information as fact. Contrast that with Jerry Stanley's *Children of the Dust Bowl: The True Story of the School at Weedpatch Camp* (1992). This historical nonfiction book documents how a school was built for migrant workers who traveled from Oklahoma to California during the 1930s.

So do we recommend using both fiction and nonfiction in a single discovery circle? Yes, but only after teaching about the differences between the two genres. For example, look at *Out of the Dust* and *Children of the Dust Bowl* side by side as a class. Browsing and thinking aloud will helps students see some immediate differences between the two books. The bottom line: Don't assume that students will know the difference between fiction and nonfiction— even older students. In Chapter 1, we described the differences in reading fiction and nonfiction and gave examples of paired sets of nonfiction and fiction titles. Here are a few more examples:

Paired Sets of Nonfiction and Fiction Titles

Nonfiction	Fiction
All About Owls by Jim Arnosky	*Owl Moon* by Jane Yolen
Chicks & Chickens by Gail Gibbons	*Cook-a-Doodle-Doo!* by Janet Stevens
Christmas in the Big House, Christmas in the Quarters by Patricia C. McKissack and Fredrick L. McKissack	*Letters From a Slave Girl: The Story of Harriet Jacobs* by Mary E. Lyons
I Am an American: A True Story of the Japanese Internment by Jerry Stanley	*Journey to Topaz* by Yoshiko Uchida

Teaching Strategies for Active and Engaged Circle Discussions

According to educator Ardith Davis Cole (2003), literary conversations help students dig deeper into what they read. She says that while engaged in them, "[students] crawl between the lines and dredge out inferences and innuendoes….They take a stand and support it with textual evidence, and…make connections to their own lives, other texts, and the craft of the author. Furthermore, kids become turned on to reading and make it an integral part of their lives. Thus, fluency grows while reading rate and vocabulary are enhanced."

We want all these things to happen for students in discovery circles. We want students to access and use all that they know about content and reading and writing nonfiction to have rich and stimulating discussions. We also want students to learn more—to deepen the way they talk with one another and to think in new and dynamic ways.

To help do that, we offer a host of strategies to teach students to use in discovery circles. You can introduce them in mini-lessons, modifying them as necessary for the grade level you teach. Or plan an instructional read aloud, think alouds, or a modeled writing lesson. From there, let your students try out the strategy in discovery circles. If

TRY DISCOVERY CIRCLE NOTEBOOKS

Discovery circle notebooks are a great way for students to keep written responses to books and discussions, and to keep track of what they do and what they read in discovery circles. Students can create their own notebooks, buy ready-made notebooks, or keep their responses and records on the computer.

they struggle, plan shared or guided instruction to learn the strategy. Each strategy description below includes a definition of the strategy, reasons for teaching it, and procedures for teaching it.

FAQ—Frequently Asked Questions

What is it? "Thick" questions to ask about nonfiction—good starting places for discovery circle discussions.

Why do it? FAQs encourage students to think about content and nonfiction features in interesting ways and provide models for questions to ask when sharing their research or writing for inquiry projects.

Procedures:

1. Have students record examples of FAQs in their notebooks to use for reference. To prepare for circle discussions, have them write responses to one or more of these as discussion starters. Balance questions you think are important for them to try in their discussions with those they choose. Teach them to ask questions that help circle members elaborate or extend their responses.

2. Remind students that when they ask questions, their peers will come up with even more to ask—it's a ripple effect! This happens naturally when we discuss something that interests us.

3. Through mini-lessons, model how to ask and respond to these questions. Apply different questions to several nonfiction texts and see how responses vary. Then let students have a try. Since the questions demand high levels of thinking, expect a range of responses.

4. Encourage students to always go back into text to verify their responses. Model this by saying things like "On page 23, the author states in the third paragraph that…." Even primary students can learn this skill.

5. Help students see that FAQs can be applied not just to their reading, but to their writing as well.

EXAMPLES OF FAQs

- What did you learn that was the most interesting? Most surprising? What questions didn't the author answer for you?
- What did you wonder about?
- What would you like to ask the author about the information? Why?
- What is the most important information that other readers need to know about this book?
- Name five words that describe the topic of what you read. Why did you choose these words?
- How would you summarize what you learned about the topic to someone younger than you?
- What did the author do to make the information interesting and easy to understand?
- How is what you read similar to something else you read on the same topic? How is it different? Compare and contrast your findings.
- What do you know about the topic now that you didn't know before you read about it?

6. Ask students to design their own questions to ask about nonfiction. Talk about these with the class or group and add them to the list.

Let's Make a Statement

What is it? An alternative to formulating a question for discussion. Students formulate and discuss a statement in discovery circles.

Why do it? J. T. Dillon's (1985) research suggests that students have lengthier discussions when they respond to declarative statements than to questions. It also gives students an alternative to questions.

Procedures:

1. If needed, teach students the differences between statements and questions. Do an instructional read aloud and then model writing a question and then a statement about the content to be discussed.

2. If students already are clear about the differences between questions and statements and how to design them, plan another instructional read aloud. Pose a question about the content. Students are obviously used to answering questions and will no doubt respond quite easily. Next, design a statement about the content and ask students to respond to that. At first they may be surprised, but give wait time and see what happens. Process with students any differences between the responses made to the question and those made to the statement. Explain to students that so often we ask questions as the only way to get a discussion started. Making statements gives them alternatives to questions and may lead to a lot more talk. To increase the challenge for students, ask them to respond to the discussion by crafting an additional statement that comes from their responses and ask students to discuss it. For example, here is a declarative statement for the book *The Truth About Great White Sharks* by Mary M. Cerullo: "The great white shark may be an animal that we need to learn more about rather than just be afraid of." As responses are made, make another statement to see if more conversation is generated. For example, if a student responds to Cerullo's statement by saying that he has heard that a lot of people get bitten every year by great whites, you might respond by reminding students of the facts—that other kinds of sharks, not only great whites, are responsible for attacks around the world. See how they respond.

3. Teach students to be patient once they've made their statement, as they need to give others in the circle time to think and respond. After the discussion, ask students to summarize major points from the conversation in a brief paragraph that an appointed scribe writes. Share the summary with the class.

Powerful Pairs, Triplets, Quads, and More

What is it? Activities that prompt students to think about a variety of perspectives on a single topic, using two, three, four, or more nonfiction titles that the teacher collects.

Why do it? This is an excellent way for students to compare and contrast how authors interpret topics (Zarnowski, 2001).

Procedures:

1. Look for books on the same topic that discuss content in varying degrees of depth, that use primary source material, and that offer different interpretations or descriptions of events. Below is an example of a group of five titles on Shackleton's Antarctic Expedition in 1914, one of the most remarkable true-life survival stories on record (Zarnowski, 2001).

2. Make sure that students are familiar with the topic before discovery circles meet to read, discuss, and write about the books. The students' ability level, the complexity of the books, and the students' familiarity with this kind of activity are all factors that the teacher will need to take into consideration while planning. The teacher will want to take the lead in getting things started. This will involve doing an instructional read aloud in which a pair of books are read aloud and compared by the class. When students are familiar with this activity, they can take on more responsibility for reading, discussing, and comparing the books.

3. Prepare students to compare and contrast pairs, triplets, quads, and more by teaching them ways to discuss and compare the books. Here are questions to use for comparing and contrasting the books:
   - What are the "big ideas" in the books?

A Text Set on the Shackleton Expedition

(Listed in order from the most comprehensive to the least comprehensive)

Shipwreck at the Bottom of the World: The Extraordinary True Story of Shackleton and the Endurance by Jennifer Armstrong

Ice Story by Elizabeth Cody Kimmel

Trial by Ice: A Photobiography of Sir Ernest Shackleton by K. M. Kostyal

Spirit of Endurance: The True Story of the Shackleton Expedition to the Antarctic by Jennifer Armstrong

Trapped by the Ice! Shackleton's Amazing Antarctic Adventure by Michael McCurdy

---

Nonfiction in Focus

- What was the author trying to accomplish by writing the book?
- To what extent does the author reveal his or her "take" on the topic or try to remain neutral?
- What is the author's perspective on the topic?
- To what extent does the author talk about his or her research?
- What primary sources were used in the book and who wrote them?
- Why were they written?
- What was the author trying to accomplish by using them?

The books can also be compared using the criteria identified by the Orbis Pictus Award Committee: accuracy, organization, design/illustration, and style (Zarnowski, 2001).

4. Assign a book from the text set for each group to read. More advanced students can read and compare two or more books in their discovery circles. But even young students can experience comparing and contrasting books if the teacher takes more of a role in the activity to scaffold students' learning. Then, gradually, students can take on more responsibility, as they are ready.

5. Once students have finished their discussions, they can create a data chart in their discovery circle and, as a class, combine the information to compare how different authors write about the same topic using some of the questions listed above. In Figure 8.3, using the Shackleton text set, each sixth-grade discovery circle used one book, collecting information on the visuals and about the Aurora Team that was sent to McMurdo to meet Shackleton after he crossed Antarctica. The class then met to combine their information and used the chart for sharing the first data they got from their books. This is only the first of many comparisons they will be doing with this text set.

Save the Last Word for Me

What is it? An effective reading and writing strategy that stimulates discussion and encourages every member of the discovery circle to participate (Short, Harste & Burke, 1996).

Why do it? The strategy helps students connect with nonfiction text on a personal level because they identify statements that match their beliefs or find points that trouble them or they feel passionate about.

Procedures:

1. On one side of an index card, have students copy a powerful statement from their reading that they react to in some way—one they agree or disagree with, one that stirs controversy, or one that can be debated. They should also write down the page number.

Figure 8.3

Comparison Chart of Shackleton Books: Visual Information and the Aurora Team

Book Titles	Maps	Photos	Illustrations	Aurora Team
Shipwreck at the Bottom of the World	2 maps, one of Antarctica and one of the expedition	original photos and plans for the Endurance	none	2 brief sentences on p. 8 to 9 that it sailed to meet the team
Ice Story	3 maps: expedition, original map of Caird's approach to South Georgia, original map of trip across South Georgia	original photos	none	No mention
Trial by Ice	1 map at end of book. Includes the trip of both teams	original photos	none	Describes the rescue of the 2nd team, p. 58
Spirit of Endurance	1 map of the expedition and inset map of Antarctica	few original photos and plans for the Endurance	primarily illustrations	no mention
Trapped by the Ice!	1 map showing the expedition journey and inset map of Antarctica	few at the end of Shackleton and 3 of his men	primarily illustrations	briefly mentioned in the foreword

2. On the other side of the card, have students record a response to the statement.

3. Ask one student to start the discussion by sharing only his or her quote and not the response. It's helpful for students to indicate the page where the quote appears, so that others can put it in context. Then, group members react to the quote, one by one.

4. Have the student who initiated the sharing read his or her response to the quote when everyone else has had a turn, thus "saving the last word" for that person. The whole process starts again with the next student in the circle. Encourage students to refer back to the text to refresh their memories, confirm statements, and answer questions that arise. Verifying responses is a good habit for students to get into.

A Response for "Save the Last Word for Me"

Alise, a sixth grader, records these statements from *Light Shining Through the Mist: A Photobiography of Dian Fossey* by Tom L. Matthews (1998):

> I decided to take some sentences out of the Afterword from page 60:
>
> "The recently discovered mountain gorillas of Uganda's Bwindi Impenetrable Forest have a large and protected habitat."
>
> "There are no guarantees that the mountain gorilla will survive forever as a species. But there is [now] much less chance that they will be wiped out by human greed or indifference."

Response on the back of the card:

> I agree with this because of all the work Dian Fossey did to save the gorillas. She punished poachers and made sure that the gorillas were safe from humans. She died doing that but all the things she did during her life will make a difference. Some people care and I hope Dian Fossey will be remembered forever.`

Anticipation Guides

What is it? An anticipation guide is comprised of statements designed to activate prior knowledge and to establish purposes for reading.

Why do it? Anticipation guides are used before and after students read a selection. The statements are written about the content and serve to challenge students' knowledge and beliefs about a topic (Brozo & Simpson, 2003). Research shows that it's important to challenge what students already know about a topic before they read to identify misconceptions they might have, as these may influence their reading and even remain after they read (Alvermann et. al., 1985; Marshall, 1989).

Procedures:

Here are steps for preparing anticipation guides based on the work of Richard T. Vacca and Jo Anne L. Vacca (2002).

1. To prepare the guide, select the main concepts about the topic students are studying—for example, bats. List each of these as a declarative statement on the anticipation guide.
2. State directions that ask students to check the statements they believe are true before they read. Also include a column for responding after they read. You might have an additional column that asks students to give evidence for what they know. See the anticipation guide

on bats, below, as an example.

3. Distribute enough guides for each student in the discovery circles and explain the purpose, which is to find out what they already know about the topic before they start reading. Then, ask them to respond to the statements in the first column.

4. Have students meet in their discovery circles to share and discuss how they responded to each statement.

5. Ask students to read their circle's selection and then respond to the statements again, this time checking the appropriate statements in the column labeled "After You Read." They also need to indicate in the third column, "How You Know," a page number where they found the information and/or a comment about how they know the statement is true.

6. Have students compare and discuss the statements they checked and how they know each is true based on what they learned from their reading.

An Anticipation Guide on Bats

Directions: Title and author of your book _____.

Before you read, put a check next to any statement about bats below that you think is true. Meet in your discovery circle and discuss your choices.

Before You Read	After You Read	How You Know
____ 1. Bats fly into people's hair.	_____	_____
____ 2. Bats are the only mammals that fly.	_____	_____
____ 3. Bats are mice with wings.	_____	_____
____ 4. The smallest mammal on Earth is a bat.	_____	_____
____ 5. Bats live everywhere in the world except in Antarctica.	_____	_____
____ 6. Bats sleep lying down.	_____	_____
____ 7. Some bats hibernate in the winter.	_____	_____
____ 8. Bats use sound to help them find food.	_____	_____
____ 9. There is a kind of bat called a vampire bat.	_____	_____
____ 10. Bats are blind.	_____	_____

After you read your nonfiction selection about bats, put a check mark next to any statement you now think is true. In the "How You Know" column, put what page helped you make your decision. What did you learn? Discuss your work with the members of your discovery circle.

A Text Set on Bats

Bats by Adrienne Mason

Batman: Exploring the World of Bats by Laurence Pringle

Bats: Night Fliers by Betsy Maestro

Bats! Strange and Wonderful by Laurence Pringle

How Do Bats See in the Dark? Questions and Answers About Night Creatures by Melvin Berger and Gilda Berger

Discovery Circles in Action

At the beginning of the chapter we discussed what happens in fifth-grade teacher Judy Bouchard's discovery circles. Next, we describe what happens in the classrooms of three other teachers. First, we describe Sue Pidhurney, who uses read alouds as a way to introduce discovery circles with her multiage students in grades 1 and 2. Next, we show how Jan Elie works with students in grades 4 through 6 in an afternoon book club. Last, we profile Bill Phillips, a third-grade teacher who uses jigsaw groups, another variation on discovery circles.

Discovery Circles With First and Second Graders: Preparing for Discussion Through Read Aloud

Teacher Sue Pidhurney is excited about how much her young students are learning about nonfiction through her work using the comprehensive framework. The children love how they can quickly identify nonfiction features and use "grown-up words," such as *access features*. Sue wants to teach them strategies for talking together independently about nonfiction, which is a big step for her students because they are just getting used to taking turns and listening to one another. So she decides to ease into discovery circles slowly by first pairing her students for discussion rather than forming larger groups. The "pair/shares," as Sue calls them, follows one of her instructional read alouds for a unit focusing on Martin Luther King, Jr. Goals for her unit include teaching students to:

- Summarize key points.
- Make connections among texts.
- Answer inferential questions verbally and in writing.

A Text Set on Martin Luther King, Jr.

Dr. Martin Luther King, Jr. by David
A. Adler

Happy Birthday, Dr. King! by Kathryn Jones

Martin Luther King Day by Linda Lowery

Scholastic News, January 2003, Vol. 59,
No. 4, Edition 2

*Young Martin Luther King, Jr.: "I Have a
Dream"* by Joanne Mattern

Sue read aloud *Dr. Martin Luther King, Jr.* by David A. Adler after sharing three other books about the civil rights leader. After pairing students, she asked them to first talk about some of the parts of the book they had questions about. This is the way Sue helped them learn about making inferences—that authors didn't include every detail—and that sometimes readers had to think hard about what the author didn't come right out and say. Here is how one pair—Genia and Kurtis—shared their thinking.

GENIA: Why did Martin Luther King get shot?

KURTIS: A guy shot him because he didn't like what Martin was trying to do.

GENIA: Some people didn't like his words.

KURTIS: The reason a guy shot him was because he didn't want the laws changed.

GENIA: The guy killed him because he didn't believe in Martin's words. He wanted the blacks to
   stay in the back of the bus.

KURTIS: That is so bad [shaking his head and looking down].

After all the pairs talk for awhile, Sue asks each to share their questions and responses. Here are two that she recorded on the board:

- Why could Martin play with his white friend before he went to school but after that, he couldn't?
- Whatever happened to his friend? The book told about what happened to Martin, but we never heard anything else about his friend!

Next, Sue asks students how readers go about making inferences or figuring out answers to their questions when the author

What Do Readers Do to Make Inferences?

- They have to look inside their minds to see what makes sense.
- They have to read a lot to know about stuff, like we did.
- They have to use their imagination and think really hard.
- They have to talk to themselves and ask those questions, and then they have to go back and read some more. Then they have to say what's in their head.

doesn't give them all the information they want. She asks them in pairs to talk about that and, on a piece of paper, to list their best ways to do this. See the box at the bottom of page 228 for responses that Sue recorded on a chart for all to see.

Sue is pleased with her students' attempts to talk about a complex reading skill. She creates a discovery circle discussion chart that lists the ways students can talk to each other in pair/shares and later in discovery circles. Asking questions and making inferences is on the list. On another day she'll have students do pair/shares to practice making connections between the books they've heard her read aloud about Martin Luther King, Jr. and making summary points. The chart will eventually serve as a list of good references for both discussing and writing nonfiction. Depending on what they study, she'll add pertinent questions. Here is the starter list of questions:

- What questions did I think of that aren't answered in the book?
- What connections did I make with other books I've read?
- How do I sum up what I read?
- What are new and interesting words that I learned?
- What was hard for me to understand? What was easy? How did the author make it hard or easy to understand?
- How do I know that what the author wrote is right?

Discovery Circles With Fourth, Fifth, and Sixth Graders: Discussing Nonfiction in an After-School Book Club

Jan Elie, a Title I teacher, heads up a weekly after-school nonfiction book club for students in grades 4 through 6. The club is open to any student who wishes to join. Jan's only requirement is that students have a deep interest in reading and discussing good nonfiction. The books she chooses often relate to careers and world cultures—two topics of special interest to her students.

Jan is currently working with a group of seven students of varying levels of reading and writing ability. She modifies her instructional support based on what she knows students can do and what they find challenging. Naturally, she wants students to read and discuss on their own as much as possible. But at times, when they need assistance, she becomes an active member of the club. At other times, when students are working well independently, she sits apart and observes or participates only occasionally. The book club is a good opportunity for Jan to teach, but also to watch, assess, and help when needed.

Jan and her students are reading the book *Anthropologist: Scientist of the People* by Mary Batten. At the club's first meeting, she distributed a copy of the book to each student and, rather than rushing into the reading, she encouraged members to read the dust jacket and browse the beautiful photographs by anthropologists A. Magdalena Hurtado and Kim Hill. The students were very intrigued. Students read some sections silently and others paired to buddy-read or share sections aloud. Jan also read aloud some sections, and a couple of students volunteered to read captions and especially interesting passages.

What is so rewarding for Jan is the amount of lively discussion the students have about the reading. Here is a sample of a session when Jan takes a more active part as a participant. They're about to begin reading the chapter entitled "Becoming an Anthropologist." The club members are used to reviewing each chapter by first reading the quote under the title. Students discovered that these quotes set the stage for understanding the chapter. Here is the quote for this chapter: "To be an anthropologist, you have to be so interested in people that you can sit in a hut for hours without being bored." Their usual next step is to go through the chapter, each taking a turn to say something about what they notice because every page contains at least one photograph and a caption. Jan's club members are learning quickly that taking a walk through the pages of a chapter of nonfiction can be helpful in understanding what is covered in the chapter. Plus, Jan is tickled because up to this point she knows that these students usually skip information like maps, photographs, and other visual information. Everyone agrees to read the first three pages and come back to the group to discuss them. Forida, Stephanie, Paul, and Oreste go to a comfortable space in the room as they buddy-read, while the rest of the circle stays at the table to read silently. Jan is going to see how the discussion goes because, in this chapter, readers need to make inferences about what it's like to be an anthropologist. Here is a sample of what they've just read: "At the beginning of her career, Magdalena realized that an anthropologist has both an enormous privilege and an enormous responsibility. 'You're essentially bothering a group of people. Your presence is intrusive, and out of respect for the people, you have to make sure that whatever you're doing is really worthwhile. Nobody ever taught me anything about this in anthropology classes, but I think it's at the crux of anthropological research.'"

ORESTE: This is just like *Survivor*. You know that show where people get followed around and watched all the time.

STEPHANIE: Well, I know once when I watched one of those shows I got so bored listening to them talk and talk and get followed around. I know I wouldn't want someone following me around all day.

[The discussion remains focused on reality shows and Jan thinks it's time to pull them back to the text. She decides to intervene.]

JAN: So Magdalena is watching the Aché people for different purposes, right? This isn't for a show.

Magdalena is a scientist.

PAUL: Yeah, but she's still watching and taking notes and stuff. I'd freak out if someone was doing that to me all day.

FORIDA: That's not what Ms. Elie is talking about. Magdalena is an anthropologist and has an important job.

JACKSON (another member of the club): She wants everyone to learn about the Aché, so they're letting her take notes and watch them.

JAN: What did Magdalena do, though, that makes it easier for her to do that?

STEPHANIE: It says on page 16 that she learned the language, so maybe that helped her.

JAN: She struggled with that, didn't she?

PAUL: She let the little kids help her. I like how it said that she had a notebook around her neck to write stuff down that they said. That must have been like a little book for her—a book of words to help her learn their language.

Jan learned a lot from listening. She thought for sure that students would have trouble making inferences about what Magdalena did to be accepted by the Aché. They were able to do this quite well once she got the discussion rerouted. She learned how easy it is for students to get off on a tangent that might not be so fruitful to the discussion. This experience fueled her to think about coming up with strategies that would allow for good, rich discussion, but not be so structured that students would end up only responding to the questions.

So at the end of the meeting that day, she asked students to reflect on how the discussion went and to share their thoughts. Stephanie piped up right away to complain about how Oreste got them off track right from the start because he talked about television shows. This gave Jan an opportunity to share how people naturally get off on digressions or conversations because they connect what they read with their own lives. She shared that as an adult reader who goes to a book club meeting once a month with her friends, the same thing happens. But then, someone usually moves the discussion back into the reading. This also showed Jan how easy these digressions can happen with nonfiction that is stimulating and thought provoking.

Unless the teacher's purpose is different, discovery circles aren't intended to be freewheeling "anything goes" conversations, but rather more structured discussions that provide students time to explore connections they make. The teacher can help by identifying a focus for the discussion, such as a question or a point to think about as they read. Then the discussion can take off from there. For example, in preparation for the discussion of Chapter 2, Jan asks students to mark pages with sticky notes that mention ways Magdalena became part of the Aché people. Jan could also teach students "Save the Last Word for Me" or other strategies. Or she could have students do some writing as a group, in pairs, or alone—they could compile a list of the things anthropologists do to build a relationship with the people they study.

This scenario is one example of how a teacher modifies the support she gives to students based on what's needed. Jan adjusted her role in the circle, starting out as a listener and observer and then became a more active participant. If Jan worked with an entire class, she could both roam and observe groups in action or sit close by to a circle to take notes on how the discussion was going. She could analyze her notes to learn the next steps she needed to take—whether it is a mini-lesson to model how to apply a strategy, a think aloud to share how to process text, or a shared reading or writing lesson.

Discovery Circles With Third Graders: Using "Jigsawing" to Comprehend Multiple Texts

Third-grade teacher Bill Phillips varies what his students read in discovery circles by choosing several different texts and using a technique called jigsawing (Aronson & Patnoe, 1997; Daniels, 2002). Bill finds it a powerful way for each student in a circle to learn many different aspects about one topic.

There are several steps in making jigsaw groups work. First, the teacher needs to select different nonfiction selections, typically on one topic, for each member of the circle. So if the whole class is involved in discovery circles and each one has five members, then there need to be five different nonfiction selections and five copies of each of those selections. When discovery circles jigsaw, each student in a circle reads a different selection. Then each student joins other members of the discovery circles who have read the same material. Their task is to discuss what they've read. The teacher can ask that students first write a summary of what they learned or a list of several important key points to bring to the group. Students share their written summaries or list of key points. In their discussion they can determine where there is consensus and what points can be added. A new summary or list can be written that synthesizes what was learned when students pooled their information. Students benefit from having to explain what they know about the topic with others and learn other perspectives on the material.

After this round of discussions, each student returns to his or her original circle to share what he or she learned about the topic. This gives each student the opportunity to be the circle expert on one aspect of a topic. There are several benefits to jigsaw groups. One is that each student has something special to contribute about the topic that no one else in the circle learned about. Another is that all students are writing pieces that summarize and synthesize what they learned.

A Text Set on Birds

Beaks! by Sneed B. Collard III

The Life Cycle of a Bird by Bobbie Kalman and Kathryn Smithyman

Birds Build Nests by Yvonne Winer

Birds: Nature's Magnificent Flying Machines by Caroline Arnold

Then they have the experience of verbally retelling or reporting out to the group what they learned. These written and oral experiences give students practice with the important strategy of retelling content information in writing and verbally.

Each of the books offers specialized information about birds—from different kinds of beaks to how birds fly. Bill's students are already into the unit and know a lot about birds. His purpose for using jigsaw groups is for students to build on their knowledge by reading about specialized topics on birds. By using jigsaw groups, students will be able to dig into a specific topic and then share what they learn with the others in their group.

When Bill uses jigsaws he needs to decide how much students will read and whether they will read on their own or with a partner. He also needs to make decisions about text selection, which are based on the content, the purposes behind doing the jigsaw groups, and the knowledge and ability level of his students. Students won't always read an entire book, as it may contain only a chapter that is pertinent. For this unit, there are four students in each jigsaw group. For each book, Bill will either flag the pages or specific chapters with a sticky note or ask the student to read the entire book.

Bill varies the materials he selects for jigsaw groups. He doesn't always choose nonfiction books. Sometimes he gathers nonfiction materials from a variety of sources— chapters from nonfiction books, articles from children's social studies and science magazines, Internet downloads, and newspaper articles. The box to the right lists nonfiction materials appropriate for a jigsaw group.

NONFICTION SELECTIONS FOR JIGSAW CIRCLES

- Chapters from nonfiction books
- Individual pages from nonfiction books
- A chapter from a biography or autobiography
- An article from *Ranger Rick*, *Cobblestone*, or other children's magazine. (See Appendix F for more examples.)
- Material from the Internet
- Newspaper articles
- Newsletters
- Brochures
- Maps

Assessing What Happens in Discovery Circles

What's going well in nonfiction discovery circles? What skills and strategies do you observe students using? What's not working? What difficulties do students have when they discuss their reading, talk about issues, or share their writing? What challenges do students have working with one another? Which students seem to work well together? What knowledge about nonfiction do students demonstrate? What needs to be taught next? These are questions that come to most teachers' minds as students work in discovery circles—and they're great starting points for assessment.

Try to observe and note all the positive things that are happening in discovery circles. You'll want to share these with students to applaud their efforts. You'll also want to keep track of what can be improved and design mini-lessons around those areas. In this section, we discuss how to use your questions to learn as much as possible about your students' abilities to read and write nonfiction. Specifically, we cover:

- Taking notes during discovery circles.
- Student self-assessment.
- Group/individual end-of-book projects and oral presentations.

Taking Notes During Discovery Circles

Brenda Power (1996) recommends taking notes in the midst of classroom action. A good way to do that is to divide a sheet of paper lengthwise. Write the names of group members at the top, along with the title of the book they're reading, and fasten the sheet to a clipboard. On one side of the paper, make general comments about how things are going with each group. On the other side, jot down specifics about how individual members are doing. Later, insert these sheets in a three-ring binder. This gives you a history of students who have worked together, a record of nonfiction selections used, and comments on what they did well and what problems they experienced.

You can also create sheets ahead of time with the following questions listed on them. Add questions as they arise, and talk to students about them. Invite students to suggest questions of their own.

- To what extent are students, as a group and as individuals, prepared to meet in discovery circles?
- To what extent do students stay on task?
- How are students interacting with one another?
- What is the quality of student talk, in general? How are individual students communicating?
- What do I need to teach students to help them talk in deeper ways about nonfiction?

- Are students able to identify and name features of nonfiction as they discuss their reading?
- What do I need to teach students next for them to understand more complex nonfiction text?
- What evidence do I have that students make connections to their lives, the world, and other things they've read? What evidence do I have that students are able to draw conclusions, synthesize information, summarize, visualize, and analyze and critique what they read?
- Do I ask students to report out what they do as readers (and writers) before, during, and after they read or write?
- What is the quality of the writing from the group? From individuals?
- What do I need to teach next to help them respond more deeply in writing?
- How do I help students write their own expository text in more sophisticated ways?

Your responses to these questions should guide your decisions about what to teach. Your next step is to plan how you want to do that. That decision is based on how much scaffolding you determine that your students need and what approach to use so you are successful. For example, do they need modeled instruction that instructional read alouds and modeled writing provide? Maybe shared reading or writing or a guided experience is the best next step.

Student Self-Assessment

It's important to provide opportunities for students to look at their own behaviors in discovery circle activities. Student self-assessments contribute another valuable piece to look at their progress. You can start with several questions like those given below and create others with students.

Create a rubric so that students can more clearly see their progress with each item and consistency of performance. Ardith D. Cole (2003) recommends starting with a rubric with three levels of performance: Three points for behaviors occurring most of the time, two points for behaviors occurring some of the time, and one point for behaviors that rarely occur. Here's an example: Which of the following statements best describes you?

___ I stayed on task today when I met in my discovery circle: Most of the time/Some of the time/Not enough

___ I need to do a better job staying on task: Most of the time/Some of the time/Not enough

___ I contributed to my discovery circle today: Most of the time/Some of the time/Not enough

___ I let others take turns: Most of the time/Some of the time/Not enough

Have students complete a self-assessment after each discovery circle session and collect and discuss them with students. This is very informative because it shows how students are progressing

Figure 8.4

Sample Questions for a Self-Assessment Form

- What did I do to prepare for work in my discovery circle today?

- What did I do well?

- What do I need to work on?

- What was easy for me?

- What was challenging?

- What did I learn from the reading I did for my discovery circle?

- What are the new words I learned from my reading and/or discussion?

- What are words from the reading that I think are tricky?

- What did I learn that was new from the discovery circle discussion?

- What did I write about?

- Was I able to retell what I read in the discussion? Was I able to retell what I read about in writing and share it with the group?

- What did I learn about reading nonfiction?

- What did I learn about writing nonfiction?

- What new nonfiction features did I learn about?

- What nonfiction features did I find in my reading that I feel comfortable teaching someone else about?

- What did I contribute in my discovery circle?

- How did others in my circle help me? How did I help them?

- What suggestions do I have for the teacher for the next discovery circles?

- What do I think the teacher wanted me to learn about reading and writing nonfiction? (adapted from Day et al., 2002)

- What do I think I need to learn next about reading and writing nonfiction? (adapted from Day et al., 2002)

and is invaluable for report card conferences. Figure 8.4 lists examples of additional questions for a student self-assessment form. Use or modify them to meet your purposes and age and level of your students. Simplify the questions and directions for very young students.

Group/Individual End-of-Book Projects and Oral Presentations

Invite students to share what they learned with the class after discovery circles, with each circle reporting out what they learned. Sharing sessions can also be the result of more ambitious undertakings, such as those described in the examples below. These projects work particularly well when units are finished or when there has been substantial reading and discussion of content. Here are examples:

Nonfiction Big Book—Have students create a nonfiction big book of the most important things learned about the topic, with each student contributing a page. This can be shared with students in other grades. Be sure to discuss with students the importance of keeping the purpose and audience for the writing in mind.

Alphabet Book—Invite students to pair up and create a class alphabet book on the topic of study. Review the features and organization of alphabet books before students design their own.

Poster Display—Have students create a collaborative poster display that describes major points of what they learned. Give each discovery circle a large, sturdy posterboard. Decide ahead of time with students what aspects each poster will cover. Each discovery circle's poster can focus on one aspect of what students learned about the topic. For example, if students just finished a unit on birds, posters can reflect topics they read and learned about, such as: What is a bird? What is its life cycle? What kinds of nests do birds make? How do birds fly? What are different kinds of birds?

Students also need to decide on the nonfiction features they will use for each topic—bulleted lists, time lines, mini-glossaries, illustrations and captions, and diagrams. Mary Evans does a variation of poster displays with her fourth graders with huge success. Each of Mary's students decides on an individual inquiry project to research. Typical topics include an animal, a country, or a famous person. They use discovery circles of pairs or triads of students to talk about what they're learning about their topics and to later share drafts of the writing that will be used on the posters.

Jackdaw Display—A jackdaw is a type of crow that gathers a variety of objects to build its nest. Thus, a jackdaw kit is a collection of objects on a single topic. Have students in each discovery circle create a jackdaw kit that includes different items—from objects, illustrations, diagrams, and maps they create to writing produced in the circle to books and other kinds of reading material that reflect the topic. Also, have students prepare a guide that describes the objects to accompany the kit. Jackdaw Publications produces large envelopes filled with materials to use in social studies. Its Web site is: http://www.jackdaws.com.

Nonfiction Visuals on Parade—Have students design and present an array of nonfiction visuals that represent the content they've studied, such as diagrams, cross sections, flow charts, maps, and illustrations and captions. Each example can be displayed and labeled to identify it and describe how to use it.

Dramatic Presentations—Get students up and moving in response to their reading. If, for example, students read a biography, they can role-play scenes from the person's life. They can write a readers theater script that reflects material from the book. See *Readers Theatre for Children: Scripts and Script Development* (Laughlin & Lathrobe, 1989) as a good source for creating and using readers theater. Also see Jeffrey Wilhelm's *Action Strategies for Deepening Comprehension* (2002) for a rich resource of ways to do role plays and other kinds of easy but powerful dramatic presentations in the classroom to explore turning points.

Invite families to see these projects. Students can write a brief script of what they want to say about their project and rehearse it before presenting it to guests. It's also important for students to rehearse before they present to the class to reinforce using good oral presentation skills. See Chapter 9 on bringing it all together, as many of the projects can be started as a result of work done in discovery circles and completed as students work in their readers' and writers' workshop.

Closing Thoughts

Discovery circles are the perfect forum for students to "try on" what they know about reading and writing nonfiction in the safe company of peers. Students can meet for a wide variety of purposes—from discussing and writing about a single nonfiction selection to exploring different books in jigsaw groups to talking about how research and inquiry writing projects are progressing.

One of the primary roles of teachers during discovery circles is to listen and learn by observing how students put into action what they know. Teachers plan instruction based on their observations. They may also participate as a member of a discovery circle, by either actively joining the discussion or observing and learning what students can do on their own and with the support of peers.

Discovery circles provide students with opportunities to demonstrate all they know about nonfiction as they read, talk, and write—and although done in collaboration with their peers, they become the gateway for independent learning and inquiry.

Chapter 9
Bringing It All Together Through Inquiry:
Observing and Assessing Independent Learning

Mentor texts become especially important as students create their own nonfiction.

erenice Knight, Title I teacher, recently involved nine second graders in a four-week-long inquiry project on the life cycle of butterflies. She used approaches from the comprehensive framework, such as instructional read alouds, shared and guided reading and writing, and readers' and writers' workshops, plus lots of opportunities to talk. Berenice was quick to tell us that her students' success was attributed both to using the framework throughout the inquiry project and to "conversation and discourse with and between students—engaging them in meaningful activities with repeated opportunities to talk about their understandings." The proof is in the products that the students created at the end of the project, which not only demonstrated how much they learned about butterflies, but how much they learned about reading and writing nonfiction. (See Vivian's brochure in Figure 9.1.)

We begin this chapter on moving toward independence with a description of Berenice's inquiry project with low-achieving second graders to show how one teacher moves through the comprehensive framework. Berenice begins her unit with the instructional read aloud of Deborah Heiligman's *From Caterpillar to Butterfly* (1996), which describes the hatching in a classroom of a painted lady butterfly as told

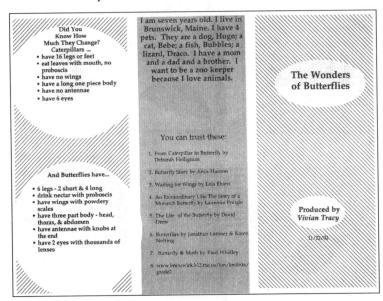

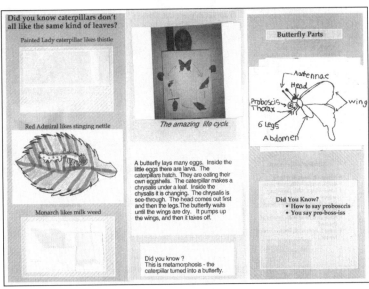

Figure 9.1: Vivian's brochure, "The Wonders of Butterflies," contains a variety of nonfiction features.

through the voices of children. Berenice chooses this book because it mirrors the students' classroom experiment of hatching a painted lady butterfly. Since she did not witness the experiment, she asks the students to describe it. Immediately, they are empowered and have lots to say. She asks them to listen and compare the information in her instructional read aloud to their experience. This sets the stage for a discussion both during and after the reading.

Berenice focuses the first reading of the book on clarifying terms—scientific words such as *metamorphosis* and terms related to anatomy and the life cycle. Berenice finds that although the language is familiar, the students still do not have it under control. They browse the rest of the book to look at appended pages to see what information they might return to in the future.

In her second reading of *From Caterpillar to Butterfly*, Berenice includes the reading of the captions that literally crawl along the plants in the illustrations. These detailed captions allow her to help the students make connections with the butterfly garden they had planted and why specific plants were chosen—individual butterflies have a preference for certain plants' nectar.

One of the primary goals of this inquiry is to understand the life cycle, so Berenice next reads Anca Hariton's *Butterfly Story* (1995), which describes the life cycle of the red admiral butterfly in the wild. Berenice encourages the students to think about how life might be different when a butterfly hatches outside. The students wonder if the butterfly could be in greater danger while drying its wings. Berenice asks the students to retell the life cycle in each book in preparation for comparing the information. The voice of *Butterfly Story* is more poetic and metaphoric, so she uses the retellings to help them gain control over describing the cycle and to encourage trying on the book's language and metaphors, such as "The caterpillar spins a silky thread that looks like a shiny trail behind it." After discussing and comparing the life cycle in the two books, the students conclude that they are the same.

With their classroom experience and these two books as background information, Berenice launches them into a shared writing session to create a KWL chart. She begins the session by creating an "I Wonder" list to find things students would like to research. Their thinking about butterflies is fresh and it is a great time to capture the questions they are mulling over. See list at right:

Berenice wants them to begin predicting what they will learn as they conduct their research. So for questions 1, 3, 4, and 5 she asks, "How many of you think the answer will be yes?" From this quick survey they make a simple bar graph with columns for yes and no for each

> **I Wonder...**
> 1. Do butterflies grow bigger?
> 2. What colors and patterns are on butterflies?
> 3. Are caterpillars all the same color?
> 4. Do chrysalises look different for different butterflies?
> 5. Are the antennae colored, too?

question and save them to compare with their findings. As they research individual topics, this will heighten their attention to details related to their questions. Berenice and the students then create a more typical "What We Think We Know" list. Having just completed the two readings, their ideas came easily. As they work in readers' and writers' workshops over the next few weeks, Berenice plans to revisit this chart often to compare their findings and revise their list. She finds this approach encourages students to think more tentatively about what they know and to be more open to information that contradicts their prior knowledge.

Berenice's next step is a shared reading of Lois Ehlert's *Waiting for Wings* (2001), which has language that rhymes, is more descriptive, and contains complex language structures. Berenice has several goals for this lesson: examining Ehlert's writing style, unraveling the poetic text, understanding the use of "we," and learning how to attend to information in the appendices, such as diagrams and a picture glossary. After they read aloud the texts, Berenice leads them to problem-solve the meaning of the descriptive language and connect it to technical vocabulary. They realize that "then make a case in which to grow" is referring to the chrysalis or pupa. The shift in voice to "We've been waiting…" also calls for problem solving to determine who "we" are. As they read together they decide "we" are the people who own the garden.

The appended pages of *Waiting for Wings,* which include a diagram of a butterfly, information on how to grow a butterfly garden, and a picture glossary, answer many of their "I Wonder" questions, especially about the colors of the butterflies and caterpillars. As they read these pages they return often to the illustrations to find the hidden butterflies and caterpillars among the dense foliage. This search of the visual text helps them to further clarify the meaning of camouflage and to see how the colors of the butterfly help protect it from predators.

Together they browse two additional books, *Butterflies: Peterson Field Guides for Young Naturalists* (Latimer & Nolting, 2000) and *Butterflies & Moths* (Whalley, 1988), to locate answers to questions and to gain an awareness of the breadth and depth of these additional resources. Berenice knows that during the research and report-writing stages the students would need these books. Since field guides are new to them, Berenice puts several pages on the overhead so they can see how this type of book works.

In an interactive writing lesson, they sequence pictures Berenice provided to create a flow chart of the life cycle of the butterfly. Initially, the students tape it on the chart in a line, but one of the students astutely notes that the butterfly could come at either end. Berenice then uses in a modeled writing lesson examples from other books and shows how life cycles are arranged as a circle with arrows. She and the students also examine these books for the language authors use to explain their flow charts and language they might add to explain the life cycle of the butterfly.

During writers' workshop, students work independently to create the first product for their reports, posters on the life cycle of butterflies. They color their illustrations of the life cycle, arrange them on a poster, label the pictures, and write a title. While conferring with one student, the issues of what colors to use becomes an important learning point about issues of accuracy. Berenice brings the group together for a brief guided writing session. They discuss the purpose of the posters. The students are quick to note that these are "teaching" posters and so accuracy is important. In other words, a monarch needs to be colored correctly. For each poster, the students write a description of the life cycle. (See Figure 9.2.)

These students now have sufficient content knowledge and control over vocabulary and nonfiction features to take on the challenges of guided reading. They read two books: *Caterpillar Diary* (Drew, 1987) and *The Life of a Butterfly* (Drew, 1987). During guided reading, Berenice supports their first reading of just the main text and the discussion. The students are given the books to continue reading independently for their research projects. Berenice also supplies them with sticky notes to place next to interesting facts that they may want to include in their final reports.

During writers' workshop, in a small-group conference on planning their final products, students decide to create a trifold brochure because the format reminds them of a butterfly's wings. Since this is a first attempt at this kind of product, Berenice works back and forth among the writing approaches, sometimes modeling, sometimes doing a portion of the task as a shared writing or guided writing, and sometimes providing low support as they successfully work independently.

For example, Berenice moves back to medium-high support and together they create a plan for the placement of the information in the brochure. As they talk, Berenice models possibilities by sharing other brochures and then guides discussion helping them work through their ideas. During a shared writing, together they create a comparison chart for butterflies and caterpillars after attempting one comparing butterflies and moths. Berenice notes they struggle with the language needed to compare butterflies and moths. When they return to the field guide for details, they notice the use of the lead in the sidebars "Did You Know?" and borrow it for the charts and brochures. The comparison chart becomes two separate sidebars with students varying the informa-

Life Cycle Chart

The amazing life cycle

The butterfly lays an egg on the bottom of the leaf. The egg opens up and a little caterpillar comes out of the egg. She eats the shell because she's hungry. The caterpillar eats and eats and she grows and grows and she turns into a chrysalis. After a few days the caterpillar comes out and it is not a caterpillar any more. It is a butterfly.

Figure 9.2: A poster and description of the life cycle of a butterfly, which each of Berenice's students creates.

tion they choose to include. To complete labeled diagrams, students again return to the field guide. Using modeled writing, Berenice shares a variety of "About the Author" samples and together they make a list of the kind of information they found interesting to help guide their own writing. During guided writing, they each attempt their first draft of their own "About the Author" with Berenice's help. They share the pieces and with the feedback from peers work on them independently. Since they plan to assemble the brochures on the computer, Berenice's support is moderate to high as they work with technical issues. Berenice said, "Seeing one's writing as a finished product was the icing on the cake for these students. Students are planning their next project."

Modified Instruction in Readers' and Writers' Workshops: Quick Points

- **Purpose:** To allow students to work independently, both individually and in small collaborative groups, to read, talk, and write about content and nonfiction features.
- **Kinds of Modified Instruction:** Readers' workshop and writers' workshop
- **Scaffolding Level:** Varied
- **Student Role/Teacher Role:** Students work on their own, with other students, or with the teacher/teacher modifies support by observing, helping, and assessing. During portions of the workshops students may work independently. Discussion occurs throughout the workshops, one on one, and in small and large groups.
- **Instructional Context:** Typically done with the entire class or small groups, with students supporting one another. Depending on the age and grade of the students, objectives of the lessons, organizational structure, and literacy approaches included, readers' workshops typically occur daily for 60 to 90 minutes and the writers' workshop daily for 30 to 60 minutes.
- **Types of Materials Typically Used:** Materials for modeled, shared, and guided instruction will be needed if these approaches are included in the workshops. (See Chapters 5 through 8.) Since students may be engaged in independent inquiry projects, an ample collection of nonfiction resources on current science and social studies units should also be made available.
- **Next Steps:** All reading and writing materials are available for students to reread independently or use for further work in inquiry projects or extension activities.

How do Berenice and other teachers we've had the privilege of working with use the approaches in the comprehensive framework to get their students reading and writing nonfiction independently? How did they create a world of inquiry and wonderment from the "get go" that propel even the most disengaged students forward? They do it by keeping inquiry at the center of instruction.

Up to this point, we've provided a comprehensive framework for teaching students how to read and write nonfiction and the tools necessary to get them there. We have offered a wide variety of lessons that can be used across the framework and in reading and writing workshops at all levels of scaffolding. We now:

- Continue our discussion of modified instruction, but in terms of readers' workshop and writers' workshop and where they fit into the framework.
- Identify the benefits of workshops to students.
- Describe the independent level of scaffolded instruction and extension activities and show where they fit in the framework.
- Identify the benefits of students working toward independence using extension activities.
- Give two additional examples of different ways teachers in grades K–6 are bringing together the comprehensive framework around inquiry.
- Review guiding principles that bring teaching and learning nonfiction together in a comprehensive literacy framework.

What Is Modified Instruction in Readers' and Writers' Workshops? Students Work on Their Own, With Other Students, and/or With the Teacher/Teacher Modifies Support

In discovery circles we described modified instruction as shifting more of the responsibility for scaffolding from yourself to your students as they work collaboratively. The level of support is based on the needs of students and the focus of instruction. But in readers' and writers' workshops, as we noticed with Berenice Knight's lessons, the level of scaffolding becomes even more varied depending on the prior experiences of the students, the nature of the inquiry, and the type of final product planned.

The content of your workshops and your levels of scaffolding also depend on how you have organized these blocks of time and what approaches of the comprehensive framework you plan to include. In both workshops, students will have opportunities to work independently on inquiry, but they may also work in collaboration with other students and with you during mini-lessons

Figure 9.3

Comprehensive Framework

Level of Scaffolding	Role of Teacher and Student	Reading Instructional Approach		Writing Instructional Approach
Modeled	• Teacher demonstrates • Students watch	Instructional Read Aloud		Modeled Writing
Shared	• Teacher leads • Students apprentice	Shared Reading		Interactive Writing and Shared Writing
Guided	• Students demonstrate • Teacher assists	Guided Reading		Guided Writing
Modified	• Students work collaboratively • Teacher modifies support by observing, helping, assessing	Reading Discovery Circles	Mini-Lessons and Extension Activities*	Writing Discovery Circles
	• Students work independently, with other students, and/or with the teacher • Teacher modifies support by observing, helping, assessing	Readers' Workshop		Writers' Workshop
Independent	• Students practice • Teacher observes and assesses independent practice activities	Extension Activities*		Extension Activities*

* Extension activities can be used as follow-up activities with all instructional approaches, but students are working independently—either individually or in small groups. Keep in mind that extension activities should match the student's ability to practice the activities independently.

and in reading and writing conferences. So you will have to adjust or modify support according to both the approaches being used as well as students' needs. For example, you might provide a high level of support by explicitly teaching students how the workshops function, using modeled instruction and mini-lessons. As students work independently on reading and writing, you adjust support according to their individual needs, ranging from high to none. If you include shared or guided instruction in the workshops, your level of support will increase appropriately. Depending on the approach, you may do the book selection, you may make suggestions, or students may independently choose. Figure 9.3 shows where modified instruction and readers' and writers' workshops fall on the comprehensive framework. Your role during the instructional time is modified to meet needs as they emerge. To make instructional decisions you will need to:

- Observe students as they work on independent reading, writing, and extension activities.
- Assess students' progress.
- Confer and help as needed or requested.
- Provide mini-lessons as needed.
- Work with small groups of students in guided reading or writing or addressing specific needs.
- Plan your next instructional steps.

Because writing approaches may be coupled with reading approaches, some teachers prefer to think of writing and reading together as the literacy block and plan instruction so it flows back and forth between reading and writing. However, they do set aside time for independent reading and writing. In independent reading, students read self-selected materials and confer with the teachers, who may also conduct running records or use some similar form of assessing how students are progressing. Independent writing still occurs during writers' workshop, but guided and shared writing may be scheduled for a separate time called literacy block. Because there are many fine teacher resources available on readers' and writers' workshops and myriad possible organizational structures, this chapter focuses only on the instruction associated with inquiry and nonfiction.

Readers' Workshop

As we explained in Chapter 2, readers' workshop is a daily block of 60 to 90 minutes in which primary reading instruction occurs. The workshop may include an instructional read aloud, shared reading, guided reading, reading and writing discovery circles, independent reading of self-selected nonfiction books, extension activities, and word-level work. Depending on your schedule, some approaches will occur daily while others may occur two or three times per week. For example, you may only do discovery circles three times a week, while shared and guided reading may occur daily. The workshop may begin with an instructional read aloud and shared reading lesson and then lead to word-level work. The teacher may follow that with independent reading and/or a guided reading group, while other students work independently on inquiry projects or extension activities. This may be followed by discovery circles.

Writers' Workshop

The organization of writers' workshop is somewhat less varied than readers' workshop. Students write on assigned or self-selected topics associated with content areas. The block usually begins with modeled writing or other types of mini-lessons, followed by students working independently or occasionally in pairs or small groups on inquiry projects, while the teacher confers with small groups and/or individuals. During this time the teacher may also provide a guided writing session for a small group of students with a similar need. The workshop usually ends with a ten-minute large-group share session where some students read their writing and receive feedback from the class. As students work on inquiry projects, they may also be reading nonfiction as they collect needed information.

Moving Toward Independence in Readers' and Writers' Workshops

Many intermediate-level teachers we know state that their students have had little exposure to reading and writing nonfiction, aside from the occasional report. This would not be the case if we open our readers' and writers' workshops to content subject matter—that is, include time in workshops to do some of the reading and writing associated with science and social studies units. This also means using nonfiction across the framework—expanding mini-lessons to include reading and writing nonfiction; including close readings and rereadings of informational text in shared and guided reading; addressing in interactive, shared, and guided writing the how's of writing nonfiction; and using nonfiction in discovery circles to collaboratively read, discuss, and complete written products. It also means providing time in the readers' and writers' workshops for students to research topics, and to read and write pieces from their social studies and science units so they can take the work through the process and receive teacher and peer support.

Providing Time for Inquiry in Readers' and Writers' Workshops

Trying to schedule the day consistently in blocks of time may ensure that students receive a comprehensive literacy program, but it may not always support students' inquiry work. Inquiry involves both reading and writing. When we are gathering information, we both read and take notes. As we write, we read notes, refer again to resources, and seek out new sources as we shape our text. When your students are conducting an inquiry project, consider reorganizing your readers' and writers' workshops so the time is seamless or extend writers' workshop. This allows students to work longer if they wish. Uninterrupted time is invaluable and will support both their work and your time to meet with them as they create products.

The Benefits of Readers' and Writers' Workshops

When using the comprehensive framework, the benefits accumulate as we move from one approach to another. Students are acquiring more knowledge, gaining control of reading, talking about and writing nonfiction features and products, and learning to work together as they participate in discovery circles and as they conduct inquiry. Because scaffolding is modified in readers' and writers' workshops, many of the benefits are similar to those already mentioned in earlier approaches and discovery circles, such as working together, learning how to solve problems, reading and writing text from different perspectives, risk taking, and assuming more responsibility for self-assessing as well as allowing the teacher to focus on assessing progress. In addition, readers' and writers' workshops offer students the opportunity to work independently as they apply what they learned to:

- Self-select their topic.
- Select resources for gathering information.
- Read independently and choose when to seek help with reading.
- Select the product and its organization for reporting their findings to others.
- Write independently and choose when to seek help with writing.
- Use rubrics to self-assess their independent work.
- Share their products with others.

What Is Independent Instruction?
Students Practice/Teacher Observes and Assesses

Even though students work independently during readers' and writers' workshops, support is available from the teacher and other students. It is during extension activities, such as seat work and center work following an explanation of the task, that we withdraw support so students can

Independent Instruction: Quick Points

- **Purpose:** To allow students to practice on their own—either individually, in pairs, or in small groups—reading, writing, and/or talking about content and nonfiction features.
- **Kinds of Independent Instruction:** Extension activities that involve reading, writing, and discussion
- **Scaffolding Level:** Lowest
- **Student Role/Teacher Role:** Students practice/teacher observes and assesses independent practice activities. The teacher briefly and explicitly shows students how to complete the extension activity, followed by them completing the task on their own during seat-work or center time. Following the activity, the teacher may quickly debrief with students. Depending upon the activity, findings may also be shared with guided reading groups or the entire class.
- **Instructional Context:** Typically done with individual students, pairs of students, or small groups of students. Activities are usually done in seats or at centers. Individual activities range from 5 to 20 minutes depending on purpose, the age and grade of students, length of the reading and writing tasks, and content.
- **Types of Materials Typically Used:** Multiple copies of informational texts often connected with an ongoing unit of content study or work with the nonfiction feature, such as nonfiction books, commercial instructional materials, magazine selections, and consumable materials such as sticky notes, worksheets, or graphic organizers for recording information.
- **Next Steps:** Products from extension activities are assessed to determine what additional instruction or practice is needed. The teacher may briefly review the work with the students or provide additional explicit instruction.

practice the strategies and understandings about types and features of nonfiction they are learning. We provide opportunities for students to practice pointing out, naming, and explaining the use of reading and writing nonfiction features and conducting limited inquiry on their own.

However, students may work with others in pairs and small groups to accomplish these tasks. Sharing the task gives students opportunities to practice working with others and constructing understandings together. It also supports the social work skills needed for discovery circles and workshops as well as life. For these reasons we recommend that you use a variety of extension activities, some done independently and some with peers. Extension activities are designed to provide additional practice with new strategies and understandings about reading and writing nonfiction. See Figure 9.4 for where independent instruction and extension activities fall on the comprehensive framework.

Independent Practice: Extension Activities for Reading and Writing

Opportunities to practice and extend new understandings learned during the instructional approaches are essential. We all know how quickly we forget new information and strategies when there aren't opportunities to apply them. In addition, the extensions are excellent learning-center and seat-work activities for students to engage in during guided reading time while you work with small groups. Extensions also support or help to expand new understandings and foster students' incorporation of them in writing.

Designing Extension Activities

Extension activities help your students practice new understandings, but what you choose for activities is dependent upon what your students know about reading and writing. You need to plan the practice work so it does not require new reading and writing skills or design your instruction so it integrates with the extension activities.

For example, say you have been reading several books on frogs and toads. You want the students to write a comparison of the two, but have only taught them how to do Venn diagrams. However, you haven't taught them how to transform the Venn diagrams into text. So the learning-center/seat-work activity might be to complete a Venn diagram on frogs and toads to bring to writing class in a couple of days. In the meantime, in writers' workshop, you would model writing a comparison of two items from a Venn diagram you have created. On the following day, using their Venn diagrams, you would do a shared writing lesson comparing frogs to toads. This could be followed by an exten-

Figure 9.4

Comprehensive Framework

Level of Scaffolding	Role of Teacher and Student	Reading Instructional Approach		Writing Instructional Approach
Modeled	• Teacher demonstrates • Students watch	Instructional Read Aloud		Modeled Writing
Shared	• Teacher leads • Students apprentice	Shared Reading		Interactive Writing and Shared Writing
Guided	• Students demonstrate • Teacher assists	Guided Reading		Guided Writing
Modified	• Students work collaboratively • Teacher modifies support by observing, helping, assessing	Reading Discovery Circles		Writing Discovery Circles
	• Students work independently, with other students, and/or with the teacher • Teacher modifies support by observing, helping, assessing	Readers' Workshop	Mini-Lessons and Extension Activities*	Writers' Workshop
Independent	• Students practice • Teacher observes and assesses independent practice activities	Extension Activities*		Extension Activities*

* Extension activities can be used as follow-up activities with all instructional approaches, but students are working independently—either individually or in small groups. Keep in mind that extension activities should match the student's ability to practice the activities independently.

The Benefits of Extension Activities

Extension activities give students the opportunity to practice what they have learned throughout the comprehensive framework. They:

- Encourage students' independence and allow them to immediately apply new strategies and understandings of content and reading and writing of nonfiction.
- Reinforce the use of literacy strategies and understandings of nonfiction features by requiring students to repeat activities similar to those completed in the group setting.
- Encourage students to interact in meaningful problem-solving, thinking, or reading and writing tasks that may have a playful or engaging quality.
- Allow the teacher to focus on small-group work, such as guided reading, and contribute to effective classroom management.
- Provide assessment of students' understandings of new concepts and allow the teacher to plan next steps.

sion activity requiring students to complete a comparison using a Venn diagram and writing a comparison on a new topic.

For early primary grades, extensions are adjusted to higher scaffolded approaches that match students' needs. For example you might need to do the Venn diagram as a group or in small groups. Follow this lesson with an interactive or shared writing with the students to create text. The point is that the decisions for extending learning by using learning centers and seat work needs to be based on what you know your students can do. As you review our examples, think about how you could modify them to ensure you scaffold the extension work to match your students' level of content knowledge, reading, and writing. We offer suggestions of how to extend understandings through identification activities, through retelling, and through innovations that transform nonfiction from one structure or style to another.

Ways to Extend Understanding Through Identification

The first steps in learning to notice are pointing out features and naming them. In centers or during seat work, provide nonfiction books, copies of pages of books (either multiple copies or laminated), or other informational resources. After introducing a type or feature in a nonfiction book during an instructional read aloud or shared reading, ask the students to:

- Sort books by type or purpose.
- Sort books by organizational features.
- Label specific parts of words or signal words in the text, using sticky notes, Wikki Stix®, or, if the text is laminated, washable transparency markers.
- Work either in pairs or independently, using the books they have read, to label diagrams associated with the topic.

Sue Pidhurney, working with her multiage first- and second-grade class, set up a nonfiction research center. After reading aloud several books on dental health, she asked students to use one of the books to complete activity sheets. She required students to label a diagram of a tooth, tell what the various teeth are used for, and identify vocabulary words associated with dental health. (See Figure 9.5.)

Name _____

Dental Health

1. Use the nonfiction books at the center.
2. Find a cross section of a tooth.
3. Label the parts of the tooth.

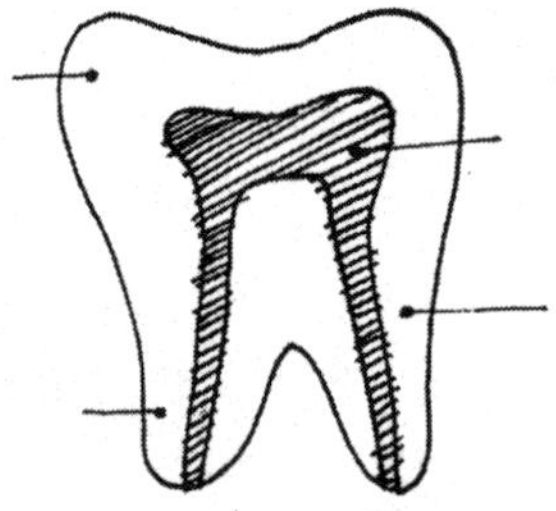

Which book did you use?

Title: _____

Author: _____

Figure 9.5: Sue's worksheet for labeling the parts of a tooth.

Ways to Extend Understanding Through Retelling

Opportunities to retell are an important part of internalizing integrated information as well as learning how to select the important information to share or summarize—key skills in doing inquiry. Students learn to acquire retelling skills initially during the instructional read aloud. Retelling can occur in oral, written, or visual form and from hearing, reading, or viewing a text independently (Brown & Cambourne, 1987). As students develop independence in retelling, this activity can be used as an extension in small groups or individually. This can be done in several ways:

- In a small group or in pairs, following a teacher or student read aloud, ask students to retell what they heard to one another. If the nonfiction piece is long or contains several subtopics, focus the retelling on one subtopic or explanation. Expand this extension by having students list the pages that support their points.

- Have students work in small groups to compose a sentence about what they thought was important to remember from the book read. Ask the children to share their ideas either in their guided reading group or with the entire class. As a group, note which ideas are repeated. Discuss the implications of why certain ideas were selected and/or repeated. Connect back to the text to examine from a language and structural perspective what the author did that caused some ideas to be emphasized and recalled by readers.

- Extend the retelling by putting the ideas on sentence strips—decide together how to order the information. As the group works on the tasks, encourage them to think of what headings they would use for similar or chunked information.

- Create visual representations of information heard or read, retell, or write a description of the visual—for example, describing in writing a process or life cycle.

- Put in sequential order a series of drawings depicting a process or life cycle.

Ways to Extend Understanding Through Innovations

Adding, transforming, or manipulating text or visuals into other structures or forms supports increased understanding of the thinking processes involved in presenting information in various types of structures for different purposes. It also reinforces students' understanding of the types and features of nonfiction and increases a sense of audience and how to manage information for different purposes and readers. In addition, reading and writing connections are strengthened.

1. Students can benefit by learning how to add new information using language, text structures, organization, and layout of the book. They can:

- Write a table of contents page, index, glossary, or additional glossary entry for a book where the item is not included.

- Create headings and subheadings in text where there were none.
- Add captions or labels written on sticky notes for visual information.
- Add within the running text definitions using a variety of strategies, such as putting the definition in parentheses, placing the definition or explanation of the word in the text prior to the word or following it in later text, or creating a sidebar that includes the definition.
- Add to the glossary a definition for key terms found in the text but not included in the original glossary.
- Write about their own experiences with the topic and add that as an introduction or item in the appendix.
- Add other entries based on the structure of the book, such as an acknowledgment, dedication, author's notes, introduction, sidebar, etc.
- Present the information through other graphic forms, such as diagrams, time lines, flow charts, or, conversely, by writing text that explains or replaces these visuals.
- Write questions that could be the basis of further research.

2. Transforming text into new forms is also beneficial. In this process, students use the language and concepts of the information, but also have to cope with using new structures. They can:
   - Change a paragraph of information into a sidebar of bulleted information or vice versa.
   - Use the glossary definition, rewrite the definition and incorporate the meaning of the word into the text within the same sentence or the next one.
   - Use a description of process to create a flow diagram.
   - Identify important information in the running text and create a summary for the end of that text.

Carrying Out the Classroom Inquiry:
Bringing It All Together, From Instructional
Read Alouds to Workshops

Clearly, the instructional task at hand is more than doing an instructional read aloud, exploring a nonfiction book in depth through shared reading, or using nonfiction in guided reading and independent reading. We have to bring it all together with the inquiry process. At the same time, we need to scaffold that learning, whether it involves understanding the content, learning how to read and write nonfiction, or learning how to engage in inquiry. Planning for such instruction needs to be deliberately engineered to ensure continuous success as students mature in the inquiry process. Berenice Knight's butterfly inquiry with second graders presented at the beginning of this chapter is an excellent example of how a teacher can bring together the comprehensive framework and workshops to successfully scaffold students' learning. We offer you three other examples of how teachers plan for the year and bring it all together.

Tracking Mini-Lessons in Third Grade

Shelly Moody and Jody Workman work together to plan their third graders' instruction in nonfiction. Early in the process, they found that they wanted to be able to keep track of:

- What they had taught about features.
- What children's literature they had used.
- Guiding questions they used to initiate the discussion.
- How they had modeled the instruction.
- Next steps they planned for the students.

Because the nonfiction instruction was spread over the year and time was split between fiction and nonfiction, they developed a chart to record their lessons. (See next page.) To match their 6+1 traits of writing assessment (Culham, 2003) for each trait they created a list of children's books to use as examples.

Creating a Plan for the School Year in Fourth Grade

Janet Nordfors, a fourth-grade teacher, has worked with nonfiction for several years. Her program has evolved from doing a unit on nonfiction features to a more integrated plan for the year. Her language arts instruction occurs in a 90-minute block, five days each week, and includes integrated reading, writing, and oral communication. A typical workshop session includes a mini-lesson, status of the class, reading, writing, and sharing. Independent reading is later in the day. Her plan was also designed to match her state's standards.

Janet begins the fall language arts instruction focused first on comprehension strategies. She states that her students' foundation in reading strategies is varied, but many lack explicit instruction in comprehension strategies for nonfiction and how to read and write nonfiction. Over the years she has learned that she needs to first put emphasis on the comprehension strategies before addressing features of nonfiction. Otherwise, her students are stuck at pointing out, naming, and describing how nonfiction is used, but comprehension of the information is limited, as is conducting inquiry.

Nonfiction Mini-Lesson Planning Form

Topic	Guiding Questions	Children's Literature	Method of Modeling	Next Steps for Students

However, she does start the year with nonfiction instructional read alouds spreading the reading of each nonfiction book over several days. One successful strategy is to leave the book available to students between the read aloud sessions. Her students browse the book and often come back to the next read aloud with questions and comments of things they've noticed. By the end of September, students are ready to embark successfully upon looking hard and deep at the nonfiction features and using them in shared reading lessons, while also comprehending the information. Like the teachers described at the end of Chapter 3, Janet has her students create a nonfiction glossary called Guide to Nonfiction Books, but her goal is to read and write the nonfiction, not just identify features. As students become more competent at reading nonfiction, she engages them in short-term experiences on how to gather information for an inquiry and create a product.

Because many of the students have not written much nonfiction, Janet starts off the year by having the students write mini nonfiction books of one or two pages. These short research projects are well within reach of the students and she builds in lots of support. She has students go through three stages to learn how to write their own nonfiction books, with students taking on increasing responsibility with each stage. In the first stage Janet selects the topic and the source. In stage two, students choose a topic from a unit of study in social studies or science and use a few resources that the whole class has already studied. By stage three, students work with any topic from the books used in the nonfiction genre study. After creating three mini-books, students move on to a longer inquiry project in which they choose a topic, make a web, and, using their Guide to Nonfiction Books as a reference about nonfiction features, create their own nonfiction book on a topic of choice.

In stage one, the students work on the topic of fossils, part of the third-grade curriculum. With their reading buddies, they read a short nonfiction article from *National Geographic Kids* magazine entitled "SuperCroc" by Peter Winkler (March, 2002), which is about a recently discovered fossil named Sarcosuchus. They highlight the key points on a photocopy of the article, which is an important skill. Think about how, as adults, we find it useful to either highlight our texts or photocopy materials so that we can mark specific points directly on the page. If your students are working with nonconsumable materials such as library books, they need alternative ways to identify key points. If they are identifying a key point on one page of text, use Wikki Stix®. For several pages of text, use highlighter tape that can be removed or narrow sticky notes along the margins to direct the reader to key points.

With lots of guidance (e.g., modeled writing mini-lessons, guided writing lessons, and much talk), the students create a draft of the important information and experiment with adding sidebars, maps, and diagrams. After conferencing over the rough draft in writers' workshop, the students create the teaching page, including visuals and the bibliography. (See Figure 9.6.)

This first experience is followed by stage two, choosing a topic from a science or social studies unit, and stage three, a genre study, with similar support, but students are increasingly given more choice on topic.

Following their work with the mini-books, students were ready to tackle a longer piece. Here is a sample of the books they created: *Dolphins; All About Spider Monkeys; Blue Whales: Giants of the Deep; The Human Digestive System; The Nintendo Gaming World;* and *Sea Turtles*. They developed unique titles and covers, title pages, dedications, tables of contents—often using their research questions as headings, sidebars for unusual information, and illustrations with captions. Janet showed them how to download or photocopy important photographs and did modeled writing lessons on photo credits and bibliographies.

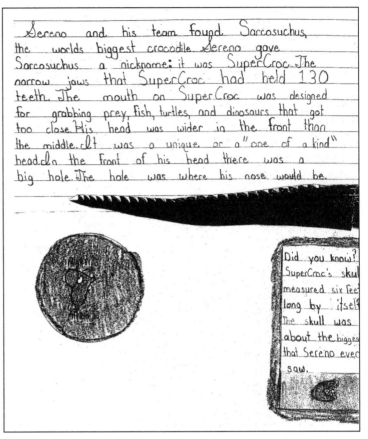

Figure 9.6: A page from Kayla's "SuperCroc" report, which contains an interesting fact in a sidebar entitled "Did You Know?"

Helping students accomplish these longer nonfiction works meant also assisting students in how to be organized. These are emergent researchers and they have much to learn. Janet uses three forms to keep her students moving forward: Writing a Nonfiction Book, Process Checklist, and Required Features Form. (See next three pages.)

To help students take an active role in assessment, Janet developed a scoring rubric that required students to assess themselves as well as be assessed by the teacher. (See page 264.) Like Janet's plan for the year, this assessment has evolved and will continue to evolve. As more teachers in her school focus on nonfiction reading and writing and inquiry, her program will shift to accommodate the changing needs of her students. As the year draws to a close students will share their nonfiction pieces at the grand finale: an "author's tea" in the evening, with families as guests.

Nonfiction in Focus

Writing a Nonfiction Book

Name _____   Topic _____

TIPS FOR SUCCESS:

- Stay organized by keeping everything in your writing folder.

- Use your Guide to Nonfiction Books as a resource.

- You do not have to do all of your own artwork. You may use photocopies, pictures from the Internet, or photographs, or you can ask a friend to do the drawing. If you use someone else's work, you must include photo or picture credits.

- Neatness counts. You may type or print your work, but it must be neat and easy to read. Remember, you will be sharing your work with others.

- Use the Process Checklist! Write in the date as you complete each task. Do each step in order and get your teacher's initials each time you have a conference.

- Remember to use the experts in the room. Think about asking students who can help you.

- Always leave a 1-inch margin on all four sides of your paper.

- Use colored pencils, not markers.

- Review this handout frequently.

- Pay attention to the rubric so that you can determine your grade before you finish.

- Bring your writing folder, this paper, and all other writing materials to every conference.

- Hand in your complete Process Checklist and Required Features Form with your book.

- Do your personal best!

Process Checklist

Complete the process in order. Do not skip steps. Keep this handout in your writing folder.

DATE
COMPLETED

TEACHER
INITIALS

_____ I made a web that includes several "big" questions about my topic.

_____ I conferenced with the teacher. (Bring folder and web.) _____

_____ I used an index card or other organizer to write summary notes for each question.

_____ I wrote the bibliography information on the "Ingredients" handout.

_____ I used 3 different types of resources.

_____ I conferenced with the teacher. (Bring folder, 3 resources, and cards.) _____

_____ I made a mock-up, draft, or storyboard for the layout of my book.

_____ I conferenced with the teacher. (Bring everything.) _____

_____ I used my notes to write first draft paragraphs and conventions.

_____ I proofread for mechanics, spelling, grammar, etc.

_____ I also asked _____ to proofread.

_____ I conferenced with the teacher. (Discuss editing, title, and cover design.) _____

_____ I typed or wrote the text neatly, making revisions when necessary.

_____ I completed all required features.

_____ I gave my book an interesting title.

_____ I designed a creative cover for my book.

_____ I conferenced with the teacher. (Discuss finished product.) _____

_____ I handed in my finished book.

_____ I AM PROUD OF MYSELF! YEAH! HIP-HIP HOORAY!

Required Features Form

Features do not have to be created in order. Date each one as you complete it.

_____	About the Author	_____	Bibliography
_____	Sidebar	_____	Table of Contents
_____	Dedication	_____	Title Page
_____	Captions	_____	Acknowledgments
_____	Cover	_____	Glossary
_____	Introduction	_____	Text w/Heading and Subheadings

VISUALS

Choose 3 different visuals from the box below. Write the date when you finish it, the type of visual, and the page on which it appears.

time line	cartoon	blueprint	chart
map	drawing	photograph	diagram with labels
graph with labels			cross section (cutaway)

_____ Visual 1 — on Page _____ Type: _____

_____ Visual 2 — on Page _____ Type: _____

_____ Visual 3 — on Page _____ Type: _____

OPTIONAL FEATURES

You will be given extra credit as long as all other requirements are complete. Put the page number on the line next to those that you create.

_____	Index	_____	Author's Research Notes
_____	Picture Credits	_____	Glossary
_____	Verso Page	_____	Photo Credits
_____	Transparent Overlay	_____	Flow Chart (cause and effect)
_____	Recommended Reading	_____	Scale Diagram or Comparison
_____	Activities, Experiments, or Quizzes	_____	Other Resources

Nonfiction Book Scoring Rubric

Fantastic   5 points— I did my very best work. My work is complete, colorful, accurate, and creative.

Very Good   4 points— I mostly did my best work. I showed good effort on this part of the book.

Average   3 points— This is average work. I could have done a bit more work, if I'd wanted to.

Needs Improvement   2 points— This is not good work for me. I could have done much better if I'd tried harder.

Poor   1 point— I didn't try very hard. I did very little work. I could do much better than this.

Missing   0 points— Not done at all.

	My scores	My scores after conferencing	Teacher scores
About the Author p. _____			
Bibliography p. _____			
Sidebar p. _____			
Table of Contents p. _____			
Dedication Page p. _____			
Title Page p. _____			
Captions p. _____			
Acknowledgments p. _____			
Cover p. _____			
Introduction p. _____			
Visual 1 p. _____ _____			
Visual 2 p. _____ _____			
Visual 3 p. _____ _____			
Glossary p. _____			
Text With Headings p. _____			
TOTALS			

These final nonfiction books are completed primarily during workshop time with some support as needed. The thoughtfully planned scaffolded instruction pays off as students conference with one another and use nonfiction books and other materials as models for their research and writing.

Creating an After-School Writer's Guild

Judy Bouchard's fifth graders want in on a special voluntary after-school project called the Nonfiction Writer's Guild. The seeds for this project were sown the day that a couple of her students remarked that there just wasn't enough time to read all the books they wanted to read and write all they wanted to write! Judy took those comments to heart and created a very special way to make more time in the day. Her Nonfiction Writers' Guild is a variation of the after-school book club, like the kind we described in Chapter 8.

This is how Judy's Nonfiction Writer's Guild works. At bimonthly meetings after school, Guild members meet in small writing groups to share their work and have writing time. At the end of the school year, each Guild member has his or her writing published in a hardcover book and shared at an author's celebration for family and friends. Their final work is a nonfiction book complete with endpapers designed to reflect the content of the book, snappy title, dedication, verso page, introduction, and many features we expect to find in well-written nonfiction, such as crisp, clear, and interesting writing, attractive page layout, diagrams, interviews, a "Did you Know?" page, and bibliographies. (See Figures 9.7 through 9.9.)

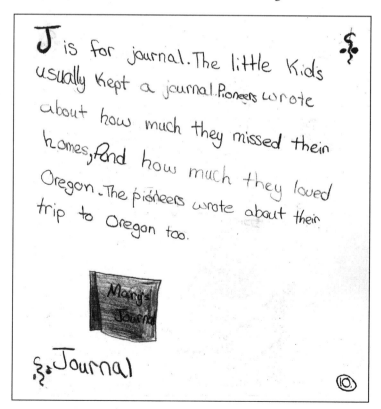

Figure 9.7: A page from a student's ABC book on the Oregon Trail.

Figures 9.8 (left) and 9.9: Examples from nonfiction books created by fifth graders.

Sample titles of their nonfiction books include: *For Girls That Are Bored!; Record Breaking Roller Coasters; Foods and Sweets Are the Real Deal; The Inside-Outside Book of Saxophones;* and *The Amazing Great Wall.*

How Do Students Become Accomplished Nonfiction Writers?

We have to look no further than their teachers to see how students become good nonfiction writers. Teachers work hard from the beginning of the school year to "marinate" their students in good nonfiction. They read aloud high-quality nonfiction so that students develop an ear for how good expository writing sounds. Their lessons about reading and writing nonfiction scaffold their learners so they feel accomplished with what they can do all along the way. Of course, they work on other genres as well, but their concentrated efforts all across the school year on nonfiction help their students build momentum for their learning. These teachers know that the impressive products their students create emerge slowly from consistent and scaffolded instruction in reading and writing nonfiction.

Nonfiction in Focus

Closing Thoughts:
Guiding Principles That Bring Teaching and Learning Nonfiction Together in a Comprehensive • Literacy Framework

Fifth grader Nathan says in the introduction to the nonfiction book he wrote called *The Amazing Great Wall,* "I love to do nonfiction because it makes my brain pump and so does this book. I hope it inspires you the way it does me." Nathan is not only excited about reading and writing nonfiction, he knows a lot about doing both. How do we make that happen for our students? The teachers we've talked with repeatedly say that it's important to continually reflect on assumptions about learning and teaching. They say that it's critical to have colleagues with whom you can share practices and ideas, and who are willing to grow and make changes in their teaching. They say that while their students conduct inquiries, it's essential that as teachers they also be engaged in their own reading and writing on topics that interest them. They say that good solid learning takes time; that to read and write nonfiction well means a commitment to teaching that supports learners all the way through the process. All of these things inform how to help students become powerfully engaged and knowledgeable readers and writers of nonfiction. In closing, we offer some guiding principles to bring it all together. (See next page.)

Guiding Principles for
Bringing It All Together

Make a commitment to:

Active, engaged, and informed teaching

- Learn about nonfiction yourself.
- Design your teaching so that it shows students how to "unpack" expository reading and writing.
- Encourage students to show you what they know about how nonfiction "works."
- Strike a sense of balance between teaching content and what students need to know about inquiry and reading and writing nonfiction.

Reading aloud nonfiction

- Share high-quality nonfiction books for the pleasure of hearing well-crafted expository writing, but don't stop there. Plan read alouds to be teaching opportunities—introducing students to how nonfiction works.

Teaching students to become strategic nonfiction readers

- Show students how to navigate nonfiction—what to expect from reading different types of nonfiction, how to determine organizational structures, how to read and understand visual information—through instructional read alouds, shared and guided reading experiences, discovery circle reading, and independent reading in readers' workshop.

Planning opportunities for students to share and talk about what they are learning

- Encourage lots of discussion about what students discover about nonfiction books.
- Invite students to see that talking and sharing with one another is a way to figure out what they understand about a topic. Sharing and talking in small groups about how their writing is going provides necessary feedback and opportunities for students to revisit their writing.

Teaching students to become effective nonfiction writers

- Write your own nonfiction book on a topic to make you more aware of your inquiry process and how what you know about expository text shapes your nonfiction writing.
- Teach students the craft of nonfiction writing through modeled, shared, interactive, and guided and modified instruction.

Appendix A
Orbis Pictus Award-Winning Books, Honor Books, and Notable Books, 1990–2003

Each year, the Orbis Pictus Committee of the National Council of Teachers of English chooses a best nonfiction title for that year, along with honor and notable books. Criteria for these awards are based on accuracy, organization, design, style, and appropriateness for K–8 classrooms. This is a list of Orbis Pictus award-winning books (AW), honor books (HB), and notable books, organized by author. See *Making Facts Come Alive: Choosing & Using Nonfiction Literature K–8, Second Edition* (Bamford & Kristo, 2003) for an annotated bibliography of these books from 1990 to 2002.

Adler, David A. (1989). *We Remember the Holocaust*

Adler, David A. (2000a). *America's Champion Swimmer: Gertrude Ederle* (HB)

Adler, David A. (2000b). *At Her Majesty's Request: An African Princess in Victorian England* (HB)

Adler, David A. (2001). *B. Franklin, Printer*

Alexander, Sally Hobart. (1990). *Mom Can't See Me*

Aliki. (1989). *The King's Day: Louis XIV of France*

Aliki. (1999). *William Shakespeare & the Globe*

Ancona, George. (1989). *The American Farm Family*

Andronik, Catherine M. (2001). *Hatshepsut: His Majesty, Herself*

Apfel, Necia H. (1991). *Voyager to the Planets*

Armstrong, Jennifer. (1998). *Shipwreck at the Bottom of the World: The Extraordinary True Story of Shackleton and the Endurance* (AW)

Arnosky, Jim. (1996). *Nearer Nature*

Arnosky, Jim. (2000). *Wild and Swampy* (HB)

Ashabranner, Brent. (1996). *A Strange and Distant Shore: Indians of the Great Plains in Exile*

Bartoletti, Susan Campbell. (1996). *Growing Up in Coal Country*

Bartoletti, Susan Campbell. (1999). *Kids on Strike!*

Bartoletti, Susan Campbell. (2001). *Black Potatoes: The Story of the Great Irish Famine 1845–1850* (AW)

Bash, Barbara. (1993). *Shadows of Night: The Hidden World of the Little Brown Bat*

Bash, Barbara. (1994). *Ancient Ones: The World of the Old-Growth Douglas Fir*

Bateman, Robert, & Archbold, Rick. (1998). *Safari*

Bausum, Ann. (2000). *Dragon Bones and Dinosaur Eggs: A Photobiography of Explorer Roy Chapman Andrews*

Beil, Karen Magnuson. (1999). *Fire in Their Eyes: Wildfires and the People Who Fight Them*

Bial, Raymond. (1995). *The Underground Railroad*

Bial, Raymond. (1996). *With Needle and Thread: A Book About Quilts*

Bial, Raymond. (2000). *A Handful of Dirt*

Bial, Raymond. (2002). *Tenement: Immigrant Life on the Lower East Side* (HB)

Blumberg, Rhoda. (1989). *The Great American Gold Rush* (HB)

Blumberg, Rhoda. (1991). *The Remarkable Voyages of Captain Cook*

Blumberg, Rhoda. (1996). *Full Steam Ahead: The Race to Build a Transcontinental Railroad* (HB)

Blumberg, Rhoda. (1998). *What's the Deal? Jefferson, Napoleon and the Louisiana Purchase*

Brandenburg, Jim. (1993). *To the Top of the World: Adventures With Arctic Wolves* (HB)

Bridges, Ruby. (1999). *Through My Eyes* (AW)

Brooks, Bruce. (1993). *Making Sense: Animal Perception and Communication* (HB)

Brown, Mary Barrett. (1992). *Wings Along the Waterway*

Burleigh, Robert. (1991). *Flight: The Journey of Charles Lindbergh* (AW)

Burleigh, Robert. (1998). *Black Whiteness: Admiral Byrd Alone in the Antarctic* (HB)

Busenberg, Bonnie. (1994). *Vanilla, Chocolate, & Strawberry: The Story of Your Favorite Flavors*

Calabro, Marian. (1989). *Operation Grizzly Bear*

Calmenson, Stephanie. (1994). *Rosie: A Visiting Dog's Story*

Carrick, Carol. (1993). *Whaling Day*

Cha, Dia. (1996). *Dia's Story Cloth: The Hmong People's Journey of Freedom*

Chester, Jonathan. (2002). *Young Adventurer's Guide to Everest: From Avalanche to Zopkio*

Cole, Joanna. (1990). *The Magic School Bus Lost in the Solar System*

Collard, Sneed B., III. (1997). *Animal Dads*

Colman, Penny. (1995). *Rosie the Riveter: Women Working on the Home Front in World War II* (HB)

Cone, Molly. (1992). *Come Back, Salmon: How a Group of Dedicated Kids Adopted Pigeon Creek and Brought It Back to Life* (HB)

Conlan, K. E. (2002). *Under the Ice*

Conrad, Pam. (1991). *Prairie Visions: The Life and Times of Solomon Butcher* (HB)

Cooper, Floyd. (1996). *Mandela: From the Life of the South African Statesman*

Cooper, llene. (1997). *The Dead Sea Scrolls*

Corey, Shana. (2000). *You Forgot Your Skirt, Amelia Bloomer! A Very Improper Story*

Cox, Clinton. (1997). *Fiery Vision: The Life and Death of John Brown*

Cummings, Pat (Ed). (1992). *Talking With Artists: Conversations with Victoria Chess, Pat Cummings, Leo and Diane Dillon, Richard Egielski, Lois Ehlert, Lisa Campbell Ernst, Tom Feelinus, Steven Kellogg, Jerry Pinkney, Amy Schwartz, Lane Smith, Chris Van Allsburg, and David Wiesner* (HB)

Curlee, Lynn. (1999). *Rushmore*

Curlee, Lynn. (2000). *Liberty*

Curlee, Lynn. (2001). *Brooklyn Bridge*

Davidson, Rosemary. (1994). *Take a Look: An Introduction to the Experience of Art*

Demi. (2001). *Gandhi*

Dewey, Jennifer Owings. (1994). *Wildlife Rescue: The Work of Dr. Kathleen Ramsay* (HB)

Donoghue, Carol. (1999). *The Mystery of the Hieroglyphics: The Story of the Rosetta Stone and the Race to Decipher Egyptian Hieroglyphs*

Dorros, Arthur. (1997). *A Tree Is Growing* (HB)

Dowden, Anne Ophelia. (1990). *The Clover & the Bee: A Book of Pollination*

Ekoomiak, Normee. (1990). *Arctic Memories* (HB)

Fisher, Leonard Evertt. (1990). *The Oregon Trail*

Fleischman, John. (2002). *Phineas Gage: A Gruesome but True Story About Brain Science* (HB)

Fleischman, Sid. (1996). *The Abracadabra Kid: A Writer's Life*

Fradin, Dennis Brindell. (1996). *"We Have Conquered Pain": The Discovery of Anesthesia*

Fradin, Dennis Brindell. (1997). *The Planet Hunters: The Search for Other Worlds*

Fradin, Dennis Brindell. (1998). *Samuel Adams: The Father of American Independence*

Fradin, Dennis Brindell. (2002). *The Signers: The 56 Stories Behind the Declaration of Independence*

Fraser, Mary Ann. (1995). *In Search of the Grand Canyon: Down the Colorado with John Wesley Powell*

Freedman, Russell. (1990). *Franklin Delano Roosevelt* (AW)

Freedman, Russell. (1991). *The Wright Brothers: How They Invented the Airplane*

Freedman, Russell. (1992). *An Indian Winter*

Freedman, Russell. (1993). *Eleanor Roosevelt: A Life of Discovery*

Freedman, Russell. (1994). *Kids at Work: Lewis Hine and the Crusade Against Child Labor* (HB)

Freedman, Russell. (1996). *The Life and Death of Crazy Horse* (HB)

Freedman, Russell. (1998). *Martha Graham: A Dancer's Life*

Freedman, Russell. (1999). *Babe Didrikson Zaharias: The Making of a Champion*

Freedman, Russell. (2002). *Confucius: The Golden Rule* (HB)

Fritz, Jean. (1989). *The Great Little Madison* (AW)

Fritz, Jean. (1991). *Bully for You, Teddy Roosevelt!*

Fritz, Jean. (2001). *Leonardo's Horse*

Garland, Sherry. (2000). *Voices of the Alamo*

Gelman, Rita Golden. (1991). *Dawn to Dusk in the Galapagos: Flightless Birds, Swimming Lizards, and Other Fascinating Creatures*

George, Jean Craighead. (1994). *Animals Who Have Won Our Hearts*

George, Jean Craighead. (1995). *Everglades*

Gherman, Beverly. (2000). *Norman Rockwell: Storyteller With a Brush*

Gherman, Beverly. (2002). *Ansel Adams: America's Photographer*

Gibbons, Gail. (1992). *The Great St. Lawrence Seaway*

Giblin, James Cross. (1990). *The Riddle of the Rosetta Stone*

Giblin, James Cross. (1993). *Be Seated: A Book About Chairs*

Giblin, James Cross. (1995). *When Plague Strikes: The Black Death, Smallpox, AIDS*

Giblin, James Cross. (1997). *Charles Lindbergh: A Human Hero* (HB)

Giblin, James Cross. (2000). *The Amazing Life of Benjamin Franklin* (HB)

Gillette, J. Lynett. (1997). *Dinosaur Ghosts: The Mystery of Coelophysis*

Gottfried, Ted. (2000). *Nazi Germany: The Face of Tyranny*

Govenar, Alan. (2000). *Osceola: Memories of a Sharecropper's Daughter* (HB)

Greenberg, Jan, & Jordan, Sandra. (1991). *The Painter's Eye: Learning to Look at Contemporary American Art*

Greenberg, Jan, & Jordan, Sandra. (2000). *Frank O. Gehry: Outside In*

Greenberg, Jan, & Jordan, Sandra. (2001). *Vincent van Gogh: Portrait of an Artist*

Hamanaka, Sheila, & Ohmi, Ayano. (1999). *In Search of the Spirit: The Living National Treasures of Japan*

Hamilton, Virginia. (1993). *Many Thousand Gone: African Americans From Slavery to Freedom*

Hampton, Wilborn. (1997). *Kennedy Assassinated! The World Mourns: A Reporter's Story* (HB)

Harrison, Barbara, & Terris, Daniel. (1992). *A Twilight Struggle: The Life of John Fitzgerald Kennedy*

Haskins, James, & Benson, Kathleen. (1999). *Bound for America: The Forced Migration of Africans to the New World*

Henderson, Douglas. (2000). *Asteroid Impact*

Holmes, Thom. (1998). *Fossil Feud: The Rivalry of the First American Dinosaur Hunters* (HB)

Hoyt-Goldsmith, Diane. (1990). *Totem Pole*

Hoyt-Goldsmith, Diane. (1991). *Pueblo Storyteller*

Hunt, Jonathan. (1989). *Illuminations*

Jacobs, Francine. (1992). *The Tainos: The People Who Welcomed Columbus*

Jaffe, Steven H. (1996). *Who Were the Founding Fathers?*

Jenkins, Steve. (1998). *Hottest, Coldest, Highest, Deepest* (HB)

Jenkins, Steve. (1999). *To the Top of the World: Climbing Mount Everest* (HB)

Jenkins, Steve. (2002). *Life on Earth: The Story of Evolution*

Jenkins, Steve, & Page, Robins. (2001). *Animals in Flight*

Johnson, Sylvia A. (1995). *Raptor Rescue! An Eagle Flies Free*

Johnson, Sylvia A. (1999). *Mapping the World* (HB)

Jurmain, Suzanne. (1989). *Once Upon a Horse: A History of Horses and How They Shaped History*

Keegan, Marcia. (1991). *Pueblo Boy: Growing Up in Two Worlds*

Keeler, Patricia A., & McCall, Francis X., Jr. (1995). *Unraveling Fibers*

Nonfiction in Focus

Kerley, Barbara. (2001). *The Dinosaurs of Waterhouse Hawkins: An Illuminating History of Mr. Waterhouse Hawkins, Artist and Lecturer* (HB)

Knight, Amelia Stewart. (1993). *The Way West: Journal of a Pioneer Woman*

Kramer, Stephen. (2001). *Hidden Worlds: Looking Through a Scientist's Microscope*

Krull, Kathleen. (1994). *Lives of Writers: Comedies, Tragedies (And What the Neighbors Thought)*

Kurlansky, Mark. (2001). *The Cod's Tale* (HB)

Lankford, Mary D. (1992). *Hopscotch Around the World*

Lasky, Kathryn. (1990). *Dinosaur Dig*

Lasky, Kathryn. (1992). *Surtsey: The Newest Place on Earth*

Lauber, Patricia. (1989). *The News About Dinosaurs* (HB)

Lauber, Patricia. (1990). *Seeing Earth From Space* (HB)

Lauber, Patricia. (1991). *Summer of Fire: Yellowstone 1988*

Lauber, Patricia. (1994). *Fur, Feather, and Flippers: How Animals Live Where They Do*

Lauber, Patricia. (1996). *Hurricanes: Earth's Mightiest Storms*

Lawrence, Jacob. (1993). *The Great Migration: An American Story*

Lawrence, R. D. (1990). *Wolves*

Levine, Ellen. (2000). *Darkness Over Denmark: The Danish Resistance and the Rescue of the Jews*

Levinson, Nancy Smiler. (1990). *Christopher Columbus: Voyager to the Unknown*

Ling, Mary, & Atkinson, Mary. (1997). *The Snake Book*

Lobel, Anita. (1998). *No Pretty Pictures: A Child of War* (HB)

Lowry, Lois. (1998). *Looking Back: A Book of Memories*

Luenn, Nancy. (1994). *Squish! A Wetland Walk*

Lyons, Mary E. (1997). *Catching the Fire: Philip Simmons, Blacksmith*

Macaulay, David. (1999). *Building the Book: Cathedral*

Maestro, Betsy, & Maestro, Giulio. (1991). *The Discovery of the Americas*

Mann, Elizabeth. (1997). *The Great Wall*

Marcus, Leonard S. (Ed.). (2000). *Author Talk*

Markle, Sandra. (1994). *Science to the Rescue*

Marrin, Albert. (1994). *Unconditional Surrender: U. S. Grant and the Civil War*

Martin, Jacqueline Briggs. (1998). *Snowflake Bentley*

Matthews, Downs. (1989). *Polar Bear Cubs*

Matthews, Tom L. (1998). *Light Shining Through the Mist: A Photobiography of Dian Fossey*

McKissack, Patricia C., & McKissack, Fredrick L. (1994). *Christmas in the Big House, Christmas in the Quarters* (HB)

McMahon, Patricia. (1995). *Listen for the Bus: David's Story*

McMillan, Bruce. (1995). *Summer Ice: Life Along the Antarctic Peninsula*

Meltzer, Milton. (1990). *Columbus and the World Around Him*

Meltzer, Milton. (1992). *The Amazing Potato: A Story in Which the Incas, Conquistadors, Marie Antoinette, Thomas Jefferson, Wars, Famines, Immigrants and French Fries All Play a Part*

Meltzer, Milton. (1993). *Lincoln: In His Own Words*

Meltzer, Milton. (1994). *Cheap Raw Material: How Our Youngest Workers Are Exploited and Abused*

Meltzer, Milton. (Ed.). (1989). *Voices From the Civil War: A Documentary History of the Great American Conflict*

Micklewaith, Lucy. (1999). *A Child's Book of Art: Discover Great Paintings*

Micucci, Charles. (1995). *The Life and Times of the Honeybee*

Miller, Debbie. (2002). *The Great Serum Race: Blazing the Iditarod Trail*

Mochizuki, Ken. (1997). *Passage to Freedom: The Sugihara Story*

Monceaux, Morgan. (1994). *Jazz: My Music, My People*

Montgomery, Sy. (1999). *The Snake Scientist* (HB)

Morimoto, Junko. (1990). *My Hiroshima*

Moser, Barry. (1993). *Fly! A Brief History of Flight Illustrated*

Murphy, Jim. (1992). *The Long Road to Gettysburg*

Murphy, Jim. (1993). *Across America on an Emigrant Train* (AW)

Murphy, Jim. (1995). *The Great Fire* (AW)

Murphy, Jim. (2000). *Pick & Shovel Poet: The Journeys of Pascal D'Angelo*

Myers, Walter Dean. (1991). *Now Is Your Time! The African-American Struggle for Freedom* (HB)

Myers, Walter Dean. (1999). *At Her Majesty's Request: An African Princess in Victorian England*

Norell, Mark A., & Dingus, Lowell. (1999). *A Nest of Dinosaurs: The Story of Oviraptor*

O'Connor, Jane. (2002). *Emperor's Silent Army: Terracotta Warriors of Ancient China* (HB)

Old, Wendie C. (2002). *To Fly: The Story of the Wright Brothers* (HB)

Osborne, Mary Pope. (1990). *The Many Lives of Benjamin Franklin*

Osborne, Mary Pope. (1996). *One World, Many Religions: The Ways We Worship* (HB)

Osofsky, Audrey. (1996). *Free to Dream: The Making of a Poet: Langston Hughes*

Pandell, Karen. (1995). *Learning From the Dalai Lama: Secrets of the Wheel of Time*

Partridge, Elizabeth. (1998). *Restless Spirit: The Life and Work of Dorothea Lange*

Patent, Dorothy Hinshaw. (1989). *Wild Turkey, Tame Turkey*

Paulsen, Gary. (1990). *Wood-Song*

Peet, Bill. (1989). *Bill Peet: An Autobiography*

Pfeffer, Wendy. (1997). *A Log's Life*

Pinkney, Andrea Davis. (1998). *Duke Ellington: The Piano Prince and His Orchestra*

Pringle, Laurence. (1991). *Batman: Exploring the World of Bats*

Pringle, Laurence. (1992). *Antarctica: The Last Unspoiled Continent*

Pringle, Laurence. (1995). *Dolphin Man: Exploring the World of Dolphins* (HB)

Pringle, Laurence. (1995). *Fire in the Forest: A Cycle of Growth and Renewal*

Pringle, Laurence. (1997). *An Extraordinary Life: The Story of a Monarch Butterfly* (AW)

Rappaport, Doreen. (2001). *Martin's Big Words: The Life of Martin Luther King, Jr.* (HB)

Reef, Catherine. (1996). *John Steinbeck*

Reef, Catherine. (2002). *This Our Dark Country: The American Settlers of Liberia*

Reich, Susanna. (1999). *Clara Schumann: Piano Virtuoso* (HB)

Reinhard, Johan. (1998). *Discovering the Inca Ice Maiden: My Adventures on Ampato*

Robbins, Ken. (1995). *Air*

Rockwell, Anne. (2000). *Only Passing Through: The Story of Sojourner Truth*

Rubin, Susan Goldman. (2001). *The Yellow House: Vincent van Gogh & Paul Gauguin Side by Side*

Ryan, Pan Munoz. (2002). *When Marian Sang: The True Recital of Marian Anderson: The Voice of a Century* (AW)

Rylant, Cynthia. (1991). *Appalachia: The Voices of Sleeping Birds*

San Souci, Robert. (1991). *N. C. Wyeth's Pilgrims*

Sattler, Helen Roney. (1989). *Giraffes, the Sentinels of the Savannas*

Sattler, Helen Roney. (1995). *The Book of North American Owls*

Severance, John B. (1999). *Einstein: Visionary Scientist*

Sill, Cathryn. (1999). *About Reptiles: A Guide for Children*

Sills, Leslie. (1989). *Inspirations: Stories About Women Artists*

Simon, Seymour. (1989). *Whales*

Simon, Seymour. (1990). *Oceans*

Simon, Seymour. (1991). *Earthquakes*

Simon, Seymour. (1997). *The Brain: Our Nervous System*

Sis, Peter. (1996). *Starry Messenger: A Book Depicting the Life of a Famous Scientist, Mathematician, Astronomer, Philosopher, Physicist*

Sloan, Christopher. (2000). *Feathered Dinosaurs*

St. George, Judith. (1989). *Panama Canal: Gateway to the World*

Stalcup. Ann. (1998). *On the Home Front: Growing Up in Wartime England*

Stanley, Diane. (1996). *Leonardo da Vinci* (AW)

Stanley, Diane. (1998). *Joan of Arc*

Stanley, Diane. (2000). *Michelangelo* (HB)

Stanley, Diane. (2002). *Saladin: Noble Prince of Islam*

Stanley, Diane, & Vennema, Peter. (1990). *Good Queen Bess: The Story of Elizabeth I of England*

Stanley, Diane, & Vennema, Peter. (1992). *Bard of Avon: The Story of William Shakespeare*

Stanley, Diane, & Vennema, Peter. (1994). *Cleopatra*

Stanley, Jerry. (1992). *Children of the Dust Bowl: The True Story of the School at Weedpatch Camp* (AW)

Stanley, Jerry. (1994). *I Am an American: A True Story of Japanese Internment*

Stanley, Jerry. (1997). *Digger: The Tragic Fate of the California Indians From the Missions to the Gold Rush* (HB)

Stanley, Jerry. (1998). *Frontier Merchants: Lionel and Barron Jacobs and the Jewish Pioneers Who Settled the West*

Stanley, Jerry. (2000). *Hurry Freedom: African Americans in Gold Rush California* (AW)

Swanson, Diane. (1994). *Safari Beneath the Sea: The Wonder World of the North Pacific Coast* (AW)

Switzer, Ellen. (1995). *The Magic of Mozart: The Magic Flute and the Salzburg Marionettes*

Tallchief, Maria, with Wells, Rosemary. (1999). *Tallchief: America's Prima Ballerina*

Thomas, Jane Resh. (1998). *Behind the Mask: The Life of Queen Elizabeth I*

Tillage, Leon Walter. (1997). *Leon's Story*

Toll, Nelly S. (1993). *Behind the Secret Window: A Memoir of a Hidden Childhood During World War II*

Verhoeven, Rian, & van der Rol, Ruud. (1993). *Anne Frank: Beyond the Diary*

Waldman, Neil. (1995). *The Golden City: Jerusalem's 3,000 Years*

Warren, Andrea. (1998). *Pioneer Girl: Growing Up on the Prairie*

Wick, Walter. (1997). *A Drop of Water: A Book of Science and Wonder* (HB)

Wright-Frierson, Virginia. (1996). *A Desert Scrapbook: Dawn to Dusk in the Sonoran Desert*

Zhensun, Zheng, & Low, Alice. (1991). *A Young Painter: The Life and Paintings of Wang Yani—China's Extraordinary Young Artist*

Appendix B
Awards and Annual Lists of Nonfiction Literature

AWARDS

Orbis Pictus Award for Outstanding Nonfiction for Children The Orbis Pictus Award Committee of the National Council of Teachers of English selects an award-winning nonfiction book, honor books, and notables each year. Winners are announced and featured in the October issue of *Language Arts*. www.ncte.org/elem/awards/orbispictus

Robert F. Sibert Informational Book Award This award is granted each year to the most distinguished informational book by the American Library Association's Association of Library Services to Children subgroup. www.ala.org

Washington Post—Children's Book Guild Nonfiction Award This award is granted each November to honor a nonfiction author or author-illustrator team for the totality of his or her work in nonfiction. www.childrensbookguild.org

Boston Globe—Horn Book Award The January/February issue of *The Horn Book Magazine* honors nonfiction titles, as well as books in other genres. www.hbook.com

ANNUAL LISTS

American Library Association Notable Children's Books The Notable Children's Book Committee for the Association of Library Services to Children, a division of the American Library Association, chooses notable nonfiction, as well as fiction. The list appears in the March 15 issue of *Booklist*, a journal of the association. www.ala.org

International Reading Association Children's Choices The Children's Choices Committee of the International Reading Association–Children's Book Council Joint Committee selects books in all genres for children. The list appears yearly in the October issue of *The Reading Teacher*. Teacher Choices and Young Adult Choices are also chosen by the International Reading Association. www.reading.org/choices/

Notable Children's Trade Books in the Field of Social Studies The annotated list of notable books is available in the April/May issue of *Social Education*, the journal of the National Council for the Social Studies. www.ncss.org/resources/notable/

Outstanding Science Trade Books for Children The annotated list of notable books is available in the March issue of *Science and Children*, the journal of the National Science Teachers Association. www.nsta.org

Appendix C
Student Assessment Checklist:
Types and Features of Nonfiction

Becoming an accomplished reader and writer of nonfiction takes time, so we recommend recording student progress across grade levels. This checklist will help. It includes features we want students to understand and apply as they read and write nonfiction.

As you observe students working within the comprehensive framework, check the appropriate boxes if the student is able to point out the feature, name it, describe how to use it, practice it in reading, and practice it in writing.

Types and Features of Nonfiction	Point It Out	Name It	Describe How to Use It	Practice in Reading	Practice in Writing
Types of Nonfiction Books					
Concept					
Photographic essay					
Identification/field guide					
Life cycle					
Biography					
Experiment, activity, craft, and how-to					
Documents, journals, diaries, and albums					
Survey					
Specialized					
Reference					
Informational picture storybook/ blended books					
Organizational Structures					
Enumerative					
Sequential					
Chronological					

Types and Features of Nonfiction	Point It Out	Name It	Describe How to Use It	Practice in Reading	Practice in Writing
Compare-contrast					
Cause-effect					
Question-answer (point-counterpoint)					
Narrative					
Access Features					
Title					
Table of contents					
Introduction, preface, prologue					
Headings and subheadings					
Sidebars					
Bulleted information					
Inset sections or pages					
Glossaries, pronunciation guides					
Bibliographies					
Index with no subtopics/with subtopics					
Afterword, epilogue, endnotes, author/illustrator notes					
Appendices					
Features for Determining Accuracy					
Dust jacket					
Copyright date					
Author's credentials					
Illustrator/photographer's credentials					
Library of Congress Cataloguing-in-Publication Data					
Acknowledgments					
Dedication					
Preface, prologue, introduction					
Use of speculative language or generalizing					

Types and Features of Nonfiction	Point It Out	Name It	Describe How to Use It	Practice in Reading	Practice in Writing
Use of fact and opinion					
Afterword, epilogue, endnotes, author/illustrator notes					
Bibliography/sources, readings for further information					
Author's comparison of content to other sources (within text or materials in the appendix)					
Style of Writing					
Clear and coherent writing					
Organization/chunked information and internal patterns of language and structure					
Language					
Figurative language/metaphors					
Vocabulary					
Voice/point of view					
Tone					
Leads					
Conclusions					
Visual Information					
Design of book/formats/layout					
Dust jackets/covers					
Endpapers (sometimes called endpages)					
Labels and captions					
Illustrations/photographs/archival materials					
Diagrams: simple, scale, cross section, cutaways, flow, tree, web					
Graphs: line, bar, column, pie					
Tables (charts)					
Maps: geographical, bird's-eye view, flow					
Time lines					

Appendix D
Checklist for Designing a K–6 Curriculum Based on Types and Features of Nonfiction

The ability to work with increasingly more sophisticated types and features of nonfiction occurs over time, and there is no "right order" in which to teach them. Mastery is determined by opportunities to work with nonfiction materials and the difficulty of those materials. To ensure students work with the array of features and have opportunities to apply them in their reading and writing, curriculum planners need to determine when and if each nonfiction feature is introduced and, from there, target grades accordingly. This checklist will help.

Types and Features of Nonfiction	K	1	2	3	4	5	6
Types of Nonfiction Books							
Concept							
Photographic essay							
Identification/field guide							
Life cycle							
Biography							
Experiment, activity, craft, and how-to							
Documents, journals, diaries, and albums							
Survey							
Specialized							
Reference							
Informational picture storybook/blended books							
Organizational Structures							
Enumerative							
Sequential							
Chronological							

Types and Features of Nonfiction	K	1	2	3	4	5	6
Compare-contrast							
Cause-effect							
Question-answer (point-counterpoint)							
Narrative							
Access Features							
Title							
Table of contents							
Introduction, preface, prologue							
Headings and subheadings							
Sidebars							
Bulleted information							
Inset sections or pages							
Glossaries, pronunciation guides							
Bibliographies							
Index with no subtopics/with subtopics							
Afterword, epilogue, endnotes, author/illustrator notes							
Appendices							
Features for Determining Accuracy							
Dust jacket							
Copyright date							
Author's credentials							
Illustrator/photographer's credentials							
Library of Congress Cataloguing-in Publication Data							
Acknowledgments							
Dedication							
Preface, prologue, introduction							
Use of speculative language or generalizing							
Use of fact and opinion							

Types and Features of Nonfiction	K	1	2	3	4	5	6
Afterword, epilogue, end notes, author/illustrator notes							
Bibliography/sources, readings for further information							
Author's comparison of content to other sources (within text or materials in the appendix)							
Style of Writing							
Clear and coherent writing							
Organization/chunked information and internal patterns of language and structure							
Language							
Figurative language/metaphors							
Vocabulary							
Voice/point of view							
Tone							
Leads							
Conclusions							
Visual Information							
Design of book/formats/layout							
Dust jackets/covers of the book							
Endpapers (sometimes called endpages)							
Labels and captions							
Illustrations/photographs							
Archival materials							
Diagrams: simple, scale, cross section, cutaways, flow, tree, web							
Graphs: line, bar, column, pie							
Tables (charts)							
Maps: geographical, bird's-eye view, flow							
Time lines							

© Bamford & Kristo, 2003

Appendix E
Checklist for Evaluating Your Instruction in Nonfiction

The purpose of this tool is to assess how well you teach features of nonfiction and strategies for reading and writing nonfiction.

1. Do I target strategies and features that my students need?
   - ❏ Does the text set for a unit include opportunities to apply the targeted strategy or feature?
   - ❏ Is the targeted strategy or feature needed to comprehend the content?
   - ❏ Is the targeted strategy or feature needed to access the text and visuals?
   - ❏ Will students need to apply the targeted strategy or feature in their writing?

2. Have I explained fully what students are learning by:
   - ❏ Pointing out the strategy or feature?
   - ❏ Naming the strategy or feature?
   - ❏ Explaining why it is important to learn the strategy or feature?
   - ❏ Explaining how to use the strategy or feature to comprehend nonfiction?
   - ❏ Explaining how and when to use this strategy or feature in their writing?

3. Have I modeled my own thinking process or use of the strategy or nonfiction feature during:
   - ❏ Instructional read aloud?
   - ❏ Modeled writing?
   - ❏ Shared reading?
   - ❏ Interactive writing?
   - ❏ Shared writing?
   - ❏ Guided reading?
   - ❏ Guided writing?
   - ❏ Discovery reading circles?
   - ❏ Discovery writing circles?

❏ Readers' workshop?

❏ Writers' workshop?

❏ Extension activities?

4. Have I encouraged students to ask questions and discuss responses among themselves during: (i.e, Do I encourage and engage students in rich talk in a problem-solving environment?)

❏ Instructional read aloud?

❏ Modeled writing?

❏ Shared reading?

❏ Interactive writing?

❏ Shared writing?

❏ Guided reading?

❏ Guided writing?

❏ Discovery reading circles?

❏ Discovery writing circles?

❏ Readers' workshop?

❏ Writers' workshop?

❏ Extension activities?

5. Am I selecting the best and most appropriate nonfiction texts that:

❏ Interest students and match their prior knowledge of the content?

❏ Are good matches for students' reading levels?

❏ Represent a good cross section of available informational materials?

❏ Offer opportunities to use comprehension strategies and nonfiction features?

6. Am I using a variety of instructional approaches to teach reading and writing of nonfiction? Am I grouping students flexibly?

7. Am I planning reading and writing tasks for instructional read alouds, shared instruction, guided instruction, discovery circles, and extension activities that are engaging and meaningful?

8. Have I provided students with repeated exposure to various features, structures, and types of visuals?

9. Am I evaluating students' progress based on:
   - ❏ Using reading strategies?
   - ❏ Comprehending nonfiction features?
   - ❏ Knowing the content?
   - ❏ Developing research skills?
   - ❏ Writing nonfiction?

10. In primary grades, am I balancing instruction in phonics, word recognition strategies, and fluency with comprehension strategies and knowledge about how nonfiction text works?

11. Am I providing students with multiple opportunities to develop new vocabulary by:
    - ❏ Developing understandings of new words through reading, talking, and real-life experiences?
    - ❏ Using explicit instruction?
    - ❏ Providing a wide variety of informational materials?
    - ❏ Encouraging the use of new words with many opportunities to discuss content?

12. Am I providing opportunities for hands-on research in developing understandings about why graphs, charts, and visuals are essential to sharing information with others?

13. Am I helping students orchestrate multiple strategies rather than using one at a time?

14. Am I working toward gradual release of responsibility from shared instruction to guided instruction to discovery circles?

15. Am I helping students unravel the complexities of nonfiction, e.g., multiple layers, simple-to-complex captions, or text that doesn't use signal words to assist readers?

16. Am I continuing to read nonfiction to keep abreast of the best available and to learn about the features and comprehension strategies my students need for reading and writing, as well as knowing about the variety of visuals, formats, text structures, and layouts?

17. Am I staying abreast of new research and how it may impact my nonfiction instruction?

Appendix F
Children's Magazines Featuring Nonfiction

Here is a sampling of magazines that feature nonfiction, which you may want to use in your teaching or make available to students for independent reading.

Chickadee Magazine (Ages 8 and up):
www.owlkids.com/chickadee/

Cobblestone/Carus Publishing Co.:
www.cobblestonepub.com
  Click (Ages 2–7)
  Appleseeds (Ages 7–9)
  Ask (Ages 7–10)
  Calliope (Ages 9–14)
  Cobblestone (Ages 9–15)
  Cricket (Ages 9–14)
  Dig (Ages 9–14)
  Faces (Ages 9–14)
  Footsteps (Ages 9–14)
  Muse (Ages 9–14)

DynaMath:
www.teacher.scholastic.com/products
/classmags/dynamath.htm

Highlights for Children (Ages 2–12):
www.highlights.com

Kids Discover (Ages 6 and up):
www.kidsdiscover.com

National Geographic:
www.nationalgeographic.com/ngkids/
  National Geographic Kids (Ages 8 and up)

National Wildlife Federation:
www.nwf.org/printandfilm
  EarthSavers (Ages 6–13)
  Ranger Rick (Ages 7–12)

Owl: The Discovery Magazine for Kids
(Ages 9 and up): www.owlkids.com/owl

Scholastic:
www.teacher.scholastic.com/scholasticnews
  Scholastic News 1
  Scholastic News 2
  Scholastic News 3
  Scholastic News 4
  Junior Scholastic

Time for Kids: www.timeforkids.com
  Big Picture (Grades K–1)
  News Scoop (Grades 2–3)
  World Report (Grades 4–7)
  Go Places (Grades 2–3; Grades 4–7)

U.S. Kids (Ages 6–10): www.cbhi.org

Weekly Reader (Grades K–12):
www.weeklyreader.com

Appendix G
Words That Signal Information

Authors use words and phrases that signal to the reader certain kinds of information. The following examples are organized into categories from *Improving Writing* by Susan Davis Lenski and Jerry L. Johns, (2000), with the exceptions of Author's Speculation, which is from Sandip Lee Ann Wilson (2001), and The Passing of Time, which is from Rosemary A. Bamford and Janice V. Kristo (2003).

WORDS AND PHRASES THAT SIGNAL:

The Passing of Time
after
before
consequently
eventually
finally
first
followed by
following day
later
next
once
soon after
subsequently
then
until
when

An Explanation or Definition
also
and
another kind
another way
are made up of
as an example
consists of
described as
first, next, then, finally
for example
for instance
here's how
in addition
is
it means
like

Compare-and-Contrast Writing
alike
also
as well as
both
but
different
however
in comparison
in the same way
instead
on the other hand
same
either...or
similar
have in common
unlike

Persuasive Writing
although
but
however
in contrast
nevertheless
on the other hand
though
while
yet

Cause-and-Effect Writing
as a result
because
consequently
due to
for that reason
if
leads to
so
then
when

An Author's Speculation
almost
appears
depending on our viewpoints
from the evidence, it seems to me that...
may
might
generally
historians are not certain
historians estimate
occasionally
no historian has been able to
not sure
perhaps
possibly
probably
we don't know for sure
we just don't know
the events will always be unclear

Professional References Cited

Allington, R. L., Johnston, P. H., & Day, J. P. (2002). Exemplary fourth-grade teachers. *Language Arts,* 79(6), 462–466.

Allington, R. L. (2000). The schools we have. The schools we need. In N.D. Padak et al. (Eds.), *Distinguished educators on reading: Contributions that have shaped effective literacy instruction* (pp. 164–181). Newark, DE: International Reading Association.

Almasi, J. F., & Gambrell, L. B. (1994). *Sociocognitive conflict in peer-led and teacher-led discussions of literature.* (Reading Research Report No. 12). Athens, GA: Universities of Maryland and Georgia, National Reading Research Center.

Alvermann, D. E., Smith, L. C., & Readance, J. E. (1985). Prior knowledge activation and the comprehension of compatible and incompatible text. *Reading Research Quarterly,* 20, 420–436.

American Association of School Librarians [and] Association for Educational Communications and Technology. (1998). *Information power: Building partnerships for learning.* Chicago: American Library Association.

Anderson, C. (2000). *How's it going? A practical guide to conferring with student writers.* Foreword by Lucy Calkins. Portsmouth, NH: Heinemann.

Aronson, E., & Patnoe, S. (1997). *The jigsaw classroom: Building cooperation in the classroom* (2nd ed.). New York: Longman.

Atwell, N. (1998). *In the middle: New understandings about writing, reading, and learning* (2nd. ed.). Portsmouth, NH: Boynton Cook/Heinemann.

Bamford, R. A., & Kristo, J. V. (2000). *Checking out nonfiction k–8: Good choices for best learning.* Norwood, MA: Christopher-Gordon.

Bamford, R. A., & Kristo, J. V. (2003). Choosing quality nonfiction literature: Examining aspects of accuracy and organization. In R. A. Bamford & J. V. Kristo (Eds.), *Making facts come alive: Choosing & using nonfiction literature k–8* (2nd ed.) (pp. 21–44). Norwood, MA: Christopher-Gordon.

Bamford, R. A., & Kristo, J. V. (Eds.). (2003). *Making facts come alive: Choosing & using nonfiction literature k–8* (2nd ed.). Norwood, MA: Christopher-Gordon.

Bamford, R. A., Kristo, J. V., & Lyon, A. (2002). Facing facts: Nonfiction in the primary classroom. *New England Reading Association Journal,* 38(2), 8–15.

Beach, R. (1994). Adopting multiple stances in conducting literacy research. In R. B. Ruddell, M. R. Ruddell, & H. Singer (Eds.), *Theoretical models and processes of reading* (2nd ed.) (pp. 1203–1219). Newark, DE: International Reading Association.

Beck, I. L., McKeown, M. G., & Kucan, L. (2002). *Bringing words to life: Robust vocabulary instruction.* New York: The Guilford Press.

Benson, V. (2002). Shifting paradigms and pedagogy with nonfiction: A call to arms for survival in the 21st century. *The New England Reading Association Journal,* 38(2), 1–6.

Bransford, J. D., Brown, A. L., & Cocking, R. R. (Eds.). (1999). *How people learn: Brain, mind, experience, and school.* Washington, DC: National Academy Press.

Brown, H., & Cambourne, B. (1987). *Read and retell.* Portsmouth, NH: Heinemann.

Brozo, W. G., & Simpson, M. L. (2003). *Readers, teachers, learners: Expanding literacy across the content areas* (4th ed.). Columbus, OH: Merrill/Prentice Hall.

Campione, J. (1981, April). *Learning, academic achievement, and instruction.* Paper presented at the second annual Conference on Reading Research of the Center for the Study of Reading, New Orleans, LA.

Carter, B. (2000). A universe of information: The future of nonfiction. *The Horn Book Magazine,* 76(6), 697–707.

Caswell, L. J., & Duke, N. K. (1998). Non-narrative as a catalyst for literacy development. *Language Arts,* 75(2), 108–117.

Clay, M. (1985). *The early detection of reading difficulties: A diagnostic survey with recovery procedures.* Portsmouth, NH: Heinemann.

Cole, A. D. (2003). *Knee to knee, eye to eye: Circling in on comprehension.* Portsmouth, NH: Heinemann.

Colman. P. (1999). Nonfiction is literature, too. *The New Advocate,* 12(3), 215–222.

Crafton, L. (1981). *The reading process as a transactional learning experience.* Unpublished doctoral dissertation. Indiana University, Bloomington, IN.

Culham, R. (2003). *6 + 1 traits of writing: The complete guide, grades 3 and up.* New York: Scholastic.

Daniels, H. (2002). *Literature circles: Voice and choice in book clubs & reading groups* (2nd. ed.). York, ME: Stenhouse.

Day, J. P., Spiegel, D. L., McLellan, J., & Brown, V. B. (2002). *Moving forward with literature circles: How to plan, manage, and evaluate literature circles that deepen understanding and foster a love of reading.* New York: Scholastic.

Dillon, J. T. (1985). Using questions to foil discussion. *Teacher and Teacher Education,* 1, 109–121.

Duke, N. K. (2000). 3.6 minutes per day: The scarcity of informational texts in first grade. *Reading Research Quarterly,* 35(2), 203–224.

Duke, N. K., & Kays, J. (1998). "Can I say 'once upon a time'?": Kindergarten children developing knowledge of informational book language. *Early Childhood Research Quarterly,* 13(2), 295–318.

Duke, N. K., & Pearson, P. D. (2002). Effective practices for developing reading comprehension. In A. E. Farstrup & S. J. Samuels (Eds.), *What research has to say about reading instruction* (pp. 205–242). Newark, DE: International Reading Association.

Ehlinger, J., & Pritchard, R. (1994). Using think alongs in secondary content areas. *Reading Research & Instruction,* 33, 187–206.

Fountas, I. C., & Pinnell, G. S. (1996). *Guided reading: Good first teaching for all children.* Portsmouth, NH: Heinemann.

Fountas, I. C., & Pinnell, G. S. (1999). *Matching books to readers.* Portsmouth, NH: Heinemann.

Fountas, I. C., & Pinnell, G. S. (2001). *Guiding readers and writers grades 3–6: Teaching comprehension, genre, and content literacy.* Portsmouth, NH: Heinemann.

Fredericks, A. (2001). *Guided reading in grades 3–6: 300+ guided reading strategies, activities, and lesson plans for reading success.* Crystal Lake, IL: Rigby Best Teacher Press.

Freeman, M. S. (1997). *Listen to this: Developing an ear for expository.* Gainesville, FL: Maupin House.

Gaskins, I. W., Anderson, R. C., Pressley, M., Cunicelli, E. A., & Satlow, E. (1993). Six teachers dialogue during cognitive process instruction. *Elementary School Journal,* 93, 277–304.

Gee, J. (2001, April). Critical literacy as critical discourse analysis. In J. Harste & P. D. Pearson (Cochairs), (book of readings for) *Critical perspectives on literacy: Possibilities and practices.* Preconvention institute conducted at the meeting of the International Reading Association, New Orleans, LA.

Gerard, P. (1996). *Creative nonfiction.* Cincinnati, OH: Story Press.

Graves, D. H. (1989). *Investigate nonfiction.* Portsmouth, NH: Heinemann.

Graves, D. H. (1994). *A fresh look at writing.* Portsmouth, NH: Heinemann.

Graves, M. F., & Graves, B. B. (2003). *Scaffolding reading experiences: Designs for student success* (2nd. ed.). Norwood, MA: Christopher-Gordon.

Harris, T. L., & Hodges, R. E. (1995). *The literacy dictionary: The vocabulary of reading and writing.* Newark, DE: International Reading Association.

Harvey, S. (1998). *Nonfiction matters: Reading, writing, and research in grades 3–8.* York, ME: Stenhouse.

Harvey, S., & Goudvis, A. (2000). *Strategies that work: Teaching comprehension to enhance understanding*. York, ME: Stenhouse.

Hayes, D. A., & Tierney, R. J. (1982). Developing readers' knowledge through analogy. *Reading Research Quarterly, 17*, 256–280.

Hepler, S. (2003). Nonfiction books for children: new directions, new challenges. In R. A. Bamford & J. V. Kristo (Eds.), *Making facts come alive: Choosing & using nonfiction literature k–8* (2nd ed.) (pp. 3–20). Norwood, MA: Christopher-Gordon.

Holdaway, D. (1979). *The foundation of literacy*. Sydney, Australia: Ashton Scholastic.

Hoyt, L. (2002). *Make it real: Strategies for success with informational texts*. Portsmouth, NH: Heinemann.

Keene, E. O., & Zimmermann, S. (1997). *Mosaic of thought: Teaching comprehension in a reader's workshop*. Portsmouth, NH: Heinemann.

Kerper, R. M. (2002). Art influencing art: The making of an extraordinary life. *Language Arts, 80*(1), 60–67.

Kerper, R. M. (2003). Choosing quality nonfiction literature: Examining access features and visual displays. In R. A. Bamford & J. V. Kristo (Eds.), *Making facts come alive: Choosing & using nonfiction literature k–8* (2nd ed.) (pp. 65–78). Norwood, MA: Christopher-Gordon.

Laughlin, M. K., & Lathrobe, K. H. (1989). *Readers theatre for children: Scripts and script development*. Englewood, CO: Libraries Unlimited.

Learning Media, Ministry of Education. (1997). *Reading for life: The learner as a reader*. Wellington, New Zealand: Learning Media.

Leland, C. H., & Harste, J. C. (2002). Critical literacy. In A. A. McClure & J. V. Kristo (Eds.), *Adventuring with books: A booklist for pre-k–grade 6* (13th ed.) (pp. 465–485). Urbana, IL: National Council of Teachers of English.

Lenski, S. D., & Johns, J. L. (2000). *Improving writing: Resources, strategies, and assessments*. Dubuque, IW: Kendall/Hunt.

Levstik, L. S. (2003). To fling my arms wide: Students learning about the world through nonfiction. In R. A. Bamford & J. V. Kristo (Eds.), *Making facts come alive: Choosing & using nonfiction literature k–8* (2nd ed.) (pp. 221–234). Norwood, MA: Christopher-Gordon.

Marshall, N. (1989). Overcoming problems with incorrect prior knowledge: An instructional study. In S. McCormick & J. Zutell (Eds.), *Cognitive and social perspectives for literacy research and instruction: 39th year book of the national reading conference* (pp. 323–330). Chicago: National Reading Conference.

Maxwell, R. J. (1996). *Writing across the curriculum in middle and high schools*. Boston: Allyn & Bacon.

Mazzoni, S. A., & Gambrell, L. B. (1996). Text talk: Using discussion to promote comprehension of informational texts. In L. B. Gambrell & J. F. Almasi (Eds.), *Lively discussions: Fostering engaged reading* (pp.134–148). Newark, DE: International Reading Association.

McCarrier, A., Pinnell, G. S., & Fountas, I. C. (2000). *Interactive writing: How language & literacy come together, k–2*. Portsmouth, NH: Heinemann.

McClure, A. A. (2003). Choosing quality nonfiction literature: Examining aspects of writing style. In R. A. Bamford & J. V. Kristo (Eds.), *Making facts come alive: Choosing & using nonfiction literature k–8* (2nd ed.) (pp. 79–96). Norwood, MA: Christopher-Gordon.

McClure, A. A., & Kristo, J. V. (2002). *Adventuring with books: A booklist for pre-k–grade 6* (13th ed.). Urbana, IL: National Council of Teachers of English.

McKenzie, M. (1986). *Journeys into literacy*. Huddersfield, Australia: Schofield & Sims, Ltd.

McMahon, S. I., & Raphael, T. E., with Goatley, V. J., & Pardo, L. S. (Eds.). (1997). *The book club connection: Literacy learning and classroom talk*. Newark, DE: International Reading Association; New York: Teachers College Press.

Moline, S. (1995). *I see what you mean: Children at work with visual information*. York, ME: Stenhouse.

Moline, S. (2002). Dominie information toolkit: Using nonfiction genres and visual texts. (Books A, B, & C). Carlsbad, CA: Dominie Press.

Mooney, M. (1990). *Reading to, with, and by children.* Katonah, NY: Richard C. Owen.

Moore, D. W., Moore, S. A., Cunningham, P. M., & Cunningham, J. W. (1998). *Developing readers & writers in the content areas K–12.* New York: Longman.

Moore, P. (2003). Choosing quality nonfiction literature: Aspects of selection for emergent, early, and transitional readers. In R.A. Bamford & J.V. Kristo (Eds.), *Making facts come alive: Choosing and using nonfiction literature k–8* (2nd ed.) (pp. 97–118). Norwood, MA: Christopher-Gordon.

Mudre, L. H. (2001). Teaching versus prompting: Supporting comprehension in guided reading. In G. S. Pinnell & P. L. Scharer (Eds.), *Extending our reach: Teaching for comprehension in reading, grades k–2* (pp. 77–85). Columbus, OH: The Literacy Collaborative at the Ohio State University.

Murray, D. (1984). *Write to learn.* New York: Holt, Rinehart and Winston.

Nagy, W. E., & Anderson, R.C. (1984). How many words are there in printed school English? *Reading Research Quarterly,* 19, 304–330.

National Council of Teachers of English, International Reading Association (1996). *Standards for the English language arts.* Urbana, IL: National Council of Teachers of English; Newark, DE: International Reading Association.

National Council of Teachers of Mathematics. (1989). *Curriculum and evaluation standards for school mathematics.* Reston, VA: National Council of Teachers of Mathematics.

National Council for the Social Studies. (1994). *Expectations of excellence: Curriculum standards for social studies.* Washington, DC: National Council for the Social Studies.

National Research Council. (1996). *National science education standards.* Washington, DC: National Academy Press.

Newkirk, T. (1989). *More than stories: The range of children's writing.* Portsmouth, NH: Heinemann.

Pappas, C. C. (1991). Fostering full access to literacy by including information books. *Language Arts,* 68, 449–462.

Paris, S. G., Wasik, B. A., & Turner, J. C. (1996). The development of strategic readers. In R. Barr, M. L. Kamil, P. Mosenthal, & P. D. Pearson (Eds.), *Handbook of reading research, vol. II* (pp. 609–640). Mahwah, NJ: Lawrence Erlbaum Associates.

Parkes, B. (2000). *Read it again!: Revisiting shared reading.* Portland, ME: Stenhouse.

Pearson, P. D., & Gallagher, M. (1983). The instruction of reading comprehension. *Contemporary Educational Psychology,* 8, 317–344.

Pearson, P. D., Roehler, L. R., Dole, J. A., & Duffy, G. G. (1992). Developing expertise in reading comprehension. In S. J. Samuels & A. E. Farstrup (Eds.), *What research has to say about reading research* (2nd ed.) (pp. 145–199). Newark, DE: International Reading Association.

Piazza, C. L. (2003). *Journeys: The teaching of writing in elementary classrooms.* Columbus, OH: Merrill/Prentice Hall.

Pinnell, G. S., & Fountas, I. C. (2003). Teaching for comprehension across the language and literacy framework. In G. S. Pinnell & P. L. Scharer (Eds.), *Teaching for comprehension in reading grades k–2* (pp. 33–54). New York: Scholastic.

Pinnell, G. S., & Scharer, P. L. (2003). *Teaching comprehension in reading grades k–2.* New York: Scholastic.

Portalupi, J., & Fletcher, R. (2001). *Nonfiction craft lessons: Teaching informational writing k–8.* Portland, ME: Stenhouse.

Power, B. (1996). *Taking note: Improving your observational notetaking.* York, ME: Stenhouse.

Pressley, M. (2002a). Metacognition and self-regulated comprehension. In A. E. Farstrup & S. J. Samuels, (Eds.), *What research has to say about reading instruction* (3rd ed.) (pp. 294–306). Newark, NJ: International Reading Association.

Pressley, M. (2002b). *Reading instruction that works: The case for balanced teaching* (2nd ed.). New York: The Guilford Press.

Rabinowitz, P. J. (1998). *Before reading: Narrative conventions and the politics of interpretation.* With foreword by James Phelan. Columbus, OH: Ohio State University Press.

Raphael, T. E., & Goatley, V. J. (1997). Classrooms as communities: Features of community share. In S. I. McMahon & T. E. Raphael with V. J. Goatley & L. S. Pardo (Eds.), *The book club connection: Literacy learning and classroom talk* (pp. 26–46). Newark, DE: International Reading Association; New York: Teachers College Press.

Raphael, T. E., Pardo, L. S., & Highfield, K. (2002). *Book club: A literature-based curriculum* (2nd ed.). Littleton, MA: Small Planet Communications.

Robb, L. (2000). *Teaching reading in middle school: A strategic approach to teaching reading that improves comprehension and thinking.* New York: Scholastic.

Roehler, L. R., & Duffy, G. G. (1984). Direct explanation of comprehension processes. In G. G. Duffy, L. R. Roehler, & J. Mason (Eds.), *Comprehension instruction: Perspectives and suggestions* (pp. 265–280). New York: Longman.

Rosenblatt, L. (1976). *Literature as exploration.* New York: Noble & Noble.

Sanacore, J. (1991). Expository and narrative text: Balancing young children's reading experiences. *Childhood Education, 67,* 211–214.

Schulman, M. B., & Payne, C. D. (2000). *Guided reading: Making it work.* New York: Scholastic.

Short, K. G., & Pierce, K. M. (Eds.) (1998). *Talking about books: Literature discussion groups in K–8 classrooms.* Portsmouth, NH: Heinemann.

Short, K. G., Harste, J. C., & Burke, C. (1996). *Creating classrooms for authors and inquirers.* (2nd ed.). Portsmouth, NH: Heinemann.

Siu-Runyan, Y. (2003). Writing nonfiction: Helping students teach others what they know. In R. A. Bamford & J. V. Kristo (Eds.), *Making facts come alive: Choosing & using nonfiction literature k–8* (2nd ed.) (pp. 209–219). Norwood, MA: Christopher-Gordon.

Strong, W. (2001). *Coaching writing: The power of guided practice.* Portsmouth, NH: Heinemann.

Swartz, S. L., Shook, R. E., & Klein, A. F. (2002). *Shared reading: Reading with children.* Carlsbad, CA: Dominie Press.

Swartz, S. L., Shook, R. E., Klein, A. F., Moon, C., Bunnell, K., Belt, M., & Huntley, C. (2003). *Guided reading & literacy centers.* Carlsbad, CA: Dominie Press.

Taberski, S. (2000). *On solid ground: Strategies for teaching reading k–3.* Portsmouth, NH: Heinemann.

Tierney, R. J., & Shanahan, T. (1996). Research on the reading-writing relationship: Interactions, transactions, and outcomes. In R. Barr, M. L. Kamil, P. Mosenthal, & P. D. Pearson (Eds.), *Handbook of reading research: Volume III* (pp. 246–280). Mahwah, NJ: Lawrence Erlbaum Associates.

Tower, C. (2000). Questions that matter: Preparing elementary students for the inquiry process. *The Reading Teacher, 53*(7), 550–558.

Vacca, R. T. (2002). Making a difference in adolescents' school lives: Visible and invisible aspects of content area reading. In A. E. Farstrup & S. J. Samuels. (Eds.), *What research has to say about reading instruction* (3rd ed.) (pp. 184–204). Newark, DE: International Reading Association.

Vacca, R. T., & Vacca, J. L. (2002). *Content area reading: Literacy and learning across the curriculum* (7th ed.). Boston: Allyn and Bacon.

Vardell, S. M. (2003). Using read aloud to explore the layers of nonfiction. In R. A. Bamford & J. V. Kristo (Eds.), *Making facts come alive: Choosing & using nonfiction literature k–8* (2nd ed.) (pp. 192–207). Norwood, MA: Christopher-Gordon.

Vygotsky, L. S. (1978). *Mind in society: The development of higher psychological processes.* Cambridge, MA: Harvard University Press.

Walpole, S. (1998). Changing texts, changing thinking: Comprehension demands of new science textbooks. *The Reading Teacher, 52*(4), 358–369.

Weaver, C. A., & Kintsch, W. (1996). Expository text. In R. Barr, M. L. Kamil, P. Mosenthal, & P. D. Pearson (Eds.), *Handbook of reading research, vol. II* (pp. 230–245). Mahwah, NJ: Lawrence Erlbaum Associates.

Wiggins, G., & McTighe, J. (1998). *Understanding by design.* Alexandria, VA: Association for Supervision and Curriculum Development.

Wilhelm, J. D. (2001). *Improving comprehension with think-aloud strategies: Modeling what good readers do.* New York: Scholastic.

Wilhelm, J. D. (2002). *Action strategies for deepening comprehension.* New York: Scholastic.

Wilhelm, J. D., Baker, T., & Dube, J. (2001). *Strategic reading: Guiding students to lifelong literacy.* Portsmouth, NH: Heinemann/Boynton-Cook.

Wilson, S. L. (2001). *Coherence and historical understanding in children's biography and historical nonfiction literature: A content analysis of selected Orbis Pictus books.* Dissertation Abstracts International, 63,(01), 121A. (University Microfilms No. AAT3039414).

Zarnowski, M. (1998). Coming out from under the spell of stories: Critiquing historical narratives. *The New Advocate, 2*(4), 345–356.

Zarnowski, M. (Spring 2001). *Creating magic, creating learning: Using nonfiction books at the middle and secondary levels.* Presentation at the National Council of Teachers of English Conference, Birmingham, AL.

Zarnowski, M. (2003). *History makers: A questioning approach to reading and writing biographies.* Portsmouth, NH: Heinemann.

Zarnowski, M., Kerper, R. M., & Jensen, J. M. (2002). *The best in children's nonfiction: Reading, writing, and teaching Orbis Pictus award books.* Urbana, IL: National Council of Teachers of English.

Children's Books Cited

Adler, David A. (2001). *Dr. Martin Luther King, Jr.* Illustrated by Colin Bootman. New York: Holiday.

Allen, Judy, & Humphries, Tudor. (2000). *Are you a snail?* New York: Kingfisher.

Allen, Judy, & Humphries, Tudor. (2002). *Are you a grasshopper?* New York: Kingfisher.

Ammon, Richard. (1998). *An Amish wedding.* Illustrated by Pamela Patrick. New York: Atheneum.

Ancona, George. (2000). *Cuban kids.* New York: Marshall Cavendish.

Andronik, Catherine M. (2001). *Hatshepsut: His majesty, herself.* Illustrated by Joseph D. Fiedler. New York: Atheneum.

Armstrong, Jennifer. (1998). *Shipwreck at the bottom of the world: The extraordinary true story of Shackleton and the Endurance.* New York: Crown.

Armstrong, Jennifer. (2000). *Spirit of Endurance: The true story of the Shackleton expedition to the Antarctic.* Illustrated by William Maughan. New York: Crown.

Armstrong, Jennifer. (2003). *Audubon: Painter of birds in the wild frontier.* Illustrated by Jos. A. Smith. New York: Abrams.

Arnold, Caroline. (2003). *Birds: Nature's magnificent flying machines.* Illustrated by Patricia J. Wynne. Watertown, MA: Charlesbridge.

Arnosky, Jim. (1995). *All about owls.* New York: Scholastic.

Arnosky, Jim. (2002a). *All about frogs.* New York: Scholastic.

Arnosky, Jim. (2002b). *Field trips: Bug hunting, animal tracking, bird watching, and shore walking with Jim Arnosky.* New York: HarperCollins.

Arnosky, Jim. (2003). *All about sharks.* New York: Scholastic.

Barbabas, Kathy. (1997). *Let's find out about toothpaste.* New York: Scholastic.

Bartoletti, Susan Campbell. (1996). *Growing up in coal country.* Boston: Houghton Mifflin.

Bartoletti, Susan Campbell. (1999). *Kids on strike!* Boston: Houghton Mifflin.

Batten, Mary. (2001). *Anthropologist: Scientist of the people.* Photographs by A. Magdalena Hurtado & Kim Hill. Boston: Houghton Mifflin.

Batten, Mary. (2003). *Aliens from Earth: When animals and plants invade other ecosystems.* Illustrated by Beverly J. Doyle. Atlanta, GA: Peachtree.

Berger, Melvin. (1996a). *The big bears.* New York: Newbridge.

Berger, Melvin. (1996b). *How do animals sleep?* New York: Newbridge.

Berger, Melvin. (1998). *Growl!: A book about bears.* New York: Scholastic.

Berger, Melvin. (2001). *Do bears sleep all winter? Questions and answers about bears.* Illustrated by Robert Osti. New York: Scholastic.

Berger, Melvin, & Berger, Gilda. (2000). *How do bats see in the dark? Questions and answers about night creatures.* Illustrated by Jim Effler. New York: Scholastic.

Berger, Melvin, & Berger, Gilda. (2002). *Where did the butterfly get its name? Questions and answers about butterflies and moths.* Illustrated by Higgins Bond. New York: Scholastic.

Bierman, Carol. (1998). *Journey to Ellis Island: How my father came to America.* Illustrated by Laurie McGaw. New York: Hyperion/Madison.

Bird, Bettina, & Short, Joan. (1997). *Insects.* Illustrated by Deborah Savin. Greenvale, New York: Mondo.

Bishop, Nic. (2002). *Backyard detective: Critters up close.* New York: Scholastic.

Blumberg, Rhoda. (2001). *Shipwrecked! The true adventures of a Japanese boy.* New York: HarperCollins.

Bolton, Faye, & Cullen, Ester. (1987). *Animal shelters.* Illustrated by Deborah Savin. Multimedia International Ltd/Scholastic.

Budhos, Marina. (1999). *Remix: Conversations with immigrant teenagers.* New York: Henry Holt.

Cahn, Rhoda, & Cahn, William. (1972). *No time for school, no time for play: The story of child labor in America.* New York: Messner.

Camper, Cathy. (1999). *Bugs before time: Prehistoric insects and their relatives.* Illustrated by Steve Kirk. New York: Simon & Schuster.

Cassie, Brian, & Pallotta, Jerry. (1995). *The butterfly alphabet book.* Illustrated by Mark Astrella. Watertown, MA: Charlesbridge.

Cerullo, Mary M. (1999). *Sea soup: Phytoplankton.* Gardiner, ME: Tilbury.

Cerullo, Mary M. (2000). *The truth about great white sharks.* Photographs by Jeffrey L. Rotman. Illustrated by Michael Wertz. San Francisco: Chronicle Books.

Cole, Joanna. (1994). *The magic school bus in the time of the dinosaurs.* Illustrated by Bruce Degen. New York: Scholastic.

Cole, Joanna. (2003). *Ms. Frizzle's adventures: Medieval castle.* Illustrated by Bruce Degen. New York: Scholastic.

Collard, Sneed B., III. (2002). *Beaks!* Illustrated by Robin Hickman. Watertown, MA: Charlesbridge.

Cooper, Michael L. (2000). *Fighting for honor: Japanese Americans and World War II.* New York: Clarion.

Corey, Shana. (2000). *You forgot your skirt, Amelia Bloomer! A very improper story.* Illustrated by Chesley McLaren. New York: Scholastic.

Crossingham, John. (2003). *Lacrosse in action.* Illustrations by Bonna Rouse. Photographs by Marc Crabtree. New York: Crabtree.

Currie, Stephen. (1997). *We have marched together: The working children's crusade.* Minneapolis, MN: Lerner.

Darling, Tara, & Darling, Kathy. (1996). *How to babysit an orangutan.* New York: Walker.

Drew, D. (1987a). *Caterpillar diary.* Australia: Rigby.

Drew, D. (1987b). *The life of a butterfly.* Australia: Rigby.

Dussling, Jennifer. (1998). *Bugs! Bugs! Bugs!* New York: DK.

Dyson, Marianne J. (1999). *Space station science: Life in free fall.* New York: Scholastic.

Ehlert, Lois. (2001). *Waiting for wings.* New York: Harcourt.

Ehrlich, Amy. (2003). *Rachel: The story of Rachel Carson.* Illustrated by Wendell Minor. San Diego, CA: Harcourt.

Facklam, Margery. (1996). *Creepy, crawly caterpillars.* Illustrated by Paul Facklam. Boston: Little, Brown.

Fleisher, Paul. (2002). *Ants.* Tarrytown, NY: Benchmark Books.

Fradin, Dennis Brindell. (2002). *Who was Ben Franklin?* Illustrated by John O'Brien. Grosset & Dunlap.

Freedman, Russell. (1994). *Kids at work: Lewis Hine and the crusade against child labor.* New York: Clarion.

Fritz, Jean. (2001). *Leonardo's horse.* Illustrated by Hudson Talbott. New York: Putnam.

Froman, Nan. (2001). *What's that bug?* Illustrated by Julian Mulock. Boston: Little, Brown.

Frost, Helen. (1999a). *Brushing well.* Oxford, UK: Capstone.

Frost, Helen. (1999b). *Food for healthy teeth.* Oxford, UK: Capstone.

Frost, Helen. (1999c). *Going to the dentist.* Oxford, UK: Capstone.

Frost, Helen. (1999d). *Your teeth.* Oxford, UK: Capstone.

Gaskins, Pearl Fuyo. (1999). *What are you? Voices of mixed-race young people.* New York: Henry Holt.

George, Jean Craighead. (2000). *How to talk to your cat.* Illustrated by Paul Meisel. New York: HarperCollins.

Gibbons. Gail. (1985). *The milk makers.* New York: Simon & Schuster.

Gibbons, Gail. (1990). *Exploring the deep, dark sea.* Boston: Little, Brown.

Gibbons, Gail. (1992). *Knights in shining armor.* New York: Holiday.

Gibbons, Gail. (1993a). *From seed to plant.* New York: Holiday.

Gibbons. Gail. (1993b). *Spiders.* New York: Holiday.

Gibbons, Gail. (1995). *The bicycle book.* New York: Holiday.

Gibbons, Gail. (1995). *How a house is built.* New York: Holiday.

Gibbons, Gail. (1997). *The honey makers.* New York: Morrow.

Gibbons, Gail. (1998). *Soaring with the wind: The bald eagle.* New York: Morrow.

Gibbons, Gail. (1999). *The pumpkin book.* New York: Holiday.

Gibbons, Gail. (2000a). *Apples.* New York: Holiday.

Gibbons, Gail. (2000b). *My soccer book.* New York: HarperCollins.

Gibbons, Gail. (2001). *Polar bears.* New York: Holiday.

Gibbons, Gail. (2002a). *The berry book.* New York: Holiday.

Gibbons, Gail. (2002b). *Giant pandas.* New York: Holiday.

Gibbons, Gail. (2002c). *Tell me, tree: About trees for kids.* Boston: Little, Brown.

Gibbons, Gail (2003). *Chicks & chickens.* New York: Holiday.

Glaser, Linda. (2000). *Magnificent monarchs.* Illustrated by Gay Holland. Brookfield, CT: Millbrook.

Glover, David. (1998). *Looking at insects.* Crystal Lake, IL: Rigby.

Goodall, Jane. (2001). *The chimpanzees I love: Saving their world and ours.* New York: Scholastic.

Gourley, Catherine. (1999). *Good girl work: Factories, sweatshops, and how women changed their role in the American workforce.* Brookfield, CT: Millbrook.

Granfield, Linda. (2001). *97 Orchard Street, New York: Stories of immigrant life.* Photographs by Arlene Alda. New York: Tundra Books.

Greenberg, Jan, & Jordan, Sandra. (2001). *Vincent van Gogh: Portrait of an artist.* New York: Delacorte.

Greenwood, Barbara. (1998). *The last safe house: A story of the underground railroad.* Illustrated by Heather Collins. Buffalo, NY: Kids Can.

Hariton, Anca. (1995). *Butterfly story.* New York: Dutton.

Harlow, Rosie, & Morgan, Sally. (2001). *The environment: Saving the planet.* New York: Kingfisher.

Hehner, Barbara. (2001). *Ice age mammoth: Will this ancient giant come back to life?* Illustrations by Mark Hallett. Toronto, ON: Madison.

Hehner, Barbara. (2002). *Ice age cave bear: The giant beast that terrified ancient humans.* Illustrated by Mark Hallett. New York: Madison Crown.

Heiligman, D. (1996). *From caterpillar to butterfly.* New York: HarperCollins.

Herberman, Ethan. (1990). *The great butterfly hunt: The mystery of the migrating monarchs.* New York: Simon & Schuster.

Hesse, Karen. (1997). *Out of the dust.* New York: Scholastic.

Hoare, Ben (Ed.). (2002). *The Kingfisher A–Z encyclopedia.* New York: Kingfisher.

Hodge, Deborah. (1997). *Whales: Killer whales, blue whales and more.* Illustrated by Pat Stephens and Nancy Gray Ogle. Tonawanda, NY: Kids Can.

Hoshino, Michio. (1993). *The grizzly bear family book.* Translated by Karen Colligan-Taylor. London: Picture Book Studio.

Jackson, Donna M. (2002). *The bug scientists.* Boston: Houghton Mifflin.

James, Sylvia M. (1996). *Meet the octopus.* Illustrated by Cynthia A. Belcher. Greenvale, NY: Mondo.

Johnson, Jinny. (1991). *Pandas.* Columbus, OH: Highlights/Two-Can.

Jones, Charlotte Foltz. (1999). *Eat your words: A fascinating look at the language of food.* Illustrated by John O'Brien. New York: Delacorte.

Jones, Kathryn. (1994). *Happy birthday, Dr. King!* Illustrated by Floyd Cooper. Modern Curriculum Press.

Kalman, Bobbie. (2002). *The life cycle of a butterfly.* Illustrated by Margaret Amy Reiach. New York: Crabtree.

Kalman, Bobbie, & Bishop, Amanda. (2002). *The life cycle of a lion.* New York: Crabtree.

Kalman, Bobbie, & Smithyman, Kathryn. (2002). *The life cycle of a bird.* New York: Crabtree.

Keenan, Sheila. (2002). *Scholastic encyclopedia of women in the United States.* New York: Scholastic.

Kimmel, Elizabeth Cody. (1999). *Ice story.* New York: Clarion.

Kostyal, K. M. (1999). *Trial by ice: A photobiography of Sir Ernest Shackleton.* Washington, DC: National Geographic Society.

Kraft, Betsy Harvey. (1995). *Mother Jones: One woman's fight for labor.* New York: Clarion.

Kramer, Stephen. (2001). *Hidden worlds: Looking through a scientist's microscope.* Photographs by Dennis Kunkel. Boston: Houghton Mifflin.

Kroll, Steven. (1995). *Ellis Island: Doorway to freedom.* Illustrated by Karen Ritz. New York: Holiday.

Kuklin, Susan. (1998). *Iqbal Masih and the crusaders against child slavery.* New York: Henry Holt.

Lang, Aubrey. (2002). *Baby lion.* Photographs by Wayne Lynch. Allston, MA: Fitzhenry & Whiteside.

Lankford, Mary D. (1998). *Dominoes around the world.* Illustrated by Karen Dugan. New York: Morrow.

Latimer, Jonathan P., & Nolting, Karen S. (2000). *Butterflies: Peterson field guides for young naturalists.* Boston: Houghton Mifflin.

Lauber, Patricia. (1996). *Hurricanes: Earth's mightiest storms.* New York: Scholastic.

Lauber, Patricia. (2002). *What you never knew about fingers, forks, & chopsticks.* Illustrated by John Manders. New York: Aladdin.

Lavies, Bianca. (1992). *Monarch butterflies: Mysterious travelers.* Photographs by Bianca Lavies. New York: Dutton.

Lawlor, Veronica. (1995). *I was dreaming to come to America: Memories from the Ellis Island Oral History Project.* New York: Viking.

Lee, Georgia. (1998). *A day with a Chumash.* Illustrated by Giorgio Bacchin. Minneapolis, MN: Runestone/Lerner.

Lessem, Don. (1999). *Dinosaurs to dodos: An encyclopedia of extinct animals.* Illustrated by Jan Sovak. New York: Scholastic.

Levine, Ellen. (1993). *...If your name was changed at Ellis Island.* Illustrated by Wayne Parmenter. New York: Scholastic.

Lewin, Ted. (2003). *Tooth and claw: Animal adventures in the wild.* New York: HarperCollins.

Livingston, Irene. (2003). *Finklehopper frog.* Illustrated by Brian Lies. Berkeley, CA: Tricycle.

Llewellyn, Claire. (1998). *Bugs.* New York: Kingfisher.

London, Jonathan. (2001). *What the animals were waiting for.* Illustrated by Paul Morin. New York: Scholastic.

Lowery, Linda. (1987). *Martin Luther King day.* Illustrated by Hetty Mitchell. New York: Scholastic.

Lowery, Linda. (1999). *Aunt Clara Brown: Official pioneer.* Illustrated by Janice Lee Porter. Minneapolis, MN: Carolrhoda.

Lyons, Mary E. (1992). *Letters from a slave girl: The story of Harriet Jacobs.* New York: Scribner's.

Maestro, Betsy. (1994). *Bats: Night fliers.* New York: Scholastic.

Maestro, Betsy. (1996). *Coming to America: The story of immigration.* Illustrated by Susannah Ryan. New York: Scholastic.

Markle, Sandra. (2000). *Growing up wild: Bears.* New York: Atheneum.

Markle, Sandra. (2002). *Growing up wild: Penguins.* Atheneum.

Martin, Jacqueline Briggs. (1998). *Snowflake Bentley.* Illustrated by Mary Azarian. Boston: Houghton Mifflin.

Marzollo, Jean. (1996). *I am water.* Illustrated by Judith Moffatt. New York: Scholastic.

Mason, Adrienne. (2003). *Bats.* Illustrated by Nancy Gray Ogle. Toronto, ON: Kids Can.

Mattern, Joanne. (1992). *Young Martin Luther King, Jr.: "I have a dream."* Illustrated by Allan Eitzen. Mahwah, NJ: Troll.

Matthews, Downs. (1989). *Polar bear cubs.* Photographs by Dan Guravich. New York: Simon & Schuster.

Matthews, Tom L. (1998). *Light shining through the mist: A photobiography of Dian Fossey.* Washington, DC: National Geographic Society.

McCurdy, Michael. (1997). *Trapped by the ice! Shackleton's amazing Antarctic adventure.* New York: Walker.

McGuffee, Michael, & Burley, Kelly. (2000). *Chasing tornadoes!* Crystal Lake, IL: Rigby/Division of Reed Elsevier.

McKissack, Patricia C., & McKissack, Fredrick L. (1994). *Christmas in the big house, Christmas in the quarters.* Illustrated by John Thompson. New York: Scholastic.

McMahon, Patricia. (1999). *One Belfast boy.* Photographs by Alan O'Connor. New York: Houghton Mifflin.

Meadows, Graham, & Vial, Claire. (2000). *The Dominie world of animals: Lions.* Carlsbad, CA: Dominie.

Meltzer, Milton. (1994). *Cheap raw materials.* New York: Viking.

Micucci, Charles. (1995). *The life and times of the honeybee.* New York: Ticknor & Fields.

Micucci, Charles. (2003). *The life and times of the ant.* Boston: Houghton Mifflin.

Moore, Helen H. (1996). *Beavers.* Illustrated by Terri Talas. Greenvale, NY: Mondo.

Murphy, Jim. (1995). *The great fire.* New York: Scholastic.

Murphy, Jim. (2000). *Blizzard!* New York: Scholastic.

Myers, Walter Dean. (1999). *At Her Majesty's request: An African princess in Victorian England.* New York: Scholastic.

Nagda, Ann Whitehead, & Bickel, Cindy. (2000). *Tiger math: Learning to graph from a baby tiger.* New York: Henry Holt.

Nagda, Ann Whitehead, & Bickel, Cindy. (2002). *Chimp math: Learning about time from a baby chimpanzee.* New York: Henry Holt.

Norell, Mark A., & Dingus, Lowell. (1999). *A nest of dinosaurs: The story of Oviraptor.* New York: Doubleday.

Orgill, Roxanne. (1997). *If I only had a horn: Young Louis Armstrong.* Illustrated by Leonard Jenkins. New York: Houghton Mifflin.

Osborne, Mary Pope. The magic tree house series. New York: Random.

Pair-it Books series. Austin, TX: Steck-Vaughn.

Parker, David L. (1998). *Stolen dreams: Portraits of working children.* With Lee Engfer and Robert Conrow. Minneapolis, MN: Lerner.

Parker, Steve. (2002). *Insects, bugs, & art activities.* New York: Crabtree.

Pascoe, Elaine. (1997). *Butterflies and moths.* Photographs by Dwight Kuhn. Woodbridge, CT: Blackbirch Press.

Patent, Dorothy Hinshaw. (1989). *Looking at ants.* New York: Holiday.

Patent, Dorothy Hinshaw. (2002). *The Lewis and Clark trail: Then and now.* Illustrated by William Muñoz. New York: Dutton.

Peterson, Cris. (1999). *Century farm: One hundred years on a family farm.* Photographs by Alvis Upitis. Honesdale, PA: Boyds Mills.

Posada, Mia. (2002). *Ladybugs: Red, fiery, and bright.* Minneapolis, MN: Carolrhoda.

Pringle, Laurence. (1991). *Batman: Exploring the world of bats.* Photographs by Merlin Tuttle. New York: Scribner's.

Pringle, Laurence. (1997). *An extraordinary life: The story of a monarch butterfly.* Illustrated by Bob Marstall. New York: Orchard.

Pringle, Laurence. (2000). *Bats! Strange and wonderful.* Illustrated by Meryl Henderson. Honesdale, PA: Boyds Mills.

Pringle, Laurence. (2001). *A dragon in the sky: The story of a green darner dragonfly.* Paintings by Bob Marstall. New York: Orchard.

Ready, Dee. (1998). *Dentists.* Oxford, UK: Capstone.

Ringgold, Faith. (1999). *If a bus could talk: The story of Rosa Parks.* New York: Simon & Schuster.

Robbins, Ken. (1994). *Water: The elements.* New York: Henry Holt.

Robert, James. (1995). *Dentists.* Vero Beach, FL: Rourke.

Roberts-Davis, Tanya. (2001). *We need to go to school: Voices of the rugmark children.* Toronto, ON: Groundwood.

Romanek, Trudee. (2003). *Achoo! The most interesting book you'll ever read about germs.* Illustrated by Rose Cowles. Tonawanda, NY: Kids Can.

Ross, Michael Elsohn. (1995). *Rolypolyology.* Photographs by Brian Grogan. Illustrations by Darren Erickson. Minneapolis, MN: Carolrhoda.

Ross, Michael Elsohn. (1996). *Cricketology.* Photographs by Brian Grogan. Illustrations by Darren Erickson. Minneapolis, MN: Carolrhoda.

Ross, Michael Elsohn. (1997). *Bug watching with Charles Henry Turner.* Illustrated by Laurie A. Caple. Minneapolis, MN: Carolrhoda.

Rowan, Kate, & McEwen, Katherine. (1999). *I know why I brush my teeth.* New York: Scholastic.

Saller, Carol. (1998). *Working children (picture the American past).* Minneapolis, MN: Carolrhoda.

Sayre, April Pulley. (1995). *If you should hear a honey guide.* Illustrated by S. C. Schindler. Boston: Houghton Mifflin.

Sayre, April Pulley. (2002a). *Army ant parade.* Illustrated by Rick Chrustowski. New York: Henry Holt.

Sayre, April Pulley. (2002b). *Secrets of sound: Studying the calls and songs of whales, elephants, and birds.* Boston: Houghton Mifflin.

Scholastic children's dictionary. (2002). New York: Scholastic.

Scholastic News, January 2003, Vol. 59, No. 4, Edition 2.

Schroeder, Alan. (1996). *Satchmo's blues.* Illustrated by Floyd Cooper. New York: Doubleday.

Seuling, Barbara. (2000). *Drip! drop!: How water gets to your tap.* Illustrated by Nancy Tobin. New York: Holiday.

Shannon, David. (1998). *No, David!* New York: Scholastic.

Sill, Cathryn. (2000). *About insects.* Illustrated by John Sill. Atlanta, GA: Peachtree.

Simon, Seymour. (1998). *Muscles: Our muscular system.* New York: Morrow.

Simon, Seymour. (1999). *Crocodiles & alligators.* New York: HarperCollins.

Simon, Seymour. (2001). *Animals nobody loves.* New York: SeaStar Books.

Singer, Marilyn. (2001). *Tough beginnings: How baby animals survive.* Illustrated by Anna Vojtech. New York: Henry Holt.

Sloan, Christopher. (2000). *Feathered dinosaurs.* Washington, DC: National Geographic Society.

Smith, Charles R., Jr. (2003). *I am an American.* New York: Scholastic.

Sobol, Richard. (1995). *One more elephant: The fight to save wildlife in Uganda.* New York: Cobblehill Books.

Solheim, James. (1997). *It's disgusting—and we ate it! True food facts from around the world—and throughout history!* Illustrated by Eric Brace. New York: Simon & Schuster.

Springer, Jane. (1997). *Listen to us: The world's working children.* Toronto, ON: Groundwood.

Stanley, Diane, & Vennema, Peter. (1994). *Cleopatra.* Illustrated by Diane Stanley. New York: Morrow.

Stanley, Jerry. (1992). *Children of the Dust Bowl: The true story of the school at Weedpatch Camp.* New York: Crown.

Stanley, Jerry. (1994). *I am an American: A true story of Japanese internment.* New York: Crown.

Stanley, Jerry. (2000). *Hurry freedom: African Americans in gold rush California.* New York: Crown.

Stefoff, Rebecca. (2002). *Bears.* Tarrytown, NY: Benchmark/Marshall Cavendish.

Stevens, Janet. (1999). *Cook-a-doodle-doo!* New York: Harcourt Brace.

Stokes, Donald, & Stokes, Lillian. (2001). *Beginner's guide to butterflies.* Boston: Little, Brown.

Stone, Lynn M. (2002). *Giant pandas.* Photographs by Keren Su. Minneapolis, MN: Lerner.

Swain, Ruth Freeman. (2002). *Hairdo! What we do and did to our hair.* Illustrated by Cat Bowman Smith. New York: Holiday.

Swanson, Diane. (1994). *Safari beneath the sea: The wonder world of the north Pacific coast.* Photographs by the Royal British Columbia Museum. Sierra Club Books.

Swinburne, Stephen R. (2003). *Black bear: North America's bear.* Honesdale, PA: Boyds Mills.

Tang, Greg. (2002). *Math for all seasons.* Illustrated by Harry Briggs. New York: Scholastic.

Tunnell, Michael O., & Chilcoat, George W. (1996). *The children of Topaz: The story of a Japanese-American internment camp based on a classroom diary.* New York: Holiday.

Uchida, Yoshiko. (1971). *Journey to Topaz.* New York: Scribner's.

Waber, Bernard. (1998). *Lyle at Christmas.* Boston: Houghton Mifflin.

Warren, Andrea. (2001). *We rode the orphan trains.* New York: Houghton Mifflin.

Wechsler, Doug. (1995). *Bizarre bugs.* New York: Cobblestone.

Whalley, Paul. (1988). *Butterflies & moths.* New York: Knopf.

Wick, Walter. (1997). *A drop of water: A book of science and wonder.* New York: Scholastic.

Wilsdon, Christina. (1998). *National Audubon Society first field guide to insects.* New York: Scholastic.

Winkler, Peter. (March 2002). Supercroc. *National Geographic for Kids, 1*(5), 4–9.

Winer, Yvonne, (2002). *Birds build nests.* Illustrated by Tony Oliver. Watertown, NY: Charlesbridge.

YES Mag. (Eds.) (2003). *The amazing international space station.* Tonawanda, NY: Kids Can.

Yolen, Jane. (1987). *Owl moon.* Illustrated by John Schoenherr. New York: Philomel.

Index

innovations, 255–256
retelling, 255

F

features of nonfiction, 53–55, 83–94
  designing curriculum based on
    (checklist), 100, 281–283
  student assessment (checklist), 101,
    278–280
  student knowledge of, 116–117
fiction
  blended books, 73
  nonfiction, vs., 47
  reading, differences in, 13–15
Forgue, TammyJo, 87
Fountas and Pinnell, 40–41, 107
framework to teach nonfiction
  benefits of, 40–44
  building momentum, 156
  discovery circles in, 210–211
  extension activities, 252
  guided instruction in, 179–180
  independent instruction in, 251–252
  modeled instruction in, 121–122
  modified instruction in readers'/
    writers' workshop, 245–247
  principles, guiding, 267–268
  reading strategies across, 105
  shared reading and writing in, 150
  theory behind, 34–39
  think alouds, 124
Fredericks, Anthony, 196
Freeman, Marcia S., 133, 145

G

Gallagher, Margaret, 25
Gambrell, Linda B., 212
Gerard, Philip (*Creative Nonfiction*), 13
Graves, Bonnie, 25
Graves, Donald, 36–39
Graves, Michael, 25
guided instruction
  benefits, 183
  definition, 179, 181
  framework, in, 180
  prompts/prompting, 181–182
  purpose, 179
  quick points, 179
guided reading, 30, 183–184
  examples, 176–178, 186–194

extension activities, 186, 190, 194, 195
framework, in, 180
planning and carrying out lesson,
  184–186
record-keeping, 185–186, 193–194
selecting material, 194–198
Guided Reading & Literacy Circles,
  (Swartz et al.), 196
guided writing, 30, 198–204
  bulleted lists, 202, 204
  considerations, 200
  example, 202–204
  framework, in, 180
  planning and carrying out lesson,
    200–202
  purpose, 198–199
  record-keeping, 202
Guiding Principles for Bringing It All
  Together (list), 268

H

Harvey and Goudvis, 107
"hedging language," 161
Hepler, Susan, 14, 16
Holdaway, Don, 151

I

Imbert, Sharon, 166–172
immersion
  books for, 83
  comparison charts, 94
  features, examining, 83–94
  read alouds, 133–134
implicit instruction, 149
*Improving Comprehension With Think-
  Aloud Strategies* (Wilhelm), 123
independent instruction
  defined, 250–251
  example, 240–245
  framework, in, 252
  purpose, 250
  quick points, 250
  readers'/writers' workshops, 247–248
  See also extension activities
independent learning, 32–33
informational literacy, developing, 49
informational text (defined), 13
inquiry, classroom, 19, 44, 96–99
  bringing it all together, 256–267
  content, 97–98, 100

creating and writing nonfiction, 97,
  99, 103
example, 240–245
framework, in, 240, 245
goals for studying nonfiction, 100–101
how nonfiction works, 101–103
interviewing, 106
learning to inquire, 104, 106
learning to read nonfiction, 104–105
questions, 98–99
readers'/writers' workshops, 249
reading/processing nonfiction, 97–98
strategies for gathering information,
  97–98
tools for, 95–117
interactive writing
  difference between shared writing
    and, 163
  example, 166–172
  procedures, general, 164–166
  purpose, 162–163
Internet, 19
intertextuality (defined), 18, 43
I See What You Mean (Moline), 146

J

jigsawing, 232–233
Johnston, Peter H., 36
"Juvenile Literature," 47, 51, 69, 73

K

Keene and Zimmermann, 107
Kerper, Richard, 16
Knight, Berenice, 240–245, 257
KWL charts, 135, 241–242

L

language, oral, 35–39
  conversation opportunities, 41
  retelling, 40
  thinking aloud, 36
  See also vocabulary
Laughlin and Lathrobe (*Readers Theatre
  for Children*), 238
Library of Congress Cataloging-in-
  Publication Data, 47, 51, 69, 73
*Listen to This: Developing an Ear
  for Expository* (Freeman), 133
literature circles, 206, 211